D1481852

Nancy

THE CLOWNS OF GOD

Also by Morris West

PROTEUS

THE NAVIGATOR

HARLEQUIN

THE SALAMANDER

SUMMER OF THE RED WOLF

SCANDAL IN THE ASSEMBLY

THE HERETIC

THE TOWER OF BABEL

THE AMBASSADOR

THE SHOES OF THE FISHERMAN

DAUGHTER OF SILENCE

THE DEVIL'S ADVOCATE

BACKLASH

CHILDREN OF THE SHADOWS

THE CLOWNS OF GOD

A novel by

MORRIS WEST

WILLIAM MORROW AND COMPANY, INC.
New York *1981*

Copyright © 1981 by Compania Financiera Perlina, S.A.

All rights reserved. No part of this book may be reproduced or utilized in any form or by any means, electronic or mechanical, including photocopying, recording or by any information storage and retrieval system, without permission in writing from the Publisher. Inquiries should be addressed to William Morrow and Company, Inc., 105 Madison Ave., New York, N. Y. 10016.

Library of Congress Cataloging in Publication Data

West, Morris L 1916–
The clowns of God.

I. Title.
PR9619.3.W4C5 1981 823 80-27153
ISBN 0-688-00449-0

Printed in the United States of America

First U.S. Edition

1 2 3 4 5 6 7 8 9 10

BOOK DESIGN BY MICHAEL MAUCERI

For
my loved ones
with
my heart's thanks

AUTHOR'S NOTE

Once you accept the existence of God—however you define Him, however you explain your relationship to Him—then you are caught forever with His presence in the center of all things. You are also caught with the fact that man is a creature who walks in two worlds and traces upon the walls of his cave the wonders and the nightmare experiences of his spiritual pilgrimage.

Who knows but the world may end tonight?

—Robert Browning,
"The Last Ride Together"

PROLOGUE

In the seventh year of his reign, two days before his sixty-fifth birthday, in the presence of a full consistory of Cardinals, Jean Marie Barette, Pope Gregory XVII, signed an instrument of abdication, took off the Fisherman's ring, handed his seal to the Cardinal Camerlengo and made a curt speech of farewell.

"So, my brethren! It is done as you demanded. I am sure you will explain it all adequately to the Church and to the world. I hope you will elect yourselves a good man. God knows you will need him!"

Three hours later, accompanied by a colonel of the Swiss Guard, he presented himself at the Monastery of Monte Cassino and placed himself under the obedience of the Abbot. The colonel drove immediately back to Rome and reported to the Cardinal Camerlengo that his mission was accomplished.

The Camerlengo breathed a long sigh of relief and set about the formalities of proclaiming that the See of Peter was vacant and that an election would be held with all possible speed.

BOOK ONE

I was in the spirit on the Lord's day and I heard behind me a great voice, as of a trumpet, saying: . . . What thou seest write in a book and send it to the seven churches.

—Revelation of St. John the Divine 1:10–11

I

She looked like a country woman, stout, apple-cheeked, dressed in coarse woollen stuff, her wispy grey hair trailing from under a straw hat. She sat bolt upright in the chair, hands folded over a large old-fashioned handbag of brown leather. She was wary but unafraid, as if she were studying the merchandise in an unfamiliar market.

Carl Mendelius, Professor of Biblical and Patristic Studies at the Wilhelmsstift, once called the Illustrious College of the University of Tübingen, stretched his legs under the desk, made a bridge of his fingertips and smiled at her over the top of it. He prompted her gently:

"You wanted to see me, madame?"

"I was told you understand French?" She spoke with the broad accent of the Midi.

"I do."

"My name is Thérèse Mathieu. In religion I am—I was—called Sister Mechtilda."

"Am I to understand that you have left the convent?"

"I was dispensed from my vows. But he said I should always wear the ring from my profession day, because I was still in the service of the Lord."

She held up a large work-worn hand and displayed the plain silver band on the wedding finger.

"He? Who is *he*?"

"His Holiness, Pope Gregory. I was with the sisters who work in his household. I cleaned his study and his private rooms. I served his coffee. Sometimes, on feast days, while the other sisters were resting, I prepared a meal for him. He said he liked my cooking. It reminded him of home. . . . He would talk to me then. He knew my birthplace very well. His family used to own vineyards in the Var. . . . When my niece was left a widow with five young children and the restaurant to keep going, I told him about it. He was very sympathetic. He said perhaps my niece needed me more than the Pope, who had too many servants anyway. He helped me to think freely and understand that charity was the most important of virtues. . . . My decision to return to the world was made at the time when the people in the Vatican began to say all those terrible things—that the Holy Father was sick in the head, that he could be dangerous—all that. The day I left Rome I went to ask his blessing. He asked me, as a special favour, to come to Tübingen and give his letter into your hands. He put me under obedience to tell no one what he had said or what I was carrying. So, I am here. . . ."

She fished in the leather bag, brought out a thick envelope and passed it across the desk. Carl Mendelius held it in his hands, weighing it. Then he laid it aside. He asked:

"You came straight here from Rome?"

"No. I went to my niece and stayed for a week. His Holiness said I should do that. It was natural and proper. He gave me money for the journey and a gift to help my niece."

"Did he give you any other message for me?"

"Only that he sent you his love. He told me, if you asked any questions, I should answer them."

"He found himself a faithful messenger." Carl Mendelius was grave and gentle. "Would you like coffee?"

"No, thank you."

She folded her hands over the bag and waited, the perfect nun, even in her country homespun. Mendelius posed his next question with casual care.

"These problems, this talk in the Vatican, when did they begin? What caused them?"

"I know when." There was no hesitation in her answer. "When he came back from his visit to South America and the United States, he looked ill and tired. Then there were the visits of the Chinese and the Russians and the people from Africa which seemed to leave him much preoccupied. After they left he decided to go into retreat for two weeks at Monte Cassino. It was after his return that the troubles began. . . ."

"What sort of troubles?"

"I never really understood. You must know I was a very small personage, a sister doing domestic work. We were trained not to comment on matters which were not our concern. The Mother Superior frowned on gossip. But I noticed that the Holy Father looked ill, that he spent long hours in the chapel, that there were frequent meetings with members of the Curia, from which they would come out looking angry and muttering among themselves. I don't even remember the words—except once I heard Cardinal Arnaldo say: 'Dear God in heaven! We are treating with a madman!' "

"And the Holy Father, how did he seem to you?"

"With me he was always the same, kind and polite. But it was clear he was very worried. One day he asked me to fetch him some aspirin to take with his coffee. I asked whether I should call the physician. He gave me a strange little smile and said: 'Sister Mechtilda, it is not a doctor I need but the gift of tongues. Sometimes it seems I am teaching music to the deaf and painting to the blind.' . . . In the end, of course, his doctor did come and then several others on different days. Afterwards, Cardinal Drexel came to see him—he's the Dean of the Sacred College and a very stern man. He spent the whole day in the Holy Father's apartment. I helped to serve them lunch. After that, well . . . it all happened."

"Did you understand anything of what was going on?"

"No. All we were told was that for reasons of health and for the welfare of souls, the Holy Father had decided to abdicate and devote the rest of his life to God in a monastery. We were asked to pray for him and for the Church."

"And he made no explanation to you?"

"To me?" She stared at him with innocent surprise. "Why to me? I was a nobody. But after he blessed me for the journey, he put his hands on my cheeks and said: 'Perhaps, little Sister, we are both lucky to have found each other.' That was the last time I saw him."

"And now what will you do?"

"Go home to my niece, help her with the children, cook in the restaurant. It is small, but a good business if we can hold it together."

"I'm sure you will," said Carl Mendelius respectfully. He stood up and held out his hand. "Thank you, Sister Mechtilda. Thank you for coming to see me—for what you have done for him."

"It was nothing. He was a good man. He understood how ordinary folk feel."

The skin of her palm was dry and chapped, from dishwater and the scrubbing pail. He felt ashamed of his own soft clerkly palms into which Gregory XVII, Successor to the Prince of the Apostles, had consigned his last, most secret memorial.

He sat late that night, in his big attic study, whose leaded windows looked out on the grey bulk of the Stiftskirche of St. George. The only witnesses to his meditation were the marble busts of Melanchthon and Hegel, the one a lecturer, the other a pupil in the ancient university; but they were dead long since and absolved from perplexity.

The letter from Jean Marie Barette, seventeenth Gregory in the papal line, lay spread before him: thirty pages of fine cursive script, impeccable in its Gallic style, the record of a personal tragedy and a political crisis of global dimension.

My dear Carl,

In this, the long dark night of my soul, when reason staggers and the faith of a lifetime seems almost lost, I turn to you for the grace of understanding.

We have been friends a long time. Your books and your letters have travelled with me always: baggage more essential than my shirts and my shoes. Your counsels have calmed me in many an anxious moment. Your wisdom has been a light to my feet in the dark labyrinths of power. Though the lines of our lives have diverged, I like to believe that our spirits have maintained a unity.

If I have been silent during these last months of purgation, it is because I have not wished to compromise you. For some time now I have been closely watched and I have been unable to guarantee the privacy even of my most personal papers. Indeed, I have to tell you that if this letter falls into the wrong hands, you may be exposed to great risk; more, if you decide to carry out the mission I entrust to you, the danger will double itself every day.

I begin at the end of the story. Last month, the Cardinals of the Sacred College, among them some I believed to be friends, decided by a large majority that I was, if not insane, at least no longer mentally competent to discharge the duties of Pontiff. This decision, the reasons for which I shall explain in detail, placed them in a dilemma both comic and tragic.

There were only two ways to get rid of me: by deposition or abdication. To depose me they must show cause, and this, I believed, they would not dare attempt. The smell of conspiracy would be too strong, the risk of schism too great. Abdication, on the other hand, would be a legal act, which, if I were insane, I could not validly perform.

My personal dilemma was a different one. I had not asked to be elected. I had accepted fearfully, but trusting in the Holy Spirit for light and strength. I believed—and I am still trying desperately to believe—that the light was given to me in a very special fashion and that it was my duty to display it to a world caught already in the darkness of the last hour before midnight. On the other hand, without the support of my most senior collaborators, the hinge-men of the Church, I was impotent. My utterances could be distorted, my directives nullified. The children of God could be cast into confusion or misled into rebellion.

Then Drexel came to see me. He is, as you know, the Dean of the College of Cardinals, and it was I who appointed him Prefect of the Sacred Congregation for the Doctrine of the Faith. He is a formidable watchdog, as you have good reason to know. In private, however, he is a compassionate and understanding man. He was at pains to be precise. He was the emissary of his brother Cardinals. He dissented from their opinion but was charged to deliver their decision. They required me to abdicate and retire to obscurity in a monastery. If I refused they would, in spite of all the risks, take steps to have me declared legally insane and placed in confinement under medical supervision.

I was, as you may imagine, deeply shocked. I had not believed they would dare so much. Then came a moment of pure terror. I knew enough of the history of this office and its incumbents to see that the threat was real. Vatican City is an independent state and for what is done within its walls there is no outside audit.

Then the terror passed and I asked, calmly enough, what Drexel himself thought of the situation. He answered without hesitation. He had no doubt that his colleagues could and would make good their threat. The damage, in a critical time, would be great, but not irreparable. The Church had survived the Theophylacts and the Borgias and the debauches of Avignon. It would survive the moon madness of Jean Marie Barette. It was Drexel's private opinion, offered in friendship, that I should bow to the inevitable and abdicate on the grounds of ill health. Then he added a rider which I quote for you verbatim: "Do what they ask, Holiness—but no more, not by a fraction! You will go. You will retire into privacy. I myself will challenge any document that attempts to bind you to more. As to this light which you claim to have been given, I cannot judge whether it is from God or whether it is the illusion of an overburdened spirit. If it is an illusion, I hope you will not cherish it too long. If it is from God, then He will enable you, in His own time, to make it manifest. . . . But if you are declared insane, then you will be totally discredited and the light will be quenched forever. History, especially Church history, is always written to justify the survivors."

I understood what he was telling me, but I still could not accept so trenchant a solution. We talked all day, examining every possible option. I prayed alone far into the night. Finally, in utter weariness, I surrendered. At nine the next morning I summoned Drexel and told him I was prepared to abdicate.

That, my dear Carl, was *how* it happened. The why will take much longer to tell; then you, too, will be forced to sit in judgment on me. Even as I write these words I fear lest your verdict may be against me. So much for human frailty! I have not yet learned to trust the Lord whose gospel I proclaim! . . .

The poignant appeal moved Mendelius deeply. The script blurred before his aching eyes. He leaned back in his chair and surrendered himself to memory. They had met in Rome more than two decades ago, when Jean Marie Barette was Cardinal Deacon, the youngest member of the Curia, and Father Carl Mendelius, S.J., was teaching his first course on the elements of scriptural interpretation at the Gregorian University. The young Cardinal had been a guest at his lecture on Judaic communities in the early Church. Afterwards, they had dined together and talked, long into the night. When they parted they were already friends.

In the bad days, after Mendelius had been delated on suspicion of heresy to the Congregation for the Doctrine of the Faith, Jean Marie Barette had supported him through long months of inquisition. When his priestly vocation no longer satisfied him he had asked to be laicized and dispensed to marry. Barette had pleaded his cause with a reluctant and irascible Pontiff. When he applied for the chair at Tübingen, the most glowing recommendation had been signed "Gregorius XVII, Pont. Max."

Now, their positions were reversed. Jean Marie Barette was in exile, while Carl Mendelius flourished in the free zone of a happy marriage and a full professional life. Whatever the cost, he must discharge the debts of friendship. He bent again to the study of the letter.

. . . You know the circumstances of my election. My predecessor, our populist Pope, had fulfilled his mission. He had centralized the Church again. He had tightened discipline. He had restated the traditional dogmatic line. His enormous personal charm—the charm of a great actor—had masked for a long time his essentially rigorist attitudes. In his old age he had become more intolerant, less and less open to argument. He saw himself as the Hammer of God, smiting the forces of the ungodly. It was hard to convince him that, unless a miracle happened, there might be no men left at all—godly or ungodly. We were in the last decade of the century and only a stride away from global war. When I assumed office, a compromise choice after a six-day conclave, I was terrified.

I do not need to read you the whole apocalyptic text; the plight of the Third World thrust to the brink of starvation, the daily risk of economic collapse in the West, the soaring cost of energy, the wild armament race, the temptation for the militarists to make their last mad gamble while they could still calculate the atomic odds. For me the most frightening phenomenon was the atmosphere of creeping despair among world leaders, the sense of official impotence, the strange atavistic regression to a magical view of the universe.

You and I had discussed many times the proliferation of new cults and their manipulation for profit and power. Fanaticism was exploding in the old religions as well. Some of our own fanatics wanted me to proclaim a Marian year, call for vast pilgrimages to all the shrines of the Virgin throughout the world. I told them

I would have none of it. A panic of devotees was the last thing we needed.

I believed the best service the Church could offer was that of mediation with reason and with charity for all. It was also the task which I, as Pontiff, was best fitted to perform. I let it be known that I would go anywhere, receive anyone, in the cause of peace. I tried to make it clear that I had no magical formulae, no illusions of power. I knew too well the deadly inertia of institutions, the mathematical madness that makes men fight to the death over the simplest equation of compromise. I told myself, I tried to convince the leaders of nations, that even one year's deferment of Armageddon would be a victory. Nevertheless, the fear of an impending holocaust haunted me day and night, sapped my reserves of courage and confidence.

Finally, I decided that, to keep any sense of perspective, I must rest awhile and rebuild my spiritual resources. So I went into retreat for two weeks at the Monastery of Monte Cassino. You know the place well. It was founded by St. Benedict in the sixth century. Paul the Deacon wrote his histories there. My namesake, Gregory IX, made there his peace with Frederick von Hohenstaufen. More than all, it was isolated and serene. Abbot Andrew was a man of singular discernment and piety. I would place myself under his spiritual direction and dedicate myself to a brief period of silence, meditation and inner renewal.

So I planned it, my dear Carl. So I began to do it. I had been there three days when the event took place.

The sentence ended at the bottom of a page. Mendelius hesitated before he turned it over. He felt a faint shiver of distaste as though he were being asked to witness an intimate bodily act. He had to force himself to continue the reading.

. . . I call it an event, because I do not wish to colour your appraisal of it, and also because, for me, it remains a fact of physical dimension. It happened. I did not imagine it. The experience was as real as the breakfast I had just eaten in the refectory.

It was nine in the morning, a clear sunny day. I was sitting on a stone bench in the cloister garden. A few yards away, one of the monks was hoeing a flower plot. I felt very placid, very relaxed. I began to read the fourteenth chapter of St. John's Gospel, which the Abbot had proposed for that day's meditation. You remember how it begins, with the discourse of Christ at his Last Supper: "Let not your heart be troubled. You believe in God; believe also in me. . . ." The text itself, full of comfort and reassurance, matched my mood. When I reached the verse "And he that loveth me shall be loved of my Father . . ." I closed the book and looked up.

Everything about me had changed. There was no monastery, no garden, no labouring monk. I was alone, on a high, barren peak. All about me were jagged mountains, black against a lurid sky. The place was still and silent as the grave. I felt no fear, only a terrible, bleak emptiness, as if the kernel of me had been scooped out and only the husk remained. I knew what I was seeing, the aftermath of man's ultimate folly—a dead planet. For what happened next I can find no adequate words. It was as if I were suddenly filled with flame, caught up in a fiery whirlwind, hurtled out of every human dimension into the center of a vast unendurable light. The light was a voice and the voice was a light, and it was as if I were being impregnated with its message. I was at the end of all, the beginning of all; the omega point of time, the alpha point of eternity. There were no symbols anymore, only the single simple Reality. Prophecy was fulfilled. Order was completed out of chaos, ultimate truth made manifest. In a moment of exquisite agony I understood that I must announce this event, prepare the world for it. I was called to proclaim that the Last Days were very near and that mankind should prepare for the Parousia: the Second Coming of the Lord Jesus.

Just when it seemed the agony would explode me into extinction it was over. I was back again in the cloister garden. The monk was hoeing his roses. The New Testament was on my lap, open now at the twenty-fourth chapter of Matthew: "For as the lightning cometh out of the east and appeareth even into the west . . . so shall the coming of the Son of Man be." Accident or omen? It did not seem to matter anymore.

And there you have it, Carl, as close as I can come to it in words, with the closest friend of my heart. When I tried to explain it to my colleagues back in Rome, I could see the shock in their faces: a Pope with a private revelation, a precursor of the Second Coming? Madness! The final explosive unreason! I was a walking time-bomb that must be defused as quickly as possible. And yet I could no more conceal what had happened to me than

I could change the colour of my eyes. It was imprinted on every fiber of my being, like the genetic patterns of my parents. I was compelled to talk about it, doomed to announce it to a world rushing, heedless, towards extinction.

I began work on an encyclical, a letter to the Universal Church. It opened with the words: "*In his ultimis annis fatalibus* . . . In these last fateful years of the millennium . . ." My secretary found the draft on my desk, photographed it in secret and distributed copies to the Curia. They were horrified. Separately and in concert, they urged me to suppress the document. When I refused, they put my apartments under virtual siege, and blocked all my communications with the outside world. Then they summoned an emergency meeting of the Sacred College, brought in a team of physicians and psychiatrists to report on my mental state, and thus set in train the events which led to my abdication.

Now, in my extremity, I turn to you, not only because you are my friend, but because you, too, have been under inquisition and you understand how reason rocks under the relentless pressure of questioning. If you judge that I am insane, then I absolve you in advance from any blame and thank you for the friendship we have been privileged to share.

If you can go halfway to believing that I have told you a simple, terrible truth, then study the two documents appended to this letter: a copy of my unpublished encyclical to the Universal Church and a list of people in various countries with whom I established friendly relations during my pontificate and who may still be prepared to trust me or a messenger from me. Try to contact them, make them aware of what they can still do in these last fateful years. I do not believe we can hold back the inevitable cataclysm, but I am commanded to continue to the end the proclamation of the good news of love and salvation.

If you accept to do this, you will be at great risk—perhaps even of your life. Remember the Gospel of Matthew: "Then they shall deliver you up to be afflicted and shall put you to death . . . and many shall be scandalized and betray one another and hate one another."

I shall soon leave this place for the solitude of Monte Cassino. I trust I may arrive safely. If not, I commend myself as I commend you and your family, to God's loving care.

It is very late. The mercy of sleep has long been denied me, but now that this letter is written, perhaps it will be granted.

I am, yours always in Christ,
Jean Marie Barette

Under the signature was scrawled a brief ironic addendum: "*Feu le Pape.*" Lately the Pope.

Carl Mendelius was numb with shock and fatigue. He could not bring himself to read the close-written text of the encyclical. The long list of names and countries might have been written in Sanskrit. He folded the letter and the documents together, then locked them in the old black safe where he kept the deeds of his house, his insurance policies and the most precious portions of his research material.

Lotte would be waiting for him downstairs, knitting placidly at the fireside. He could not face her until he had composed himself and framed some kind of answer to her inevitable questions: "What did the letter say, Carl? What really happened to our dear Jean Marie?"

What indeed . . . ? Whatever else Carl Mendelius might be—failed priest, doting husband, puzzled father, skeptical believer—he was a scholarly historian, rigid in his application of the rules of internal and external evidence. He could smell a textual interpolation a mile away, trace it with meticulous accuracy back to its source, Gnostic, Manichean or Essene.

He knew that the doctrine of the Parousia—the Second Coming of the Redeemer which would mark the end of all temporal things—was the oldest and most authentic in tradition. It was recorded in the Synoptic Gospels, enshrined in the Creed, recalled every day in the liturgy: "Christ died, Christ is risen, Christ will come again." It represented the deepest hope of the believer for the final justification of the divine plan, the ultimate victory of order over chaos, of good over evil. That Jean Marie Barette, lately a Pope, should believe it, preach it as an article of faith, was as natural and necessary as breathing.

But that he should be committed to the narrowest, most primitive form of the belief—an imminent universal cataclysm, followed by a universal judgment, for which the elect must prepare themselves—was, to say the least, disquieting. The millenarian tradition took many forms, not all of them religious. It was implicit in Hitler's idea of the thousand-year Reich, in the Marxist promise that capitalism would wither away and give place to the universal brotherhood of socialism. Jean Marie Barette had needed no vision to shape his version of the millennium. He could have plucked it ready-made out of a hundred sources, from the Book of Daniel to the Cévenol prophets of the seventeenth century.

Even his purported vision was a familiar and disturbing element in the pattern. The minister of an organized religion was called and ordained to expound, under authority, a doctrine fixed and agreed long since. If he exceeded his commission he could be silenced or excommunicated by the same authority that called him.

The prophet was another kind of creature altogether. He claimed a direct communication with the Almighty. Therefore, his commission could not be withdrawn by any human agent. He could challenge the most sacred past with the classic phrase, used by Jesus himself: "It is written thus . . . but I tell thus and thus." So the prophet was always the alien, the herald of change, the challenger of existing order.

The problem of the Cardinals was not the madness of Jean Marie Barette, but that he had accepted the official function of high priest and supreme teacher, and then assumed another, possibly a contradictory, role.

In theory, of course, there need be no contradiction. The doctrine of private revelation, of a direct personal communication between Creator and creature, was as ancient as that of the Parousia. The Spirit descending on the apostles at Pentecost, Saul struck down on the road to Damascus, John caught up to apocalyptic revelation on Patmos—all these were events hallowed in tradition. Was it so unthinkable that in this last fateful decade of the millennium, when the possibility of planetary destruction was a proven fact and a vivid danger, God might choose a new prophet to renew His call to repentance and salvation?

In theological terms it was, at least, an orthodox proposition. To Carl Mendelius, the historian, called to sit in judgment on the sanity of a friend, it was a highly dangerous speculation. However, he was too tired now to trust his judgment on the simplest matter; so he locked the door of his study and went downstairs.

Lotte, blond, plump, affectionate and contented as a cat in

her role as mother of two and Frau Professor Mendelius, smiled up at him and lifted her face to be kissed. Caught in a sudden surge of passion he drew her to him and held her for a long moment.

She gave him a quizzical look and said, "What was that for?"

"I love you."

"I love you, too."

"Let's go to bed."

"I can't go yet. Johann telephoned to say he's forgotten his key. I said I'd wait up for him. Would you like a brandy?"

"Well, it's the next best thing."

As she poured the liquor she asked exactly the questions he had dreaded. He knew he could not fence with her. She was too intelligent for half-truths, so he told her flatly:

"The Cardinals forced him to abdicate, because they thought he was mad."

"Mad? Dear God! I should have said no one was more sane."

She handed him his drink and sat on the mat beside him, resting her head on his knees. They toasted each other. Mendelius stroked her forehead and her hair. She asked again:

"Why did they think he was mad?"

"Because he claimed to them—as he has to me—that he had a private revelation that the end of the world was near and that he was the precursor of the Second Coming!"

"What?" She gagged on the liquor. Mendelius passed her his handkerchief to mop her blouse.

"It's true, liebchen. He describes the experience in his letter. He believes it absolutely. Now that he is silenced he wants me to help spread the news."

"I still can't believe it. He was always so—so French and practical. Perhaps he has gone crazy."

"A crazy man could not have written the letter he wrote to me. A delusion, a fixed idea—that I could accept. It can happen, as a result of stress, or even as a result of a defective exercise in logic. Sane men once believed the world was flat. Sane people run their lives by the horoscopes in the evening papers. . . . Millions, like you and me, believe in a God they can't prove."

"But we don't go round saying the world's going to end tomorrow!"

"No, liebchen, we don't. But we do know it could, if the Russians and the Americans press the red button. We all live under the shadow of that reality. Our children are as aware of it as we are."

"Don't, Carl, please!"

"I'm sorry." He bent and kissed the top of her hair and then she pressed his hand against her cheek.

A few moments later she asked, quietly, "Are you going to do what Jean Marie wants?"

"I don't know, Lotte. Truly I don't. I'll have to think about it carefully. I'll need to talk to people who were close to him. Afterwards I'll want to see him . . . I owe him that much. We both owe it to him."

"That means you'll have to go away."

"Only for a little while."

"I hate it when you're away. I miss you so much."

"Come with me then. It's ages since you've been to Rome. You'd have lots of people to see."

"I can't, Carl. You know that. The children need me. This is a big year for Johann and I like to keep an eye on Katrin and her young man."

It was the small familiar contention between them: Lotte's constant clucking over her grown children, and his own middle-aged jealousy of her attention. But tonight he was too tired for argument, so he deferred the issue.

"We'll talk about it another time, liebchen. I need some professional counsel before I move a step out of Tübingen."

At fifty-three, Anneliese Meissner had achieved a variety of academic distinctions—the most notable of which was to be voted unanimously the ugliest woman in any faculty of the university. She was squat, fat and sallow, with a frog mouth and eyes scarcely visible behind thick myopic lenses. Her hair was a Medusa mess of faded yellow and her voice a hoarse rasp. Her dress was mannish and always ruinously untidy. Add to all that a sardonic wit and a merciless contempt for mediocrity and you had, as one colleague put it, "the perfect profile of a personality doomed to alienation."

Yet, by some miracle, she had escaped the doom and established herself as a kind of tutelary goddess in the shadow of the old castle of Hohentübingen. Her apartment on the Burgsteige was more like a club than a dwelling place, where students and faculty perched on stools and boxes to drink wine and make fierce debate until the small hours. Her lectures in clinical psychology were packed and her papers were published in learned journals in a dozen languages. She was even credited in student myth with a lover, a troll-like creature who lived in the Harz Mountains and who came to visit her in secret on Sundays and the greater holidays of the university calendar.

The day after he received Jean Marie's letter, Carl Mendelius invited her to lunch in a private booth at the Weinstube Forelle. Anneliese Meissner ate and drank copiously, yet still managed to deliver waspish monologues on the administration of university funds, the local politics of Land Baden-Württemberg, a colleague's paper on endogenous depression, which she dismissed as "puerile rubbish," and the sexual lives of Turkish labourers in the local paper industry. They were already at the coffee before Mendelius judged it wise to ask his question.

"If I were to show you a letter, would you be able to offer a clinical opinion on the person who wrote it?"

She fixed him with a myopic stare and smiled. The smile was terrifying. It was as if she were about to gobble him up with the crumbs of her strudel. "Are you going to show me the letter, Carl?"

"If you'll accept it as a professional and privileged communication."

"From you, Carl, yes. But before you give it to me, you'd better understand a few axioms in my discipline. I don't want you to communicate a document that's obviously important to you and then complain because my commentary's inadequate. Understood?"

"Understood."

"First then: handwriting, in serial specimens, is a fairly reliable indicator to cerebral states. Even simple hypoxia—the inadequate oxygen supply to the brain—will produce rapid deterioration of the script. Second: even in the gravest psychotic illnesses, the subject may have lucid periods in which his writings or utterances are completely rational. Hölderlin died in this town of ours a hopeless schizophrenic. But would you guess it from reading *Bread and Wine* or *Empedocles on Etna*? Nietzsche died of general paralysis of the insane, probably due to syphilitic infection. Could you diagnose that, solely on the evidence of *Thus Spake Zarathustra*? Third point: any personal letter contains indications of emotional states or even psychic propensities; but they are indicators only. The states may be shallow, the propensities well within the confines of normality. Do I make myself clear?"

"Admirably, Professor!" Carl Mendelius made a comical gesture of surrender. "I place my letter in safe hands." He passed it to her across the table. "There are other documents as well, but I have not yet had time to study them. The author is Pope Gregory the Seventeenth, who abdicated last week."

Anneliese Meissner pursed her thick lips in a whistle of surprise but said nothing. She read the letter slowly, without comment, while Mendelius sipped his coffee and munched petits fours—bad for the waistline but better than the cigarette habit which he was trying desperately to abandon. Finally Anneliese finished her reading. She laid the letter on the table in front of her and covered it with her big pudgy hands. She chose her first words with clinical care.

"I am not sure, Carl, that I am the right person to comment on this. I am not a believer, never have been. Whatever may be the faculty that enables one to make the leap from reason to faith, I have never had it. Some people are tone-deaf; others are colour-blind. I am incurably atheist. I have often regretted it. In clinical work I have sometimes felt handicapped when dealing with patients who have strong religious beliefs. You see, Carl" —she gave a long, wheezing chuckle—"according to my lights, you and all your kind live in a fixed delusional state, which is, by definition, insanity. On the other hand, since I can't disprove your delusions, I have to accept that I may be the sick one."

Mendelius grinned at her and popped the last petit four into her mouth.

"We've already agreed that your conclusions will be subject to large qualification. Your reputation will be safe with me."

"So, the evidence as I read it." She picked up the letter and began her annotation. "Handwriting: no evidence of disturbance. It's a beautiful regular script. The letter itself is precise and logical. The narrative sections are classically simple. The emotions of the writer are under control. Even when he speaks of being under surveillance, there is no overemphasis to indicate a paranoid state. The section dealing with the visionary experience is, within its limits, clear. There are no pathological images, with either a violent or a sexual connotation. . . . Prima facie, therefore, the man who wrote the letter was sane when he wrote it."

"But he does express doubts about his own sanity."

"In fact he does not. He recognizes that others may have doubts about it. He is absolutely convinced of the reality of his visionary experience."

"And what do you think of that experience?"

"I am convinced that he had it. How I would interpret it is another matter. In the same fashion I am convinced that Martin Luther believed he saw the Devil in his cell and pitched an inkwell at him. That doesn't mean I believe in the devil, only in the reality of the experience to Luther." She laughed again, and went on in a more relaxed fashion. "You're an old Jesuit, Carl. You know what I'm talking about. I deal with delusional patients all the time. I have to start with the premise that their delusions are real to them."

"So you're saying Jean Marie is a delusional subject?"

"Don't put the words in my mouth, Carl!" Her reproof was instant and sharp. She thrust the letter towards him. "Take another look at the vision passage again, and the pieces before and after. It falls exactly into a daydream structure. He is reading and meditating in a sunny garden. All meditation involves some degree of auto-hypnosis. He dreams in two parts: the aftermath of the cataclysm on an empty earth, and then the whirling fiery passage to outer space. Both these images are vivid but essentially banal. They could have been culled from any good science fiction film. He has cerebrated them many times before. Now he daydreams them. When he wakes he is back in the garden. It's a common phenomenon."

"But he believes it is a supernatural intervention."

"He *says* he does."

"What the hell do you mean?"

"I mean," said Anneliese Meissner flatly, "he could be lying!"

"No! It's impossible! I know this man. We're close as brothers."

"An unfortunate analogy," said Anneliese Meissner mildly. "Sibling relationships can be infernally complicated. Simmer down, Carl! You wanted a professional opinion, you're getting it. At least take time to examine a reasonable hypothesis."

"This one is pure fantasy!"

"Is it? You're an historian. Think back. How many convenient miracles can you name? How many most timely revelations? Every sect in the world has to provide them for its devotees.

The Mormons have Joseph Smith and his fabulous golden plates; the Reverend Sun Myung Moon made himself the Lord of the Second Advent, even Jesus bowed down to worship him. So suppose, Carl—just suppose!—your Gregory the Seventeenth decided that this was crisis time for the institution and that the moment was ripe for some new manifestation of divine involvement."

"Then he was taking a hell of a gamble."

"And he lost it. Might he not now be seeking to recover something out of the wreckage, and using you to do it?"

"It's a monstrous idea!"

"Not to me. Why are you choking on it? I'll tell you. Because, though you like to believe you're a liberal thinker, you're still a member of the Roman Catholic family. For your own sake you have to protect the mythos. I noticed you didn't wince when I mentioned the Mormons and the Moonies. Come on, my friend! Where's your mind?"

"It seems I've mislaid it." Carl Mendelius was grim.

"If you take my advice, you'll drop the whole affair."

"Why?"

"You're a scholar with an international reputation. You want no truck with madness or folk magic."

"Jean Marie is my friend. I owe him at least an honest enquiry."

"Then you'll need a *Beisitzer*—an assessor to help you weigh the evidence."

"How would you like the job, Anneliese? It might give you some new clinical insights."

He said it as a joke to take the sting out of their discussion. The joke fell flat.

Anneliese weighed the proposition for a long moment and then announced firmly, "Very well. I'll do it. It'll be a new experience to play inquisitor to a Pope. But, dear colleague"—she reached out and laid her big hand on his wrist—"I'm much more interested in keeping you honest!"

When his last lecture was over, late in the afternoon, Carl Mendelius walked down to the river and sat a long time, watching the stately passage of swans on the grey water.

Anneliese Meissner had left him deeply disturbed. She had challenged not only his relationship with Jean Marie Barette, but his integrity as a scholar, his moral stance as a seeker after truth. She had probed shrewdly at the weakest point in his intellectual armour: his inclination to make more tender judgments about his own religious family than about others. For all his skeptic bent, he was still god-haunted, conditioned to the pavlovian reflexes of his Jesuit past. He would rather conform his findings as an historian with orthodox tradition than deal bluntly with the contradictions between the two. He preferred the comfort of a familiar hearth to the solitude of the innovator. So far, he had not betrayed himself. He could still look in the mirror and respect the man he saw. But the danger was there, like a small prickling lust, ready to take fire at the right moment with the right woman.

In the case of Jean Marie Barette, the danger of self-betrayal could be mortal. The issue was clear and he could not gloss or hedge it. There were three possibilities, mutually exclusive. Jean Marie was a madman. Jean Marie was a liar. Jean Marie was a man touched by God, charged to deliver a momentous revelation.

He had two choices: refuse to be involved—which was the right of any honest man who felt himself incompetent—or submit the whole case to the most rigid scrutiny, and act without fear or favour on the evidence. With Anneliese Meissner, brusque and uncompromising, as his *Beisitzer* he could hardly do otherwise.

But what of Jean Marie Barette, longtime friend of the heart? How would he react when the harsh terms of reference were set before him? How would he feel when the friend he sought as advocate presented himself as the Grand Inquisitor? Once again Carl Mendelius found himself flinching from the confrontation.

Far away towards the Klinikum an ambulance siren sounded—a long, repetitive wail, eerie in the gathering dusk. Mendelius shivered under the impact of a childhood memory: the sound of air-raid sirens, and after it, the drone of aircraft and the shattering explosions of the fire bombs that rained down on Dresden.

When he arrived home, he found the family huddled around the television screen. The new Pope had been elected in an afternoon session of the conclave and was now being proclaimed as Leo XIV. There was no magic in the occasion. The commentaries were without enthusiasm. Even the Roman crowd seemed listless and the traditional acclamations had a hollow ring.

Their Pontiff was sixty-nine years old, a stout man with an eagle's beak, a cold eye, a rasping Aemilian accent and twenty-five years' practice in Curial business behind him. His election was the outcome of a careful but painfully obvious piece of statecraft.

After two foreign incumbents, they needed an Italian who understood the rules of the papal game. After an actor turned zealot and a diplomat turned mystic the safest choice was Roberto Arnaldo, a bureaucrat with ice water in his veins. He would raise no passions, proclaim no visions. He would make none but the most necessary pronouncements; and these would be so carefully wrapped in Italian rhetoric that the liberals and the conservatives would swallow them with equal satisfaction. Most important of all, he suffered from gout and high cholesterol and, according to the actuaries, should enjoy a reign neither too short nor too long.

The news kept the conversation going at Mendelius' dining table. He was glad of the diversion, because Johann was moody over an essay that would not come right, Katrin was snappish and Lotte was at the low point of one of her menopausal depressions. It was an evening when he wondered with wry humour whether the celibate life had not a great deal to recommend it, and a noncelibate bachelor existence, even more. However, he was practiced enough in marriage to keep that kind of thought to himself.

When the meal was over he retired to his study and made a telephone call to Herman Frank, director of the German Academy of Fine Arts in Rome.

"Herman? This is Carl Mendelius. I'm calling to ask a favour. I'm coming to Rome for a week or ten days at the end of the month. Could you put me up?"

"Delighted!" Frank was a silver-haired courtly fellow, an historian of Cinquecento painters, who kept one of the best tables in Rome. "Will Lotte be coming with you? We've got acres of space."

"Possibly. It's not decided yet."

"Bring her! Hilde would be delighted. She needs some girl company."

"Thanks, Herman. You're very kind."

"Not at all. You might be able to do me a favour, too."

"Name it."

"While you're here the Academy will be playing host to a group of Evangelical pastors. The usual thing—daily lectures, evening discussions, afternoon bus rides. It would be a great feather in my cap if I could announce that the great Mendelius would give a couple of lectures, perhaps conduct a group discussion . . . ?"

"Happy to do it, my friend."

"Wonderful! Wonderful! Let me know when you're arriving and I'll pick you up at the airport. . . ."

Mendelius put down the receiver and gave a chuckle of satisfaction. Herman Frank's invitation to lecture was a stroke of good fortune. The German Academy was one of the oldest and most prestigious national academies in Rome. Founded in 1910 in the reign of Wilhelm II of Prussia, it had survived two wars and the mindless ideologues of the Third Reich and still managed to maintain a reputation for solid Germanic scholarship. It offered Mendelius, therefore, a base of operations and a highly respectable cover for his delicate enquiries.

The German contingent at the Vatican would respond happily to a dinner invitation from Herman Frank. His guest book was an elaborate tome resplendent with exotic titles like "Rector Magnificent of the Pontifical Biblical Institute" and "Grand Chancellor of the Institute of Biblical Archaeology." How Lotte would respond to the idea was another matter. He needed a more propitious moment to open that little surprise packet.

His next step was to prepare a list of contacts to whom he should write and announce his visit. He had been a denizen of the city long enough to assemble a miscellany of friends and acquaintances, from the crusty old Cardinal who disapproved his defection but was still generous enough to appreciate his scholarship, to the Custodian of Incunabula in the Vatican Library and the last dowager of the Pierleoni, who directed the gossips of Rome from her wheelchair. He was still dredging up names when Lotte came in, carrying a tray of coffee. She looked penitent and forlorn, uncertain of her welcome.

"The children have gone out. It's lonely downstairs. Do you mind if I sit up here with you?"

He took her in his arms and kissed her. "It's lonely up here too, liebchen. Sit down and relax. I'll pour the coffee."

"What are you doing?"

"Arranging our holiday."

He told her of his talk with Herman Frank. He enthused about the pleasures of the city in summer, the opportunity to meet old friends, do a little touring. She took it all with surprising calm. Then she asked:

"It's really about Jean Marie, isn't it?"

"Yes; but it's also about us. I want you with me, Lotte. I need you. If the children want to come, I'll arrange hostel accommodation for them."

"They have other plans, Carl. We were arguing about them before you came home. Katrin wants to go to Paris with her boyfriend. Johann is going hiking in Austria. That's fine for him; but Katrin . . ."

"Katrin's a woman now, liebchen. She'll do what she wants whether we approve or not. After all . . ." He bent and kissed her again. "They're only lent to us; and when they leave home we'll be left where we started. We'd better start practicing to be lovers again."

"I suppose so." She gave a small shrugging gesture of defeat. "But, Carl . . ." She broke off, as if afraid to put the thought into words.

Mendelius prompted her gently. "But what, liebchen?"

"I know the children will leave us. I'm getting used to the idea, truly I am. But what if Jean Marie takes you away from me? This—this thing he wants of you is very strange and frightening." Without warning she burst into convulsive sobbing. "I'm afraid, Carl . . . terribly, terribly afraid!"

II

"In these last fateful years of the millennium . . ." Thus the opening line of Jean Marie Barette's unpublished encyclical. "In this dark time of confusion, violence and terror, I, Gregory, your brother in the flesh, your servant in Christ Jesus, am commanded by the Holy Spirit to write you these words of warning and of comfort. . . ."

Mendelius could hardly believe the evidence of his own eyes. Papal encyclicals, for all their portentous authority, were usually commonplace documents—stating traditional positions on matters of faith or morals. Any good theologian could frame the argument. Any good Latinist could make it eloquent.

The pattern was still that of the old rhetoricians. The argument was laid down. Scripture and the Fathers were quoted in support. Directives were given, binding the conscience of the faithful. There was a closing exhortation to faith, hope and continuing charity. The formal "we" was used throughout, not merely to express the dignity of the Pontiff but to connote a community and a continuity in the office and in the teaching. The implication was plain: the Pope taught nothing new; he expounded an ancient and unchangeable truth, simply applying it to the needs of his time.

At one stroke Jean Marie Barette had broken the pattern. He had abrogated the role of exegete and assumed the mantle of the prophet. "I, Gregory, am commanded by the Holy Spirit . . ." Even in the formal Latin, the impact of the words was shocking. No wonder the men of the Curia had blanched when they read them for the first time. What followed was even more tendentious:

. . . The comfort which I offer you is the abiding promise of our Lord Jesus Christ: "I will not leave you orphans. Behold I am with you all days, even to the end of the world." The warning I give you is that the end is very near, that this generation shall not pass until all these things be fulfilled . . . I do not tell you this of myself, or because I have predicated it upon human reason, but because it was shown to me in a vision, which I dare not conceal but am commanded to tell openly to the world. But even that revelation was no new thing. It was simply an affirmation, clear as sunrise, of what was revealed in the Holy Scriptures. . . .

There followed a long exposition of texts from the Synoptic Gospels, and a series of eloquent analogies between the biblical "signs" and the circumstances of the last decade of the twentieth century: wars and rumours of wars, famines and epidemics, false Christs and false prophets.

To Carl Mendelius, deeply and professionally versed in apocalyptic literature from the earliest times to the present, it was a disturbing and dangerous document. Emanating from so high a source it could not fail to raise alarm and panic. Among the militant it might easily serve as a rallying cry for one last crusade of the elect against the unrighteous. To the weak and the fearful it might even be an inducement to suicide before the horrors of the last times overtook them.

He asked himself what he would have done had he, like the secretary, seen it, new-written, on the Pontiff's desk. Without a doubt he would have urged its suppression. Which was exactly what the Cardinals had done: suppressed the document and silenced the author.

Then a new thought presented itself. Was not this the fate of all prophets, the price they paid for a terrible gift, the bloody seal of truth upon their soothsaying? Out of the welter of biblical eloquence another text echoed in his mind; the last lamentation of Christ over the Holy City.

"Jerusalem, Jerusalem, thou that killest the prophets and stonest them that are sent to thee! How often would I have gathered thy children as a hen gathers her chickens under her wings, but thou wouldst not! . . . Therefore the day will come when thine enemies will cast a trench about thee, and beat thee flat to the ground, and thy children who are in thee; and they shall not leave in thee a stone upon a stone, because thou hast not known the things that are to thy peace!"

It was an eerie thought for the midnight hour, with the moonlight streaming through the leaded windows and the cold wind searching down the Neckar valley and round the alleys of the old town where poor Hölderlin died mad and Melanchthon, sanest of men, taught that "God draws; but he draws the willing ones."

All his experience affirmed that Jean Marie Barette was the most willing, the most open of men, the least likely to fall victim to a fanatic's illusion.

True, he had written a wildly imprudent document. Yet, perhaps this was the core of the matter: that in the hour of extremity only such a folly could command the attention of the world.

But command it to what? If the final catastrophe were at hand, its date computed irrevocably into the mechanism of creation, then why proclaim it at all? What counsel could prevail against the nightmare knowledge? What prayer had potency against a rescript written from eternity? There was a deep pathos in Jean Marie's response to the questions:

. . . My dear brothers and sisters, my little children, we all fear death, we shrink from the suffering which may precede it. We quail from the mystery of the last leap, which we must all make, into eternity. But we are followers of the Lord, the Son of God who sufferered and died in human flesh. We are the inheritors of the good news which he left with us: that death is the gateway to life, that it is a leap, not into darkness, but into the hands of Everlasting Mercy. It is an act of trust, an act of love, by which, as lovers do, we abandon ourselves to, become one with, the Beloved. . . .

The knock at the door startled Mendelius. His daughter, Katrin, entered, hesitant and timid. She was in her dressing gown, her blond hair tied back with a pink ribbon, her face scrubbed clean of make-up, her eyes red with weeping. She asked, "May I talk with you, Papa?"

"Of course, sweetheart." He was instantly solicitous. "What's the matter? You've been crying." He kissed her gently and led her to a chair. "Now tell me what's bothering you."

"This trip to Paris. Mother's still very angry about it. She says I have to discuss it with you. She doesn't understand, Papa—truly she doesn't. I'm nineteen. I'm a woman now, just as much as she is and . . ."

"Take it easy, little one! Let's start from the beginning. You want to go to Paris for the summer. Who's going with you?"

"Franz, of course! You know we've been going together for ages now. You said you liked him very much."

"I do. He's a very nice young man. A promising painter, too. Are you in love with him?"

"Yes, I am." There was a note of defiance in the answer. "And he's in love with me!"

"Then I'm very happy for you both, little one!" He smiled and patted her hand. "It's the best feeling in the world. So what comes next? You've talked about marriage? You want to become engaged? Is that it?"

"No, Papa." She was very firm about it. "Not yet anyway. . . . And that's the point—Mama refuses to understand."

"Have you tried explaining it to her?"

"Over and over! But she just won't listen."

"Try *me* then," said Mendelius gently.

"It's not easy. I'm not good with words like you. The thing is, I'm afraid; we're both afraid."

"Of what?"

"Of always . . . just that. Of getting married and having children and trying to make a home, while the whole world could tumble round our ears in a day." Suddenly she was passionate and eloquent. "You older ones don't understand. You've survived a war. You've built things. You've had us; we're grown up. But look at the world you've left us! All along the borders there are rocket launchers and missile silos. The oil's running out so we're using atom power and burying the waste that will one day poison our children. . . . You've given us everything except tomorrow! I don't want my baby to be born in a bomb shelter and die of radiation sickness! All we've got is today and loving each other and we think we've got a right at least to that!"

Her vehemence shocked him like water dashed in his face. The little blond *Mädchen* he had dandled on his knee was gone forever. In her place was an angry young woman, filled with a deep resentment against himself and his whole generation. The grim thought struck him that perhaps it was for her and all the others like her that Jean Marie Barette had written his prescription for life in the last days. Certainly it was not the young ones who had suppressed it, but the men of his generation, the elders, the seeming wise, the perennial pragmatists, living, in any case, on borrowed time. He breathed a silent prayer for wisdom of the tongue and began softly and tenderly to reason with her.

". . . Believe me, little one, I understand how you feel, both of you. Your mother understands, too, but in a different way, because she knows how a woman can be hurt, and how the consequences can be longer for her than for a man. She fights with you because she loves you and she's afraid for you. . . . You see, whatever mess the world's in—and I've been sitting here reading how much more horrible it may get—you've had the experience of loving and being loved. Not the whole experience, yet, but some of it; so you do know what loving's about: giving and taking and caring and never grabbing the whole cake for yourself. . . . Now you're beginning the next chapter with your Franz, and only the pair of you can write it, together. If you botch it, the best your mother and I can do is dry your tears and hold your hand until you're ready to begin living again. . . . We can't tell you how to arrange your emotional lives, or even your sexual lives. All we can tell you is that if you waste your hearts and waste that special joy that makes sex so wonderful, it's something you can't renew. . . . You can find other experiences, other joys, too, but never again that first, special, very exclusive ecstasy that makes this whole confusion of living and dying worthwhile. . . . What more can I say, little one? Go to Paris with your Franz. Learn your loving together. As for tomorrow? . . How's your Latin?"

She gave him a tearful smile "You know it's always been terrible."

"Try this. '*Quid sit futurum cras, fuge quaerere.*' Old Horace wrote it."

"It still means nothing."

"It's very simple. 'Forbear to ask what tomorrow may bring.' . . . If you spend your whole life waiting for the storm, you'll never enjoy the sunshine."

"O Papa!" She threw her arms round his neck and kissed him. "I love you so much! You've made me very happy."

"Go to bed, little one," said Carl Mendelius softly. "I've still got an hour's work ahead of me."

"You work too hard, Papa."

He gave her a small admonitory pat on the cheek and quoted lightly, "A father without work means a daughter without a dowry. Good night, my love. Golden dreams!"

When the door closed behind her, he felt the prickling of unbidden tears—tears for all the youthful hope in her, and all her threatened innocence. He blew his nose violently, picked up his spectacles and settled back to his reading of Jean Marie's apocalypse.

. . . It is clear that in the days of universal calamity the traditional structures of society will not survive. There will be a ferocious struggle for the simplest needs of life—food, water, fuel and shelter. Authority will be usurped by the strong and the cruel. Large urban societies will fragment themselves into tribal groups, each hostile to the other. Rural areas will be subject to pillage. The human person will be as much a prey as the beasts whom we now slaughter for food. Reason will be so clouded that man will resort for solace to the crudest and most violent forms of magic. It will be hard, even for those founded most strongly in the Promise of the Lord, to sustain their faith and continue to give witness, as they must do, even to the end. . . . How then must Christians comport themselves in these days of trial and terror?

. . . Since they will no longer be able to maintain themselves as large groups, they must divide themselves into small communities, each capable of sustaining itself by the exercise of a common faith and a true mutual charity. Their Christian witness must be given by spreading that charity outwards to those who are not of the faith, by aiding the distressed, by sharing even their most meager means with those who are most deprived. When the priestly hierarchy can no longer function, they will elect to themselves ministers and teachers who will maintain the Word in its integrity, and continue to conduct the Eucharist. . . .

"God Almighty! He's really done it now!" Mendelius heard his own voice echo round the attic room. Fiction or predestined fact, this, from the pen of a Pope, was the unsayable, the absolutely unprintable. If the press of the world got hold of it, they would make Jean Marie Barette look like the maddest of mad mullahs, the craziest of all prophets of doom. And yet, in the context of an atomic calamity, it was a matter of simple logic. It was a scenario which, in one form or another, every national leader kept locked in his most secret files, the script for the aftermath of Armageddon.

Which brought Mendelius, by a round turn, to the third and final document: the list of those who, Jean Marie thought, would be prepared to believe his message and his messenger. This was perhaps the most startling deposition of all. Unlike the letter and the encyclical it was typewritten, as if it had once formed part of an official file. It contained names, addresses, titles, telephone numbers, methods of private contact, and terse, telegraphic notes on each individual. There were politicians, industrialists, churchmen, leaders of dissident groups, editors of well-known journals, more than a hundred names in all. Two sample entries set the tone of the record.

U.S.A.

Name:	Michael Grant Morrow
Title:	Secretary of State
Private Address:	593 Park Avenue, New York
Telephone:	(212) 689-7611
Religion:	Episcopalian

Met at presidential dinner. Firm religious convictions. Speaks Russian, French and German. Respected in Russia but Asian relations weak. Deeply aware of hair-trigger situation on European frontiers. Has written a private monograph on the function of religious groups in a disintegrating social framework.

U.S.S.R.

Name: Sergei Andrevich Petrov
Title: Minister for Agricultural Production
Private Address: Unknown
Telephone: Moscow 53871

Private visit Vatican with nephew of Premier. Aware of need for religious and ethnic tolerance in U.S.S.R. and satellites, but unable make headway against party dogmatists. Concerned that Russia's problems with food supplies and oil may precipitate conflict. Close friends in high military; enemies in K.G.B. Vulnerable in event bad harvest or economic blockade.

On the last page was a note in Jean Marie's own handwriting:

All of the people on this list are known to me personally. Each in his own fashion has demonstrated an awareness of the crisis, and a willingness to confront it in a spirit of human compassion, if not always from the standpoint of a believer. Whether they will change under the pressure of coming events, I do not know. However, each has reposed a degree of trust in me and I have tried to return the gesture. As a private person you will be regarded at first with suspicion and they will be much more reserved with you. The risks of which I have warned you will begin at your first contact, because you will have no diplomatic protection, and the language of politics is contrived for the concealment of truth. J.M.B.

Carl Mendelius took off his spectacles and tried to palm the sleep out of his eyes. He had read his brief with the devotion of a friend and the care of an honest scholar. Now, in this lonely hour after midnight, he must pass judgment on the text, if not yet on the man who had written it. A sudden cold fear took hold of him, as if the shadows of the room were haunted by old accusing ghosts: the ghosts of men burned for heresy and women drowned for witchcraft and nameless martyrs bewailing the vanity of their sacrifice.

In these skeptical years of middle age, prayer did not come easily to him. Now he felt the need of it; but the words would not come. He was like a man locked in darkness so long that he had forgotten the sound of human speech.

"Now, we're really in cloud-cuckoo-land!" Anneliese Meissner munched on a pickled gherkin and washed it down with red wine. "This so-called encyclical is a nonsense—a hotchpotch of folklore and mysticism!"

They were sitting in her cluttered apartment, with the documents spread before them on the table and a bottle of Assmanshausen to keep down the dust that lay everywhere. Mendelius had refused to let the documents out of his sight, while Anneliese had demanded, with equal vehemence, the right of the assessor to read every line of evidence. Mendelius protested her curt dismissal of the document.

"Let's stop right there! If we're going to debate the issue let's be scientific about it. First of all there's a whole body of millenarian literature from the Book of Daniel in the Old Testament to Jakob Boehme in the seventeenth century and Teilhard de Chardin in the twentieth. Some of it is nonsense—yes! Some of it is high poetry like that of the Englishman William Blake. Some of it represents a critical interpretation of one of the oldest traditions in the world. Second, any serious scientist will tell you that there may be a term, by evolution or catastrophe, to human existence as we know it on the planet. What Jean Marie has written falls well within the saner confines of the codex. The scenario of catastrophe is already a matter of informed speculation by the scientists and military strategists."

"Agreed. But your man still makes a mishmash of it! Faith, hope and charity while the wolf-children are snarling at the gates! A loving God brooding over the chaos he himself has engineered. Balls, Professor!"

"What would happen if the text were published?"

"Half the world would laugh it out of court. The other half would catch the dancing madness and go waltzing out to meet the redeemer on his 'cloud of glory.' Seriously, Carl, I think you ought to burn the damned thing and forget it!"

"I can burn it; but I can't forget it."

"Because you're a victim of the same God-madness!"

"What about this third document—the list of names?"

"I don't see that it has any significance at all. It's an aide-mémoire pulled out of the filing cabinet. Every politician in the world keeps records like that. What does he expect you to do with it? Trot round the world visiting all these people? What will you say to them? 'My friend Gregory the Seventeenth, the one they tossed out of the Vatican, believes the end of the world is coming. He's had a vision about it. He thought you should have advance notice.' Come on, Carl! They'd have you in a straitjacket halfway through the first interview!"

Suddenly he saw the funny side of it and laughed, a great bellow of mirth that subsided finally into a helpless giggle. Anneliese Meissner splashed more wine into the glasses and lifted her own in salute.

"That's better! For a while I thought I'd lost a good colleague."

"Thank you, Frau Beisitzer." Mendelius took a long swallow of wine and set down his glass. "Now let's get back to business. I'm going to Rome in a couple of weeks."

"The hell you are!" She stared at him in disbelief. "And what good do you expect to do there?"

"Have a holiday, give a couple of lectures at the German Academy, talk to Jean Marie Barette and people who were close to him. I'll make tapes during or after each interview and send them back to you. Afterwards, I'll decide whether to drop the affair or not. At least I'll have discharged my duty as a friend—and I'll have kept my assessor honest, too!"

"I hope you realize, my friend, that even when you've done all that, your evidence will still be incomplete."

"I don't see why it need be."

"Think about it." Anneliese Meissner speared another gherkin and waved it under his nose. "How are you going to talk to God? Will you put him on tape, too?"

He was a tidy man by nature and he prepared for his visit to Rome with finical care. He made telephone calls to friends, wrote letters to acquaintances, armed himself with introductions to Vatican officials, made dates far in advance for lunches, dinners and formal interviews. He was careful to stress the overt purpose of his visit: a search in the Vatican Library and the Biblical Institute for fragments of Ebionite literature and a short series of discourses at the Academy on the apocalyptic tradition.

He had chosen the subject not only because it provided a cue on which to begin his enquiries about Jean Marie, but because it might elicit from his Evangelical audience some emotional response to the millennial theme. In his younger days he had been deeply stirred by the Jungian idea of the "great dreaming," the persistence of tribal experience in the subconscious, and its perennial influence on the individual and on the group. There was a striking similarity between this notion and that which the theologians called the "Infusion" and the "Indwelling of the Spirit." It raised also the question of Anneliese Meissner, his *Beisitzer*, and her obdurate rejection of any transcendental experience whatsoever. Her gibe about talking to God still rankled —the more because he had found no adequate answer to it.

He spent a long time over a letter to the Abbot of Monte Cassino, who was now Jean Marie's religious superior. This was a most necessary courtesy. Jean Marie had placed himself under obedience, and the exactions of authority could extend to his physical movements and even to his private correspondence. Mendelius, a onetime subject of the system, had a nice perception of religious protocol. His letter told of his long friendship with Jean Marie Barette, his diffidence about intruding upon his present privacy. However, if the Abbot had no objection and the former Pontiff were willing to receive him, Professor Carl Mendelius would like to pay a visit to the monastery at a mutually convenient date.

He enclosed a note which he begged the Abbot to deliver into the hands of Jean Marie Barette. This, too, he had composed with studious discretion.

My dear friend,

Please forgive the informality, but I am ignorant of the protocol for correspondence with a retired Pope, who has made himself a humble son of St. Benedict.

I have always regretted that it was not possible for me to share the burdens of your final days in the Vatican; but German professors are two marks a dozen and their sphere of influence seldom extends beyond the lecture hall.

However, I shall soon be in Rome—still researching the Ebionites and giving some lectures on the doctrine of the Parousia at the German Academy—and it would give me a great pleasure to see you again, if only for a little while.

I have written to the Father Abbot asking his permission to visit you, provided always that you are in the mood to receive me. If we can meet I shall be grateful and happy. If the time is not opportune, please do not hesitate to say so.

I trust you are well. With the world in such a mess I think you were wise to retire from it. Lotte sends you her most affectionate greetings and my children their respectful salutations. As for myself, I remain always

Yours in the Fellowship of the Lord,
Carl Mendelius

The answer came back in ten days, delivered by a clerical messenger from the Cardinal Archbishop of Munich: the Very Reverend Abbot Andrew would be happy to receive him at Monte Cassino, and, if his health permitted, the Very Reverend Jean Marie Barette, O.S.B., would be delighted to see his old friend. He should telephone the Abbot immediately upon his arrival in Rome, and an appointment would be arranged.

There was no response at all from Jean Marie.

The evening before he left for Rome with Lotte he asked his son, Johann, to have coffee with him in his study. They had been uneasy together for a long time now. The boy, a brilliant student in economics, was uncomfortable in the shadow of a father who was also a senior member of the faculty. The father was often clumsy in his eagerness to foster so obvious a talent. The result was secrecy on the one side, resentment on the other, with only a rare display of the affection that still existed between them. This time Mendelius was determined to be tactful. As usual he managed only to be heavy-handed. He asked:

"When do you leave on your trip, son?"

"Two days from now."

"Have you planned a route yet?"

"More or less. We go by train to Munich, then start hiking—through the Obersalzburg and over the Tauern into Carinthia."

"It's beautiful country. I wish I were coming with you. By the way"—he fished in his breast pocket and brought out a sealed envelope—"this is to help with the expenses."

"But you've already given me my holiday money."

"That's something extra. You've worked very hard this year. Your mother and I wanted to show our appreciation."

"Well . . . thanks." He was obviously embarrassed. "But there was no need. You've always been generous with me."

"There's something I want to say to you, son." He saw the boy stiffen immediately. The old mulish look came over his face. "It's a personal matter. I'd rather you didn't discuss it with your mother. One of the reasons I'm going to Rome is to investigate what brought about the abdication of Gregory the Seventeenth. As you know he was my dear friend. . . ." He gave a small wry smile. "Yours, too, I suppose, because without his help your mother and I might never have married and you wouldn't be here. . . . However, the enquiries may take a long time and entail a great deal of travel. There may also be certain risks. If anything happens to me, I want you to know my affairs are in order. Doctor Mahler, our lawyer, holds most of the documents. The rest are in the safe over there. You're a man now. You would have to step into my shoes and take care of your mother and sister."

"I don't understand. What sort of risks are you talking about? And why do you have to expose yourself to them?"

"It's difficult to explain."

"I'm your son." His tone was resentful. "At least give me a chance to understand."

"Please! Try to relax with me. I need you now, very much."

"I'm sorry, it's just that . . ."

"I know. We rub each other the wrong way. But I love you, son. I wish I could tell you how much." Emotion welled up in him and he wanted to reach out and embrace the young man, but he was afraid of a rebuff. He went on quietly, "To explain, I have to show you something secret and bind you on your honor not to reveal it to anyone."

"You have my word, Father."

"Thank you." Mendelius crossed to the safe, took out the Barette documents and handed them to his son. "Read those. They explain everything. When you're finished, we'll talk. I've got some notes to write up."

He settled himself at his desk while Johann sat in the armchair, poring over the documents. In the soft glow of the reading lamp he reminded Mendelius of one of Raffaello's young models, obedient and immobile, while the master made him immortal on canvas. He felt a pang of regret for the wasted years. This was the way it should have been, long ago: father and son, content and companionable, all childish quarrels long forgotten.

Mendelius got up and refilled Johann's coffee cup and brandy glass. Johann nodded his thanks and went on with his reading. It was nearly forty minutes before he turned the last page, sat for a long moment in silence, then folded the documents deliberately, got up and laid them on his father's desk. He said quietly:

"I understand now, Father. I think it's a dangerous nonsense and I hate to see you involved with it; but I do understand."

"Thank you, son. Would you care to tell me why you think it's a nonsense?"

"Yes." He was firm but respectful. He held himself very erect, like a subaltern addressing his commander. "There's something I've wanted to tell you for a long while. Now seems as good a time as any."

"Perhaps you'd like to pour me a brandy first." Mendelius smiled at him.

"Of course." He refilled the glass and set it on the desk. "The fact is, Father, I'm no longer a believer."

"In God, or specifically in the Roman Catholic Church?"

"In neither."

"I'm sorry to hear it, son." Mendelius was studiously calm. "I've always felt the world must be a bleak place without some hope of a hereafter. But I'm glad you told me. Does your mother know?"

"Not yet."

"I'll tell her, if you like—but later. I'd like her to enjoy this holiday."

"Are you angry with me?"

"Dear God, no!" Mendelius heaved himself out of his chair and clamped his hands on the young man's shoulders. "Listen! All my life I've taught and written that a man can walk only the path he sees at his own feet. If you cannot honestly assent to a faith then you must not. Rather you should consent to be burned like Bruno in the Field of Flowers. As for your mother and me, we have no more right than anyone else to dictate your conscience. . . . But remember one thing, son. Keep your mind open, so that the light can always come in. Keep your heart open so that love will never be shut out."

"I—I never thought you'd take it like this." For the first time his control cracked and he seemed about to burst into tears. Mendelius drew him close and embraced him.

"I love you, boy! Nothing changes that. Besides . . . you're in a new country now. You won't really know whether you like it until you've spent a winter there. . . . Let's not fight each other anymore, eh?"

"Right!" Johann disengaged himself from the embrace and reached for his brandy glass. "I'll drink to that."

"*Prosit,*" said Carl Mendelius.

"About the other thing, Father."

"Yes?"

"I can see the risks. I know what Jean Marie's friendship means to you. But I think you have to get the priorities right. Mother has to come first; and, well, Katrin and I need you, too."

"I'm trying to keep things in their right order, son." Mendelius gave a small, rueful chuckle. "You may not believe in the Second Coming, but if it happens, it will change the priorities somewhat . . . no?"

From the air the Italian countryside was a pastoral paradise, the orchards in full bloom, the meadows bright with wild flowers, the farmland flush with new green, the old fortress towns placid as pictures from a fairy tale.

By contrast, Fiumicino Airport looked like a rehearsal for final chaos. The traffic controllers were working to rule; the baggage handlers were on strike. There were long queues at every passport barrier. The air was filled with a babel of voices shouting in a dozen languages. Police with sniffer dogs moved among the harassed crowd looking for drug carriers; while young conscripts, armed with machine guns, stood guard at every exit, watchful and uneasy.

Lotte was near to tears and Mendelius was sweating with anger and frustration. It took them an hour and a half to barge their way through to the customs room and out into the reception area, where Herman Frank was waiting, dapper and solicitous as always. He had a limousine, a vast Mercedes borrowed from the German Embassy. He had flowers for Lotte, an effusive welcome for the Herr Professor, and champagne to drink during the long ride back to town. The traffic would be hell as always; but he wanted to offer them a small foretaste of heavenly peace.

The peace was granted to them at last in the Franks' apartment, the top floor of a seventeenth-century palazzo with high frescoed ceilings, marble floors, bathrooms large enough to float a navy and a stunning view over the rooftops of old Rome. Two hours later, bathed, changed and restored to sanity, they were drinking cocktails on the terrace, listening to the last bells and watching the swifts wheeling around the cupolas and attics, russet in the sunset glow.

"Down there it's murder. . . ." Hilde Frank pointed at the cluttered thoroughfares jammed with automobiles and pedestrians. "Sometimes real murder, because the terrorists are very bold now and the crust of law and order has worn thin. Kidnapping is the biggest private industry. We don't go out at night as we used, because there's always danger from purse-snatchers and motorcycle gangs. But up here"—her gesture embraced the whole ancient skyline—"it's still the same as it's been for centuries: the washing on the lines, the birds, the music that comes and goes, and the calls of the women to their neighbours. Without it I don't think we could bear to stay any longer."

She was a small dark woman, bubbly with talk, elegant as a mannequin, twenty years younger than the white-haired husband who followed her every movement with adoration. She was affectionate, too, cuddlesome as a kitten. Mendelius caught the flash of jealousy in Lotte's eyes, when Hilde took his hand and led him to the corner of the terrace to point out the distant dome of St. Peter's and the Castle of Sant'Angelo. She told him in a loud stage whisper:

"Herman's so happy you've agreed to lecture for him. He's getting near to retirement and he hates the idea. His whole life has been wrapped up in the Academy—both our lives really, because we've never had any children. . . . Lotte looks very well. I hope she likes shopping. I thought I'd take her to the Condotti tomorrow while you and Herman are at the Academy. The seminar people haven't arrived yet but he's dying to show you the place. . . ."

". . . And we've got fine things to show this year!" Herman Frank, with Lotte on his arm, walked into their talk. "We're giving the first comprehensive exhibition of Van Wittel ever held in this country, and Piero Falcone has lent us his collection of antique Florentine jewellery. That's an expensive venture because we need armed guards all the time. . . . Now let me tell you who's coming to dinner tonight. There's Bill Utley and his wife, Sonia. He's the British envoy to the Holy See. Bill's a dry old stick but he really knows what's going on. Also he speaks good German, which helps things along. Sonia's a cheerful gossip with no inhibitions. You'll enjoy her, Lotte. Then there's Georg Rainer, who's the Rome correspondent for *Die Welt*. He's a relaxed fellow who talks well. It was Hilde's idea to invite him because he's got a new girl friend whom nobody's seen yet. A Mexican, I believe, and reputed to be rich! . . . We'll sit down about nine-thirty. . . . By the way, Carl, there's a pile of mail for you. I asked the maid to leave it in your room. . . ."

It was the warmest of welcomes and a reminder of happier times before the oil war began, and the Italian miracle turned sour, and all the bright hopes of European unity were tarnished beyond repair. By the time the dinner guests arrived, Lotte was completely relaxed and chatting happily with Hilde about a trip to Florence and another to Ischia, while Carl Mendelius outlined, to an enthusiastic Herman, the schema of his discourses to the Evangelicals.

Dinner was a comfortable meal. Utley's wife was a scandalously entertaining talker. Georg Rainer's girl, Pia Menendez, was an instant success—a stunning beauty who knew how to defer graciously to the matrons. Georg Rainer wanted news; Utley liked to reminisce; so it was easy for Mendelius to steer the talk to recent events in the Vatican. Utley, the Britisher, who in his mother tongue had elevated obscurity to a fine art, was very precise in German.

". . . Even to the outsider it was plain that Gregory the Seventeenth had everyone in a panic. The organization is too big and therefore too fragile to support an innovator or even a too flexible man at the top. It's like the Russians with their satellites, and their comradely governments in Africa and South America. They have to preserve, at any cost, the illusion of unanimity and stability. . . . So Gregory had to go."

"I'd be interested," said Carl Mendelius, "to know exactly how they got him to abdicate."

"Nobody's prepared to talk about that," said Utley. "This was the first time in my experience when there were no real leaks from Monte Vaticano. Obviously there was some very rough bargaining; but one got the impression there were some very uneasy consciences afterwards."

"They blackmailed him!" said the man from *Die Welt* flatly. "I had the evidence; but I couldn't publish it."

"Why not?" The question came from Utley.

"Because I got it from a medical man, one of the doctors they called in to examine him. Obviously he was in no position to make a public statement."

"Did he tell you his findings?"

"He told me what the Curia wanted him to find: that Gregory the Seventeenth was mentally incompetent."

"Did they put it as bluntly as that?" Mendelius was surprised and dubious.

"No. That was the problem. The Curia were very subtle about it. They asked the medicos—there were seven in all—to establish, beyond reasonable doubt, whether the Pontiff was mentally and physically competent to carry on the duties of his office in this critical time."

"That's a catch-all brief," said Utley. "Why did Gregory fall for it?"

"He was caught in a trap. If he refused, he was suspect. If he accepted he was subject to the medical consensus."

"And what was that?" Mendelius asked.

"My man couldn't tell me. You see, that was the other smart thing they did. They asked each doctor to render an independent opinion in writing."

"Which left the Curia free to write its own assessment afterwards." Bill Utley gave a small dry chuckle. "Very smart! So what was your man's verdict?"

"Honest, I believe; but not very helpful to the patient. He was suffering from gross fatigue, constant insomnia and elevated, though not necessarily chronic, blood pressure. There were clear indications of anxiety and alternating moods of cheerfulness and depression. Obviously if these symptoms persisted in a man of sixty-five, there would be reason to fear graver complications. . . ."

"If the other reports were like that . . ."

"Or," said Mendelius softly, "if they were less honest and a shade more slanted . . ."

"The Cardinals had him in checkmate," said Georg Rainer. "They picked the choicest bits of the reports, constructed their own final verdict and presented Gregory with an ultimatum: go or be pushed!"

"Loving God!" Mendelius swore softly. "What choice did he have?"

"A beautiful piece of statecraft though." Bill Utley chuckled wryly. "You can't impeach a Pope. Short of assassination, how do you get rid of him? You're right, Georg, it was pure blackmail! I wonder who dreamed up the ploy."

"Arnaldo, of course. I do know he was the one who instructed the physicians."

"And now he's the Pope," said Carl Mendelius.

"He'll probably make a very good one," said Utley with a grin. "He knows the rules of the game."

Reluctantly, Carl Mendelius, the onetime Jesuit, was forced to agree with him. He also thought that Georg Rainer was a very smart journalist and that it would pay to cultivate his acquaintance.

That night he made love with Lotte in a huge baroque bed, which, Herman swore on his soul, had belonged to the elegant Cardinal Bernis. Whether it had or it hadn't made small matter. Their mating was the most joyous in a long time. When it was over, Lotte curled up in the crook of his arm and talked in drowsy contentment.

"It's been a lovely evening—everybody so bright and welcoming! I'm glad you made me come. Tübingen's a nice town; but I'd forgotten there was such a lot of world outside."

"Then let's start seeing it together, liebchen."

"We will, I promise. I feel happier now about the children. Katrin was very sweet. She told me what you'd said to her and how Franz had taken the news."

"I didn't hear about that."

"Apparently, he said, 'Your father's a big man. I'd like to bring him back one good canvas from Paris.' "

"That's nice to hear."

"Johann seemed happier, too; though he didn't say very much."

"He got a few things off his chest, including the fact that he wasn't a believer anymore. . . ."

"Oh, dear! That's sad."

"It's a phase, liebchen." Mendelius was sedulously casual. "He wants to find his own way to the truth."

"I hope you made him aware that you respected his decision."

"Of course! You mustn't worry about Johann and me. It's just the old bull and the young one sparring with each other."

"Old bull is right!" Lotte giggled happily in the darkness. "Which reminds me, if I catch Hilde playing pat-hands with you too often, I'll scratch her eyes out!"

"Nice to know you're still jealous."

"I love you, Carl. I love you so very much."

"And I love you, liebchen."

"That's all I need to finish a perfect day. Good night, my dear, dear man!"

She rolled away from him, curled herself under the covers and lapsed swiftly into sleep. Carl Mendelius clasped his hands under his head and lay a long time staring up at the ceiling, where amorous nymphs and rapacious demigods disported themselves in the darkness. For all the sweet solace of loving, he was still haunted by what he had heard at dinner and by the last letter in the pile which the maid had left on his dressing table.

It was in Italian, handwritten on heavy notepaper, embossed with the official superscription of the Sacred Congregation for the Doctrine of the Faith.

Dear Professor Mendelius,

I am informed by our mutual friend the rector of the Pontifical Biblical Institute that you will shortly be visiting Rome for the purpose of scholastic research, and that you will be delivering some discourses at the German Academy of Fine Arts.

I understand also that you plan to pay a visit to the recently retired Pontiff at the Monastery of Monte Cassino.

Since I have always had the greatest admiration for your scholarly work, it would give me great pleasure to entertain you to coffee one morning in my private apartment in Vatican City.

Perhaps you would be kind enough to call me at the Congregation any evening between four and seven so that we may arrange a mutually convenient day, preferably before you go to Monte Cassino.

I send you my salutations and my best wishes for a pleasant sojourn.

Yours in Christ Jesus,
Anton Drexel,
Cardinal Prefect

It was beautifully done, as always: a courteous gesture and a tart reminder that nothing, but nothing, that went on in the sacred circle escaped the watchdogs of the Lord. In the old days of the Papal States they would have sent a summons and a detachment of gendarmes to enforce it. Now it was coffee and sweet biscuits in the Cardinal's apartment and sweet seductive talk afterwards.

Well, well! *Tempora mutantur . . .* ! He wondered which the Cardinal Prefect wanted more: information or an assurance of discretion. He wondered also what conditions might be laid down before they would permit him to visit Jean Marie Barette.

III

Herman Frank had good reason to be proud of his exhibition. The press had been generous with praise, compliments and illustrations. The galleries of the Academy were thronged with visitors —Romans and tourists—and there was a quite astonishing number of young people.

The works of Gaspar Van Wittel, a seventeenth-century Dutchman from Amersfoort, were little known to the Italian public. Most of them had been jealously preserved in the private collections of the Colonna, the Sacchetti, the Pallavicini and other noble families. To assemble them had taken two years of patient research and months of delicate negotiation. The provenance of many was still a closely guarded secret—witness the large number still denominated *"raccolta privata."* Together they constituted an extraordinarily vivid pictorial and architectural record of seventeenth-century Italy. Herman Frank's enthusiasm had the rare and touching innocence of childhood.

"Just look at that! So delicate yet so precise! Almost a Japanese quality in the colour. A magnificent draftsman, a complete master of the most intricate perspective . . . Study these sketches. . . . Notice how patiently he builds the composition. . . . Strange! He lived in a dark little villa out on the Appia Antica. It's still there. Terribly claustrophobic. Mind you, it was all meadowland in those days, so probably he had all the space and light he needed. . . ." He broke off, suddenly embarrassed. "I'm sorry, I'm talking too much; but I love these things!"

Mendelius laid a gentle hand on his shoulder.

"My friend, it's a delight to listen to you! Look at all these young people! You've lifted them out of their resentments and confusions and set them down in another world, simpler, more beautiful, with all its ugliness forgotten. You have to be proud of that!"

"I am, Carl. I confess it. But I'm also scared of the day when all these canvases are down, and the packers arrive to ship them back to their owners. I'm getting old. I'm not sure whether I'll have the time, or the energy—the luck for that matter!—to do anything like this again."

"But you'll still be trying. That's the important thing."

"Not for long, I'm afraid. I retire next year. I won't know what to do with myself. We can't afford to go on living here; and yet I hate the idea of going back to Germany."

"You could take up writing as a full-time occupation. You've already got an established reputation as an art historian. I'm sure you could get a better publishing deal than you've had. . . . Why don't you let me talk to my agent and see what he can set up for you?"

"Would you?" He was almost pathetically grateful. "I'm not very good at business and I worry about Hilde."

"I'll call him as soon as we get home. Which reminds me, can I use your telephone now? There is a call I must make before midday."

"Come to my office. I'll have some coffee sent in. . . . Oh, before you go you simply must look at this view of the Tiber. There are three versions of it: one from the Pallavicini collection, one from the National Gallery and this one came from an old engineer who bought it for a song in the flea market. . . ."

It was another fifteen minutes before Mendelius was free to make his call to the Monastery of Monte Cassino. It took an unconscionable time to find the Abbot and bring him to the telephone. Mendelius fumed and fretted and then reminded himself that monasteries were designed to separate men from the world, not to keep them in touch with it.

The Abbot was cordial, if not exactly effusive. "Professor Mendelius? This is Abbot Andrew. Kind of you to call so promptly. Would you be able to arrange your visit for Wednesday next? It's a feast day for us, and so we shall be able to offer you a little more generous hospitality. I suggest you arrive about three-thirty and stay to dinner. It's a long drive from Rome; so if you care to remain overnight we'll be happy to accommodate you."

"That's very kind. I'll stay then and drive back on Thursday morning. How is my friend Jean?"

"He's been unwell; but I hope he will be recovered in time for your visit. He looks forward to seeing you."

"Please give him my most affectionate greetings and say that my wife asks to be remembered to him."

"I'll do that with pleasure. Until Wednesday then, Professor."

"Thank you, Father Abbot."

Mendelius put down the receiver and sat a moment lost in thought. There it was again: the courteous response, the veiled caution. Wednesday was a week ahead—more than enough time to cancel the invitation, should circumstances change or authority intervene. Jean Marie's illness, real or diplomatic, would provide an adequate excuse.

"Something wrong, Carl?" Herman set down the coffee tray and began pouring.

"I'm not sure. It seems the Vatican is more than a little interested in my activities."

"I would have thought that was natural enough. You've given them a few headaches in the past; and every new book causes a flutter in the pigeon loft. . . . Milk and sugar?"

"No sugar. I'm trying to lose weight."

"I've noticed. I noticed also you were pushing a little last night, for information on Gregory the Seventeenth."

"Did it show that much?"

"Only to me, I think. Was there any special reason?"

"He was my friend. You know that. I wanted to find out what really happened to him."

"Didn't he tell you himself?"

"I hadn't heard from him in months." Mendelius hedged his answer. "I imagine he had little time for private correspondence."

"But you'll be seeing him while you're here?"

"It's been arranged. Yes."

The answer was a shade too curt. Herman Frank was too tactful a man to press the matter. There was an awkward moment of silence; then he said quietly, "Something's been puzzling me, Carl. I'd like your opinion on it."

"Tell me, Herman."

"About a month ago I was called to our embassy. The ambassador wanted to see me. He showed me a letter from Bonn: a circular instruction to all academies and institutes abroad. Many of them, as you know, have valuable material on loan from the Republic: sculptures, pictures, historic manuscripts, that sort of thing. . . . All directors were told to arrange secret safe-deposits in the host countries where these things could be stored in the event of civil disorder or international conflict. We were all given a budget, available immediately, to buy or lease suitable storage."

"It sounds like a reasonable precaution," said Mendelius mildly. "Especially since you can't insure against war or civil violence."

"You miss the point." Herman Frank was emphatic. "It was the tone of the document that worried me. There was a note of real urgency, and a threat of stringent penalties for neglect. I got the impression our people are genuinely worried that some terrible thing may happen very soon."

"Do you have a copy of the instruction?"

"No. The ambassador was very firm that it must not leave the embassy. Oh, and that's another thing. Only most senior staff were to know its contents. I thought that was rather sinister. I still do. I know I'm a worrier; but all the time I think of Hilde and what might happen to her if we were separated in some emergency. I'd like your honest opinion, Carl."

For a moment, Mendelius was tempted to put him off with some facile encouragement; then he decided against it. Herman Frank was a good man, too soft for a rough world. He deserved a sober and honest answer.

"Things are bad, Herman. We're not at panic stations yet; but very soon we may be. Everything points that way: public disorder, the breakdown of political confidence, the huge recession —and the fools in high places who think they can solve the problem by a well-timed but limited war. You're right to be concerned. What you can do about it is another matter. Once the first missiles are launched there's no safe hiding place anywhere. Have you talked to Hilde about it?"

"Yes. She doesn't want to go back to Germany, but she agrees we ought to consider moving out of Rome. We've got that little farmhouse in the Tuscan hills. It's isolated; but there's fertile ground around it. I suppose we could survive just on what we grew ourselves. . . . But it seems an act of despair even to contemplate such a thing."

"Or an act of hope," said Mendelius gently. "I think your Hilde's a very wise girl—and you shouldn't worry about her as much as you do. Women are much better at survival than we are."

"I suppose they are. I've never thought about it that way. . . . Don't you wish sometimes we could find a great man to take control and lead us out of the filthy mess?"

"Never!" said Carl Mendelius somberly. "Great men are dangerous. When their dreams fail, they bury them under the rubble of cities, where simple folk once lived in peace!"

"I want to be open with you, Mendelius. I want you to be open with me."

"How open, Eminence? And on what subject?"

The courtesies were over now. The sweet biscuits were all eaten. The coffee was cold. His Eminence Anton Cardinal Drexel, grey-haired, straight as a grenadier, stood with his back to his visitor, looking out on the sunlit gardens of the Vatican. He turned slowly and stood a moment longer, a faceless silhouette against the light. Mendelius said:

"Please, Eminence, why don't you sit down? I'd like to see your face while we talk."

"Forgive me." Drexel gave a deep growling chuckle. "It's an old trick—and not very polite. . . . Would you prefer we speak German?"

In spite of his name, Drexel was Italian, born in Bolzano, long a territory in dispute between Austria and the Italian Republic. Mendelius shrugged. "As your Eminence pleases."

"Italian then. I speak German like a Tyrolese. You might find it comical."

"The mother tongue is the best one to be honest in," said Mendelius drily. "If my Italian fails me, I'll speak German."

Drexel moved away from the window and sat down facing Mendelius. He arranged the folds of his cassock carefully across his knees. His seamed face, still handsome, might have been carved from wood. Only his eyes were alive, vivid blue, amused yet appraising. He said, "You always were a tough customer." He used the colloquial phrase: *un tipo robusto*. Mendelius smiled at the left-handed compliment. "Now, tell me. How much do you know about what happened here recently?"

"Before I answer that, Eminence, I should like an answer from you. Do you intend to set any impediment to my contact with Jean Marie?"

"I? None at all."

"Does anyone else, to your knowledge?"

"To the best of my knowledge, no one; though there is obviously an interest in the encounter."

"Thank you, Eminence. Now, the answer to your question: I know that Pope Gregory was forced to abdicate. I know the means that were used to exact his decision."

"Which were?"

"A series of seven independent medical reports, which were then consolidated by the Curia into a final document designed to cast grave doubts upon the mental competence of his Holiness. . . . Is that accurate?"

Drexel hesitated a moment and then nodded assent. "Yes, it's accurate. What do you know of my own role in the matter?"

"It is my understanding, Eminence, that while dissenting from the decision of the Sacred College you agreed to convey it to the Pontiff."

"Do you know why they reached their decision?"

"Yes."

There was a flicker of doubt in Drexel's eyes; but he went on without hesitation. "Do you agree with it or not?"

"I think the means of enforcing it were base: flat blackmail. As to the decision itself, I find myself in dilemma."

"And how would you express that dilemma, my friend?"

"The Pope is elected as Supreme Pastor and Custodian of the Deposit of Faith. Can that office be reconciled with the role of prophet proclaiming a private revelation, even if that revelation be true?"

"So you do know!" said the Cardinal Prefect softly. "And, fortunately, you understand."

"So where does that leave us, Eminence?" asked Mendelius.

"Facing the second dilemma: how do we prove whether the revelation is true or false?"

"Your colleagues have already resolved that one," said Mendelius tartly. "They judged him a madman."

"Not I," said Anton Cardinal Drexel firmly. "I believed, I still believe, his position as Pontiff was untenable. There was no way he could have functioned in the face of so much opposition. But mad? Never!"

"A lying prophet, then?"

For the first time Drexel's mask-like visage betrayed his emotion. "That's a terrible thought!"

"He asked me to judge him, Eminence. I had to consider every possible verdict."

"He is not a liar."

"Do you think he is deluded?"

"I would like to believe it. Everything would be so much simpler. But I cannot; I simply cannot!"

Suddenly he looked exactly what he was: an old lion with the strength ebbing out of him.

Mendelius felt a surge of sympathy for the anguish scored in his face. Still he could not relent in his own inquisition. He asked firmly, "How have you tested him, Eminence? By what criteria?"

"By the only ones I know: his speech, his conduct, his writings, the tenor of his spiritual life."

Mendelius chuckled. "There speaks the Hound of God."

Drexel smiled grimly. "The wounds still smart, eh? I admit we gave you a rough time. At least we taught you to understand the method. What do you want to know first?"

"It was the writing that finally damned him. I have a copy of the encyclical. How did you read it, Eminence?"

"With great misgiving, obviously. I had not a doubt in the world that it must be suppressed. But I agree it contains nothing, absolutely nothing, that is contrary to traditional doctrine. There are interpretations that might be considered extreme, but they are certainly not heterodox. Even the question of an elective ministry, when ordination by a bishop is totally impossible, is a very open one—if rather delicate for Roman ears."

"Which brings us to the tenor of his spiritual life." There was a faint hint of irony in Mendelius' tone. "How did you judge that, Eminence?"

For the first time, Drexel's harsh face softened into a smile. "It measured better than yours, my dear Mendelius. He remained faithful to his vocation as a priest. He was a totally unselfish man, all of whose thoughts were directed to the good of the Church and of human souls. His passions were under control. In high office he was humble and kind. His anger was always against malice and never against frailty. Even at the end he did not rail against his accusers, but went with dignity and accepted the role of a subject without complaint. I am told by the Abbot that his life in Monte Cassino is a model of religious simplicity."

"He is also silent. How does that conform with the obligation, which he says he has, to spread the news of the Parousia?"

"Before I answer that," said Drexel, "I think we should clear up one question of fact. Obviously he wrote to you and sent you a copy of the suppressed encyclical. Correct?"

"Correct."

"Was this before or after his abdication?"

"He wrote it before. I received it after the event."

"Good! Now let me tell you something which you do not know. When my brother Cardinals had secured Gregory's consent to abdication, they were sure they had broken him, that he would do whatever they wanted. First they tried to write into the instrument of abdication a promise of perpetual silence on any issue affecting the public life of the Church. I told them that they had neither a moral nor a legal right to do so. If they persisted I would fight them to the death. I would resign my office and make a full public statement on the whole sorry affair. Then they tried another tack. His Holiness had agreed to enter the order of Saint Benedict and live the life of a simple monk. Therefore, he would be bound to obey his religious superior. Therefore, said my clever colleagues, the Abbot would be instructed to bind him to silence under the vow."

"I know that one," said Carl Mendelius with cold anger. "Obedience of the spirit! The worst agony you can impose on an honest man. We've taught it to every tyranny in the world."

"So," said Drexel quietly, "I was determined they should not impose it on our friend. I pointed out that this was an intolerable usurpation of the right of a man to act freely in the light of his private conscience, that the most stringent vow could not bind him to commit a wrong, or to stifle his conscience in the name of good. Once again I threatened exposure. I bargained with my vote in the coming conclave and I instructed Abbot Andrew that he, too, was bound under mortal sanction to protect the free conscience of his new subject."

"I'm happy to hear it, Eminence." Mendelius was grave and respectful. "It's the first light I've seen in this dark affair. But it still doesn't answer my question. Why is Jean Marie still silent? Both in his letter to me and in the encyclical, he speaks of his obligation to proclaim the news that he claims has been revealed to him."

Drexel did not answer immediately. Slowly, almost painfully, he rose from his chair, walked to the window and stood again, staring out into the garden. When he turned finally, his face was in shadow as before; but Mendelius made no protest. The man's distress was all too evident in his voice.

"The reason, I think, is because he is now undergoing the experience of all the great mystics, which is called 'the dark night of the soul.' It is a period of utter darkness, of howling confusion, of near despair, when the spirit seems bereft of every support, human or divine. It is a replica of that terrible moment when Christ Himself cried out: 'My God! Why have you abandoned me?' . . . This is the news I hear from Abbot Andrew. This is why he, and I, wanted to speak with you before you see Jean Marie. . . . The fact is, Mendelius, I think I failed him, because I tried to compromise between the promptings of the Spirit and the demands of the system to which I have been committed for a lifetime. . . . I hope, I pray, you may prove a better friend than I."

"You talk of him as a mystic, Eminence. That seems to predicate a belief in his mystical experience," said Carl Mendelius. "I'm not ready for that yet, much as I love him."

"I hope you will tell him that first and ask your questions afterwards. . . . Perhaps you'll be kind enough to call me after you've seen him?"

"You have my promise, Eminence." Mendelius stood up. "Thank you for inviting me here. I hope you'll forgive me if I seemed rude at the beginning."

"Not rude, just robust." The Cardinal smiled and held out his hand. "You were much less reasonable in the old days. Marriage must be good for you."

Lotte and Hilde had driven out to Tivoli for lunch, so he was treating himself to a solitary meal in the Piazza Navona. When he left the Vatican it was a quarter to midday; so he decided to walk. Halfway down the Via della Conciliazione he stopped and turned back to look at the great basilica of San Pietro, with the encircling colonnades that symbolized the all-embracing mission of Mother Church.

For half a billion believers this was the center of the world, the dwelling place of Christ's vicar, the burial place of Peter the

Fisherman. When the IBM's were launched from the Soviet perimeters, it would be obliterated in the first blast. What would happen to the half-billion faithful once this visible symbol of unity, authority and permanence were destroyed?

They had been conditioned for so long to regard this time-worn edifice as the navel of the world, its ruler as the sole, authentic legate of God to men; to whom would they look when the house and the man were reduced to a glaze on the pavement?

These were no idle questions. They were possibilities hideously imminent—to Jean Marie Barette, to Anton Cardinal Drexel, to Carl Mendelius, who knew the apocalyptic literature by heart and saw it rewritten in every line of the daily press. He felt sorry for Drexel, old, still powerful, but bereft of all his certainties. He felt sorry for all of them: cardinals, bishops, curial clerics, all trying to apply the Codex Juris Canonicus to a mad planet, whirling itself towards extinction.

He turned away and strolled, in leisurely fashion, through the crowd of pilgrims, across the Victor Emmanuel Bridge and down the Corso. Halfway along the thoroughfare he found a bar, with tables spread along the sidewalk. He sat down, ordered a Campari and watched the passing show.

This was the best time in Rome: the air still soft, the flowers fresh on the vendors' stalls, the girls flirting their new summer finery, the shops filled with bright baubles for the tourist season.

His attention was caught by a young woman standing on the curb a few paces to his left. She was dressed in dark blue slacks and a white silk blouse that displayed high-tilted breasts. Her black hair was held back by a red scarf. She looked like a southerner, slight and olive-skinned; with a calm, Madonna face, singularly beautiful in repose. She carried a folded newspaper in one hand, and in the other a small handbag of blue leather. She seemed to be waiting for someone.

As he watched, a small red Alfa backed into the space near her. The driver parked it awkwardly, with the nose pointing out into the traffic. He opened the door and leaned across to speak to the girl. For a moment it looked like a pickup; but the girl responded without protest. She passed her handbag to the driver and, still holding the newspaper, turned back to face the sidewalk. The driver waited, with the door open and the engine running.

A few moments later a man, middle-aged, fashionably dressed and carrying a leather briefcase, walked swiftly down the Corso. The girl stepped forward, smiled and spoke to him. He stopped. He seemed surprised; then he said something which Mendelius could not hear. The girl shot him three times in the groin, tossed the newspaper into the gutter and leapt into the car, which roared away down the Corso.

For a single, stunned moment, Mendelius sat shocked and immobile; then he lunged towards the fallen victim and rammed his fist into the man's groin to stanch the blood pumping from the femoral artery. He was still there when the police and the ambulance men pushed their way through the crowd to take charge of the victim.

A policeman dispersed the gaping onlookers and the photographers. A street sweeper cleaned the blood from the pavement. A plainclothes man hustled Mendelius into the bar. A waiter brought hot water and clean napkins to mop his bloody clothes. The proprietor offered a large whisky with the compliments of the house. Mendelius sipped it gratefully as he made his first deposition. The investigator, a young, poker-faced Milanese, dictated it immediately over the telephone to headquarters. Then he rejoined Mendelius at the table and ordered a whisky for himself.

". . . That was most helpful, Professor. The description of the assailant, detailed and closely observed, is very useful to us at this early stage. . . . I'm afraid, however, I'll have to ask you to come to headquarters and look at some photographs—maybe work with an artist on an identikit picture."

"Of course. But I'd like to do it this afternoon if possible. As I explained, I have engagements to fulfil."

"Fine. I'll take you down when we've finished our drinks."

"Who was the victim?" asked Mendelius.

"His name's Malagordo. He's one of our senior Senators, Socialist and Jewish. . . . A filthy business, and we're getting more of it every week."

"It seems so pointless—a gratuitous barbarity."

"Gratuitous, yes; but pointless, no! These people are dedicated to anarchy, a classic and total breakdown of the system by a destruction of public confidence. . . . And we're getting very close to that point now. You may find this hard to believe, Professor. At least twenty other people saw the shooting today; but I'll bet a month's salary yours will be the only deposition that tells us anything concrete . . . and you're a foreigner! The others have to live in this mess; but they won't lift a finger to clean it up. So"—he shrugged in weary resignation—"in the end they'll get the country they deserve. . . . Which reminds me, you'd better be prepared to see yourself spread all over the newspapers."

"That's the last thing I need," said Mendelius glumly.

"It could also be dangerous," said the detective. "You will be identified as a key witness."

"And therefore a possible target. Is that what you're telling me?"

"I'm afraid so, Professor. This is a propaganda game, you understand—black theatre. They have to shoot the leading man. The girl in the ticket office has no publicity value. . . . If you take my advice you'll move out of Rome, preferably out of Italy."

"I can't do that for at least a week."

"As soon as possible then. Meantime, change your address. Move into one of the bigger hotels where the tourists congregate. Use another name. I'll arrange the passport problem with the management."

"It wouldn't help much. I'm booked for lectures at the German Academy. So, I'm still exposed."

"What can I say then?" The detective shrugged and grinned. "Except watch your step, vary your routine, and don't talk to pretty girls in the Corso!"

"No chance of police protection, at least for my wife?"

"Not a hope. We're desperately short of manpower. I can give you the name of an agency that hires bodyguards; but they charge millionaire rates."

"Then to hell with it!" said Mendelius. "Let's go look at your photographs."

As they drove through the midday chaos, he could still smell the blood on his clothes. He hoped Lotte was having a good lunch at Tivoli. He wanted her to enjoy this holiday; there might not be too many more in the future.

Later in the afternoon, while he waited for Lotte and Hilde to return from their outing, he sat on the terrace and taped a memorandum to Anneliese Meissner. He set down the new facts he had learned from Georg Rainer and from Cardinal Drexel and only then added his own comments.

". . . Rainer is a sober and objective reporter. His medical evidence though secondhand proved reliable. Clearly Jean Marie Barette was under great mental and physical strain. Clearly, too, there was no consensus on his mental incapacity. . . . As Rainer put it: 'Had they wanted to keep him, the most he would have needed was a decent rest and a reduction of his workload.' . . .

"Cardinal Drexel's point of view surprised me. Remember I was under inquisition for a long time, and I knew him as a formidable and quite relentless dialectician. However, even in our worst encounters, I never had the slightest doubt of his intellectual honesty. I would love to see you and him lock horns in a public debate. It would be a sell-out performance. He rejects utterly any idea of insanity or of fraud on Jean Marie's part. He goes further and puts him in the category of the mystics like Teresa of Avila, John of the Cross and Catherine of Siena. By inference, Drexel commits himself to a belief—not yet clearly categorized—in the authenticity of Jean Marie's visionary experience. So now it is I who am the skeptic or, at least, the agnostic. . . .

"I am to see Jean Marie next Wednesday and Thursday and I shall report to my assessor after those meetings. I give my first Academy lecture tomorrow. I am looking forward to it. The Evangelicals are an interesting group. I admire their way of life. And, of course, Tübingen has always been one of the heartlands of the Pietist tradition, which has had such a huge influence in England and the United States. . . . But I forget. You are tone-deaf to this music. . . . None the less I trust you and am glad to have you as my *Beisitzer*. My most affectionate salutations from this wonderful, but now very sinister, city. *Auf wiedersehen.*"

The audience was already seated when he entered the auditorium; twenty-odd Evangelical pastors, most of them in their early thirties, a dozen wives, three deaconesses, and half a dozen guests whom Herman Frank had invited from the local Waldensian community in Rome. Carl Mendelius felt comfortable with them. The theological faculty at Tübingen had been one of the early forcing-grounds for the Pietist movement in the Lutheran

Church; and Mendelius was personally attracted by its emphasis on personal devotion and works of pastoral charity. He had once written a long paper on the influence of Philipp Jakob Spener and the "College of Piety" which he founded in Frankfurt during the seventeenth century.

When Herman Frank had finished his introduction and the applause had subsided, Mendelius laid out his papers on the lectern and began to speak. His manner was relaxed and informal.

"I don't want to give a lecture. I should prefer, if you agree, to explore our subject in a Socratic dialogue, to see what we can tell each other and what the historical evidence can tell us all. . . . In broad terms we are dealing with eschatology, the doctrine of last things: the ultimate destiny of man, of social organizations and of the whole cosmic order. We want to consider these things in the light of both Old and New Testament writings, and the earliest Christian traditions. . . .

"There are two ways of looking at the Doctrine of Last Things. Each is radically different from the other. The first is what I call the consummatory view. Human history will end. Christ will come a second time, in glory, to judge the living and the dead. The second is what I call the modificating view. Creation continues, but is modified by man working in concert with his creator, towards a fulfilment or perfection, which can be expressed only by symbol and analogy. In this view Christ is ever present, and the Parousia expresses the ultimate revelation of His creative presence. . . . Now I'd like to know where you stand. What do you tell your people about the Doctrine of Last Things? Show hands if you want to answer and let's hear your name and your home-place. . . . You sir, in the second row . . ."

"Alfred Kessler from Köln . . ." The speaker was a short sturdy young man with a square-cut beard. "I believe in continuity and not consummation for the cosmos. The consummation for the individual is death and union with the Creator."

"How then, Pastor, do you interpret the Scriptures to the faithful? You teach them as the Word of God—at least, I presume you do. How do you expound the Word on this subject?"

"As a mystery, Herr Professor: a mystery which, under the influence of divine grace, gradually unfolds its meaning to each individual soul."

"Can you clarify that—perhaps express it as you would to your congregation?"

"I usually put in this way. Language is a man-made instrument and therefore imperfect. Where language stops, music, for example, takes over. Often a hand's touch says more than a volume of words. I use the example of each man's personal consummation. Instinctively we fear death. Yet, as all of us know from pastoral work, man becomes familiar with it, prepares himself, subconsciously, for it, understands it through the universe about him—the fall of a flower, the scattering of its seeds on the wind, the rebirth of spring. . . . In this context, the Doctrine of Last Things is, if not explainable, at least conformable to physical and psychic experience."

"Thank you, Pastor. Next."

"Petrus Allmann, Darmstadt." It was an older man this time. "I disagree totally with my colleague. Human language is imperfect, yes; but Christ the Lord used it. I think we err when we try to turn His utterances into some kind of double-talk. Scripture is absolutely clear on this subject." He quoted solemnly: " 'And immediately after the tribulation of those days, the sun shall be darkened and the moon shall not give her light and the stars shall fall from the sky and the powers of heaven shall be moved. And then shall appear the Sign of the Son of Man in heaven. . . .' What else does that mean but consummation, the end of temporal things?"

There was a surprising burst of applause from one section of the audience. Mendelius let it run on for a moment, then held up his hand for silence. He gave them a good-humored smile. "So now, ladies and gentlemen, who would like to decide between these two men of goodwill?"

This time it was a grey-haired woman who held up her hand. "I am Alicia Herschel, deaconess, from Heidelberg. I do not think it matters which colleague is right. I have worked as a missionary in Muslim countries and I have learned to say 'Inshallah.' Whatever is the will of the Lord will be done, however we humans read his intentions. Pastor Allman quoted from Matthew twenty-four; but there is another saying in that same chapter: 'But of that day and hour no one knoweth; no, not the angels of heaven, but the Father alone.'

She was an impressive woman and there was more applause when she sat down. She was followed by a young man from Frankfurt. This time he addressed a question to Mendelius.

"Where do you stand on this question, Herr Professor?"

He was pinned now, as he had expected to be; but at least it forced him to some kind of definition. He paused a moment, collecting his thoughts, then outlined his position.

"As you know, I was ordained a priest in the Roman Catholic Church. However, I left the ministry and engaged myself in academic work. For a long time, therefore, I have been absolved from the obligation of pastoral interpretation of Scripture. I am now an historian, still a professing Christian, but dedicated to a purely historical study of biblical and patristic documents. In other words, I study what was written in the past, in the light of our knowledge of that past. . . . So, professionally speaking, I should not make predications on the truth or otherwise of prophetic writings, only on their provenance and authenticity."

They were silent now. They accepted his disclaimer; but if he ducked the issue of a personal testimony they would reject him out of hand. The knowing was not enough for them. True Evangelicals, they demanded that it be fruitful in word and action. Mendelius went on.

"By temperament and training I have always been inclined to interpret the future in terms of continuity, modification, change. I could not come to terms with consummation. . . . Now, however, I find myself drawn to the view that consummation is possible. It is an experiential fact that mankind has all means to create a global catastrophe of such dimensions that human life as we know it would be extinguished on the planet. Given the other experiential fact of man's capacity for destructive evil, we are faced with the fearful prospect that the consummation may be imminent. . . ."

There was an audible gasp from the audience. Mendelius added a footnote to the affirmation.

"But whether it would be wise to preach such a message is another question altogether, and I confess that, at this moment, I am not competent to answer it."

There was a moment of silence and then a small forest of hands shot up. Before he called for more questions Mendelius reached for the water glass and took a long swallow of liquid. He had a sudden incongruous vision of Anneliese Meissner peering at him through her thick spectacles and grinning all over her ugly face. He could almost hear her mocking verdict.

"I told you, didn't I, Carl? God-madness! You'll never be cured of it!"

The session was scheduled to end at midday, but the discussion was so lively that it was a quarter to one before Mendelius was able to escape for a pre-lunch drink in Herman Frank's office. Herman was lavish with compliments; but Mendelius was less than happy with the headlines in the newspapers stacked on his desk.

They ranged from the extravagant to the malicious: "Hero of the Corso"; "Distinguished scholar in shooting affray"; "Ex-Jesuit chief witness against terrorist brigades." The photographs were lurid: Mendelius spattered with blood, kneeling beside the victim, Malagordo being hoisted into the ambulance, Mendelius and the detective huddled in talk over their whisky. There was also an identikit picture of the assassin, carefully captioned: "Impression of the assassin by Professor Carl Mendelius of Tübingen University." The copy was orchestrated in Italian operatic style: grandiloquent horror, high heroics and heavy irony. . . . "It is, perhaps, not without a certain poetic justice that a Jewish Senator should owe his life to a German historian. . . ."

"God Almighty!" Mendelius was pale with anger. "They've set me up like a decoy duck!"

Herman Frank nodded unhappily. "It is bad, Carl. The embassy called to warn you that there are strong links between local terrorists and similar groups in Germany."

"I know. We can't stay at your place any longer. Call back to the embassy, get them to use their influence to book us a double room in one of the better hotels, the Hassler perhaps or the Grand . . . I absolutely refuse to expose you and Hilde to danger on my account."

"No, Carl! I will not bend to this kind of threat. Hilde would never permit it either."

"Herman, please! This is no time for heroics."

"It's not heroics, Carl." Herman was surprisingly resolute. "It's simple common sense. I refuse to live underground like a mole. That's what these bastards want! Besides, it's only for a week. The girls can go to Florence as they planned. A couple of old stagers like you and me should be able to look after ourselves."

"But listen . . . !"

"No 'buts,' Carl. Let's put it to the girls over lunch and see how they feel."

"Very well. Thanks, Herman."

"Thank you, my friend. This morning was a special triumph for me. In all my years at the Academy, I've never seen such an animated debate. They can't wait for your next appearance. . . . Oh, I almost forgot. There were two telephone calls for you. One was from Cardinal Drexel. He'll be in his office until one-thirty. The other was from the wife of Senator Malagordo. She'd like you to call her back at the Salvator Mundi hospital. . . . Those are the numbers. Make the calls now and get them off your mind. I'd like you to enjoy your lunch."

As he dialled Drexel's number, Mendelius was filled with misgivings. The Vatican placed a high premium on discretion. Drexel might well see the threat to Mendelius as a threat to the privacy of Jean Marie Barette. He was surprised to find the old warrior cordial and solicitous.

"Mendelius? . . . I presume you've seen this morning's papers?"

"I have, Eminence. I've just been discussing them with my host. An embarrassment to say the least."

"I have a suggestion. I hope you'll accept it."

"I'd be happy to consider it, Eminence."

"For the rest of your stay I'd like you to have the use of my car and my driver. His name's Francone. He used to be in the Carabinieri. He understands security work and he's alert and capable."

"It's a kind thought, Eminence, but I can't really accept."

"You can. You must. I have a vested interest in your safety, my friend. I propose to protect it. Where are you now?"

"At the Academy. I'm going back to the Franks' for lunch. The address is . . ."

"I have the address. Francone will report to you at four and will remain at your disposal during the rest of your stay. . . . No arguments now! We can't afford to lose the Hero of the Corso, can we?"

Much lighter in heart, Mendelius called the Salvator Mundi hospital and asked for the wife of Senator Malagordo. He was put through first to a very brusque German nun and then to a male security man. After a long silence the Senator's wife came on the line. She wanted to tell him her thanks for saving the Senator's life. He was badly hurt but his condition was stable. As soon as he was in a condition to receive visitors he would like to see the Professor and offer his thanks in person.

Mendelius promised to call later in the week, thanked her for her courtesy and rang off. When he heard the news, Herman Frank was happy again.

"You see, Carl! That's the other side of the medal. People are kind and grateful. And the Cardinal's a canny old fox. You probably don't know it, but the Vatican has a staff of very tough security boys. They have no inhibitions about breaking heads in the service of God. This Francone is obviously one of them. I feel better now—much better! Let's go home to lunch."

During the meal, Lotte was very quiet; but afterwards, when the Franks had retired for their siesta, she made her position plain.

"I'm not going to Florence, Carl, not to Ischia or anywhere out of Rome, unless you're with me. If you're in danger I have to share it; otherwise I'm nothing but a piece of furniture in your life."

"Please, liebchen, be sensible! You don't have to prove anything to me."

"Have you never thought I might have to prove it to myself?"

"Why, for God's sake?"

"Because, ever since we married, I've been on the comfortable side of the bed; the wife of a notable scholar first, and then the Frau Professor at Tübingen. I've never had to think too much about anything, except having my babies and running the house. . . . You were always there, a strong wall against the wind. I've never had to test myself without you. I've never had a rival. It was wonderful, all of it; but now, looking at other women my age, I feel very inadequate."

"Why should you? Do you think I could have made this career without you, without the home you provided, and all the loving inside it?"

"I think so, yes. Not quite in the same way perhaps—but yes, you'd have made it without me. You're not just a stuffy scholar. There's an adventurer in you, too. Oh, yes! I've seen him peeping out sometimes—and I've shut the door on him because he frightened me. Now, I want to see more of him, know him better, enjoy him before it's too late."

She was weeping now, quiet tender tears. Mendelius reached out and drew her to him, coaxing her softly.

". . . There's nothing to be sad about, liebchen. We're here, together. I don't want to push you away. It's just that suddenly, yesterday, I saw the face of evil—real evil! That girl—she couldn't have been much older than Katrin—looked like one of Dolci's Madonnas. But she shot a man in cold blood, not to kill him but to maim him in his manhood . . . I don't want you exposed to that sort of cruelty."

"But I am exposed to it, Carl! I'm part of it, just as much as you are. When Katrin went off to Paris with her Franz, I wished I were young again and going in her place. I was jealous; because she was getting something I never had. When you and Johann used to fight, a part of me was glad, because he would always turn to me afterwards. He was like a young lover with whom I could make you jealous. . . . There! It's out now; and if you hate me I can't help it."

"I can't hate you, liebchen. I've never ever been able to be angry with you for very long."

"That's part of the problem, I suppose. I knew it and I needed you to fight me."

"I still won't fight you, Lotte." Suddenly he was somber and remote. "Do you know why? Because, all of my early life, I was bound—by my own choice, I agree—but bound nonetheless. When I became free I prized it so much, I couldn't bear to impose a servitude on anyone else . . . I wanted a partner, not a puppet. I saw what was happening, but until you saw it yourself, and wanted to change it, I couldn't, I wouldn't force you. Right or wrong, that's how I felt."

"And now, Carl? What do you feel now?"

"Scared!" said Carl Mendelius. "Scared of what may be waiting for us out there in the streets; even more scared of what's going to happen when I meet Jean Marie."

"I was asking about us—you and me."

"That's what I'm talking about, liebchen. Every way we move now, we're at risk. I want you with me; but not to prove something to me or to yourself. That's like having sex just to show you can do it. . . . It may be magnificent but it's a long way from loving. In short, it's up to you, liebchen."

"How many ways do I have to tell you, Carl? I love you. From now on, where you go, I go."

"I doubt the monks will offer you a bed in Monte Cassino;

but apart from that, fine! We go together."

"Good!" said Lotte with a grin. "Then come to bed, Herr Professor. It's the safest place in Rome!"

In principle, it was an excellent idea; but before they could put it into practice the maid knocked on the door to tell him that Georg Rainer was on the line from the bureau of *Die Welt*. Rainer's approach was good-humoured but crisp and businesslike.

"You're a celebrity now, Carl. I need an interview for my paper."

"When?"

"Right now, on the telephone. I have a deadline to meet."

"Go ahead."

"Not so fast, Carl. We're friends of a friend, so I'll give you the ground rules, once only. You can decline to answer; but don't tell me anything off the record. Whatever you give me I print. Clear?"

"Clear."

"This conversation is being recorded with your consent. Agreed?"

"Agreed."

"We're running. Professor Mendelius, your prompt action yesterday saved the life of Senator Malagordo. How does it feel to be an international celebrity?"

"Uncomfortable."

"There have been some rather provocative headlines about your act of mercy. One calls you the Hero of the Corso. How do you feel about that?"

"Embarrassed. I did nothing heroic. I simply applied elementary first aid."

"What about this one: 'Ex-Jesuit chief witness against terrorist brigades'?"

"An exaggeration. I witnessed the crime. I described it to the police. I presume they have taken testimony from many others."

"You also gave them a description of the girl who fired the shots."

"Yes."

"Was it accurate and detailed?"

"Yes."

"Did you not feel that you were taking a big risk by giving that evidence?"

"I should have taken a much bigger one by remaining silent."

"Why?"

"Because violence can only flourish when men are afraid to speak and act against it."

"Are you afraid of reprisals, Professor?"

"Afraid, no. Prepared, yes."

"How are you prepared?"

"No comment."

"Are you armed? Do you have police protection, a private bodyguard?"

"No comment."

"Any comment on the fact that you are German and the man whose life you saved is a Jew?"

"Our Lord Jesus Christ was a Jew. I am happy to have served one of His people."

"On another matter, Herr Professor, I understand you gave a very dramatic lecture at the German Academy this morning."

"It was well received. I shouldn't have called it dramatic."

"Our report runs as follows and I quote: 'Asked by one questioner whether he believed that the end of the world as foretold in the Bible was a real and possible event, Professor Mendelius replied that he considered it not only a possibility but an imminent one.'"

"How the hell did you get that?"

"We have good sources, Professor. Is the report true or false?"

"It's true," said Mendelius. "But I wish to God you wouldn't print it."

"I told you the ground rules, my friend; but if you'd like to amplify the statement I'll be happy to report you verbatim."

"I can't, Georg. At least not at this time."

"And what's that mean, Herr Professor? Did you really take yourself so seriously?"

"In this case, yes."

"All the more reason then to print the report."

"How good a journalist are you, Georg?"

"I'm doing all right so far, aren't I?" Rainer's laugh crackled over the wire."

"I'm offering you a deal, Georg."

"I never make them—well, hardly ever. What do you have in mind?"

"Kill the end-of-the-world story and I'll give you a much bigger one."

"On the same subject?"

"No comment."

"When?"

"A week from today."

"That's a Friday. What do you expect to give me—the date of the Second Coming?"

"You get lunch at Ernesto's."

"And the story exclusive?"

"That's a promise."

"You have your deal."

"Thanks, Georg."

"And I still have the tape to remind us of it. *Auf wiedersehen*, Herr Professor."

"*Auf wiedersehen*, Georg."

He put down the receiver and stood, brooding and perplexed, under the indifferent gaze of the fauns and shepherdesses on the ceiling. All unwittingly he had walked himself into a minefield. One more uncautious move and it would explode under his feet.

IV

Domenico Giuliano Francone, chauffeur and man of confidence to his Eminence, was, in looks and character, an original. He was six feet tall, with an athlete's body, a grinning goat's face and a mop of reddish hair kept sedulously dyed. He claimed to be forty-two years old, but was probably on the wrong side of fifty. He spoke a German he had learned from the Swiss Guards, an atrocious Genovese French, English with an American accent and Italian with a Sorrentine singsong lilt.

His personal history was a litany of variables. He had been an amateur wrestler, a champion cyclist, a sergeant in the Carabinieri, a mechanic of the Alfa racing team, a notable boozer and wencher until, after the untimely death of his wife, he had found religion and taken a job as sexton in the titular church of His Eminence.

His Eminence, impressed by Francone's industry and devotion—and possibly by his raffish good humour—had promoted him into his personal household. Because of his police training, his skill as a driver, his knowledge of weapons and his experience in hand-to-hand combat, he had assumed, almost by natural right, the duties of bodyguard. In these rough and godless times, even a prince of the Church was not safe from the sacrilegious threats of the terrorists. While a religious man dared not show himself afraid, the Italian government made no secret of its fears and demanded commonsense precautions.

All this and more Domenico Francone elaborated eloquently, as he drove the Mendelius' and the Franks on a Saturday afternoon excursion to the Etruscan tombs of Tarquinia. His authority established, he then laid down the rules:

". . . I am responsible to His Eminence for your safety. So you will please do as I say, and do it without question. If I tell you to duck, you get your heads down fast! If I drive madly, you hang on tight and don't ask why. In a restaurant you let me pick the table. If you, Professor, go on foot in Rome, you wait until I have parked the car and am ready to follow you. . . . That way you keep your mind on your own affairs and let me do the worrying. I know the way these *mascalzoni* work. . . ."

"We have every confidence in you," said Mendelius amiably, "but is there anyone following us now?"

"No, Professor."

"Then perhaps you'd take it a little more slowly. The ladies would like to look at the countryside."

"Of course! My apologies! . . . This is a very historic zone, many Etruscan tombs. There is, as you know, a ban on excavation without permission, but still there is looting of hidden sites. When I was in the Carabinieri . . ."

The torrent of his eloquence poured over them again. They shrugged and smiled at each other, and drowsed the rest of the way to Tarquinia. It was a relief to leave him standing sentinel by the car while they followed a soft-voiced custodian through the wheatfields, to visit the people of the painted tombs.

It was a tranquil place, filled with lark song and the low whisper of the wind through the ripening wheat. The prospect was magical: the fall of the green land to the brown villages, with the blue sea beyond, and the scattered yachts, spinnakers filled with the land breeze, heading westward to Sardinia. Lotte was entranced, and Mendelius tried to re-create for her the life of a long-vanished people.

". . . They were great traders, great seafarers. They gave their name, the Tyrrhenian, to this part of the Mediterranean. They mined copper and iron and smelted bronze. They farmed the rich lands from here to the Po valley and as far south as Capua. They loved music and dancing and made great feasts; and when they died, they were buried with food and wine and their best clothes, and pictures of their life painted on the walls of their tombs. . . ."

"And now they're all gone," said Lotte quietly. "What happened to them?"

"They got rich and lazy. They hid behind their rituals and trusted to gods who were already out of fashion. Their slaves and commoners revolted. The rich fled with their wealth to buy the protection of the Romans. The Greeks and the Phoenicians took over their trade routes. Even their language died out." He quoted softly the epitaph: " 'O ancient Veii! Once you were a kingdom and there was a golden throne in your forum. Now the idle shepherd plays his pipes within your walls; and, above your tombs, they reap the harvest of the fields . . . !' "

"That's pretty. Who wrote it?"

"A Latin poet, Propertius."

"I wonder what they'll write about our civilization?"

"There may not be anyone left to write a line . . ." said Mendelius moodily, "and there certainly won't be pastorals painted on the side of our sepulchers. At least these people expected continuity. We look forward to a holocaust. . . . It took a Christian to write the 'Dies Irae.' "

"I refuse to think any more gloomy thoughts," said Lotte firmly. "It's beautiful here. I want to enjoy my day."

"My apologies." Mendelius smiled and kissed her. "Get ready to hide your blushes. The Etruscans enjoyed sex, too, and they painted some very pretty reminders of it."

"Good!" said Lotte. "Show me the naughty ones first. And make sure it's my hand you're holding, not Hilde's!"

"For a virtuous woman, liebchen, you have a very dirty mind!"

"Be glad of it, my love." Lotte giggled happily. "But for God's sake don't tell the children!"

She took his hand and trotted him up the slope towards the beckoning custodian. He was a young fellow with agreeable manners, a recent laureate in archaeology and full of enthusiasm for his subject. Awed by the presence of two distinguished scholars, he devoted his attention to the women, while Mendelius and Herman Frank chatted quietly in the background. Herman was in the mood for confidences.

"I've talked things out with Hilde. We've decided to take your advice. We'll shift ourselves out to the farm—gradually of course—and I'll work out a program of writing. If I could get a contract for a series of volumes, it would give me a continuity of work and some sense of financial security."

"That's what my agent recommends." Mendelius encouraged him. "He says publishers like that sort of project because it gives them time to build a readership. When we get back to Rome, I'll call him and see what progress he's made. He always spends weekends at home."

"There's only one thing that worries me, Carl . . ."

"What's that?"

"Well, it's slightly embarrassing . . ."

"Come on! We're old friends. What's the problem?"

"It's Hilde. I'm a lot older than she is. I'm not as good in bed as I used to be. She says it doesn't worry her and I believe it—probably because I want to, anyway. We do have a good life in Rome: lots of friends, many interesting visitors. It . . . well, it seems to balance things out. Once we leave, I'll have my work; but she'll be stuck in a cottage in the hills like a farmer's wife. I'm not sure how that will work out. It would be easier if we had children or grandchildren; but as things are . . . it would kill me to lose her, Carl!"

"What makes you think you will?"

"That!" He pointed ahead to the two women and the custodian, who was just unlocking the next sepulcher. Hilde was joking with him and her high bubbling laugh echoed across the quiet hills. "I'm an old fool, I know; but I get jealous—and scared!"

"Swallow it, man!" Mendelius was curt with him. "Swallow it and keep your mouth shut. You have a good life together. Hilde loves you. Enjoy it, day by day! Nobody gets eternal reassurance. Nobody has a right to it! Besides, the more scared you get, the worse you'll be in bed. Any physician will tell you that."

"I know, Carl. But it's rough sometimes to . . ."

"It's always rough." Mendelius refused to bend to him. "It's rough when your wife seems to pay more attention to the children than she does to you. It's rough when the kids fight you for the right to grow up in a different way from yours. It's rough when a man like Malagordo walks out to lunch and a pretty girl puts a bullet in his balls! Come on, Herman! How much sugar do you need in a cup of coffee?"

"I'm sorry."

"Don't be. You've got it off your chest. Now forget it." He leafed through his catalogue. "This one's the Tomb of the Leopards, with the flute player and the lutanist. Let's go in and join the girls."

As they stood inside the ancient chamber, listening to the custodian expound the meaning of the fresco, Mendelius pondered another random thought. Jean Marie Barette, lately a Pope, was driven to proclaim the Parousia; but did people really want to know about it? Did they really want to listen to the gaunt prophet shouting from the mountaintop? Human nature had not changed much since 500 B.C., when the old Etruscans buried their dead to the sound of lutes and pipes, and locked them in a perpetual present, with food and wine and a tame leopard for company, under the painted cypresses.

That night Mendelius and Lotte dined out in a trattoria on the old Appian Way. The garrulous Francone drove them there, and when they protested his long hours he silenced them with the now familiar phrase: "I am responsible to His Eminence." He ordered them to sit with their backs to the wall, then retired to eat in the kitchen, whence he could survey the yard and make sure no one planted a bomb under the Cardinal's limousine.

Their host for the evening was Enrico Salamone, who published Mendelius' works in Italy; a middle-aged bachelor with a taste for exotic and preferably intelligent women. His escort for this time was one Mme. Barakat, the divorced wife of an Indonesian diplomat. Salamone was a shrewd and successful editor who admired scholarship but never disdained a topical and sensational subject.

". . . Abdication, Mendelius! Think about it. A vigorous and intelligent Pope, still only in his mid-sixties, quits in the seventh year of his reign. There has to be a big story behind it."

"There probably is." Mendelius was elaborately casual. "But your author would break his back finding it. The best journalists in the world got only stale crumbs."

"I was thinking of you, Carl."

"Forget it, Enrico!" Mendelius laughed. "I've got too much on my plate already."

"I tried to tell him," said Mme. Barakat. "He should be looking outward. The West is a small and incestuous world. Publishers should be opening new windows—to Islam, to the Buddhists, to India. All the new revolutions are religious in character."

Salamone nodded a reluctant agreement. "I see it. I know it. But where are the writers who can interpret the East to us? Journalism is not enough; propaganda is a whore's trade. We need poets and storytellers steeped in the old traditions."

"It seems to me," said Lotte ruefully, "everyone shouts too loud and too often. You can't tell stories in a mob. You can't write poetry with the television blaring."

"Bravo, liebchen!" Mendelius squeezed her hand.

"It's true!" She was launched now and ready to engage in combat. "I don't have many brains, but I know Carl's always done his best work in a quiet, provincial situation. Haven't you always told me, Carl, too many people argue their own books out of existence? You, too, Enrico! You said once you'd like to lock your authors up until they were ready to walk out with a finished manuscript."

"I said it, Lotte. I believe it." He gave her a swift sidelong grin. "But even your husband here isn't the hermit he pretends to be. . . . What are you really doing in Rome, Carl?"

"I told you: research, a couple of lectures, and having a holiday with Lotte."

"There's a rumor," said Mme. Barakat sweetly, "that you were given some kind of mission by the former Pope."

"Hence my suggestion for a book," said Enrico Salamone.

"Where the hell did you pick up that nonsense?" Mendelius was nettled.

"It's a long story." Salamone was amused but wary. "But I assure you it is authentic. You know I'm a Jew. It's natural that I entertain the Israeli ambassador and any visitors he wants to present in Rome. It's also natural that we talk about matters of mutual concern. So now! . . . The Vatican has always refused diplomatic recognition to the State of Israel. The refusal is pure politics. They don't want to quarrel with the Arab world. They would like, if they could, to assert some kind of sovereignty over the Holy Places in Jerusalem. Echoes of the Crusades! There was hope that this position might change under Gregory the Seventeenth. His personal response to diplomatic relations with Israel was believed to be favourable. So, early this spring, a private meeting was arranged between the Israeli ambassador and the Pontiff. The Pope was frank about his problems, inside his own Secretariat of State and outside, with Arab leaders. He wanted to continue exploring the situation. He asked my ambassador whether a personal and unofficial envoy would be welcome in Israel. Their answer was naturally in the affirmative. Yours was one of the names suggested by the Pontiff. . . ."

"Good God!" Mendelius was genuinely shocked. "You have to believe me, Enrico. I knew absolutely nothing about it."

"That's true!" Lotte was instant in support. "I would have known. This thing was never, never mentioned—not even in his last . . ."

"Lotte, please!"

"I'm sorry, Carl."

"So there was no mission." Mme. Barakat was soothing as honey. "But there was communication?"

"Private, madame," said Mendelius curtly. "A matter of old friendship . . . And I'd like to change the subject."

Salamone shrugged and spread his hands in surrender. "Fine! But you mustn't blame me for trying. That's what makes me a good publisher. Now tell me, how's the new book coming?"

"Slowly."

"When can we expect the manuscript?"

"Six, seven months."

"Let's hope we're still in business by then!"

"Why shouldn't you be?"

"If you read the papers, my dear Professor, you'll know the great powers are talking us all into a war."

"They need another twelve months," said Mme. Barakat. "I keep telling you, Enrico. Nothing before twelve months. After that . . ."

"Nothing ever again," said Salamone. "Pour me the rest of the wine, Carl! I think we could use another bottle!"

The bloom was already off the evening; but they had to sit it out to the end. As they drove home through the sleeping city, they sat close and talked softly, for fear of rousing Francone to another oration.

Lotte asked, "What was the meaning of all that, Carl?"

"I don't know, liebchen. Salamone was trying to be smart."

"And Madame Barakat is a bitch!"

"He does collect some odd ones, doesn't he?"

"Old friends and new bedmates don't mix."

"I agree. Enrico should have known better."

"Do you think it was true about Jean Marie and the Israelis?"

"Probably. But who knows? Rome's always been a whispering gallery. The hard thing is to put the right names to the voices."

"I hate that kind of mystery-making."

"I, too, liebchen."

He was too tired to tell her how he truly felt: a man caught in toils of gossamer, the trailing wisps of a nightmare from which he could neither flee nor wake.

"What are we doing tomorrow?" asked Lotte drowsily.

"If you don't mind I thought we'd go to mass in the Catacombs; then we'll go out to Frascati for lunch. Just the two of us."

"Couldn't we hire a car and drive ourselves?"

Mendelius gave a rueful chuckle and shook his head. "I'm afraid not, liebchen. That's another lesson you learn in Rome. There's no escape from the Hounds of God."

Garrulous he might be, but Domenico Francone was a very good watchdog. He drove twice around the block before dropping them at the Franks' apartment, then stood watch until the ancient door closed behind them, sealing out the dangers of the night.

In the garden of San Callisto the bougainvillaea was in flame, the rose gardens in first flush and the doves still fluttered in their cote behind the chapel, all just as he remembered it from his first visit, long years before. Even the guides still looked the same: old devotees from a dozen countries, who dedicated their services as translators to the pilgrim groups who came to pay homage at the tombs of ancient martyrs.

There were no ghosts in the tiny chapel, only an extraordinary tranquillity. There were no baroque horrors, no mediaeval grotesques. Even the symbols were simple and full of grace: the anchor of faith, the dove carrying the olive twig of deliverance, the fish that bore the loaves of the Eucharist on its back. The inscriptions all spoke of hope and peace: *Vivas in Christo. In pace Christi.* The word *Vale*—farewell—was never used. Even the dim labyrinths below held no terrors. The *loculi*, the wall niches where the dead were laid, held only shards and dusty fragments.

In the Chapel of the Popes, they attended a mass said by a German priest for a group of Bavarian pilgrims. The chapel was a large, vaulted chamber, where, in 1854, Count de Rossi had discovered the resting place of five of the earliest Pontiffs. One had been deported as a mine slave to Sardinia and died in captivity. His body was brought back and buried in this place. Another had been executed in the persecution of Decius, yet another was put to the sword at the entrance to the burial place. Now, the violence in which they had perished was almost forgotten. They slept here in peace. Their memory was celebrated in a tongue they never knew.

As he knelt with Lotte on the tufa floor, responding to the familiar liturgy, Mendelius remembered his own priesthood and felt a pang of resentment that he should now be debarred from its exercise. It had not been so in the early Church. Even now, the Uniats were permitted a married clergy; while the Romans clung obstinately to their celibate rule, and reinforced it with myth and historic legend and canonical legislation. He had written copious argument about it, still fought it in debate; but, married himself, he was a discredited witness, and the lawmakers paid no heed to him.

But what of the future—the near future—when the supply of celibate candidates would dry up, and the flock would cry out for ministry—by man or woman, married or single, it made no matter, just so they heard the Word and shared the Bread of Life in charity? Their Eminences at the Vatican still ducked the issue, hiding behind a carefully edited tradition. Even Drexel ducked it, because he was too old to fight and too well-drilled a soldier to challenge the high command. Jean Marie had faced the question in his encyclical and this was yet another reason for suppressing it. Now the dark days were coming again. The shepherd would be struck down, the flock scattered. Who would bring them together again and hold them in love, while the rooftrees of the world toppled about them?

When the celebrant raised the host and the chalice after the Consecration. Mendelius bowed his head and made a silent, heartfelt prayer: "O God, give me light enough to know the truth, courage enough to do what will be asked of me!" Suddenly he found himself weeping, uncontrollably. Lotte reached out and took his hand. He held to her, mute and desperate, until the mass was ended and they walked out into the sunlight of the rose arbour.

Early on Monday morning, while Lotte was taking her bath, Mendelius telephoned the Salvator Mundi hospital and enquired about the progress of Senator Malagordo. He was passed, as before, from reception to the ward sister, to the security man. Finally he was told that the Senator was much improved and would like to see him as soon as possible. He made an appointment for three that same afternoon.

He was getting restless now—more and more convinced that his Wednesday meeting with Jean Marie would be some kind of turning point in his life. If he could not accept Jean Marie's revelation, their relationship would change irrevocably. If he did accept it, then he must accept the mission as well, no matter what form it might take. Either way, he must soon be gone and he wanted as few social encumbrances as possible.

He had done some research, but he was too preoccupied to concentrate on the new material, which, in any case, was fragmentary and of little importance. Tuesday would see him out with the Evangelicals. He was still irritated by the leaking of conference material to the press; but he needed to test the reaction of a Protestant audience to certain of Jean Marie's propositions. He still had to make good his promise of a news story for Georg Rainer. So far, he had no idea in the world what he would tell him.

Lotte was still bathing, so he gathered up his notes and walked out to breakfast on the terrace. Herman had left early for the Academy. Hilde was alone at the table. She poured his coffee and then announced firmly:

"Now, you and I can have a little talk. Something's bothering you, *Carlo mio*. What is it?"

"Nothing I can't deal with."

"Herman looks at pictures. I read people. And there's trouble written all over your face. Is everything all right with you and Lotte?"

"Of course."

"Then what's the matter?"

"It's a long story, Hilde."

"I'm a good listener. Tell me!"

He told her, haltingly at first, then in a rush of vivid words, the story of his friendship with Jean Marie Barette and the strange pass to which it had led him. She listened in silence; and he found it a relief to express himself without the burden of reasoning or polemic. When he had finished he said simply, "So that's it, my love. I won't know anything more until I meet Jean Marie on Wednesday."

Hilde Frank laid a soft hand on his cheek and said gently, "That's a hell of a load to carry around—even for the great Mendelius! It helps to explain some other things, too."

"What things?"

"Herman's romantic idea of living on beans and broccoli and goat cheese up in the mountains."

"Herman doesn't know what I've just told you about Jean Marie."

"Then what the devil is he talking about?"

"He's scared of a new war. We all are. He worries about you."

"And how he worries! You know his latest idea? He wants to

rush off to Zurich for a hormone implant, to improve our sex life. I told him not to bother. I'm perfectly happy the way we are."

"And are you happy, Hilde?"

"Would you believe, yes! Herman's a dear and I love him. As for the sex part, the fact is I'm not really good at it myself—never have been. Oh, I love the warm snuggly part, but the rest of it—I'm not frigid but I'm slow and hard to rouse, and what I get at the end is hardly worth the bother. So you see, Herman's really got nothing to worry about."

"Then you'd better tell him as often as you can." Mendelius tried to be casual about it. "He's feeling very uncertain of himself just now."

"Forget about us, Carl. We'll work it out. I've been managing Herman ever since we married. . . . Let's get back to your story."

"I'd like to hear your reaction to it, Hilde."

"Well, first, I've lived in Italy a long time so I'm skeptical about saints and miracles and weeping virgins and friars who levitate at Mass. Second, I'm a pretty contented woman, so I've never been drawn to fortune-tellers or séances or encounter groups. I'd much rather be doing fun things. Finally, I'm pretty self-centered. So long as my little corner of the universe makes sense, I put the rest out of my mind. There's nothing I can do to change it anyway."

"Let's put it another way then. Suppose I come back on Thursday from Monte Cassino and say: 'Hilde, I've just seen Jean Marie. I believe he's had a true revelation, that the world is going to end soon and the Second Coming of Christ will occur.' What will you do?"

"Hard to say. I certainly wouldn't go rushing off to church, or hoarding food or climbing the Apennines to wait for the Saviour or watch the last sunrise. And you, Carl? How will you react?"

"I don't know, Hilde my love. I've thought about it every day, every night, since I read Jean's letter; but I still don't know."

"There's one way to look at it, of course . . ."

"What's that?"

"Well, if somebody's really going to shut down the world, everything becomes pointless. Rather than wait for the last big bang, why not buy a bottle of whisky and a big bottle of barbiturates and put ourselves to sleep? I think a lot of people would decide to do just that."

"Would you?" asked Mendelius softly. "Could you?"

She refilled their cups and began calmly buttering a croissant. "You're damn right I could, Carl! And I wouldn't want to wake up and meet a God who incinerated His own children."

She said it with a smile; but Carl Mendelius knew that she meant every word.

As they drove out to the Salvator Mundi hospital, Domenico Francone, the garrulous one, was taciturn and snappish. When Mendelius pointed out that they seemed to be taking a complicated route, Francone told him bluntly:

"I know my business, Professor. I promise you will not be late."

Mendelius digested the snub in silence. He himself was feeling none too happy. His talk with Hilde Frank had raised more and deeper questions on the veracity of Jean Marie and the wisdom of his encyclical. It had also cast new light on the attitude of the Cardinals who deposed him.

All through the literature of apocalyptic, in the Old and the New Testament, in Essene and Gnostic documents, one special theme persisted: the elect, the chosen, the children of light, the good seed, the sheep, beloved by the shepherd, who would be separated forever from the goats. Salvation was exclusive to them. Only they would endure through the horrors of the last time, and be found worthy of a merciful judgment.

It was a perilous doctrine, full of paradoxes and pitfalls, easily appropriated by fanatics and charlatans and the wildest of sectaries. A thousand of the elect had committed ritual suicide in Guyana. Ten million of the elect made up the Soka Gakkai in Japan. Another three million were chosen to salvation in the Unification Church of the Reverend Moon. . . . All of them and other millions, in ten thousand exotic cults, believed themselves the chosen, practiced an intense indoctrination, a fierce, exclusive and fanatical bonding. . . .

In the event of a universal panic, such as the publication of Jean Marie's encyclical might raise, how would such sectaries perform? The history of every great religion offered only the gloomiest forecast. It was not so long ago that Mahdist Moslems had occupied the Kaaba in Mecca and held hostages and spilled blood in the holiest place of Islam. It was a nightmare possibility that the Parousia might be preceded by a vast and bloody crusade of the insiders against the outlanders. Against such a horror, a swift and painless suicide might seem to many the most rational alternative.

This was the nub of the problem he must thresh out with Jean Marie. Once you invoked private revelation, reason was out the window. To which the rationalists would reply that once you invoked any kind of revelation—however hallowed by tradition—you were committed to an ultimate insanity.

Francone swung the car into the circular drive of the Salvator Mundi and stopped immediately outside the entrance. He did not get out, but simply said, "Go straight inside, Professor. Move fast."

Mendelius hesitated a split second, then opened the nearside door and went straight into the reception area. When he looked out, he saw Francone park the car in the space reserved for medical staff, get out and walk briskly to the entrance. Mendelius waited until he was inside, then asked, "What was all that about?"

Francone shrugged. "Just a precaution. We're in an enclosed space, nowhere to run. You go upstairs and see the Senator. I have a phone call to make."

An elderly nun with a Swabian accent escorted him to the elevator. On the fifth floor a security man checked his papers and passed him to the ward sister, a very brusque lady who clearly believed that the sick were best healed by the firm hands of authority. She told him he might spend fifteen minutes, no more, with the patient, who must not, in any case, be excited. Mendelius bowed his head in meekness. He, too, had suffered under the handmaidens of the Lord and knew better than to argue against their resolute virtue.

He found Malagordo propped up on his pillows, with a glucose drip strapped to his left arm. His lean, handsome face lit up with pleasure at the sight of his visitor.

"My dear Professor! Thank you for coming. I wanted so much to see you."

"You seem to be making a good recovery." Mendelius pulled a chair to the bedside. "How do you feel?"

"Better each day, thank God. I owe you my life. I understand you are now in danger because of me. What can I say? The newspapers can be so irresponsible. May I order you some coffee?"

"No, thank you. I had a late lunch."

"What do you think of my sad country, Professor?"

"It was mine, too, for a number of years, Senator. At least I understand it better than most foreigners."

"We have gone back four centuries, to the bandits and the *condottieri*! I see small hope for betterment. Like all the other Mediterraneans, we are lost tribes, squabbling on the shores of a putrid lake."

The threnody had a familiar ring to Mendelius. The Latins were great mourners of a past that never existed. He tried to lighten the conversation.

"You may be right, Senator; but I must tell you the wines are still good in Castelli, and Zia Rosa's spaghetti alla carbonara is magnificent as always. My wife and I lunched there on Sunday. The nice thing was she remembered me from my clerical days. She seemed to approve the change."

The Senator brightened immediately. "I'm told she used to be a great beauty."

"Not any longer. But she's a great cook and she rules that place with an iron fist."

"Have you been to the Pappagallo?"

"No."

"That's another very good place."

There was a moment's silence, then Malagordo said with wry humour, "We talk banalities. I wonder why we waste so much life on them."

"It's a precaution." Mendelius grinned. "Wine and women are safe topics. Money and politics lead to broken heads."

"I'm retiring from politics," said Malagordo. "As soon as I get out of here my wife and I are emigrating to Australia. Our two sons are there, doing very well in business. Besides, it's the last stop before the penguins. I don't want to be in Europe for the great collapse."

"Do you think it will collapse?" asked Mendelius.

"I'm certain of it. The armaments are nearly all ready. The latest prototypes will be operational in a year. There's not enough oil to go round. More and more governments are in the hands of gamblers or fanatics. It's the old story: if you're faced with riots at home, start a crusade abroad. Man is a mad animal, and the madness is incurable. Do you know where I was going when I got shot? To plead for the release of a woman terrorist who is dying of cancer in a Palermo jail!"

"God Almighty!" Mendelius swore softly.

"I think He'll be happy to see this race of imbeciles eliminate itself. . . ." Malagordo made a wry mouth as a sudden pain took hold of him. "I know! From a Jew that's blasphemy. But I don't believe in the Messiah anymore. He's delayed too long. And who needs this bloody mess of a world anyway?"

"Take it easy," said Mendelius. "If you get excited, they'll have me thrown out. That ward sister is a real dragon."

"A missed vocation." Malagordo was good-humoured again. "She's got quite a good body under all that drapery. Before you go . . ." He reached under his pillow and brought out a small package wrapped in bright paper and tied with a gold ribbon. "I have a gift for you."

"It wasn't necessary." Mendelius was embarrassed. "But thank you. May I open it?"

"Please!"

The gift was a small gilt box with a glass lid. Inside the box was a shard of pottery inscribed with Hebrew characters. Mendelius took it out and examined it carefully.

"Do you know what it is, Professor?"

"It looks like an *ostracon.*"

"It is. Can you read the words?"

Mendelius traced them slowly with his fingertip. "I think it spells Aharon ben Ezra."

"Right! It came from Masada. I am told it is probably one of the shards which were used to draw lots when the Jewish garrison killed each other, rather than fall into the hands of the Romans."

Mendelius was deeply moved. He shook his head. "I can't take this. Truly, I can't."

"You must," said Malagordo. "It's the nearest I can get to a proper thank-you—all that's left of a Jewish hero, for the life of a lousy Senator, who isn't even a man anymore. . . . Go now, Professor, before I make a fool of myself!"

When he reached the ground floor he found Francone waiting for him. As he moved towards the exit Francone laid a restraining hand on his arm.

"We'll wait here for a few minutes, Professor."

"Why?"

Francone pointed out through the glass doors. There were two police cars parked in the driveway and four more outside in the road. Two orderlies were loading a stretcher into an ambulance under the eyes of a curious crowd. Mendelius gaped at the scene. Francone explained tersely.

"We were followed here, Professor. One car. Then a second one arrived and parked just outside the gates. They had both entrances covered. Fortunately I spotted the tail just after we left town. I telephoned the *Squadra Mobile* as soon as we arrived. They blocked both ends of the street and caught four of the bastards. One's dead."

"For God's sake, Domenico! Why didn't you tell me?"

"It would have spoiled your visit. Besides, what could you have done? Like I told you, Professor, I know how these *mascalzoni* work. . . ."

"Thanks!" Mendelius held out a damp and unsteady hand. "I hope you won't tell my wife."

"When you work for a Cardinal," said Francone with grave condescension, "you learn to keep your mouth shut."

"Dear colleagues!" Carl Mendelius, smiling and benign, adjusted his spectacles and surveyed his audience. "I begin today with a mild censure on person or persons unknown. . . .

"I know that travel is expensive. I know that ministers of the gospel are paid very little. I know that it is a common practice to supplement one's income, or one's travel allowance, by supplying conference reports to the press. I have no objection to the practice, provided it is open and declared; but I think it is an abridgment of academic courtesy to file press reports in secret and without notice to colleagues. One of our members has caused me considerable embarrassment by reporting to a senior journalist that I believed the end of the world could be imminent. True, I said so in this room; but, out of the context of our assembly and its specialist discussions, the statement could be interpreted as frivolous or tendentious. I do not ask for a confession from the reporter. I do, however, seek an assurance that what is said here today will be reported only with our full knowledge. . . . Will all those who agree please raise their hands? . . . Thank you. Any dissenters? None. Apparently we understand each other. So let us begin. . . .

"We have talked about the Doctrine of Last Things: consummation or continuity. We have expressed differing views on the subject. Now let us accept, as hypothesis, that the consummation is possible and imminent: that the world will end soon. How should the Christian respond to that event? . . . You, sir, in the third row."

"Wilhelm Adler, Rosenheim. The answer is that the Christian—or anyone else for that matter—cannot respond to a hypothesis, only to an event. This was the mistake of the schoolmen and the casuists. They tried to prescribe moral formulae for every situation. Impossible! Man lives in the here and the now, not in the perhaps."

"Good! . . . But does not human prudence dictate that he should prepare for the perhaps?"

"Could you give an example, Herr Professor?"

"Certainly. The earliest followers of Christ were Jews. They continued to live a Jewish life. They practiced circumcision. They observed the dietary laws. They frequented the synagogues and read the Scriptures. . . . Now Paul—Saul that was—of Tarsus embarks on his mission to the Gentiles, the non-Jews, to whom circumcision is unacceptable and the dietary laws are unexplainable. They see no point in bodily mutilation. They have to eat what they can get. Suddenly they are out of theory into practice. . . . The question simplifies itself. Surely salvation does not hang on a man's foreskin; nor does it depend on his starving himself to death. . . ."

They laughed at that and applauded the rabbinical humour. Mendelius went on.

"Paul was prepared for the event. Peter was not. In the absence of scriptural dictate, he had to find justification for his new position in a vision—'Take and eat'—remember?"

They remembered, and gave a murmur of approval.

"So now, our 'perhaps.' The Last Days are upon us. How prepared are we?"

They hung back now. Mendelius offered them another example.

"Some few of you here are old enough to remember the last days of the Third Reich; a country in ruins, a monstrosity of crimes revealed, a generation of men destroyed, a whole ethos corrupted, the only visible goal, survival! To those of us who remember, is it not at least a fair analogue of the millennial catastrophe? . . . But you are here today because, somewhere, somehow, faith and hope and charity survived and became fruitful again. . . . Do I explain myself?"

"Yes." The answer came back in a muted chorus.

"How then . . ." He challenged them strongly. "How do we

ensure that faith and charity survive, if and when the Last Days come upon us? Forget the Last Days if you must. Suppose that, as many predict, we have atomic war within a twelvemonth, what will you do?"

"Die!" said a sepulchral voice from the back; and the room dissolved into a roar of laugher.

"Ladies and gentlemen!" Mendelius chuckled helplessly. "There speaks a true prophet! Would he like to come up here and take my place?"

No one stirred. After a few moments the laughter died into silence. More quietly now, Mendelius went on.

"I should like to read to you now an extract from a document prepared by a dear friend of mine. I cannot name him. I ask you to accept that he is a man of great sanctity and singular intelligence; one, moreover, who understands the usages of power in the modern world. After the reading I shall ask for your comments."

He paused to wipe his spectacles and then began to read from Jean Marie's encyclical: ". . . It is clear that in the days of universal calamity the traditional structures of society will not survive. There will be a ferocious struggle for the simplest needs of life—food, water, fuel and shelter. Authority will be usurped by the strong and the cruel. Large urban societies will fragment themselves into tribal groups. . . ."

He felt the words take hold of them, the tension begin to build again. When the reading was done the silence was like a wall before him.

He stepped back from the rostrum and asked simply, "Any comment?"

There was a long pause and then a young woman stood up.

"I am Henni Borkheim from Berlin. My husband is a pastor. We have two young children. I have a question. How do you show charity to a man who comes with a gun to rob you and take the last food from your children?"

"And I have another!" The young man next to her stood up. "How do you continue to believe in a God who contrives or permits so universal a calamity—and then sits in judgment on its victims?"

"So perhaps," said Carl Mendelius gravely, "we should all ask ourselves a more fundamental question. We know that evil exists, that suffering and cruelty exist, that they may well propagate themselves to extremity like cancer in the body. Can we really believe in God at all?"

"Do you, Professor?" Henni Borkheim was on her feet again.

"Yes, I do."

"Then will you please answer my question!"

"It was answered two millennia ago. 'Father, forgive them, for they know not what they do!' "

"And that's the answer you would give?"

"I don't know, my dear." He was about to add that he had not yet been crucified; but he thought better of it. He stepped down from the rostrum and walked down through the audience to where the girl was sitting with her husband. He talked calmly and persuasively.

". . . You see the problem we get when we demand a personal testimony on every issue? We do not, we cannot, know how we will act. How we *should* act, yes! But how we will, in an immediate situation, there is no way to know in advance. . . . I remember as a youth in Dresden my mother talking to my aunt about the coming of the Russians. I was not supposed to hear; but I did. My mother handed her a jar of lubricant jelly and said: 'Better relax and survive than resist and be murdered.' . . . Either way it's rape, and there is no miracle promised to prevent it; no legislation to cover the time of chaos." He smiled and held out his hand to the young woman. "Let's not contend· but discuss in peace."

There was a small murmur of approval as they joined hands; then Mendelius put another question.

"In a plural world, who are the elect? We Romans, you Lutherans, the Sunnis or the Shi'ites in Islam, the Mormons of Salt Lake City, the Animists of Thailand?"

"In respect of the individual, it is not for us to distinguish." A grey-haired pastor rose painfully to his feet. His hands were knotted with arthritis. He spoke haltingly but with conviction. "We are not appointed to judge other men by our lights. We are commanded only to love the image of God in our fellow pilgrims."

"But we are also commanded to keep the faith pure, to spread the good news of Christ," said Pastor Allman of Darmstadt.

"When you sit down at my table," said the old man patiently, "I offer you the food I have. If you cannot digest it, what should I do—choke you with it?"

"So, my friends!" Mendelius took command of the meeting

again. "When the black night comes down, in the great desert, when there is neither pillar of cloud nor spark of fire to light the path, when the voice of authority is stilled, and we hear nothing but the confusion of old argument, when God seems to absent himself from his own universe, where do we turn? Whom can we sanely believe?"

He walked slowly back to the rostrum and, in a long hush, waited for someone to answer.

"I'm scared, liebchen! So damn scared, I'd like to walk out of here and take the next plane back to Germany!"

It was thirty minutes after midday and they were eating an early lunch in a quiet restaurant near the Pantheon, before Mendelius left for Monte Cassino. Two tables away, Francone shovelled spaghetti into his mouth and kept a vigilant eye on the door. Lotte leaned across to Mendelius and wiped a speck of sauce from the corner of his mouth. She chided him firmly:

"Truly, Carl, I don't know what the fuss is about! You're a free man. You're going to see an old friend. You don't have to accept any commission, any obligations, beyond this one visit."

"He's asked me to judge him."

"He had no right to demand that."

"He didn't demand—he asked, begged! Look, liebchen. I've thought round and round this thing. I've talked it up and down; and still I'm no nearer to an answer. Jean Marie's asking for an act of faith just as big as . . . as an assent to the Resurrection! I can't make that act."

"So tell him!"

"And do I tell him why? 'Jean, you're not mad; you're not a cheat; you're not deluded; I love you like a brother—but God doesn't have dialogues in country gardens about the end of the world; and I wouldn't believe it if you came complete with the stigmata and a crown of thorns!' "

"If that's what you mean, say it."

"The problem is, liebchen, I think I mean something else altogether. I'm beginning to believe the Cardinals were right to get rid of Jean Marie."

"What makes you say that?"

"It arises out of my dialogues at the Academy—and even a talk I had with Hilde Frank. The only finality people can cope with is their own. . . . Total catastrophe is beyond their comprehension and probably their capacity to deal with. It's an invitation to despair. Jean Marie sees it as a call to evangelical charity. I think it would lead to an almost complete breakdown in social communication. Who was it who said: 'The veil that hides the face of the future was woven by the hand of Mercy'?"

"Then I think," said Lotte firmly, "you have to be as honest with Jean Marie as you're trying to be with yourself. He asked you for a judgment. Give it to him!"

"I want to ask you a straight question, liebchen. Do you think I'm an honest man?"

She did not answer him directly. She cupped her chin on her hands and looked at him for a long time without speaking. Then very quietly she told him:

"I remember the first day I met you, Carl. I was with Frederika Ullman. We were walking down the Spanish Steps, two German girls on their first visit to Rome. You were there, sitting on the steps next to a lad who was painting a very bad picture. You were dressed in black pants and a black roll-necked sweater. We stopped to look at the picture. You heard us talking in German and you spoke to us. We sat down beside you, very glad to have someone to chat with us. You bought us tea and buns in the English Tea Shop. Then you invited us to go for a ride in a *carrozza*. Off we went, clip-clopping, all the way to the Campo dei Fiori. When we got there you showed us that marvellous brooding statue of Giordano Bruno and told us about his trial and how they burned him for heresy on the same spot. Then you said: 'That's what they'd like to do to me!' I thought you were drunk or a little crazy until you explained that you were a priest under suspicion of heresy. . . . You looked so lonely, so haunted, my heart went out to you. Then you quoted Bruno's last words to his judges: 'I think, gentlemen, that you are more afraid of me than I of you.' . . . I'm looking at the same man I saw that day. The same man who said: 'Bruno was a faker, a charlatan, a muddled thinker, but one thing I know: he died an honest man!' I loved you then, Carl. I love you now. Whatever you do, right or wrong, I know you'll die an honest man!"

"I hope so, liebchen!" said Carl Mendelius gravely. "I hope to God I can be honest with the man who married us!"

V

At three-thirty precisely Francone set him down at the portals of the great Monastery of Monte Cassino. The guestmaster welcomed him and led him to his room, a plain whitewashed chamber furnished with a bed, a desk and chair, a clothes closet and a prie-dieu over which was hung a crucifix carved in olive wood. He threw open the shutters to reveal a dizzying view across the Rapido valley to the rolling hills of Lazio. He smiled at Mendelius' surprise and said:

"You see! Already we are halfway to heaven! . . . I hope you enjoy your stay with us."

He waited while Mendelius laid out his few belongings and then led him along the bare, echoing corridors to the Abbot's study. The man who rose to greet him was small and spare with a lean, weathered face and iron-grey hair and the smile of a happy child.

"Professor Mendelius! A pleasure to meet you! Please, sit down. Would you like coffee, a cordial perhaps?"

"No, thank you; we stopped for a coffee on the autostrada. It's very kind of you to receive me."

"You come with the best recommendations, Professor." There was a hint of irony in the innocent smile. "I don't want to keep you too long from your friend; but I thought we should talk first."

"Of course. You told me on the telephone he had been ill."

"You will find him changed." The Abbot chose his words carefully. "He has survived an experience that would have crushed a lesser man. Now he is going through another—more difficult, more intense, because it is an interior struggle. I counsel him as best I can. The rest of the brethren support him with their prayers and their attentions; but he is like a man consumed by a fire inside him. It may be he will open himself to you. If he does, let him see that you understand. Don't press him. I know that he has written to you. I know what he has asked. I am his confessor and I cannot discuss that subject with you, because he has not given me permission to do so. . . . You, on the other hand, are not my subject and I cannot presume to direct your conscience either."

"Perhaps then, you and I could open our minds to each other."

"Perhaps." Abbot Andrew's smile was enigmatic. "But first, I think you should talk to our friend Jean."

"Certain questions arise. Does he truly want to see me?"

"Oh, yes, indeed."

"Then why, when I wrote to you both, did he not write back as well as you? When I called on the telephone, why did you not invite him to speak with me?"

"It was not discourtesy, I promise you."

"What was it?"

The Abbot sat silent for a long moment, studying the backs of his long hands. Finally he said, slowly, "There are times when it is not possible for him to communicate with anyone."

"That sounds ominous."

"On the contrary, Professor. It is my belief, based on personal observation, that your friend Jean has reached a high degree of contemplation, that state, in fact, which is called 'illuminative,' in which, for certain periods, the spirit is totally absorbed in communication with the Creator. It is a rare phenomenon; but not unfamiliar in the lives of the great mystics. During these periods of contemplation the subject does not respond to any external stimuli at all. When the experience is over, he returns immediately to normality. . . . But I am telling you nothing you don't know from your own reading."

"I know also," said Carl Mendelius drily, "that catatonic and cataleptic states are very well known in psychiatric medicine."

"I, too, am aware of it, Professor. We are not altogether in the Dark Ages here. Our founder, Saint Benedict, was a wise and tolerant legislator. It may surprise you to know that one of our fathers is a quite eminent physician with degrees from Padua, Zurich and London. He entered the order only ten years ago after the death of his wife. He has examined our friend. He has, on my direction, consulted with other specialists on the matter. He is convinced, as I am, that we are dealing with a mystic and not a psychotic."

"Have you so informed the people who declared him a madman?"

"I have informed Cardinal Drexel. For the rest . . ." He gave a small chuckle of amusement. "They're very busy men. I prefer not to disturb them in their large affairs. Any more questions?"

"Only one," said Mendelius gravely. "You believe Jean Marie is a mystic, illuminated by God. Do you also believe that he was granted a relevation of the Parousia?"

The Abbot frowned and shook his head.

"Afterwards, my friend! After you've seen him. Then I'll tell you what I believe. . . . Come! He's waiting in the garden. I'll take you to him.

He was standing in the middle of the cloister garden, a tall slim figure in the black habit of St. Benedict, feeding crumbs to the pigeons that fluttered at his feet. At the sound of Mendelius' footfall he turned, stared for a single moment, and then hurried towards him, arms outstretched, while the pigeons wheeled in panic above his head. Mendelius caught him in midstride and held him in a long embrace, shocked to feel, even through the coarse stuff of the habit, how thin and frail he was. His first words were a stifled cry:

"Jean . . . Jean, my friend!"

Jean Marie Barette clung to him, patting his shoulder and saying over and over, "*Grâce à Dieu . . . Grâce à Dieu!*"

Then they held each other at arms' length, looking into each other's face.

"Jean! Jean! What have they done to you? You're as thin as a rake."

"They? Nothing." He fished a handkerchief from the sleeve of his habit and dabbed at Mendelius' cheeks. "Everybody's been more than kind. How are all your family?"

"Well, thank God. Lotte's here in Rome. She sends you her best love."

"Thank her for lending you to me. . . . I prayed you would come quickly, Carl!"

"I wanted to come sooner; but I couldn't leave Tübingen until end of term."

"I know . . . I know! And now I read that you are involved in a terrorist shooting in Rome. That troubles me. . . ."

"Please, Jean! It's a nine-day wonder. Tell me about yourself."

"Shall we walk awhile? It's very pleasant here. One gets the breeze from the mountains, cool and clean, even on the hottest day."

He took Mendelius' arm and they began to stroll slowly round the cloisters, making small tentative talk, as the first rush of emotion ebbed and the calm of an old friendship took hold of them.

"I am very much at home here," said Jean Marie. "Abbot Andrew is most considerate. I like the rhythm of the day; the hours of the office sung in choir, the quiet work. . . . One of the fathers is an excellent sculptor in wood. I sit in his workshop and watch. I love the smell of wood shavings! It's a feast day today. I prepared the dessert you will be having for supper. It's an old recipe my mother used. The fruit is from our own orchard. In the kitchen they have decided I'm better as a cook than as a Pope. . . . And how is life with you, Carl?"

"It's good, Jean. The children are beginning to make their own lives. Katrin is head over heels in love with her painter. Johann is brilliant in economics. He's decided he's not a believer anymore. One hopes he will grope his way back into faith; but he's a good lad just the same. Lotte and I, well, we're just beginning to enjoy being middle-aged together. . . . The new book's moving ahead. At least it was, until you put it all out of my head. . . . I don't think there's been an hour when you were absent from my thoughts. . . ."

"And you were never far from mine, Carl. It was as if you were the last spar to which I could cling after the shipwreck. I dared not let you go. I look back on those last weeks in the Vatican, with real horror."

"And now, Jean . . . ?"

"Now I am calm—if not yet at peace, because I am still struggling to divest myself of the last impediments to a conformity with God's will. . . . You cannot believe how hard it is, when it should be so simple, to abandon yourself absolutely to His designs, to say and mean it: 'Here I am, a tool in your hands. Use me any way you want.' The trust has to be absolute; but always one tries—without even knowing—to hedge the bet."

"And I was part of the hedge?" Mendelius said it with a smile and a hand's touch to soften the question.

"You were, Carl. I suppose you still are; but I believe also that you are part of God's design for me. Had you not written, had you declined to come, I would have been forced to think otherwise. I prayed desperately for strength to face the possibility of a refusal."

"It's still a possibility, Jean," said Mendelius with grave gentleness. "You asked me to judge you."

"Have you reached a verdict yet?"

"No. I had to talk to you first."

"Let's sit down, Carl. Over there, on the stone bench. That's where I was sitting when it happened. But, first, there are other things to tell you. . . ."

They settled themselves on the bench. Jean Marie scooped up a handful of pebbles from the path and began tossing them at an imaginary target. He talked casually, in a tone of wry reminiscence.

". . . Let me say outright, Carl, that in spite of all the ritual disclaimers and the public acts of humility, I really wanted to be Pope. All my life I had been a careerist in the Church. I use the word in the French sense. I was built for what I did. As a youth I fought with the Maquis. I came to the seminary a man, sure of his vocation and of his motives. More, I understood instinctively how the system works. It's like Saint Cyr or Oxford or Harvard . . . If you know the rules of the game, the averages are in your favour. There's no discredit . . . that's not what I'm saying. I simply point out that there is, there has to be, an element of ambition, an element of calculation . . . I had the ambition. I also had a good, tidy French mind. . . .

"So, I was a good priest, a good diocesan bishop. I mean that! I worked hard at it. I spent a lot of love. I held the people together, even the young. I set up social experiments. I was attracting vocations to the ministry while others were losing them. My people told me they felt a sense of unity, of religious purpose. In short, I had to be, sooner or later, a candidate for the red hat. In the end it was offered to me, on condition that I came to Rome and joined the Curia. Naturally, I accepted. I was appointed Prefect of the Secretariat for Christian Unity and Subprefect of the Secretariat for Nonbelievers. . . . These were minor offices as you know. The real power was vested in the important Congregations: Doctrine of the Faith, Episcopal and Clerical Affairs.

"Still I was very happy. I had access to the Pontiff. I had an open brief, the opportunity to travel, to make contacts far outside the Roman enclave. . . . This was when we met, Carl. You remember the excitements we shared. It was like having a box at the opera! . . . And there were good and great things to be done. . . .

"But then, slowly I began to see how very little I had accomplished—or could ever accomplish for that matter. At home, if I founded a school or a hospital, the results were there, tangible and consequential. I saw the dying comforted by the sisters. I saw the children taught in a religious tradition. . . . But as a Cardinal in Rome—what? Plans and projects and discussions and a new printing press to roll out the documents, but between me and the people a wall was thrown up. I was no longer an apostle. I was a diplomat, a politician, a go-between, and I did not like the man who walked in my shoes. . . . I liked the system even less: cumbersome, archaic, costly and full of cozy corners where slothful men could sleep their lives away and intriguers flourish like exotic plants in a hothouse.

"However, if I wanted to change it—and I did, believe me!—I had to stay inside the Curia. I had to work within the limits of my own character. I am a persuader, not a dictator. I hate rudeness. I have never pounded a table in my life! . . .

"So, when my predecessor died and the conclave was deadlocked, they chose me, Jean Marie Barette, Gregory the Seventeenth, Successor to the Prince of the Apostles!" He tossed the last pebbles onto the pathway and eased himself painfully to his feet. "Do you mind, Carl, if we go to Father Edmund's workshop? It's warmer there, and we can still be private. When evening comes I feel the cold. . . ."

Inside the workshop, amid the cheerful clutter of wood billets and shavings and tools and a shaggy Baptist half born from a block of oak, they perched themselves like schoolboys on the bench while Jean Marie continued his story.

". . . And there I was, my dear Carl, suddenly as high as man could climb in the City of God. My titles assured me of my eminence and my authority: Supreme Pontiff of the Universal Church, Patriarch of the West, Primate of Italy . . . *et patati et patata!*" He gave a laugh of genuine amusement. "I tell you, Carl, when you stand for the first time on that balcony and look across Saint Peter's Square and hear the applause of the crowd, you really believe you're someone! It's very easy to forget that

Christ was a wandering prophet who slept in caves, and Peter was a fisherman from a lakeside in Galilee and John the Precursor was murdered in a prison cell.

". . . After that, of course, you learn very fast. The whole system is designed to surround you with the aura of absolute authority, and resolutely to obstruct your use of it. The long liturgical ceremonies and the public appearances are theatre pieces in which you are stage-managed like an actor. Your private audiences are diplomatic occasions. You talk banalities. You bless medals. You are photographed for the posterity of your visitors. . . .

"Meantime, the bureaucracy grinds on, filtering what comes to your desk, editing and glossing what you hand down. You are besieged by counsellors whose sole object seems to be to delay decision. You cannot act except through intermediaries. There are not enough hours in the day to digest a tenth of the information presented to you—and the language of Curial documents is as carefully designed as American officialese or the double-talk of the Marxists. . . .

"I remember speaking about this to the President of the United States and, later, to the Chairman of the People's Republic of China. Each told me the same thing in different words. The President, a very salty fellow, said: 'They geld us first and then expect us to win the Kentucky Derby.' The Chairman put it rather more politely: 'You have five hundred million subjects. I have nearly twice that number. That is why you need hellfire and I need the punishment camps—and death takes us both before the work is half done.' . . . That's the other thing, Carl, our own mortality makes us desperate; and desperate leaders are very vulnerable. We either surround ourselves with sycophants or we weary ourselves in a daily battle with men as resolute as we are. . . ."

"Or we begin to look for miracles," said Carl Mendelius quietly.

"Or we are tempted to create them." Jean Marie gave him a swift shrewd look. "The politicians have their propaganda pieces. The Pope has his wonder-workers. That's what you're really saying, isn't it, Carl?"

"It's a point at issue, Jean. I had to put it to you."

"The answer's simple. Yes, you wish for miracles. You pray for God to show His hand sometimes on this cruel planet. But to create them for yourself, or find yourself a ready-made magus, or adopt one from the annual crop of *soi-disant* saints—no, Carl! Not I! What happened to me was real, and uninvited. It was a torment and not a gift."

"But you did try to exploit it?"

"Do you believe that, old friend?"

"I ask because others believe it—still others could say it in the future."

"And I can offer no proof to the contrary."

"Precisely, Jean! To use the terms of biblical analysis, you claim a private disclosure experience, but you cannot ask for an act of faith in your unsupported testimony. Therefore, there has to be a legitimizing sign. . . . The Cardinals were scared you would get it by invoking the dogma of infallibility. They were desperate to get rid of you before you could do it. . . ."

Jean Marie frowned over the idea for a moment, then nodded agreement.

"Yes, I accept your definitions. I claim a disclosure experience. I lack a legitimizing sign which authorizes me to proclaim it . . ."

"Correction." Mendelius frowned over the phrase. ". . . which authorizes you to proclaim it as Pontiff of the Universal Church."

"But look at our Baptist here." Jean Marie ran his hand over the half-finished sculpture. "He came out of the desert, preaching that the Kingdom of God was at hand, that men should repent and be baptized. What was his patent of authority? I quote: 'The word of the Lord came to John the son of Zachary in the desert. . . .' " He smiled and shrugged. "At least there are precedents, Carl! But let me go on. . . . We were talking about power and its limitations. One thing I did have as Pope was access to information—and from the highest sources. I travelled. I talked to heads of state. They sent emissaries to me.

"All of them, without exception, faced the same dreadful dilemma. They were appointed to serve a national interest. If they failed to do that, they would be deposed. But they knew that at some point they had to compromise national interest with other interests equally imperative; and if the compromise failed, the world would be plunged into an atomic war. . . .

"They knew more, Carl, more than they ever dared to make public: that the means of destruction are so vast, so deadly, so far beyond antidote, that they can obliterate mankind and make the planet itself unfit for human habitation. . . . What these high men told me was the stuff of nightmares and I was haunted by them, day and night. Everything else became petty and irrelevant: dogmatic disputes, some poor priest hopping into bed with a housemaid, whether a woman should take a pill or carry a little card to count her lunar periods to avoid making gun-fodder for the day of Armageddon. . . . Do you understand, my friend? Do you really understand?"

"I understand, Jean," said Mendelius with somber conviction. "Better than you perhaps, because I have children and you have not. On this matter we are not at odds. But I have to put it to you, that you didn't need a vision to show you the last disaster. It was already burned into your brain. You, yourself, called it the stuff of nightmares—and you can have those, waking or sleeping!"

"And the rest of it, Carl? The final deliverance, the last justification of God's redeeming plan, the Parousia? Did I dream that, too?"

"You could have." Mendelius pieced out his answer slowly. "I tell you as an historian, I tell you as a man and as a student of mankind's beliefs, the dream of the last things haunts the folk-memory of every race under the sun. It is expressed in every literature, in every art, in every death ritual known to man. The forms are different; but the dream persists, haunting our pillows in the dark, forming itself by day out of the storm clouds and the lightning flash. I share the dream with you; but when you say, as you do in your encyclical: 'I . . . am commanded by the Holy Spirit to write you these words,' then I have to ask, as your colleagues did, whether you are speaking in symbol or of fact. If of fact, then show me the rescript and the seal; prove to me that the message is authentic!"

"You know I can't do that," said Jean Marie Barette.

"Exactly," said Carl Mendelius.

"But if you admit, Carl, that catastrophe is possible and even imminent, if you admit that the Doctrine of Last Things is an authentic dream of all mankind—and a clear tradition in Christian doctrine, why should I not say so—vision or no vision?"

"Because you determine it!" Mendelius was implacable. "You determine it by circumstance, by approximate time. You demand immediate and specific preparations. You close out all hope of continuity—and you lock yourself into so narrow a doctrine of election that it will be rejected by most of the world and half our own church as well. For those who accept it the consequences may be disastrous—mass panic, public disorders, and most certainly a rash of suicides. . . ."

"My compliments, Carl!" Jean Marie gave him a smile of ironic approbation. "You've made a splendid case, better even than my Cardinals presented."

"I rest it there," said Carl Mendelius.

"And you expect me to answer it?"

"You asked me in your letter to spread the message which you could no longer proclaim. You have to prove to me that it is authentic."

"How, Carl? What evidence would convince you? A burning bush? A rod turned into a serpent? Our Baptist here, stepping alive out of this block of wood?"

Before Mendelius had time to frame an answer the monastery bell began to toll. Jean Marie slipped off the bench and dusted the sawdust from his robe.

"It's a feast day. Vespers are half-an-hour early. Are you going to join us in the chapel?"

"If I may," said Mendelius quietly. "I've run out of human answers."

"There are none," said Jean Marie Barette, and quoted softly: " '*Nisi dominus aedificaverit domum. . . .* Unless the Lord build the house, the builders labour in vain!' "

In the chapel, the ancient hierarchic order still prevailed. The Abbot sat in the place of honour with his counsellors about him. Jean Marie, lately a Pope, was seated with the juniors. Carl Mendelius was placed among the novices, with a borrowed breviary in his hands. It was a strange, poignant experience, as if he had stepped back thirty years, to the old monkish life in which he had been trained. Every cadence of the Gregorian chant was familiar. The words of the Psalms called up vivid pictures of his student days; lectures and disputations and long, painful discussions with superiors in the period before his exit.

"*Ad te domine, clamabo . . .*" the choir intoned. "To thee O Lord I will cry out. O my God be not silent to me, lest, if thou be silent to me, I become like those who go down into the pit. Hear O Lord the voice of my supplication when I pray to thee, when I lift up my hands to thy holy temple."

The invocations had a new meaning for him as well. The silence which had fallen between himself and Jean Marie was sinister. Suddenly they were strangers, met in a no-man's-land, each speaking a language alien to the other. The God who spoke to Jean Marie was silent to Carl Mendelius.

"According to the works of their hands . . ." the chant echoed through the vaulted nave, "render to them their reward." And the response came back, somber and menacing: "Because they have not understood the works of the Lord . . . thou shalt destroy them and not build them up."

But . . . but—against the counterpoint of the psalmody Mendelius wrestled his way through the argument—whose understanding was the right one? If the leap of faith were not a rational act, it became an insanity, to which he could not commit, even if his refusal meant the rupture of the bond between himself and Jean Marie. It was a thing sad to contemplate, late in life, when the simple abrasion of time wore out so many cherished relationships.

He was glad when the service was over and he joined the community for the feast-day meal in the refectory. He could laugh at the small community jokes, applaud Jean Marie's dessert, discuss with the father archivist the resources of the library, and with the Abbot, the quality of the wines of the Abruzzi. When the meal was over and the monks moved into the common room for evening recreation, Jean Marie approached the Abbot and asked:

"May we be excused, Father Abbot? Carl and I still have things to discuss. Afterwards we'll read Compline together, in my cell."

"Of course. . . . But don't keep him up too late, Professor! We're trying to get him to take care of himself."

Jean Marie's cell was as bare as the guest room. There were no ornaments save the crucifix, the only books were the Bible, a copy of the Rule, a book of hours and a French edition of *The Imitation of Christ*. Jean Marie took off his habit, kissed it and hung it in the closet. He pulled a woollen jersey over his shirt and sat on the bed, facing Mendelius. He said with a touch of irony:

"So here we are, Carl! No popery, no monkery; just two men trying to be honest with each other. Let me ask you some questions now. . . . Do you believe I am a sane man?"

"Yes, I do, Jean."

"Am I a liar?"

"No."

"And the vision?"

"I believe the experience you described in your letter was real to you. I believe you are totally sincere in your interpretation of it."

"But you will not commit yourself to that interpretation."

"I cannot. The best I can do is keep an open mind."

"And the service I asked of you?"

"To spread the word of the catastrophe and the Coming? I cannot do it, Jean. I will not. Some of the reasons I've explained to you; but there are others as well. You abdicated over this issue! You wore the Fisherman's ring. You held the seal of the Supreme Teacher. You surrendered them! If you could not proclaim as Pope what you believe, what do you want of me? I'm not a cleric anymore. I'm a secular scholar. I am deprived of authority to teach in the Church. What do you expect me to do? Go round forming little sects of millenarian Christians? That's been done before, as far back as Montanus and Tertullian—and the consequences have always been disastrous. . . ."

"That's not what I mean, Carl."

"It's what would happen! Like it or not, you'd have charismatic anarchy."

"There will be anarchy in any case!"

"Then I refuse to contribute to it."

"I will tell you something more, Carl! The mission you refuse now, you will one day accept. The light you cannot see will be shown to you. One day you will feel God's hand on your shoulder, and you will walk wherever it leads you."

"For the love of God, Jean! What are you? Some kind of oracle? You can't pile prophecy on prophecy and make anything but a madness. Now, listen to me! I'm Carl Mendelius, remember? You asked me to make a judgment. So I make it! I judge that you tell us too much and too little! You were the Pope. You say you had a vision. In the vision you were called by God to proclaim the imminence of the Parousia. . . . Now, face this fact. You did not proclaim it! You bent to a power group. Why did you let them silence you, Jean? Why are you silent now? You abdicated the one rostrum from which you might have spoken to the world! Why do you expect a middle-aged professor from Swabia to recover what you threw away?" Mendelius' anger and frustration vented itself in a final, bitter tirade. "Drexel tells me you've become a mystic. That's a fine, traditional thing to be—and it saves the Establishment a whole lot of trouble, because even the newspapers shy away from God-madness! But what you wrote in your encyclical signified life or death for millions on this small planet. Was it fact or fiction? We need full testimony! We can't wait around while Jean Marie Barette plays hide-and-seek with God in a monastery garden!"

The moment the words were out he was ashamed of his brutality. Jean Marie was silent for a long moment, staring down at the backs of his hands. Finally he answered with wintry restraint.

"You ask me why I abdicated. . . . The conflict between me and the Curia was more desperate than you can imagine. If I had decided to stay in office, there would almost certainly have been a schism. The Sacred College would have deposed me and elected a rival. Our claims would have been disputed for half a century. Popes and anti-popes are an old story, which could have been repeated in this case. But, to live and die with that on my conscience—no! . . . Just now you used a savage metaphor: 'Jean Marie, playing hide-and-seek with God in a monastery garden.'"

"I'm sorry, Jean. I didn't mean . . ."

"On the contrary, Carl, you meant exactly what you said; but you missed the point. I am not playing hide-and-seek. I am sitting very still, waiting for the Lord to speak again and tell me what I must do. I know the need for a legitimizing sign—but I can't give that sign myself. Again, I wait. . . . We talked about miracles, Carl—signs and wonders! You asked whether I had ever prayed for them. Oh, yes! When the Cardinals came to argue with me, day after day, when the doctors came, all grave and clinical, I prayed then: 'Give me something to show them I am not crazy, not a liar!' Before you came, I begged and begged: 'At least make my Carl believe me.' Well! . . ." He smiled and gave a very Gallic shrug. "It seems I must wait longer to be legitimized. . . . Shall we read Compline now?"

"Before we do, Jean, let me say one thing. I came as a friend. I want to leave as a friend."

"And so you shall. What do we pray for?"

"The last wish of Goethe—*Mehr Licht,* more light!"

"Amen!"

Jean Marie reached for his breviary. Mendelius sat beside him on the narrow bed and, together, they recited the psalms for the last canonical hour of the day.

In the morning it was easier to talk. The hardest words had been said. There was no ground of contention, no fear of misunderstanding. In the garden of the vision, the gardener swung his mattock. The father sacristan cut new roses for the altar bowls; while Jean Marie Barette, lately a Pope, tossed bread crumbs to the strutting pigeons and Carl Mendelius stated his own position.

". . . In the matter of your private revelation, Jean, I am agnostic. I do not know. Therefore I cannot act. But in the matter of us—old friends of the heart!—if I have little faith, I still have much love. Believe that, please!"

"I believe it."

"I cannot accept a mission in which I do not believe—and on which you have no authority to send me. But I can do something to test your ideas of an international audience."

"And how would you propose to do that, Carl?"

"Two ways. First, I could arrange with a Georg Rainer, a journalist of authority, to publish an accurate account of your abdication. Second, I myself would write, for the international press, a personal memoir on my friend the former Gregory the Seventeenth. In this memoir I should draw attention to the ideas expressed in your encyclical. Finally, I could ensure that the two pieces were brought to the notice of the people on your diplomatic list. . . . Understand what I am offering, Jean. It is not an advocacy, not a crusade, but an honest history, a sympathetic portrait, a clear exposition of your ideas as I have understood them . . . with a chance for total disclaimer if you don't like whatever is written."

"It's a generous offer, Carl." Jean Marie was touched.

Mendelius cautioned him. "It falls far short of what you asked. It will also expose the gaps and weaknesses in your position. For instance, even to me in this meeting you have explained very little of your spiritual state. . . ."

"What can I tell you, Carl?" The implied challenge seemed to surprise him. "Sometimes I am in a darkness so deep, so threatening, that it seems I have been stripped of all human form and damned to an eternal solitude. At other times I am bathed in a luminous calm, totally at peace, yet harmoniously active, like an instrument in the hands of a great master. . . . I cannot read the score; I have no urge to interpret it, only a serene confidence that the dream of the composer is realized in me at every moment. . . . The problem is, my dear Carl, that the terror and the calm both take me unaware. They go as suddenly as they come, and they leave my days as full of holes as a Swiss cheese. Sometimes, I find myself in the garden, or in chapel or in the library, with no idea how I came there. If that is mysticism, Carl, then God help me! I'd rather plod along in the purgative way like ordinary mortals! . . . How you explain that to your readers is your affair."

"Then you do agree to the kind of publication I suggest?"

"Let's be very precise about it." There was a mischief in his eyes. "Let's be very Roman and diplomatic. A journalist does not require my permission to speculate about current history. If you, my learned friend, choose to memorialize me or my opinions, I cannot prevent your doing so. . . . Let's leave it like that, shall we?"

"With pleasure!" Mendelius chuckled with genuine amusement. "Now, one more question. Could you, would you, consider coming to me for a vacation in Tübingen? Lotte would love to have you. For me, it would be like having a brother in the house."

"Thank you, dear friend; but no! If I asked, the Abbot would be embarrassed. The diplomatic problems would be far too delicate to handle. . . . Besides, we can never be closer than we are at this moment. . . . You see, Carl, when I was in the Vatican, I saw the world in panorama—a vast planet with its teeming millions, labouring and fearful, under the threat of the mushroom cloud. Here, I perceive everything in little. All the love and the longing and the caring that I have is concentrated on the nearest human face. At this moment it is your face, Carl; you in all and all in you. It is not easy to express—but that was the agony I experienced in the vision: the stark simplicity of things, the splendid, terrifying oneness of the Almighty—and His designs."

Mendelius frowned and shook his head.

"I wish I could share that vision, Jean. I can't. I think we have enough terrors without the God of the final holocaust. I have met good people who would prefer eternal blackness to the vision of Siva the Destroyer."

"Is that how you see Him, Carl?"

"Back in Rome," said Mendelius quietly, "there are assassins waiting to kill me. I am less afraid of them than of a God who can slam the lid on His own toy box and toss it into the fire. That's why I can't preach your millennial catastrophe, Jean . . . not if it is inevitable, a horror decreed from eternity."

"It is not God who is the assassin, Carl—not God who will press the red button."

Carl Mendelius was silent for a long moment. He took the bread crumbs from Jean Marie's hands and began pitching them to the birds. When, finally, he spoke again it was to utter a banality.

"Cardinal Drexel asked me to call him after this visit. What do you want me to say?"

"That I am content; that I bear no one any ill will; that I pray for them all each day."

"Pray for me, too, Jean. I am an arid man in a darkling desert."

"The darkness will pass. Afterwards you will see the day-spring and the well of sweet water."

"I hope so." Mendelius stood up and stretched out a hand to lift Jean Marie to his feet. "Let's not linger on the farewells."

"Write to me sometimes, Carl."

"Every week. I promise."

"God keep you, my friend."

They held to each other in a last silent embrace. Then Jean Marie walked away, a frail dark figure whose footsteps rang hollowly on the pavement of the cloister.

"You asked me a question, Professor." The Father Abbot was walking him to the monastery gate. "I told you I would give you my answer today."

"I am curious to hear it, Father Abbot."

"I do believe that our friend was granted a vision of the Parousia."

"Another question then. Do you feel obliged to do anything about it?"

"Nothing special," said the Abbot mildly. "After all, a monastery is a place where men come to terms with the last things. We watch; we pray; we hold ourselves ready, according to the commandment; we dispense charity to the community and to the voyager."

"You make it sound very simple." Mendelius was unimpressed.

"Too simple, too bland." The Abbot gave him a quick sidelong look. "That's what you really mean, isn't it? What would you suggest I do, my friend? Send my monks out into the mountain villages to preach the Apocalypse? How many do you think would listen? They'll still be watching Lazio play football when the last trumpet sounds! . . . What will you do now?"

"Finish the vacation with my wife. Go back and prepare for next year's lectures. . . . Look after Jean for me."

"I promise."

"With your permission I'll write to him regularly."

"Let me assure you your correspondence will be private."

"Thank you. May I leave an offering with the guestmaster?"

"It would be appreciated."

"I'm grateful for your hospitality."

"A word of advice, my friend."

"Yes?"

"You cannot wrestle with God. He is too large an adversary. . . . You cannot manage His universe either, only the small garden He has given you. Enjoy it while you can. . . ."

"This has been a very painful episode for you."

Drexel poured the dregs of the coffee into Mendelius' cup and handed him the last sweet biscuit.

"Yes, it has, Eminence."

"And now that it is ended . . . ?"

"That's the problem." Mendelius heaved himself out of the chair and walked to the window. "It isn't ended at all. For Jean Marie, yes! He has made the final acts of a believer: an act of submission to his own mortality, an act of faith in the continued beneficent working of the Spirit in human affairs. I have not come to that yet. God knows if I ever shall. I hated coming back to the Vatican today. I hated the pomp and the power, the historic impedimenta of Congregations and Tribunals and Secretariats, all dedicated to what? The most elusive abstracttion: man's relationship to an unknowable Creator! I am glad Jean is quit of it all. . . ."

"And you, my friend." The Cardinal's tone was very gentle. "Do you want to be quit of it, too?"

"Oh, yes!" Mendelius swung round to face him. "But I cannot, any more than I be quit of my mother or my father or my furthest ancestors. I cannot dispense with the traditions that have shaped me. I cannot adopt another man's history or fabricate a new mythos for myself. I loathe what this family does, often, to its children; but I cannot leave it and I will not traduce it. So I wait. . . ."

He made a shrugging gesture of defeat, and then stood, bowed and silent, staring out at the placid garden.

"You wait . . ." Drexel pressed him, "for what, Mendelius?"

"God knows! The last day-spring before the holocaust. The fiery finger writing on the wall. I wait, that's all! Did I tell you —no, I must have forgotten—Jean Marie made a prophecy about me, too?"

"What did he say?"

"He said," Mendelius quoted the words in a flat voice, " . . . 'The mission you refuse now, you will one day accept. The light you cannot see will be shown to you. One day you will feel God's hand on your shoulder, and you will walk wherever it leads you.' "

"And did you believe him?"

"I wanted to. I could not."

"I believe him," said Drexel quietly.

Mendelius' control snapped and he challenged Drexel harshly. "Then why in God's name didn't you believe the rest of it? Why did you let the others destroy him?"

"Because I could not risk him." There was an infinite pathos in his voice. "Like you—more than you perhaps—I needed the reassurance of being what I am, a high man in an old system that has stood the test of centuries. I was afraid of the dark. I needed the calm cool light of tradition. I wanted no mysteries, only a God I could cope with, an authority to which, in good conscience, I could bend. When the moment came I was unready. I could neither repeal the past nor abdicate my function in the present. . . . Don't judge me too curtly, Mendelius! Don't judge any of us. You are more free and more fortunate."

Mendelius bowed to the reproof and said, with bleak humility, "I was rude and unjust, Eminence. I had no right to . . ."

"Please! No apologies!" Drexel stayed him with a gesture. "At least we have managed to be open with each other. Let me explain something more. In ancient days, when the world was full of mystery, it was easy to be a believer—in the spirits who haunted the grove, in the god who cast the thunderbolts. In this age we are all conditioned to the visual illusion. What you see is what exists. Remove the visible symbols of an established organization —the cathedrals, the parish church, the bishop in his miter—and the Christian assembly, for many, ceases to exist. You can talk until you're blue in the face about the abiding Spirit and Mystical Body; but even among the clergy, you'll be talking to the deaf. Subconsciously they associate these things with the cultists and the charismatics. Discipline is the safe word—discipline, doctrinal authority and the Cardinal's High Mass on Sunday! There's no place anymore for wandering saints. . . . Most people prefer a simple religion. You make your offering in the temple and carry away salvation in a package. Do you think any cleric in his right mind is going to preach a charismatic church or a Christian diaspora?"

"Probably not." Mendelius gave a small reluctant smile. "But they do have to come to terms with one fact."

"Which is?"

"We all belong to an endangered species: millennium man!"

Drexel pondered the phrase for a moment and then nodded approval. "A sobering thought, Mendelius. It merits a meditation."

"I'm glad you think so, Eminence. I propose to include it in my essay on Gregory the Seventeenth."

Drexel showed no surprise. He asked, almost as if it were a matter of academic interest, "Do you think such an essay is opportune at this moment?"

"Even if it were not, Eminence, I believe it is a matter of simple justice. The meanest functionary is memorialized on his retirement, even if only by five lines in the *Government Gazette*. . . . I hope I may be free to consult your Eminence on matters of fact—perhaps even coax you into an expression of opinion on certain aspects of recent history."

"On matters of fact," said Drexel calmly, "I am happy to assist, by directing you to appropriate sources. As for my opinions— I'm afraid they are not for publication. My present master would hardly approve. . . . But thank you for the invitation. And good luck with your essay."

"I'm glad you like the idea." Mendelius was bland as honey.

"I didn't say I liked it." Drexel's craggy face was lit by a fleeting smile. "I recognize it as an act of piety, which, morally, I am bound to commend. . . ."

"Thank you, Eminence," said Carl Mendelius. "And thank you

for the protection you have afforded me and my wife in this place."

"I wish I could extend it," said Drexel gravely. "But where you are going my writ does not run. Go with God, Professor!"

It was five in the afternoon when Francone dropped him off at the apartment. Lotte and Hilde were at the hairdresser; Herman had not yet returned from the Academy; so he had time and privacy to bathe, rest and set his thoughts in order before reporting to the others his experiences at Monte Cassino. He was happy about one thing: he was no longer bound to secrecy. He could discuss the issues involved; test his opinions against those of devotees and cynics alike, talk out his puzzlements in the language of simple folk, instead of the loaded dialect of the theologians.

He was still far from satisfied by the explanations Jean Marie had given him. The description of his mystical states, which obviously others had witnessed, seemed too bland, too familiar, too—he groped for the word—too derivative from the vast body of devotional writing. Jean Marie was precise about the possibilities of catastrophic conflict. He was, even in visionary terms, vague about the nature of the Parousia itself. Most apocalyptic writings were vivid and detailed. The revelation of Jean Marie Barette was too open and general for credence.

In psychological terms there was a contradiction also, between Jean Marie's view of himself as a natural careerist and his tragic failure to exercise power in a crisis. His willingness, not to say his eagerness, to accept even a partial defense in the popular press was sad, if not faintly sinister in a man who claimed a private dialogue with Omnipotence.

And yet, and yet . . . as he stepped out into the sunset glow on the terrace Mendelius was forced to admit that Jean Marie Barette was easier to damn in absence than to demean face to face. He had not retreated one pace from his claim of a disclosure experience or from his calm conviction that the legitimizing sign would be given. Beside him, Carl Mendelius was the small man, the courier who carried secrets of state in his body belt, but had no personal convictions beyond the state of the beds and the cost of the wine in the posthouses. . . .

All this and more Mendelius talked out eagerly with Lotte and the Franks over cocktails. He was surprised that they all put him under rigid inquisition. Herman Frank was the most anxious questioner.

"Aren't you really saying, Carl, that you believe half the story at least? Discount the vision, discount the Second Coming, which is a primitive myth anyway; but the catastrophe of global war is very close to us."

"That's about the size of it, Herman."

"I don't think it is." Hilde's smile carried more than a hint of irony. "You're still a believer, Carl. So you're still plagued by the presence of a God in every proposition. You've been like that as long as I've known you—half rationalist, half poet. That's true, isn't it?"

"I suppose so." Mendelius reached for his drink. "But the rationalist says all the evidence isn't in yet and the poet says there's no time for versifying when the assassins are at the gates."

"There's something more." Lotte reached out and stroked his wrist. "You love Jean Marie like a brother. Rather than reject him outright, you are prepared to split yourself in two. . . . You've told him you will write this memoir about him. Are you sure you can do it with such a divided mind?"

"No, I'm not, liebchen. Rainer will do a good job on his part. It's a plum for any journalist—a big exclusive that will go round the world. As for my part—the personal portrait, the interpretation of Jean's thoughts—I'm not at all sure I can do it right."

"Where will you work on it?" asked Hilde. "You're welcome to stay with us as long as you like."

"We must get home to Tübingen." Lotte was a shade too anxious. "The children will be back early next week."

"Carl could stay awhile longer . . ."

"It's not necessary." Mendelius was firm. "Thanks for the offer, Hilde; but I'll work better at home. I'll talk to Georg Rainer on Friday. We'll leave on Sunday for Tübingen. This place is too seductive—I need a strong dose of Protestant common sense."

"Delivered in a Swabian accent!" said Herman with a grin. "As soon as summer's over, Hilde and I will start preparing our place in Tuscany."

"Take it easy, Herman." Hilde sounded irritable. "Nothing's going to happen that fast. Is it, Carl?"

Mendelius grinned and refused to be drawn. "I'm married, too, girl! We males have to stick together sometimes. I'd be inclined to get your place in order as soon as you can. If there's a whiff of crisis, materials and manpower will double in price overnight. Besides, you'll need to plant this winter for the next summer harvest."

"And what are you going to do, Carl?" Hilde asked pointedly. "Your friend Jean Marie is safe in his monastery. If anything happens, Germany will be the first battle zone. What are you going to do about Lotte and the children?"

"I haven't really thought about it."

"Tübingen's only a hundred and eighty kilometers from the Swiss border," said Herman. "It would pay you to have some of your royalties accumulate there."

"I refuse to talk about this anymore." Lotte was suddenly close to anger. "These are our last days in Rome. I want them to be happy ones."

"And so they shall be!" Herman was instantly penitent. "So we dine here. Afterwards we go listen to folk music at the Arciliuto. It's a quaint place. They say Raffaello kept a mistress there. Who knows? At least it proves the Roman talent for survival."

There were still loose ends to be tucked away before Lotte and he could pack and be gone. He spent all of Friday morning preparing his final tape for Anneliese Meissner: an account of his visit to Monte Cassino, a frank admission of his own perplexities and a somewhat terse envoi:

". . . You now have the full record as honestly as I can set it down. I want you to study it carefully before we meet again in Tübingen. . . . There is much more to tell; but it will keep. See you soon . . . I am sick of this febrile and inbred city. Carl."

He packed the tapes carefully and instructed Francone to deliver them to a courier service which plied daily between Rome and various German cities. Then Francone drove him to his luncheon appointment with Georg Rainer. At one o'clock, tucked into a private booth at Ernesto's, he began the ritual fencing match. Georg Rainer was a very practiced performer.

"You've been a busy man, Mendelius. It's hard to keep track of your movements. That affair at the Salvator Mundi, when the police shot one man and arrested three others . . . you were at the hospital?"

"Yes. I was visiting Senator Malagordo."

"I guessed as much. I didn't print anything because I thought you shouldn't be exposed any more."

"That was generous. I appreciate it."

"Also I didn't want to spoil today's story. . . . You do have one for me, I hope?"

"I do, Georg. But before I give it to you, I want to see if we can agree some ground rules."

Rainer shook his head. "The rules are already in operation, my friend. What you give me I check first and then put it on the telex. I guarantee an accurate rendering of the facts and the quotes and I reserve the right to make whatever comment I choose for the guidance of my editors. . . . I can't guarantee your immunity from editorial emphasis, dramatic or misleading headlines, or distorted versions of the same story by other hands. Once we start this interview you're on the witness stand and everything you say goes into the court record. . . ."

"In this case," said Mendelius deliberately, "I'd like to see if we could agree the way the story is to be presented."

"No," said Georg Rainer flatly. "Because I can make no agreement about what happens after the copy leaves my office. I'm happy to show you what I file, and I'll gladly change any rendering that seems inaccurate. . . . But if you're thinking there's some way to control the consequences of a news release, forget it! It's like Pandora's box: once you open it, all the mischiefs fly out. . . . Why are you giving me this story anyway?"

"First, you kept your word to me; I'm trying to keep mine to you. Second, I want the truth about a friend put on public record before the mythmakers get to work. And, third, I want to do a companion piece to your story in the form of a personal memoir. I can't do that if your version goes wildly off the rails. So, let me frame my question another way. How can we get together to meet my needs and yours?"

"Tell me the name of the story first."

"The abdication of Gregory the Seventeenth."

Georg Rainer gaped at him in undisguised amazement. "The true story?"

"Yes."

"Can you document it?"

"Provided we can agree an appropriate use or non-use of the documents, yes . . . and to save you further trouble, Georg, I've just spent twenty-four hours with Gregory the Seventeenth in the Monastery of Monte Cassino!"

"And he agrees to the disclosures?"

"He offers no impediment, and relies on my discretion in the choice of a reporter for the exclusive story. We have been close friends for a long time. So you see, Georg, I have to be very sure of the ground rules before we start."

A waiter hurried up flourishing his pad and pencil.

Georg Rainer said, "Let's order first, shall we? I hate waiters hovering around while I'm doing an interview."

They settled for a pasta, saltimbocca and a carafe of Bardolino. Then Georg Rainer laid his miniature tape recorder on the table and pushed it towards Mendelius. He said quietly:

"You handle the recording. You keep the tape until we've agreed a final text. We'll work on it together. All out-takes will be destroyed immediately. Satisfactory?"

"Fine!" said Mendelius. "Let's begin with two documents, handwritten by Gregory the Seventeenth and delivered to me by personal messenger. The one is a letter to me describing the events which led to his abdication. The other is an unpublished encyclical which the Curia suppressed."

"Can I see them?"

"At an appropriate time, yes. Obviously I don't carry them around."

"What is the key message?"

"Gregory the Seventeenth was forced to abdicate because he claimed to have had a vision of the end of the world—the holocaust and the Second Coming. He believed he was called to be the precursor of the event." He gave a wry-mouthed grin and added, "Now you understand why I ducked the story on the end of the world. I was testing the theme on an audience of Evangelical clerics before I went to Monte Cassino. . . ."

Georg Rainer sipped at his wine and munched a crust of dry bread. Finally he shrugged, like a losing poker-player, and said, "Now of course it all makes sense. The Curia simply had to get rid of him. The man's a lunatic."

"That's the problem, Georg." Mendelius poured more wine and signalled the waiter to remove the pasta plates. "He's as sane as you or I."

"Who says so?" Rainer stabbed a finger at his chest. "You, his friend?"

"I, yes. And Cardinal Drexel and Abbot Andrew, who directs his life at Monte Cassino. These two accept him as a mystic like

John of the Cross. Drexel's going through a crisis of conscience because he didn't defend him against the Curia and the Sacred College."

"You've talked to Drexel?"

"Twice. And twice to the Abbot of Monte Cassino. The odd thing is they're the believers and I'm the skeptic."

"Which is just the way they want it," said Rainer with tart humour. "They've removed a troublesome Pope—now they can afford to praise his obedient virtue. . . . You know, Mendelius, for a notable scholar you're sometimes very naïve. You even accept to be driven around by the Cardinal's chauffeur in the Cardinal's car; so Drexel knows every move you've made in Rome—including this lunch with me."

"The point is, Georg, I don't care a curse what he knows."

"Does he know you've got the documents?"

"Yes. I told him."

"And?"

"Nothing."

"You don't think he might drop a word to have them recovered—or diverted to more orthodox hands?"

"Frankly, I can't see Drexel as a spymaster or a receiver of stolen manuscripts."

"Then you're more trusting than I am." Rainer shrugged. "I read history, too, and the usages of power don't change in the Church or anywhere else. However . . . let's talk about Gregory the Seventeenth. How do you judge him?"

"I believe he's sane—and sincere in his own convictions."

"There's nobody more dangerous than a sincere visionary."

"Jean Marie recognized that. He abdicated to avoid a schism. He is silent because he has no legitimizing sign to prove his vision authentic."

"Legitimizing sign? I don't recall the expression."

"It's a term that's become popular in modern biblical analysis. Basically it means that when the prophet or the reformer claims to speak in the name of God he needs to show some patent of authority. . . ."

"Neither you nor I can give him that."

"No; but between us we should be able to guarantee him an honest publication of the facts and an enlightened interpretation of his message. We can set down the events that led to the abdication. The documents will demonstrate the why of the matter. We can record what Jean Marie Barette has told me about his alleged vision."

"So far so good. But that vision deals with mighty matters: the end of the world, the Second Coming, the Last Judgment. What can you and I tell our readers about those things?"

"I can tell them what people in the past believed and wrote about these things. I can direct their attention to the existence of millenarian sects in today's world. . . ."

"Nothing else?"

"After that, Georg, it's your turn. You're the man who writes the bulletins about the state of the nations. How close are we now to Armageddon? The world is full of prophets. Could anyone of them be the One who is to come? If you look at it in concordance with all the crazy social phenomena, Jean Marie's prediction is far from irrational."

"I agree." Rainer was thoughtful. "But to get this story into readable shape will take a hell of a lot of work. Can you stay on in Rome?"

"I'm afraid not. I have to prepare for the opening of the University. What's the chance of your spending a few days in Tübingen? You'd be very welcome to stay in my house. We could work better there. I have all my texts and filing systems."

"I need to work fast. It's my training to grab the idea, test the logic and write it for the telex the same day. . . ."

"I'm probably much slower," said Mendelius, "but I at least am prepared in the subject. . . . Anyway, I'll leave here Sunday and begin work the next day."

"I could be with you by Wednesday. I'll get a stringer to cover for me here. But I don't want to discuss this story with my editor until you and I have written it together and tested every phrase of it. . . . So I'll have to work up an excuse for a few days' absence."

"There's one thing we should discuss," said Mendelius. "You and I have to act jointly. There should be a contract between us. And I'd like to use my agent in New York to arrange our joint contracts with publishers."

"That's fine."

"Then I'll call him tonight and ask him to meet us both in Tübingen."

"Can I give you a piece of advice, Mendelius? For God's sake be careful with those documents. Lodge them in the bank. I know people who'd kill you to get hold of them."

"Jean Marie warned me of that in his letter. I'm afraid I didn't take him too seriously."

"Then you'd better be very serious from now on. This story will make you just as famous or notorious as the shooting on the Corso. Even when you're back in Tübingen, watch your step. You're still a key witness against the girl, and you've cost the underground four men. . . . These operators have long arms and long memories."

"The terrorist thing, I understand." Mendelius was genuinely puzzled. "But the documents—a private letter to me, an unpublished encyclical—I can see their news value, but they're certainly not worth a man's life."

"No? Look at it another way. The encyclical brought about a papal abdication. It could equally have brought about a schism or caused Gregory the Seventeenth to be certified insane. . . ."

"True, but . . ."

"So far," Rainer silenced him brusquely, "all you've thought about is your personal reaction to his affair, and your concern for your friend. But what about all the thousands of other people with whom Gregory the Seventeenth had dealings during his pontificate? How have they reacted? How might they react if they knew the true facts? Some of them must have had very close relationships with him. . . ."

"They did. He sent me a list . . ."

"What kind of list?" Rainer was instantly alert.

"People in high places all over the world, who he believed would be receptive to his message."

"Can you give me some of the names on it?" Mendelius thought for a moment and then recited half a dozen names, which Rainer wrote in his notebook. Then he asked, "Has any one of these tried to contact him in Monte Cassino?"

"I don't know. I didn't ask. However, they'd certainly be thoroughly screened before they got through. I was. In fact I never did speak to Jean Marie on the telephone. There were moments when I thought I was being carefully steered away from him; but Drexel was definite. There were no impediments to my visit, just a lot of official interest."

"Which is hardly likely to wane, now that they know you've talked to me."

"Let's be fair, Georg. Drexel didn't enquire what I proposed to do. He didn't make any further mention of the documents—and he took some very rough talk from me."

"So what does that prove? Nothing except that he's a patient man. And, remember, he was the one the Cardinals chose to be their messenger. Think about that! As for other friends or acquaintances of Gregory the Seventeenth, I'm going to be doing some digging on my own account before I come to Tübingen. . . . No! No! I'm paying for lunch. I'm going to make so much money out of you it's almost obscene!"

"You'll work for it, my friend." Mendelius laughed. "Two things I learned from the Jesuits were the rules of evidence and a respect for stylish writing. I want this to be the best story you've ever delivered!"

As soon as he reached the apartment, Mendelius made a guarded telephone call to his agent, Lars Larsen, in New York. Larsen's immediate reaction was a whistle of excitement and then a howl of anguish. . . . The idea was wonderful. It was worth a mint of money—but why the hell did Mendelius have to share it with a journalist? Rainer had nothing to contribute but his connection with a big German news empire. This story should be launched from America. . . .

And so on, and so on, for ten minutes of impassioned pleading, after which Mendelius explained patiently that the whole purpose of the exercise was to present a sober account of recent events and direct serious attention to the core of Jean Marie's last message. Therefore, would Lars please come to Tübingen and discuss the matter with the gravity it deserved? . . .

Lotte, listening to the one-sided conversation, tut-tutted unhappily.

". . . I warned you, Carl! All these people have personal concerns that must conflict with yours. The agent smells big money. Georg Rainer's reputation as a newsman will be enormously enhanced. But you . . . You're writing about a friend. You're treating a subject which you know has haunted man through his history. You can't let yourself be treated like an overnight film star. . . . You hold the trump card: the documents. Don't display them to anyone until you've got all the terms you need to protect yourself and Jean Marie."

Later, cradled in his arms in the big baroque bed, she mused drowsily:

". . . It's ironic really. In spite of all your skepticism, you've given Jean exactly what he asked in the first place. Because you're his friend you can't fail to give him sympathetic treatment. Because you're a scholar of world repute, your commentaries will protect him from the clowns. If Anneliese Meissner is willing to go into print with you, she'll be at least clinically honest. . . . All in all, my love, you're making a handsome payment on our debts to Jean Marie. . . . By the way, I bought a gift today for Herman and Hilde. It was rather expensive but I knew you wouldn't mind. They've been so generous with us."

"What is it, liebchen?"

"A piece of old Capo di Monte, Cupid and Psyche. The dealer said it was quite rare. I'll show it to you in the morning. I hope they'll like it."

"I'm sure they will." He was grateful for the quiet aimless talk.

"Oh, and I forgot to tell you. Katrin sent us a card from Paris. It doesn't say much except: 'Love is wonderful. Thanks to you both from both of us.' There's also a long letter and some colour prints from Johann."

"That's a surprise! I thought he'd be the one to send the postcard."

"I know. Funny, isn't it? He's quite lyrical about his vacation. They didn't get very far, though—not even into Austria. He and his friend discovered a little valley high up the Bavarian Alps. It has a lake and a few ruined cabins . . . not a soul for miles around. They've been camping there ever since, just going into town for supplies. . . ."

"It sounds wonderful. I wouldn't mind changing places with him. I don't want to see Rome again for a long, long time. I'll write to Jean Marie as soon as we get back to Tübingen. . . . By the way, we must do something for Francone. I think a gift of money would be best. I don't imagine he gets paid too much. Remind me, will you, liebchen?"

"I will. Close your eyes now and try to sleep."

"I'll drowse off in a little while. Oh, that's another thing. I have to send Cardinal Drexel a thank-you note for the use of the car and of Francone."

"I'll remind you. . . . Now go to sleep. You looked absolutely worn out tonight. I want you around for a long while yet."

"I'm fine, liebchen, truly. You mustn't worry about me."

"I do worry. I can't help it. Carl, if Jean Marie is right, if there is a last great war, what will we do? What will become of the children? I'm not being foolish. I just want to know what you think."

There was no way he could qualify the answer and he knew it. He heaved himself up on his elbow and looked down at her, glad of the dark that hid the pain in his eyes.

"This time, my love, there will be no banners and no trumpets. The campaign will be short and terrible; and afterwards no one will care where the frontiers used to be. If we survive, we'll try to hold together as a family; but you have to remember we can't dictate what our children do. If we're separated from them, then we gather some good souls together and do what we can to hold out against the assassins in the streets! That's all I can tell you."

"'It's strange!" Lotte reached up to touch his cheek. "When we first talked about this, before we came away, I was afraid all the time. Sometimes I wanted to sit in a corner and cry about nothing at all. Then, while you were in Monte Cassino, I took out that little piece of pottery the Senator gave you and held it in my hands. I traced the name that was written on it. I remembered how the lots were drawn to see who would die, and who would perform the act of execution, on Masada. Suddenly I felt very calm—fortunate somehow. I understood that if you hold too tightly to anything—even to life—you become a captive. So you see, you mustn't worry about me either. . . . Kiss me good night and let's go to sleep."

As he lay wakeful through the small, cold hours, he wondered at the change in her: the air of new confidence, the curious calm with which she seemed to accept an unspeakable prospect. Had Aharon ben Ezra bequeathed a last magical courage to the potsherd which bore his name? Or was it perhaps a small wind of grace blown from the desert, where Jean Marie Barette communed with his Creator?

VI

It was good to be home. In the countryside the harvest was safely gathered; the blackbirds were pecking contentedly over the brown stubble. The Neckar flowed silver under a summer sky. Traffic was sparse in the city, because the holiday-makers had not yet returned from their sojourn in the sun. The halls and cloisters of the University were almost empty. The rare footfalls of janitor or colleague sounded hollow in the hush. It was possible to believe—provided one read no newspapers, switched off radio and television—that nothing would ever change in this quiet backwater, that the old Dukes of Württemberg would sleep forever in peace under the floor stones of the Stiftskirche.

But the peace was an illusion, like the painted backdrop of a pastorale. From Pilsen to Rostock the armies of the Warsaw Pact were arrayed in depth: shock troops and heavy tank formations and, behind them, the rocket launchers with tactical atomic warheads. Facing them were the thin lines of the NATO forces, prepared for a fallback under the first onslaught, trusting, but none too confidently, that their own tactical warheads would hold up the advance until the big bombers came in from the British Isles and the IBM's were launched from their silos on mainland United States.

There was no mobilization yet, no call-up of reserves, because the crisis had not matured to the point where democratic governments could rely on their depressed and uneasy populations to answer a call to arms, or respond to the rhetoric of the propaganda machine. German industry still depended on guest-workers, who, deprived of tenure and citizenship, could hardly be expected to render liege service in a lost cause. At the other side of the world a new axis had been formed: industrial Japan was pouring plant and technical experts into China, in return for oil from the northern fields and the new wells in the Spratleys. Islam was in ferment from Morocco to the high passes of Afghanistan. South Africa was an armed camp, beleaguered by the black republics. . . . No leader, no junta, no parliamentary assembly could compass or control the complex geo-polity of a world haunted by depletion and the debasement of every currency of human intercourse. Reason rocked under the barrage of contradictions. The corporate will seemed frozen in a syncope of impotence.

After the first relief of homecoming, Carl Mendelius found himself tempted to the same despair. Who would hear one small voice above the babel cry of millions? What was the point of propagating ideas which would immediately be swept away like sand-motes in a tempest? What was the profit in expounding a past that would soon be as irrelevant as the magical animals of the cavemen?

This, he understood clearly, was the syndrome that produced spies, defectors, fanatics and professional destructors. Society is a stinking slum; blow it up! Parliament is a nest of nincompoops and hypocrites; destroy the filthy brood! God is dead; let's polish up Baal and Ashtaroth, call back the Witch of Endor, to make the spells we need.

The best remedy was the sight of Lotte, busy and cheerful, dusting and polishing and chatting with women friends on the telephone, knitting a winter jersey for Katrin. He had no right to trouble her with his own dark dreaming. So he retired to his study and addressed himself to the pile of work that had accumulated in his absence.

There was a stack of books, which he was begged to read and recommend. There were student reports to be assessed, revisions to be made in his lecture texts, the inevitable bills to be paid.

There was a note from the President of the University, inviting him to an informal meeting with a few senior colleagues on Tuesday forenoon. The President's "informal meetings" were well known. They were designed to pre-empt any problems before they were raised at the full meeting of the faculties in mid-August. They were also intended to persuade the gullible that they were privileged members of an inner cabinet. . . . Mendelius had small taste, but a reluctant admiration, for the President's skill in academic intrigue.

The next letter was a communication from the Bundeskriminalamt, the Federal Criminal Bureau in Wiesbaden.

. . . We are informed by our Italian colleagues that as a result of recent incidents in Rome, you may become the target of attack, either by foreign terrorist agents or by local groups affiliated with them.

We advise you, therefore, to take the precautions outlined in the enclosed pamphlet, which we circulate normally to government officials and senior executives in industry. In addition, we advise you to exercise special vigilance within the precincts of the University, where political activists may easily conceal themselves in a large congregation of students.

Should you notice any suspicious activity, either in your neighbourhood or at the University, please contact the Landeskriminalamt in Tübingen without delay. They have already been apprised of your situation. . . .

Mendelius read the pamphlet carefully. It told him nothing he did not know; but the final paragraph was a chill reminder that violence was as infectious as the Black Death.

. . These precautions should be strictly observed, not only by the subject, but by all members of his household. They, too, are under threat, because the subject is vulnerable through them. A common and concerted vigilance will reduce the risk.

There was a brutal irony in the fact that an act of mercy in a Roman street should expose a whole family to violent invasion in a provincial town in Germany. There was an even grimmer corollary: that a shot fired on the Amur River in China could plunge the whole planet into war.

Meantime, there were more pleasant thoughts to distract him. The Evangelicals had written a joint letter expressing their thanks for "your openness in discussion and your emphatic affirmation of Christian charity as the binding element in our diverse lives." There was also a second letter from Johann, addressed to him personally.

. . . Before I left on this vacation I was in deep depression.

Your gentleness about my religious problem helped very much; but the rest of it I couldn't explain. I was worried about my career. I couldn't see any point to what I was doing. I didn't want to join some big company, planning the economics of a world that could blow up in our faces. I was afraid of being called up for military service in a war that would produce nothing but universal disaster. . . . My friend Fritz felt exactly the same way. We were angry with you and your generation because you had a past to look back on, while we had only a question mark before us. . . . Then we found this place—Fritz and I and two American girls we met in a *Bierkeller* in Munich.

It's a small valley, with only a footpath leading into it. There are high cliffs all around, covered with pines to the snow line. There is an old hunting lodge and a few cabins grouped around a lake, surrounded by lush meadows. There are deer in the woods and the lake is full of fish. There's an old mine tunnel that goes a long way into the mountain. . . .

Fritz, who is an amateur archaeologist, says it was worked in the Middle Ages for bloodstone. We've found broken tools and a leather jerkin, and a pewter drinking mug and a rusted hunting knife. . . .

Last time we went into town I made enquiries and found that the place is private property, owned by a very old lady, the Gräfin von Eckstein. . . . .Her husband used to use it as a hunting preserve. We traced her to Tegernsee and went to see her. . . . She's a spry old girl, and after she got over her surprise at being invaded by four young people she'd never met before, she gave us English tea and cakes and told us she was happy we were enjoying the place. . . .

Then, purely on impulse, I asked her whether she'd consider selling it. She asked what for. I told her it would make a wonderful holiday place for students like us. . . . At the beginning it was just something to talk about; but she took it quite seriously. . . .

Anyway, the upshot of it all was she named a price—a quarter of a million deutschmarks. I told her there was no way we could raise money like that. . . . Then she said, if we were serious, she'd consider leasing it to us. I said we'd think about it and get back to her. . . .

I'd love to do it. It's so quiet, so remote from today; and it could be made to pay for itself. . . . It's one of the things we've talked about often in class: the small, self-contained economy where a quality of life can be preserved. When we come back I'd like to talk to you about it and see what you think.

I spend my nights by lamplight trying to set down a plan. I find it a much more satisfying exercise than the currency problems of the European community or the relations between the oil producers and the industrial economies and the agricultural nations. . . . Somehow, as Fritz says, we have to scale things down to human size again, otherwise we all go mad, or become indifferent robots in a system we can never control. . . I'm running on, I know; but this is the first time I've felt free to open myself to the father I truly love. It's a pleasant sensation. . . .

Later, as they ate supper together, Mendelius read the letter to Lotte. She smiled and nodded approval.

"That's good! He's coming out of the dark forest, at last. It isn't easy to be young these days. I'd encourage the idea, Carl; even if nothing comes of it. We can't afford money like that; but still . . ."

"We might," said Mendelius thoughtfully. "We just might. I've got some big royalties due in September; and once the new book is delivered . . . Besides, Johann isn't the only one with a private dream."

Lotte gave him a swift reproachful glance. "You wouldn't care, perhaps, to share yours with your wife?"

"Come on, liebchen!" Mendelius laughed. "You know I hate talking about things until I've got them clear in my head. This one's been simmering for a long time. What happens to elderly professors when they give up the chair? I can go on writing, I know; but I'd like to go on teaching, too, with small, selected groups of advanced students. I've had thoughts of founding a private academy, offering annual specialist courses to postgraduates. Musicians do it all the time—violinists, composers, conductors. . . . A place like the one Johann describes could be ideal."

"It could." Lotte was dubious. "Don't misunderstand me. I love your idea, Carl; but it would be a mistake to mix it up with Johann's project. Show him you're interested; but don't meddle. Let him follow his own star."

"You're right of course." Mendelius leaned across and kissed her cheek. "Don't worry! I'll keep my big hands out of the pie dish. Besides, we've got another problem to face. . . ."

He told her about the letter from the police in Wiesbaden. Lotte frowned and sighed unhappily.

"How long will we have to live like this, always looking over our shoulders?"

"God knows, liebchen! But we can't panic. We just have to make it a routine—like watching traffic lights and locking the house at night, and driving within the speed limit. After a while it will become automatic." He changed the subject abruptly. "Georg Rainer called. He's arriving Wednesday evening. Lars Larsen arrives in the morning from Frankfurt. That gives us a chance to talk before Rainer gets here."

"Good!" Lotte nodded a vigorous approval. "You must see the terms are right before you go one step further with Rainer."

"I will. It's a promise. Do you need any extra help in the house?"

"I've got it. Gudrun Schild is coming in each day."

"Good. . . . I wonder what our noble president has in mind for Tuesday's meeting?"

"He worries me, that one." Lotte was terse. "He's a conjuror. He makes you think he's pumping wine out of his elbow. What you really get is . . ."

"I know what you get, liebchen," said Mendelius with a grin. "The trick is never to drink the stuff. . . ."

The President's notion of an informal gathering was strictly Old Empire. Each colleague was treated to a firm handshake, a solicitous enquiry about his wife and his family, a cup of coffee and a slice of apple cake, freshly baked by the President's wife and served by a maid in a starched apron.

The ceremony was a careful contrivance. With a cup of coffee in one hand and a plate in the other, the guests had to sit down. The chairs, each with a tabouret table beside it, were arranged in a semicircle facing the President's desk. The President did not sit down. He perched himself on the edge of the desk in an attitude intended to suggest informality, intimacy and openness among colleagues. The fact that he spoke from three feet above their heads and had his hands free for gestures and punctuation was only a gentle reminder of his primacy. His speech was unctuous and usually banal.

". . . I am in need of your expert advice. The—ah—responsibilities of my office preclude me from the day-to-day contact which I should like to have with the junior faculty and the students. I look to you, therefore, to interpret them to me and me to them. . . ."

Brandt, from Latin Language, leaned across to Mendelius and whispered, "He's the *fons et origo*—and we're the bloody water carriers."

Mendelius stifled a grin behind his paper napkin.

The President went on, "Last week I was invited, with the heads of other universities, to a private meeting with the Minister of Education and the Minister for the Interior, in Bonn. The purpose of the meeting was to discuss the—ah—academic implications of the present international crisis. . . ."

He paused a moment to let them consider the solemnity of the occasion in Bonn and what the—ah—academic implications might be. They were startling enough to dispel any boredom in his audience.

". . . In September this year the Bundestag will authorize full mobilization of both men and women for military service. We are asked to prepare recommendations for exempted categories of students, and to supply lists of those with specialist qualifications in physics, chemistry, engineering, medicine and related disciplines. . . . We are further asked to consider how courses in these subjects may be accelerated to meet the needs of industry and the armed services. We have also to face the depletion of students and junior staff as a result of the call-up. . . ." There was a ripple of surprise in the audience. The President hushed it with a gesture. "Please, ladies and gentlemen, let me finish! There will be time for discussion afterwards. In this matter we have no choice. We, like everyone else, will have to comply with regulations. There is, however, a more contentious issue. . . ." He paused again. This time he was obviously embarrassed and groping for the right words. ". . . It was raised by the Minister for the Interior, prompted, I believe, by pressure from our NATO allies. It is the question of internal security, of protection against subversion, espionage, and—ah—the activities of disaffected elements, in the student body. . . ." The only reaction was a hostile silence. He took a deep breath and hurried on. "In short, we are asked to cooperate with the security service by supplying them with copies of student dossiers and any other information which may be required from time to time, in the interest of public security."

"No!" The sound erupted from the gathering. Someone dropped a coffee cup, which shattered on the parquet.

"Please! Please!" The President pushed himself off the desk and raised his hands in a pleading gesture. "I have conveyed the Minister's request. It is now open for discussion."

Dahlmeyer from Experimental Physics was the first on his feet, a big shaggy fellow with a jutting jaw. He challenged the President harshly. "I think we have a right to know, sir, what response you made to the Minister."

There was a chorus of approval. The President shuffled uneasily.

"I told the Minister that while we were all conscious of the need for—ah—adequate security in a critical time, we were—ah—at least equally concerned to preserve the—ah—principles of academic freedom."

"Oh, Christ!" Dahlmeyer exploded.

There was an audible groan from Brandt. Mendelius stood up. He was white with anger but he spoke with quiet formality.

"I wish to make a personal statement, sir. I hold tenure to teach in this place. I do not hold, nor will I accept, a commission to investigate the private lives of my students. I am ready to resign rather than do so."

"I would point out, Professor"—the President was cold—"that I have conveyed a request, not a ministerial order; which would, in the present circumstances at least, be illegal. However, you must understand that in conditions of national emergency, the situation may change radically."

"In other words"—Hellman from Organic Chemistry was on his feet—"we have a threat, as well as a request."

"We are all under threat, Professor Hellman—the threat of armed conflict, when civil liberties must inevitably be curtailed in the national interest."

"There's another threat, which you should also consider," said Anneliese Meissner. "Student revolt, expressing total loss of faith in the integrity of the academic faculty. I remind you of what happened to our universities in the thirties and forties when the Nazis ran the country. . . . Do you want to see that again?"

"Do you think you will not see it when the Russians come?"

"Ah! So you have already committed yourself, sir."

"I have not." The President was fuming now. "I told the Minister I would refer the request to my staff and report their reactions."

"Which puts us all straight into the computer bank of the security service. Well, so be it! I'm with Mendelius. If they want me to spy on my students, I'm out!"

"With respect to the President and to my esteemed colleagues." A small mousy fellow stood up. It was Kollwitz, who taught forensic medicine. "I suggest that such a situation can be avoided very simply. The President reports that his senior faculty is unanimously against the proposed measure. He does not have to give names."

"It's a good idea," said Brandt. "If the President himself stands firm with us, then we're in a strong position: and other universities may be encouraged to follow suit."

"Thank you, ladies and gentlemen." The President was obviously relieved. "As usual, you've been most helpful. I'll give some thought to—ah—an appropriate answer to the Minister!"

After that no one had very much to say and the President was eager to be rid of them. They left the coffee dregs and the last of the apple cake and straggled out into the sunlight. Anneliese Meissner fell into step beside Mendelius. She was snorting with fury.

"God Almighty! What an old humbug! . . . An appropriate answer to the Minister! . . . Balls!"

"They've got his balls in a nutcracker," said Mendelius with a sour grin. "He's only two years off retirement. You can't blame him for trying to compromise. . . . Anyway, he's got a united faculty behind him. That has to give him some courage."

"United?" Anneliese snorted again. "My God, Mendelius! How simple can you get? That was just choir practice—all of us noble souls chanting 'A Mighty Fortress Is Our God'! How many will stand firm when the security boys really put the pressure on? . . . 'Isn't it true, Professor Brandt, that you've been laying little Mary Toller? . . . And you, Dahlmeyer? Does your wife know about your Saturdays in the Love Hotel in Frankfurt? . . . And for you, Heinzl, or Willi, or Traudl, if you don't cooperate we've got some lovely filthy jobs—like sanitation scientist or bath attendant in the nut-house . . . !' Don't make any mistake, my friend. If we get three out of ten in the final count, we'll be damn lucky."

"You're forgetting the students. The moment they hear of it, they'll be up in arms."

"Some, yes! But how many will still be standing up after the first baton charge, and the tear gas and the water cannon? Not too many, Carl! And there'll be fewer still when the police cut loose with live ammunition."

"They'll never do it!"

"What have they got to lose? Once the propaganda machine starts blaring who will hear the shots in the alley? Besides, one itty-bitty atom bomb on Tübingen and the slate is wiped clean. . . . Will you have lunch with me? If I eat alone I'll probably get drunk."

"We can't have that, can we?" Mendelius hooked his arm through hers and drew her thick body close to him. "There's only one consolation, girl: every university in the world is probably facing the same pressure at this moment."

"I know! Philistines of the world, unite! The eggheads will be crushed at last! My God, Carl! Your Jean Marie wasn't too far wrong!"

"Have you listened to the tapes I sent you?"

"Over and over. I've been doing a lot of reading, too."

"And . . . ?"

"And I'm not going to say another word until I've got a big drink inside me. I'm a bitch, Carl—cynical and old and too ugly to believe in a God who makes monsters like me. . . . But now, I'm so damned scared I could cry."

"Where do you want to eat?"

"Anywhere! The first *Bierkeller* we find. Sausage and sauerkraut, beer and a double schnapps! Let's join the happy proletariat!"

He had never seen her so upset. She ate ravenously and drank with a desperate determination; but even after a liter of beer and two very large schnapps she was still cold sober. She called the waitress to clear the dishes and bring another shot of liquor, then announced that she was ready for a rational discussion.

"About you first, Carl . . ."

"What about me?"

"I understand you better now. I like you more."

"Thank you." Mendelius grinned at her. "I love you, too!"

"Don't make fun of me. I'm not in the mood for it. Those tapes shook me up. You sounded so damned desperate, trying to come to terms with the impossible."

"What about Jean Marie?"

"Well, now, that was another surprise. Your portrait of him was too vivid to be a fake. I had to accept that it was authentic . . . I saw him. I felt him."

"How did you judge him?"

"He's a very lucky man."

"Lucky?"

"Yes! . . . I spend half my life dealing with sick minds. Leaving aside organic defects, most cases boil down to a fragmentation of the personality, a loss of identity. Life—interior and exterior—is a jigsaw, with the pieces scattered all over the table. . . . The clinician spends his time trying to create a condition of self-recognition—a condition in which even the confusion makes sense. The patient has to see that the jigsaw is designed to make you work at putting it together. . . . Whatever happened to your Jean Marie had just that saving effect. I made sense of everything—conflict, failure, your rejection, even his present darkness. . . . God! If I could do that with my patients, I'd be the greatest healer in the world. If I could do it with myself, I'd be a hell of a lot happier than I am now. . . ."

"I'd say you were a pretty integrated personality."

"Would you, Carl? Look at me now—half drunk on cheap liquor, because I'm scared of tomorrow and I hate the fat frog my mother brought into the world! . . . I've learned to live with me, but not to like me—not ever!"

"I'm proud to know you, Anneliese," said Carl Mendelius gently. "You're a dear friend and a great woman."

"Thanks!" She closed up again instantly. "I told you I've been doing a lot of reading: comparative religion, the basis of mystical experience in various cults. It's still strange country to me; but the idea of salvation begins to make sense. We all experience pain, fear, injustice, confusion, death. We struggle to stay whole through the experience. Even when we fail, we try to salvage our selves out of the wreckage. We can't do it alone. We need support. We need more—a module or exemplar to show us what a whole human being looks like. . . . Hence the prophet, the Messiah, the Christ figure. The same thing applies to the communities of believers. The Church—whatever church!—says: 'Truth is here; light is here; we are the chosen; join us!' . . . Yes or no, Professor?"

"Yes," said Mendelius. "But the important question is, which module do you choose, and why?"

"I don't know yet," said Anneliese Meissner. "But I do know that the final assent is simple, as it was for your Jean Marie. The catch is that you have to be absolutely desperate before you make your submission. The patient I can help quickest is the desperate one who knows he's sick. . . . The best candidate for the cults is the person at the end of his rope."

"Which brings us to the next problem." Mendelius reached out to touch her hand. "What are we going to do, you and I, about the situation at the University? If the President sells us out to the politicos, as he probably will, if half our colleagues surrender to the witch-hunters, what then?"

"We go underground." Anneliese Meissner had no doubts on that score. "We start organizing for it now."

"You see?" Mendelius chuckled and lifted his glass in salute. "Even you, Frau Professor, are prepared to bury the sacred scrolls and take to the mountains!"

"Don't count on it, Carl. It's the drink talking. . . ."

"*In vino veritas* . . ." said Mendelius with a grin.

"Oh, Christ!" Anneliese Meissner glowered at him. "We've had more than enough clichés for one day! Let's walk awhile. It's stifling in here."

As he strolled homeward through the placid streets of the old town, Mendelius found himself faced with a new dilemma. In a pointless conflict, a war that would be fought to extinction, where did a man's loyalties belong? To the blasted, sterile earth that had once been a homeplace? To the men who rode the juggernaut chariot, heedless of the victims under its wheels? To the nation-state, soon to be as meaningless to the living as to the dead? To race, blood, tribe, tradition, *Gott und Vaterland*? If not to these, then to what? And when should Carl Mendelius begin to disengage himself from the system of which he had been so long a beneficiary?

Katrin and Johann would be called to the colours before the year was out. How should he advise them to answer? Yes, to the mad imperative? Or no, we will not serve, because there is no possible end but catastrophe? Once again, childhood memories rose up to haunt him: the bodies of boy soldiers hanged from lampposts in Dresden because they had given up a hopeless cause, in the last days of a crazed despot.

Now he was truly caught in the closed circuit of Jean Marie's predetermined cosmos. So long as you could still flip a coin on a 50–50 chance, you could live, at least, in hope. But once you discovered that the coin had two heads and the Creator wasn't offering any odds at all, when you were in a gull's game, and the quicker you got out, the better . . . So which do you think it is, Herr Professor? Continuity or chaos? And if you opt out of coming chaos, on what far planet and with what remnant creatures will you build your new Utopia?

It was a treadmill argument and he was soon weary of it. He needed distraction; so he turned down a narrow lane, pushed open a worm-eaten door and climbed three flights of stairs to the studio of Alvin Dolman, onetime master sergeant in the U. S. Army of the Rhine, onetime husband of the Bürgermeister's daughter, now happily divorced and working as an illustrator for a local publisher. He was a big, laughing fellow with ham fists and a game leg, the result of an accident on the autobahn. He also had a shrewd eye for old prints; and Mendelius was one of the regular clients to whom he served Rhine wine, knackwurst and gratuitous advice on women, politics and the art market.

". . . You've come at the right time, Professor. Trade is so goddam slow, I'm thinking of going into the porno business. . . . Look at these! I spotted them in a junk shop in Mannheim—three pen-and-ink drawings by Julius Schnorr von Carolsfeld. . . . See! There's the signature and the date, 1821. Beautiful draftsman, isn't he? And the models are pretty, too. . . . How about five hundred marks for the lot?"

"How about three hundred, Alvin?" Mendelius munched happily on his knackwurst.

"Four—and it's a steal!"

"Three fifty—they're foxed anyway."

"You're taking the bread out of my mouth, Professor!"

"I'll throw in a rye loaf."

"You've got a deal. Do you want 'em framed?"

"The usual price?"

"Would I steal from a friend?"

"His wife, maybe," said Mendelius with a grin. "But not his watch. How is life with you, Alvin?"

"Not bad, Professor! Not bad!" He splashed wine into his glass. "How's the family?"

"Fine! Fine!"

"That young fellow—your daughter's boyfriend—he's got the makings of a good artist. I've been giving him lessons in dry-point. He learns fast. . . . It's a shame, though, what's going to happen to these kids."

"What is going to happen, Alvin?"

"I only know what I hear, Professor. I keep in touch with our soldier boys in Frankfurt, sell 'em a print or two occasionally, when they're drunk enough. There's lots of war talk. They're filtering in fresh troops and new equipment. Back in Detroit they're switching to military vehicles. . . . I'm thinking of pulling up stakes and heading home. It's nice to be the artist-in-residence in a university town—but hell!—who wants to get his ass shot off for the sake of the *Fräuleins*! If anything happens, Tübingen will be a battle zone inside a week. But then, so will Detroit, I guess. . . . Help yourself to the wine. I want to show you something."

He rummaged in a cupboard and brought out a small square package, wrapped in oilcloth. He unpacked it carefully to reveal a small duplex portrait of a sixteenth-century nobleman and his wife. He set it on the easel and adjusted the light.

"Well, Professor, what do you say?"

"It looks like a Cranach."

"It is. Lucas Cranach the Elder. He painted it in Wittenberg in 1508."

"Where the devil did you get it?"

Dolman grinned and laid his forefinger along his nose. "I smelled it, Professor—in a woman's bedroom if you want to know. She was so happy with my company she gave it to me. I cleaned it up and—presto!—a ready-made insurance policy! No way I'm selling it in Germany though. It goes home with me. . . ."

"What about the lady? Doesn't she share the profits?"

"Hell, no! She's beautiful but dumb; and her husband's got money running out of his ears. Besides, it was a fair trade. I made her very happy."

"You're a rogue, Alvin." Mendelius chuckled.

"Aren't I though! . . . But with inflation the way it is, an army pension hardly buys pretzels!"

"If things get bad, maybe they'll pull you back into the Army."

"No way, Professor!" Dolman began rewrapping his treasure.

"I'm out and I'm staying out! Next time it won't be a war, just one big firestorm and then—bingo!—I'll be back to painting buffalo on the walls of a cave!"

". . . The fear is everywhere, Jean . . ." Mendelius was at his desk writing, while Lotte sat quietly knitting in the corner and listening to a Brahms concerto, broadcast from Berlin. "It is like a dark mist rising from the marshes, spreading through the streets, permeating every dwelling place. It taints the most casual talk. It enters into the simplest domestic calculation.

"Our faculty members are now asked to report to the security service on the political affiliations of our students. So, this most elementary of relationships is corrupted and may be utterly destroyed. I have already given notice that I shall resign if the request is made an order. But you see how subtly the corruption works: if I rely on the police for personal protection, how can I, with sound reason, refuse them my cooperation in a national emergency? The answer is clear to me. It will be clear to very few others, when the propagandists raise what Churchill called 'the bodyguard of lies.'

". . . But if fear is an infection, despair is a plague. Your vision of the end of temporal things obsesses us all; but the rest of it—the final redeeming act, the ultimate demonstration of divine justice and mercy—how does one express these, in terms that will keep human hope alive? Your closed-out cosmos, my dear friend, will be a terrible place without it. . . ."

The telephone rang. Lotte laid down her knitting to answer it. Georg Rainer was on the line. When Mendelius picked up the phone Rainer launched immediately into monologue.

"I'm in Zurich. I flew up just to make this telephone call. I couldn't trust the Italian circuits. Now, listen carefully and don't make any comments at all. Do you remember, at our last meeting, we discussed a list?"

"Yes."

"Do you have it close by?"

"Upstairs. Hang on."

Mendelius hurried up to his study, unlocked the old safe and fished out Jean Marie's list. He picked up the receiver. "Right. I have it in front of me."

"Is it arranged by countries?"

"Yes."

"I'm going to mention four names from four countries. I want to know whether the names are on your list. Clear?"

"Go ahead."

"U.S.S.R. . . . Petrov?"

"Yes."

"U.K. . . . Pearson?"

"Yes."

"U.S.A. . . . Morrow?"

"Yes."

"France . . . Duhamel?"

"Yes."

"Good That means my informant is reliable."

"You're talking in riddles, Georg."

"I sent you a letter from the General Post Office in Zurich. It will explain the riddles."

"But you're coming here on Wednesday."

"I know. But I'm a pessimist. I hope for the best and prepare for the worst. Somebody's had a tail on me since Saturday. Pia thought she spotted a changeover at the airport which means we could be under surveillance in Zurich as well. So we're going to try a little evasive action and come overland instead of by air. Can you accommodate both of us? No way I would leave Pia alone in Rome."

"Of course! This is all very sinister, Georg!"

"I warned you it might be. Sit tight and light a candle for us. *Auf wiedersehen.*"

Mendelius set down the receiver, and began absently leafing through the typewritten pages of Jean Marie's list. Right from the beginning he had accepted Anneliese Meissner's dismissive description of it as "an aide-mémoire pulled out of a filing cabinet." He had given no thought at all to the stretch and potency of friendship between high men. But Rainer had understood its importance; Rainer had opened a whole new area of investigation and was now at risk because of it. . . .

Lotte stuck her head around the door and asked, "What did Rainer want?"

"He was rather cryptic. He wanted me to confirm that four names were on this list from Jean Marie. He also wanted to tell me he was coming overland to Tübingen and bringing Pia with him."

It was on the tip of his tongue to say that Rainer was under surveillance but he thought better of it.

"Oh, dear!" Lotte was instantly the housewife. "That does make complications. I'll have to change the rooms about. Do you think we could put Lars Larsen up here in the study?"

"Whatever you want, liebchen. . . . Any chance of some coffee?"

"Chocolate," said Lotte firmly. "I don't want you tossing about all night." She kissed him and went out.

Mendelius turned back to his letter. He was tempted to make reference to Rainer's phone call and ask for further explanation of the significance of the list, but he thought better of it. Italian mails were never secure and he did not wish to be too specific.

. . . So I find myself returning again and again to your letter and annexures and I am exercised by the problem of presenting your ideas in open forum. I wonder how you would wish them presented, for example, to the people on your list. . . .

In what terms do we discuss the Parousia with a twentieth-century audience of believers and nonbelievers? I ask, my dear Jean, whether we have not corrupted its meaning out of all recognition. We talk of triumph, judgment, "the Son of Man coming on the clouds of heaven, with great power and majesty. . . ."

I wonder whether the power and the majesty and the glory may not demonstrate themselves far otherwise than we expect. I remember the phrase in your letter: "a moment of exquisite agony" and how you explained it as a sudden perception of the oneness of all things. . . . Like the dying Goethe, I cry still for more light. I am a sensual man, burdened with too much learning and too little real understanding. At the end of a long day, I know I am very content with Lotte's hot chocolate and her arms around me in the dark. . . .

Lars Larsen, brusque, dapper and voluble, arrived an hour before midday after a night flight from New York and a breakneck drive from Frankfurt. Within fifteen minutes he was closeted with Mendelius, reading him the facts of life within the literary establishment.

". . . Yes, I'll represent you and Rainer but not until I've worked out a satisfactory contract between you both—and that has to be at least sixty–forty in your favour. Before we even get that far Rainer has to disclose his arrangements with *Die Welt.* If he's a staff man, pure and simple, the Springer group can claim full ownership of anything he contributes to this project. . . . So, first I talk to Rainer alone. You stay away until I'm ready. . . . Now, don't give me any arguments, Carl. Fifty–fifty just isn't acceptable. You have to control this thing, and you can't do that unless you own the votes. . . . Besides, it's you the customers want to buy. I've got three bids for world rights to serial and book publication with a million and a half up front—and that's on your name, and your association with Gregory the Seventeenth, not on Rainer! Once I see what you've got we can probably raise the floor to two million . . . plus a whole lot of healthy spin-offs. So get it clear, Carl! You're making Rainer a wealthy man. You don't have to apologize for the terms. . . ."

"I wasn't thinking about Rainer." Mendelius was suddenly moody. "I was thinking about myself. When this story is published, a lot of people will want to discredit me as they discredited Jean Marie. Two million dollars could make me look like a very expensive Judas."

"If you do it for nothing," said Lars Larsen, "they'll think you're a schnook—too crazy to be believed. Money always smells clean. However, if it bothers you, talk to your lawyer, maybe he'll advise you to set up a benefice for fallen women! That's not my problem. The money I get you guarantees that your publishers have to get you a big readership . . . and that, in the end, is what you want. Now, can I look at the documents, please?"

Mendelius unlocked the old safe and brought out the envelope containing Jean Marie's letter and the encyclical. Larsen glanced at the documents and then asked bluntly:

"These are genuine?"

"Yes."

"You can authenticate the handwriting?"

"Of course—and I've verified them in personal discussion with the author."

"Good. I'll want a notarized deposition to that effect. I'd also like to photograph some specimen passages . . . not necessarily the important ones. For this kind of money the clients demand boiler-plate protection. And the last thing they want is a run-in with the Vatican over phony attributions."

"I've never known you so careful before, Lars."

"We're only at the beginning, Carl." Larsen was not amused. "Once this story breaks, your past and present will be under the microscope. So will Rainer's—and professionally, at least, he'd better be squeaky clean. . . . Now do you think you could get me another cup of coffee and leave me alone to study this stuff . . ."

"While you're doing it," said Mendelius with a grin, "make a few notes on the internal evidence: the handwriting, the polished French style, the quality of the reasoning and the rendering of personal emotion."

"I know about internal evidence," said Larsen tartly. "One of my earliest clients was a master plagiarist. . . . He was sued for a million and lost. I had to return my commissions. . . . Now, what about that coffee?"

When he came down to lunch at one-thirty, Larsen was a different man, shaken and subdued. He picked at his food, and talked disjointedly.

". . . I'm usually detached when I read. I have to be. . . . No one can sustain the impact of all those student personalities clamouring at you from the manuscripts. . . . But that letter, Lotte! It had me in tears. I never go to church except for weddings and funerals. But my grandfather on my mother's side was an old-fashioned Swedish Lutheran. When I was little he would sit me on his knee and read the Bible to me. . . . Upstairs, it was as if I were listening to him again. . . ."

"I know what you mean." Lotte picked up the discussion eagerly. "That's why I keep saying to Carl that this account of Jean Marie must be done with love and fidelity. . . . No one must be allowed to make it cheap or vulgar."

"How do you feel, then, about Georg Rainer?"

"I don't know him very well. He's charming and witty. I think he's very knowledgeable about Italy and the Vatican. However, I do say Carl must stay in control of this project."

"Let's be clear about this." Mendelius was suddenly edgy and irritable. "Georg Rainer arrives here this afternoon as our guest. The important thing is that he and I work happily and productively together. I don't want any arguments about money to spoil that. And I don't want to offer him a halfhearted welcome either."

"*Jawohl*, Herr Professor!" Lotte made a mocking mouth at his solemnity.

"Trust me, Carl." Lars Larsen grinned at him. "I'm a very good surgeon. I cut clean and all my patients recover! . . . Now I want to tie up your phone for a couple of hours. They're open for business in New York; and after what I've read—oh, boy!—do we have business!"

Afterwards, in the kitchen, Lotte giggled helplessly to Mendelius.

"Lars is so funny! As soon as he starts talking money, you can feel the electricity. His eyes sparkle and you almost expect his hair to stand on end. . . . I'm sure he'd be shocked if you told him; but he's like the fat man at the circus gate, shouting his head off, selling tickets for Judgment Day!"

Lars Larsen's sales campaign went on all the afternoon. At five-thirty, with the bidding at two and a quarter million, he closed the market. As he explained to Mendelius, he now had a handsome cash guarantee with which to begin discussions with Georg Rainer. But Georg Rainer was late. At seven, he called in from a roadhouse twenty miles south of Tübingen. He explained that they had been followed out of Zurich, that he had shaken the surveillance team before the border post, and then driven half the country roads in Swabia to make sure they had not been picked up again. At eight-thirty he arrived with Pia, windblown and travel-worn. An hour later, relaxed over Lotte's ample supper, he explained the melodrama.

". . . The most extraordinary thing about the abdication was the secrecy with which it was accomplished. Nobody, but nobody, was willing to talk. . . . Which prompted us in the press corps to believe that Gregory the Seventeenth must not only have made powerful enemies, but also alienated most of his friends inside and outside the Vatican. We knew him as you did, Carl, for a man of singular charm. So where had all his friends gone? . . . Then you told me about this list and it seemed to me that it must have a special importance. . . . You said it was typewritten. So it had to have come from a file. I asked myself who would know about Gregory the Seventeenth's private file. . . . I came up with his private secretary. . . . In my records he was listed as Monsignor Bernard Logue, who, in spite of his Irish name, is a Frenchman, a descendant of one of the wild geese who fled to France to fight the English. . . . I enquired what had happened to him after the abdication. . . ."

"That was clever of you, Georg. Logue was the man who denounced the encyclical to the Curia and started the whole affair.

I never thought to ask how he was rewarded."

"Apparently not well. He was moved out of the papal household into the Secretariat for Public Communications. I had been told he was a rather unhappy fellow who might be prepared to air his grievances. . . . On the contrary! He was the perfect clerical functionary—precise, patronizing, absolutely convinced that the finger of God guided every scribe in Vatican City. . . . Clearly he was not about to spill secrets on my plate. So, I told him I was working on an account of the last days of Gregory the Seventeenth, in which he, Monsignor Logue, had played a key role. . . . That shook him. He asked me to define the role he was supposed to have played. I told him that he had informed the Curia of the contents of Gregory the Seventeenth's last unpublished encyclical. That really upset him. He denied any such act. He disclaimed knowledge of any encyclical. Then I mentioned the list and quoted from it the names which you had confirmed to me. He demanded to know where I had seen that document. I told him I had to protect my sources; but clearly, I might be prepared to trade some information with him. He told me he knew about the list but he had never seen it. He went on to explain Gregory the Seventeenth was a great believer in personal diplomacy. He was altogether too vulnerable to gestures of friendship. The Secretariat of State saw great dangers also in his attitude towards *Les Amis du Silence*. . . ."

"The what?" It was almost a shout from Mendelius. Rainer threw back his head and laughed.

"I thought that would get to you, Carl! It certainly did to me. Who were the Friends of Silence? I asked. But our little Monsignore realized that he had made a big blunder and urged me to forget that I had ever heard such a phrase. . . . I tried to reassure him. He refused to be comforted. The interview was over. I was left with the four names: Petrov and the others and something called *Les Amis du Silence*. . . . That night, Saturday, I took Pia to dinner at Piccola Roma and afterwards to a discothèque. We left about two in the morning. The streets were almost deserted. That was when we realized we were being followed. . . . We've been under surveillance ever since."

"But no mischief?" asked Larsen. "No violence?"

"Not yet," said Rainer dubiously. "But once they know where the list is . . ."

"Who are 'they'?" asked Lotte.

"I have no idea." Rainer's gesture was one of weary puzzlement. "Unlike Carl here, I am not surprised by anything the Vatican does. But in this case we are dealing with a single cleric, a zealot, a known informer, who was willing to topple his own master. He may be serving other interests than the Vatican. Pia has her own opinion."

"Please!" Mendelius urged her into the discussion. "We could use some fresh thoughts."

Pia Menendez hesitated for a moment and then explained quietly, "My father was a diplomat. He used to say that diplomacy was possible only between established institutions, good or bad. In a revolutionary situation you could not negotiate, only gamble. . . . Now, from what Georg has told me, Gregory the Seventeenth believed that a worldwide revolutionary situation would follow an atomic catastrophe and that he or others would have to gamble on men of goodwill inside and outside the Church. They might be presently obscure, but such as could survive into positions of power."

"Men presently obscure." Larsen seized on the phrase. "Or perhaps out of favour, or even considered dangerous to existing régimes. That would make another reason for pushing Gregory the Seventeenth off the throne."

"But it doesn't tell me who is having us shadowed," said Georg Rainer.

"Let's reason a little." Mendelius entered the talk again. "Monsignor Logue said he had never seen the list. That's possible. Once Jean Marie knew him for an informer he would obviously try to protect his documents. But Logue knew the list existed. . . . Once he knew you had access to it, Georg, whom would he tell: his present masters in the Vatican—or those other unspecified interests? Round-the-clock surveillance doesn't sound like a Vatican tactic. As Pia points out, they, above all, play the institutional game. So, my guess is the outside interest. What's your view on that, Georg?"

"None until I've read all your documents. I'd like to take them to bed with me."

"Before you go to bed," said Lars Larsen hastily, "I'd like a short chat about contracts."

"I'll save you the trouble," said Georg Rainer with a grin. "Mendelius is the Jesuit among us. If your contracts satisfy his sense of justice, I'll sign 'em."

"I'll get the stuff Jean Marie sent me," said Mendelius. "I warn you, it will keep you awake all night."

"For once," said Pia, the diplomat's daughter, "I'm happy to be sleeping alone!"

That night Mendelius lay wakeful, long into the small, sinister hours after midnight, trying, as any good historian should, to think himself back into the ancient battles of Christendom: the battle to establish a codex of belief, a constitution for the assembly and to hold them secure against the encroachments of the fantasists and the forgers.

The battles were always bitter and sometimes violent. Men of goodwill were sacrificed without mercy. Complaisant rogues flourished under the umbrella of orthodoxy. Marriages of convenience were made between Church and State. There were harsh divorcements of nations and communities from union with the elect.

The battle continued still. Jean Marie Barette, lately a Pope, was one of its casualties. He had invoked the Spirit; the Cardinals had invoked the assembly—and the assembly had won, as always, by the weight of numbers and the strength of the organization. This was the lesson the Romans had taught the Marxists: keep the codex pure and the hierarchy exclusive. With the one you smoke out the heretic; with the other you crush him.

Which brought Mendelius by swift turnabout to this question: who were The Friends of Silence? It was tempting to adopt Pia Menendez' theory of men waiting in the shadows to be called to salvage a situation of revolution or catastrophe. On the other hand, he remembered a letter from the long-ago when Jean Marie, still a Cardinal, had inveighed against elitist movements in the Church.

. . . I distrust them, Carl! If I were Pope I should discourage actively anything that remotely resembled a secret society, a hermetic association, a privileged cadre in the Church. Of all societies, the assembly of the people of God should be the most open, the most sharing. There are enough mysteries in the universe without our fabricating any more. . . . But the Romans love their whispers and their gossip in the corridors and their secret archives!

It was hard to believe that the man who had written those

words would set up his own elite club and give it so obvious a name. Was it not more probable that *Les Amis du Silence* was an outside group whose French title was designed to create the impression of approval by a French Pope? Years ago the Spaniards had set the example when they created their own authoritarian elite and called it *Opus Dei*—God's work.

Still restless, Mendelius began rummaging in his memory for anything that would associate with The Friends of Silence. The word friends produced some odd correlatives: from the Society of Friends, to *amicus curiae*, and the Marquis de Mirabeau's "Friend of Man." The word silence produced a greater variety of associations. In the Mamertine Prison in Rome a dusty lamp burned in memory of the "Church of Silence": the faithful denied the liberty to worship or persecuted for their adherence to the old faith. There was the Amyclean Silence, which forbade the citizens of Amyclae to speak of the Spartan threat, so that when the invasions did come, the city fell easy prey. There was the sinister Italian proverb: "Noble vengeance is the daughter of deep silence." . . .

Drowsy at last, Mendelius decided that this might be the occasion to test Drexel on his promise to supply reference points on matters of fact. Lotte stirred and reached out in the dark for reassurance. He folded himself into her warmth and lapsed swiftly into sleep.

There were unexpected problems in Georg Rainer's contract with *Die Welt*, so immediately after breakfast Lars Larsen left for Bonn and Berlin to talk with executives of the Springer group. He was jaunty and confident as always.

"They have to play ball. No agreement, no newsbreak—and Georg resigns! Leave it to me. You guys settle down and put the story together. I want to carry it back by hand to New York."

Mendelius and Rainer closed themselves in the study to set their materials in order: Rainer's files on the pontificate of Gregory XVII, Mendelius' private correspondence with him, before and during his reign, lecture notes and bibliography on the millennial tradition, and, for cornerstone to the edifice, the three most recent documents: the letter, the encyclical and the list of names. On these last Georg Rainer rendered a curt judgment.

". . . If you're not a believer—and I'm at best a vestigial Lutheran—the letter and the encyclical are like poetry, beyond rational discussion. Either you feel them or you don't. I felt the man's agony. However, for me, he was walking on the moon, far out of reach. . . . But the list of names—that was a different matter. I recognized most of them. I knew enough about them to observe certain common factors, and guess that a computer run might show even more. I want to work through the list again this morning before I commit to any conclusions. . . ."

"Can you see them as Friends of Silence?"

"No way at all. They've all been very vocal people, some of whom have suffered checks in their careers and may or may not recover."

"I'm going to try the name on Drexel."

Mendelius reached for the phone, dialled the number of Vatican City and asked to be connected with Cardinal Drexel. His Eminence sounded surprised and a little wary.

"Mendelius? You're stirring early. What can I do for you?"

"I am working on my memoir. You were kind enough to offer your assistance on matters of fact."

"Yes?"

"Who are *Les Amis du Silence*?"

"I'm sorry." Drexel was brusque. "I can give you no information at all on that question."

"Can you refer me, as you promised, to any other source?"

"That would not be opportune."

"Others have informed me that the subject may be dangerous."

"As to that, I can offer no opinion."

"Thank you, Eminence, at least for accepting my call."

"My pleasure, Mendelius. Good morning!"

Rainer was not surprised. "No luck?"

Mendelius gave a snort of disgust. "The subject is inopportune!"

"I love that word! They use it to bury all sorts of bodies. . . . Why not ring Monte Cassino and ask your friend for clarification?"

"Because I don't want him to bear any responsibility for what we write. You're the reporter. Where else can we try?"

"I suggest we forget it for the moment and block out the argument of the piece. As I see it we start with the abdication itself, a large, consequential act, the reason for which is still a mystery. We have now accumulated enough evidence to affirm that the members of the Sacred College engineered the situation. We demonstrate how it was done. Finally we come to the why; which depends on your testimony, the final three documents and your interviews with Drexel in Rome and the former Gregory the Seventeenth in Monte Cassino. I report all that and cite the evidence. Immediately our readers make judgments. The cynics say the man was mad and the Cardinals were right to get rid of him. The devout rest tranquil on the official line that whatever happened, the Holy Spirit will make it come right in the end. The curious and the critical will want to know more. . . . Which is where you take up the narrative with a portrait of the man and an examination of what he said and wrote. I know you're a very lucid writer, but this time you'll really have to spell things out in simple language—even for our sub-editors! . . . Well, do you agree the form?"

"As a beginning, yes. Let's see how it looks in typescript. . . . You make yourself comfortable. I'm going to take a walk before I start work."

As he was walking through the lounge the telephone rang. The man on the other end of the line identified himself as Dieter Lorenz, senior investigator with the Landeskriminalamt. A matter of some importance had come up; he would like to discuss it with the Herr Professor.

He arrived ten minutes later, a gangling shabby-looking fellow dressed in blue jeans and a leather jacket. While Lotte prepared coffee he displayed to Mendelius a grubby sheet of mimeograph paper on which was a line-drawn portrait of Mendelius with his name, address and telephone number. The paper was folded several times as if it had been carried in a wallet. Lorenz explained its provenance.

". . . There's a beer hall frequented by Turkish workmen from the paper factory. It's one of the centers for drug traffic in the city and among the students. Last night there was an affray between some Turks and a bunch of young Germans. A man was knifed. He was dead before they got him to hospital. We've identified him as Albrecht Metzger, onetime clerk at the paper-works, sacked six months ago for petty theft. We found that paper in his wallet."

"What does it mean?"

"In brief, Professor, it means you are under terrorist surveillance. The sketch is mimeographed, which indicates it has been circulated to a number of people. The paper is German. The drawing was probably done in Rome. It was made from one of the photographs of you which appeared in the Italian press. . . . The rest of the story is not yet clear. We do know that some underground groups finance themselves by trafficking in drugs which originate in Turkey. There are twenty thousand students at the University—so that's a highly significant market for the dealers. The dead man was not on any of our wanted lists. However, the terrorist groups do use fringe operators, paid in cash, in order to protect the central organization. The way things are now—with high unemployment and social unrest—there's no trouble finding pickup labour for jobs like this. . . ."

Lotte brought the coffee and while she served it Mendelius explained the situation. She took it calmly enough; but her face was pale and her hand trembled as she set down the coffeepot. Lorenz continued his exposition:

". . . You have to understand how the terrorist system works. Using people like our deceased friend Metzger—we call them 'spotters'—they build up a picture of the habits and movements of the intended victim. In a big city it's more difficult; but in a small one like Tübingen and with a professional man like yourself, it's comparatively easy. You go always to the same place of work. You shop at the same stores. . . . You can't introduce too many variations. So you get inattentive and careless. Then, one day, they move in a hit team—three, four people, with a couple of vehicles, and—poof!—the thing is done."

"It's not a very hopeful picture, is it?" Lotte's voice was unsteady.

"No, dear lady, it is not." Lorenz offered no comfort at all. "We can give your husband a pistol permit; but unless he's prepared to take small-arms training, it's not much use. You can hire bodyguards, but they're ruinously expensive—unless of course your students are prepared to help."

"No!" Mendelius refused flatly.

"Then the only answer is personal vigilance, and constant contact with us. You must report even the most trivial incident that appears strange or out of the ordinary. I'll leave you my card. . . . Call that number at any time, day or night. There's always a man on desk duty."

"One thing I can't understand," said Lotte. "Why do they pursue Carl like this? He made his depositions in Rome. The information is already on file. Dead or alive he can't change that."

"You miss the point, dear lady," Lorenz explained patiently. "The whole object of terror is to create fear and uncertainty. If the terrorist does not exact retribution, he loses his influence. . . . It's the old idea of vendetta, which never stops until one side is wiped out. In a settled society, our job as policemen was easier. Now it gets harder every day—dirtier, too!"

"That's what bothers me," said Mendelius moodily. "You know, I presume, that the University staff may be asked to supply security information on our students?"

Lorenz gave him a swift hooded glance and nodded. "I know. . . . I gather you don't like the idea."

"I loathe it."

"It's a question of priorities, isn't it? How much are you prepared to pay for safety in the streets?"

"Not that much," said Carl Mendelius. "Thank you for your help. We'll keep in touch."

He handed back the sketch. Lorenz folded it carefully and put it back in his wallet. He gave Mendelius his card and repeated:

"Remember! Anytime, day or night. . . . Thank you for the coffee, ma'am."

"I'll walk you to your car," said Mendelius. "Back in a minute, liebchen. I want to walk awhile before I begin work with Georg."

"Who is Georg?" The policeman was suddenly cautious.

"Georg Rainer. He's the Rome correspondent for *Die Welt*. We are doing a story together on the Vatican."

"Then please don't let him print this story. There's too much attention focused on you already."

As they strolled up the Kirchgasse towards the Old Market, Dieter Lorenz added a brusque afterthought to their discussion.

"I didn't want to say this in front of your wife. You've got two children. From the terrorist point of view kidnapping is an even better bargain than murder. It gives them a huge press and it puts them in funds. When your kids get back from vacation, you'd better teach them the drill, too."

"We're really getting back to the jungle, aren't we?"

"We're deep inside it," said Dieter Lorenz drily. "This used to be a nice quiet town; but if you could see some of the stuff that crosses my desk, it would make your hair stand up."

"What's the answer?"

"Christ knows. Maybe we need a good war to kill off some of the bastards and let us start clean again!"

It was a wild sad thought from an overworked man. It did nothing to allay the prickling fear that filled Mendelius as he walked down to the newsstand, that made him jump when a housewife jostled him and a boy on a motorcycle roared past him with an open exhaust. There was no Francone now to shepherd him. Point, flanks and rear, he was exposed to the silent hunters, who carried his image like a juju doll wherever they walked.

VII

Rainer was a fast worker, trained to meet daily deadlines with clean, accurate copy. Mendelius was accustomed to the ambling gait of an academic author. He finicked over points of style, argued over the refinement of a definition. He insisted on writing his copy in longhand; his corrections demanded two or three drafts of typescript.

In spite of their apparent incompatibility they produced, at the end of four days, the first and most important stage of the project—a twenty-thousand-word version for immediate serial publication in newspapers and magazines. Before handing it over to the translator—an English version being mandatory under the contracts—they had it read in turn by Lotte, Pia Menendez and Anneliese Meissner. The readings elicited some frank and unexpected comments.

Lotte tried hard to be gentle but succeeded only in devastating the scribes.

". . . There's something wrong. I can't say exactly what it is . . . or perhaps I can. I know Jean Marie. He's a warm man, complex and always interesting to a woman. I don't feel him in anything that you've written there. It's too detached, too . . . I don't know! I'm quite uninterested in the character you've described! I don't really care what happens to him."

Pia Menendez weighed in with a qualified agreement and an explanation.

". . . I think I see what has happened. I know how Georg's mind works. . . . You've always said, darling, that you're reporting from Rome for believers and unbelievers alike. You can't indulge the one, for fear of alienating the other. So you have to show a touch of the cynic. I think Professor Mendelius has fallen into the same trap. He's trying so hard to be detached from a dear friend that he sounds like a censor of morals. And he's trying so hard to be scholarly about the Doctrine of Last Things that it sounds like an exercise in higher mathematics. I don't mean to be rude, but . . ."

"Don't apologize!" Anneliese Meissner was brusque as always. "I agree with you and Lotte. We've lost the man who is, after all, the center-point, the pivot of this whole historic episode. In his discussion of a prophet Carl has abdicated poetry for pedantry. . . . I've got another complaint, too, Carl! I believe this one may be very important. In your discussion of the Last Things you duck two important questions: the nature of evil, the presence of evil in a man-made cataclysm, and the nature of the Parousia itself. What are we going to see? Or, more accurately, what do the apocalyptic prophets—Jean Marie among them—promise that we will see? What will distinguish the Christ from the Antichrist? . . . I'm your reader now, even if I'm not a believer! Once you open the box, I'm as anxious as anyone to see what's inside. . . "

Mendelius and Rainer looked at each other in dismay. Rainer grinned and made a gesture of defeat.

"If the readers don't like us, Carl, we're dead. And if we can't move them to pity and terror with this subject, we deserve to be dead."

"Back to the desk then." Mendelius began restacking the manuscript.

"Not tonight!" Lotte was very firm. "I've booked dinner for the five of us at the Hölderlinhaus. The food's good and the atmosphere seems to do something for Carl. It's the only place I've seen him tipsy enough to recite *Empedocles on Etna* with the roast and sing Schubert with the dessert. . . . Both very well, I might add!"

"I might get drunk again tonight," warned Mendelius. "I'm profoundly discouraged. I'm only glad Lars Larsen didn't read this version."

"A word of advice then," said Anneliese Meissner. "Scrap your part of the piece, Carl! Start from the beginning. Let your heart speak as it did on the tapes you sent me from Rome!"

"Bravo!" said Lotte. "And if a little drinking helps the heart to speak, I'm all in favour!"

"And what's your prescription for me?" asked Georg Rainer.

"For you it's less difficult," said Anneliese Meissner boldly. "I think you'll do better if you stick to the history of the event, leave the interpretation to Carl and then simply swing back at the end with a straight question that makes the readers judge and jury."

Georg Rainer thought about it for a moment and then nodded agreement. "You could be right. I'll try it. . . . But tell me one thing, Frau Doctor Meissner. You're a nonbeliever. You deal with the sick and the deluded. Why do you care so much about this piece of religious history?"

"Because I'm scared," said Anneliese Meissner curtly. "I read the omens in every newspaper. I hear the distant drums and the mad trumpets. . . . I think we'll have our Armageddon. I dream about it every night—and I wish I could find a faith to comfort me in the dark."

The air was still soft with summer. The Neckar flowed tranquil under the willows, while the lovers plied their lazy traffic of punts and rowboats under the windows of the Bursa and the Old Hall, where once Melanchthon had taught and the great Johannes Stöffler had lectured in astronomy and mathematics—and designed the Town Hall clock!

The Hölderlinhaus was a small antique villa with a round tower that looked across the river to the botanical gardens. Friedrich Hölderlin had died there in 1843, a sad, mad genius overshadowed by his contemporary Uhland, in whom, as Goethe had prophesied, the politician would gobble up the poet.

The alleys were quiet now, because the University was still in recess; but the restaurant was busy with a dinner party for staff from the Evangelical Institute and another for a group of actors in town for rehearsals at the University theatre. Mendelius presented Georg Rainer and Pia to his colleagues, and as the meal went on and the wine flowed, there were constant exchanges of talk between the three tables.

As the well-known correspondent of a famous newspaper, Rainer was the center of attention and Mendelius noted with admiration how skilfully he drew the scholars into talk, baiting them with scraps and snippets of information about the Roman scene. Finally, in a sedulously casual aside, he asked:

"Has any of you ever heard of an organization called The Friends of Silence?" He did not use the original French phrase but the German one: *Die Freunde des Schweigens.*

He was talking to the academics; but a response came in startling fashion from the actors at the other table. A tall, cadaverous young man stood up, and in a ceremonious announcement introduced himself and his troupe.

"We," he told them, "we are the friends of silence. To understand us, you must be silent, too. We will, in silence still, tell you a tale of love and fear and pity. . . ."

And there, in the old room, where poor Hölderlin had tried to grasp the last tatters of his dreams, they played out a mimed version of the man who lost his shadow and the woman who gave it back to him again.

It was one of those strange, spontaneous encounters that turned a sober evening into a magical event, that went on with wine and singing and tale-telling until Master Stöffler's clock struck two in the morning from the tower of the Town Hall. As they were saying their good-nights an elderly colleague from the Institute tugged at Mendelius' sleeve and volunteered a suggestion.

". . . Your friend Rainer really didn't get an answer to his question. We were all distracted by those talented young people. You take the *Review of Patristic Studies,* don't you? . . . There's an article in the April issue on the Discipline of the Secret. It makes a couple of references that may help his enquiry. . . ."

"Thank you. I'll look them up in the morning."

"Oh, and there's one more thing, Mendelius . . ."

"Yes?" He was anxious to be gone. Lotte and the others were already drawing away.

"I heard about your stand on the question of student surveillance. I agree with it; but you should be warned; the President is less than happy. He claims you affronted him. My guess is he's scared of a faculty revolt—which is the last thing he needs before his retirement. Well . . . good night, my dear fellow. Walk carefully. A man can break an ankle on these damned cobbles!"

At three and at four in the morning Mendelius was still tossing restlessly between sleep and waking. At five he got up, made himself coffee and settled himself at his desk with the April edition of the *Review of Patristic Studies.* The edition had been published before the abdication and clearly had been in preparation several months before.

The article on the Discipline of the Secret was datelined Paris and signed by someone called Jacques Mandel. It dealt with a practice in the early Christian communities called *disciplina arcani.* The phrase itself was not coined until the seventeenth century; but the discipline was one of the earliest in the Christian community—a mandatory concealment of the more mysterious rites and doctrines of the Church. These were never to be mentioned to the unbeliever or even to aspirants under instruction. Any necessary reference was to be made in cryptic, enigmatical or even misleading terms. The most famous example of such language was the inscription discovered at Autun in 1839: "Take the honey-sweet food of the Saviour of the holy ones; eat and drink holding the fish in your hands." The word fish was an anagram for Jesus Christ, Son of God, Saviour. The "honey-sweet food" was the Eucharist.

The first part of Mandel's article was a scholarly assessment of evidence on the practice and the resulting scarcity of early patristic evidence on doctrinal and sacramental matters. However, there was nothing new in it beyond one or two curious sidelights on the Synod of Antioch, where the orthodox condemned the Arians for admitting catechumens and even pagans to a discussion of "the mysteries." Mendelius found himself wondering why the writer had taken the trouble to write a rehash of such old material. Then suddenly the tenor of the writing changed. Jacques Mandel, whoever he might be, was using the Discipline of the Secret as a text on which to hang a very modern argument.

He claimed that within the hierarchy of the Roman Catholic Church, there existed a powerful group who wished to stifle all debate on doctrinal matters, and impose a twentieth-century version of the Discipline of the Secret. He pointed to the suppressive action taken against certain Catholic theologians in the seventies and early eighties and the rigorist attitudes of certain contemporary bishops in France and elsewhere. He wrote:

. . . One has heard that there exists a clandestine fraternity of these bishops, who have high friends in the Curia, and are able to bring great pressure to bear even on the Pontiff. . . . So far, Gregory XVII, himself a Frenchman, has navigated successfully between the rigorists and the innovators; but he makes no secret of his disapproval of what he calls "a freemasonry of senior clerics, the friends of silence and of darkness." The author has seen a copy of a letter from the Pontiff to a senior Archbishop in which these terms of censure are used. . . .

They were blunt words for such a sober and specialist journal; but Mendelius understood their import. Jacques Mandel was flying a kite to see who would shoot at it or who might salute it. But, clearly, he had information that explained much of the background to the abdication.

Long before the vision and the abdication, Jean Marie had been under enormous pressure. The possibility of schism had been real. Bishops were powerful men both in the religious and in the secular orders. In the one they were leaders of large congregations. In the other they were a discreet but potent force, controllers of a confessional vote on contentious issues. In the outcome—because the Cardinals would not have moved without majority support from the bishops—they had proved strong enough to topple a Pope. . . .

In the light of this new information, Georg Rainer's story of surveillance and pursuit made a certain grim sense. Not all clerics were divorced from politics. Not all were strangers to its more violent practices. History was full of shabby deals made by high men for holy purposes. And, sitting in his own high place, Jean Marie knew the mischiefs that could be concealed or condoned under the discipline of the secret or within a confraternity of silence.

Mendelius marked the relevant passages in the article and scribbled a memo for Georg Rainer.

. . . This isn't evidence; but add it to the indiscretion of Monsignor Logue and we have a strong indicator as to the nature of The Friends of Silence. My feeling is to incorporate a reference into our story as Mandel has done and see what reactions we get. I'm going to draft a small section on another aspect of the phenomenon: that in times of acute crisis, the public leans always to dictators and juntas as the sick man leans to the reassuring doctor however incompetent he may be. . . . If I'm not here when you start work, you'll find the new stuff on my desk.

He pinned the note to Rainer's copy of the draft, then drew his own copy of the manuscript towards him, and under the heading "The Time-frame of Gregory XVII," he began to write:

Psychic epidemics are no new phenomenon in human history. The germs which cause them lie encapsulated, like the anthrax bacillus, until conditions are ripe for their rebirth. These conditions are fear, uncertainty, the breakup of social systems too fragile for the loads imposed on them. The symptoms are as various as the illusions of mankind: the self-mutilation of the flagellants and the castrate priests, the murderous fury of the *sicarii*, the sexual perversion of the witch-hunters, the methodical madness of the inquisitors who think to confine truth in a phrase and burn any contumacious fellow who dares dissent from their definition. But the effects of the disease are always the same. The patient becomes fearful and irrational, subject to nightmare terrors, addicted to pleasurable illusions—an easy prey to peddlers of nostrums, magical incantations and the collective follies of the other afflicted ones. . . .

To chart the origin and the course of the disease is one thing; to cure it is quite another. The most drastic remedy is extermination. The only problem is that you are never sure who will emerge from the slaughterhouse: the lunatics or the sane. Propaganda is another potent medicine. You pump the patients full of healing thoughts from dawn to dusk, and even through their sleeping hours. You tell them, over and over, that all is for the best in this most benign of all creations. And they will believe you too, gladly and gratefully—until the day when they first smell fire in the wind and see blood on the altar stone. Then they will turn and rend you limb from limb in a manic fury of resentment.

It was for this reason that the Sacred College decided to silence Jean Marie Barette and suppress the account of his vision. They knew that the backlash of a millennial proclamation could be enormous. Yet it was for exactly the same reason that Jean Marie proposed in his encyclical a preparation of the spirit against an inevitable period of social insanity. He wanted physicians and places of asylum already established before the epidemic took hold. And, in principle, at least, I believe he was right.

Even in ancient times asylum was a mystic word. It connoted a sacred place, a temple, a shrine, a forest grove where a criminal or a runaway slave would find sanctuary from his pursuers and sleep safe under the numen of the resident god. It was not merely the ingathering which was important. It was the outgoing, as well; the outgoing of the power, the hope, the life-thrust, which sustained the panting fugitive for the last mile as the hounds bayed closer and closer at his heels. . . .

A new thought took hold of Mendelius. He laid down his pen to meditate on it. Everything he had just written about the causes and symptoms of psychic epidemic might be applied with equal justice to Jean Marie. He had abdicated reason for the wildest revelations. He had abdicated the place from which alone power could be exercised. He offered no hope, only a cataclysm and a final judgment on the survivors. His adversaries, whatever they called themselves, had at least pragmatic common sense on their side. Traditional organizations had been tested by time and had survived the vast stresses of the centuries. Traditional interpretations commanded respect, if only for their antiquity and durability. When the roof was falling in you needed a tiler and not a prophet.

And here precisely was the weakness which Lotte, Anneliese and Pia had all found in his portrait of Jean Marie. It carried no conviction because its author had none. It excited no passion because it was bathed in the flat white light of pure reason. . . . Or perhaps, as Anneliese Meissner had warned him long ago, he was still too much the Jesuit to embarrass the family of the faith with an unpopular truth! Enough then! He picked up a red pencil and began savagely and methodically to cut his copy of the manuscript to pieces. Then he pulled a clean brief-pad towards him and began again with a simple stark testimony.

I write of a man I love. I am, therefore, a suspect witness. For this reason, if for no other, I offer only such testimony as may be accepted under the strictest rules of evidence. Where I present an opinion I call it so. I express my doubts as honestly as my certainties. But, I repeat, I am writing of a man I love, to whom I am in debt for some of the best things in my life, who is closer to me than a brother—and whose present agonies I have been unable fully to share. . . .

Suddenly, it was as if he were endowed with a grace of eloquence. He knew exactly what he must say about Jean Marie and how he must say it to touch the hearts of the most simple. When he came to expound the doctrine of last things and how closely Jean Marie adhered to it, he was lucid and persuasive. Jean Marie had been silenced without a hearing. Now, said Mendelius, the unwilling advocate, he must have open judgment.

But when he came to answer the questions which Anneliese had asked, the nature of evil and the mode of the Second Coming, he was forced to a moving admission.

. . . I know that evil exists. I am already marked as a victim of its destructive power. I pray daily to be delivered from it. I do not know why there is evil and pain in a world designed by a beneficent creator. The vision of Gregory XVII described only the effects of that evil, it cast no light upon the mystery of its existence. So, too, with the Second Coming. He tells us nothing of the how, the when, the where of the event, which Christians believe is implicit in and irrevocably guaranteed by the doctrine of the Resurrection. . . . So it would be quite just to say that the vision of Gregory XVII tells us nothing that we do not know already. But this does not discredit the vision or the visionary, any more than a painter is discredited because he shows us light and landscape as we have never seen them before. I wish I could interpret the meaning of my friend's moment of private rapture. I cannot. The best I can do is to show how for good reasons or bad Jean Marie Barette, Pope Gregory XVII, was prevented from offering his own interpretation to the world. . . . Are we the richer or the poorer? Only time will tell.

Three days later, with the help of four typists and two translators, the thing was done. The English and the German versions were boxed for the couriers. The affidavits and the photographic copies of the documents were all attested. Lars Larsen was making a farewell toast before driving to Frankfurt to pick up his flight to New York.

". . . Always, when I've sold a big one like this, I'm scared. My head's on the block. If my judgment's discredited, I'm out of a job. If my author delivers me a turkey, what do I say to the publishers? . . . But this time, I can drop a package on the publisher's desk and swear on my mother's memory he's getting his money's worth. . . . We've got worldwide agreement. Simultaneous publication next Sunday. After that, sit tight for the backlash. But you're sturdy fellows, you'll weather it well. When the going gets rough, remember every television interview is dollars and deutschmarks and yen in the bank. . . . Georg, Carl, I take off my hat to you both. Lotte, my love, thanks for your hospitality. Pia, may your man bring you to New York. And you, Professor Meissner, it's been a pleasure to know you. When I finally crack under the strain I hope you'll undertake my treatment."

"You'll never crack." Anneliese Meissner gave him her most wolfish smile. "Not until they abolish money and go back to barter!"

"Be glad of me!" said Lars Larsen cheerfully. "I like the game, so I play it well. I hope you fellows get as much fun out of spending the money as I had getting it for you. Cheers! . . ."

It was a good exit line and Mendelius gave him full marks for it. Even Anneliese offered amends and asked whether Larsen would consent to represent her works in the American market. Georg Rainer admitted that feeling rich was a novel and pleasant experience. He was reluctant to agree with Pia that there was now no impediment to his getting married—preferably to her. He changed the subject hastily.

". . . There's a couple of matters that still bother me, Carl. We've mentioned The Friends of Silence. We've introduced Gregory the Seventeenth's list of sympathetic politicians; but we've offered no firm conclusions about either. Sooner or later we're going to be questioned in these areas. So, I'll continue digging in Rome and if I get anything new I'll call."

"I'll be more interested to know if you're still under surveillance when you get back to Rome."

"So will I. The dumbest spy has had time to trace me here. But now that the story's written and with so many copies in circulation, I don't see what anyone can do about it. I'm taking Pia to Bonn to deliver a safety copy. Even if they hijacked that, the news would still break. I'm not worried . . . just curious. I hate loose ends."

After that, there was a flurry of farewells and the inevitable anticlimax. Anneliese left to keep appointments at the clinic. Lotte was impatient to get to her housekeeping so that the place would be shining for the return of her brood. Mendelius took one look at his littered study and opted for a walk in the botanical gardens to feed the ducks and the swans.

The next day the children came home. Katrin, bubbling with happiness, arrived in the morning. She presented her mother with an expensive scarf and Mendelius with the promised picture from Franz—a fully worked canvas of the Place du Tertre. Then she took a deep breath and delivered the big news. She and Franz had decided to set up house in Paris. They would be independent and modestly prosperous. Franz had been taken up by a well-known art dealer. She herself would be employed by a German import house in Paris. Yes, she and Franz had discussed the question of marriage. They both agreed it would be wiser to wait awhile—and please! please! would Mutti and Papa try to understand!

Lotte was shaken, but managed to retain her composure. It was Mendelius who tried to reason with Katrin the problems of an unmarried couple, living in a foreign country in a period of impending disorder. Yet, somehow, the arguments lacked conviction. At bottom he was glad to see her removed from the threat which hung over them all in Tübingen. He wanted her to enjoy what happiness she could before the dark times came and the world fell apart.

In the end, it was agreed that Lotte would go with her to Paris to help her find an apartment and see her settled and that Mendelius would provide a personal capital fund which would sustain her if the love affair turned sour. All three of them were aware—though none dared put it into words—that it was at bottom a cold-blooded talk about survival, and the best terms that could be arranged to hold the family together and let the leaven of the old pieties continue to work in an unsatisfactory situation.

Afterwards, while Katrin was unpacking, Lotte wept quietly and Mendelius groped for words of comfort.

". . . I know you're disappointed, liebchen; but at least this way the family holds together and she will still turn to us in the bad times. . . . I know you'd love a white wedding and a grandchild the first year afterwards. I'm afraid I wouldn't. I'm glad to see her still free. And I'm glad we now have enough money to make her independent. . . ."

"But she's so young, Carl—and Paris seems so far away."

"The farther the better at this moment," said Mendelius bitterly. "You and I can look after each other; but the last thing I want is our children taken hostages. Dry your eyes now. Go upstairs and talk with her. She needs you just as much as you need her. . . ."

By the time Johann arrived they were all calm again and ready to interest themselves in the account of his Alpine retreat. He showed them his photographs, and enthused about the possibilities of development.

". . . The entrance is hidden at the end of a timber cutter's track. It's a long, narrow defile that opens into this strange valley, which is like an axe-cut, straight down the center of the ridge. . . . All around the lake are meadows a meter deep in good soil. . . . The woods are full of deer—but they need culling. The waterfall is here . . . and to the left of it is the entrance to the old mine workings, which are nearly half a mile long, with lots of natural passages which we didn't explore, because we're not trained and we hadn't the proper equipment. . . ."

Mendelius let him talk himself out and then put the blunt question:

"Are you still interested to acquire the place and develop it?"

"Interested—sure! But it would cost a mint of money to develop. You need labour for farming and building. You need expert advice on engineering, plumbing and even on Alpine cultivation. I got out some figures. Even if we leased the place, it would still take something like three hundred thousand deutschmarks to make it a going concern. I know we can't come up with that sort of money."

"Suppose we could. What then?"

Johann considered the question and then asked another. "Have I missed something while I've been away?"

"Quite a lot," Katrin told him ruefully. "These parents of ours have been embroiled in some rather explosive affairs. You'd better tell him from the beginning, Papa."

Mendelius told him. Johann listened intently, asking few questions, masking his feelings, as he always did. Finally Mendelius came to the postscript of his tale.

"As a result of what I have written about the abdication of Gregory the Seventeenth, I've made a lot of money. Therefore we're able to think more freely about our immediate futures. . . . But there are certain things beyond our control. We may well be at war within the next twelve months. . . . You and Katrin will be liable for military call-up in September."

"If we are," said Johann grimly, "there won't be much future to discuss."

"There may be," said Mendelius with bleak humor, "if you're interested in becoming an Alpine farmer. Agricultural workers and proprietors are normally exempt from military service. . . . If you're still keen to acquire that property in Bavaria, do it now. Start to develop it immediately. It could be a refuge as well as a productive property."

"It's a hell of a price to pay for a bomb shelter." Johann was thoughtful. "Not to mention the development costs. But, yes, it bears thinking on. Mother could come there and Franz and Katrin. We need labour anyway."

"Tell him the other thing, Carl!" Lotte cut into the talk. "This can wait."

"What other thing, Father?"

"There are people who want to kill me, son. So long as we are here together in Tübingen we are all in danger. That's why I think we should disperse for a while. Your mother's going to Paris to get Katrin settled. If you take up my offer on this property that gets you out of the way."

"And you, Father? Who takes care of you?"

"I do," said Lotte, "and I've changed my mind about Paris. If Katrin's old enough to take a lover instead of a husband, she's old enough to find and furnish her own lodgings. You and I will stay here, Carl . . . Johann can make his own decisions."

"Frankly, son, I'd much rather you were out of the University." Mendelius was suddenly eager to persuade him. "Things are going to get rough. There's a move to have security dossiers on all students. Faculty members will be required to contribute information. I've refused to go along. That means sooner or later—if I survive the assassins—I'm under fire from the security boys."

"It seems to me," said Johann deliberately, "all this is predicated on a belief that war is inevitable—global war!"

"That's right. It is."

"And do you truly believe mankind will commit to that monstrosity?"

"Mankind will have very little to do or to say about it," said Mendelius. "According to Jean Marie's vision war is already written into our futures. That's why I found myself at odds with him in Rome. On the other hand, everything I see and hear tells me that the nations are hell-bent on a confrontation over fuel and resources, and that the risk of conflict grows greater every day. So, what can I say to my adult children? Your mother and I have lived the best part of our lives. We'd like to offer you free choice about the disposition of your own."

"You are part of our lives. We can't just go about our own affairs as if you both didn't exist. . . . I'm very grateful for your offer, Father, but I want to think about it very carefully. I want to talk with you, too, little sister. There are things I have to arrange with your Franz!"

"Franz is my business." Katrin was instantly defensive. "I don't want a fight between you two."

"There'll be no fight," said Johann calmly. "But I want to be sure Franz knows what he's getting into—and what he'll have to share by way of a family responsibility. . . . It would be good, for instance, if we could recruit some sort of bodyguard for Father and Mother, from within the student body."

"Absolutely not!" Mendelius was very emphatic. "That's an immediate gain for the terrorist. He has disrupted our lives, forced us to take public precautions. Therefore he is important, potent and to be feared. No! No! No! Your mother and I—and you, too, so long as you are here—will protect each other. The handbook the police gave us is very good. I want you both to read it and . . ."

The doorbell rang. Mendelius went to answer it. Johann followed him. Mendelius recited the simple drill.

". . . Always use the spyhole in the door. If you cannot identify the caller, leave the chain bolt on when you open the door. If you receive a package you are not expecting, or an especially bulky letter, call the Kriminalamt and ask for a bomb expert to examine them. You may feel foolish if the packages are harmless but it's better than opening a booby trap which will blow your face off. . . ."

This time the caller and his package were both harmless. Alvin Dolman had come to deliver the framed prints. While Mendelius poured his drink he displayed them proudly to Lotte and the family.

". . . They look good, eh? I had a fellow in my studio yesterday who offered three times the price you paid. You see, you do get favoured-nation treatment, Professor!"

"With this family, I need it, Alvin."

"Be glad of this family, Professor. I wish I had one like it. I'm getting too old for hunting in the wildwood! Which reminds me, I was at a party last night in honour of the mime troupe. Your name came up. The leading man said they had performed for you and some journalist fellow at a party in the Hölderlinhaus."

"That's right. It turned into a long night."

"Anyway, I mentioned that I knew you and your family. Everybody seemed to know about your adventure in Rome. Then this girl buttonholed me and started asking questions."

"What girl?" Mendelius frowned. "What sort of questions?"

"Her name is Alicia Benedictus. She works for the *Schwabisches Tagblatt*. She said she was writing a profile on you for the paper."

"Did she offer any identification?"

"Why should she? We were both guests at the same party. I took her at face value—and the value was pretty good, believe me!"

In spite of his concern, Mendelius laughed. The light of lechery in Alvin Dolman's eyes was beacon-bright. Mendelius repeated his query. "What sort of questions did she ask?"

"Oh, the usual stuff: what sort of man you are; how were you regarded in the town; who were your most important friends . . . that sort of thing."

"Strange! If she works for the *Tagblatt*, she has a file full of that material. I think I'd like to check her out."

"Why, for God's sake?" Dolman was completely at a loss. "This was cocktail talk. I just thought you'd be interested that someone was doing a piece on you."

"I'm very interested, Alvin. Let's call the paper now."

He leafed through the directory and made the call, while Dolman and the family looked on. The call was brief; the information negative. There was no one on the staff called Alicia Benedictus. No one had been assigned to do a feature on Carl Mendelius. Mendelius put down the receiver and told them the news. Dolman gaped at him.

"Well, how do you like that?"

"I don't like it at all, Alvin. I'm calling Inspector Dieter Lorenz in the Kriminalamt. He'll want to see us both."

"The police? Hell, Professor! I live a nice quiet life here. I'd like to keep it that way till I go home. Why do you need the police?"

"Because there's a contract out on my life, Alvin. I was a key witness to a shooting in Rome. We know the terrorists have spotters covering me and my family in Tübingen. This girl could be one of them."

Alvin Dolman shook his head as if he were trying to clear it of cobwebs. He swore softly, "Christ! Who'd have believed it? They're gunning for academics now—and in Tübingen yet! O.K., Professor, let's call the cops and get it over with."

Fifteen minutes later they were in the office of Dieter Lorenz at the Landeskriminalamt. Lorenz put Dolman through a lengthy interrogation, then settled him in an interview room with a cup of coffee, a sketch pad and an instruction to produce a likeness of the girl who called herself Alicia Benedictus. Then, back in his own office, he asked Mendelius:

"How close are you to this Dolman?"

Mendelius shrugged. "Not that close; but I've known him for years. I've had him to drinks many times but rarely to dinner. I buy prints from him. I drop in at his studio sometimes for a glass of wine and a chat. I find him an agreeable jester. Why do you ask? Do you have anything against him?"

"Nothing." Lorenz was frank about it. "But he's one of those characters who always bother a policeman in a provincial town like this. A criminal you can deal with. You can ship home a guest-worker who gets into trouble. But this type is different. You can see no good reason why he stays. He's an American. He's divorced from a local girl. He's gainfully employed but there's no way he can make a reputation or a fortune. Also he's a raffish type. When he gets bored, you find him in the boozy bars and the wilder student nightclubs. His house parties make a lot of noise, and we get complaints from neighbours. So, because he's popular and a bit rowdy and a high spender, we wonder if he's got any sidelines like hash or heroin or receiving stolen goods. To this point he's clean. . . . But I still have to ask whether he could be spotting for the group that is out to get you or whether he's connected with these mysterious folk who, you told me, were supposed to be shadowing Mr. Rainer. . . ."

"It sounds a little far-fetched to me," said Mendelius.

"It probably is," Lorenz agreed patiently. "But sometimes in this business you get nasty surprises. Dolman's an artist. We've found a sketch of you in the pocket of a dead man. Wouldn't it be odd if it were done by Alvin Dolman?"

"Impossible! I've known the man for years!"

Lorenz shrugged off the objection. "It's the impossible that happens every day. Anyway, he's making another sketch now. It will be instructive to compare the two."

Mendelius was suddenly edgy and irritable. "You've put me in an intolerable position, Inspector. I can't continue to be friendly with Dolman and not tell him what you've told me."

"I don't mind your telling him." Lorenz seemed mildly surprised. "It helps me. If he's innocent, he'll go out of his way to cooperate and he's got a lot of useful contacts in town. If he's guilty, then he'll get restless and begin making mistakes."

"Don't you ever get sick of this game, Inspector?"

"I like the game, Professor; I dislike the people with whom I have to play it. . . . Excuse me, I'll see how Dolman's coming along with his art work."

As they left the police station and strolled homewards through the warm summer air, Dolman seemed philosophic about his situation. He brushed aside Mendelius' apologies with weary humour.

". . . Don't fret about it, Professor! I understand Lorenz and his kind. I'm a fringe operator, always have been, even in the Army. The only time I'm surprised is when someone drops a coin in the blind man's hat instead of kicking him in the teeth. . . . However, just between you and me, I have no interest in getting you knocked off and no connection with any group. I'm strictly a loner—and I'm sure Lorenz is bright enough to see it. What he figures is that because I get around and meet a lot of oddballs, I might stumble on some useful information. . . . Because it's you that's involved, I'm prepared to cooperate. Also, I don't like being played for a sucker—which is what Miss Alicia Benedictus tried to do. . . . All in all, Professor, this has been one lousy day! This used to be a nice cozy town. You could wrap it round yourself like strudel pastry. Now . . . ? I don't like it anymore. I think I'll start packing very soon. . . . You go on home, Professor. I know a girl who keeps a bottle of brandy warm just for Alvin Dolman!"

He turned away and strode across the bridge, a big aggressive man thrusting heedless through the shoppers and the loiterers. Mendelius turned down the path that led to the gardens. He did not want to go home yet. He needed time and quiet to set his thoughts in order. The family needed privacy to discuss the radical proposals he had made to them.

It was a warm, bright day and the burghers of Tübingen were sunning themselves on the lawns. Down by the lake a small crowd had gathered to watch the theatrical troupe working with a group of very young schoolchildren. It was a charming scene—the youngsters wide-eyed and wondering, totally absorbed in the tale of a sad clown who blew beautiful bubbles but could never coax one of them to rest on his hand. The clown was the cadaverous fellow who had entertained them at the Hölderlinhaus. The rest of the troupe played the bubbles who mocked his efforts to catch them. . . .

Mendelius sat on the grass and watched the small, innocent opera, fascinated to see how the children, timid at first, were drawn to participate in the mimicry. After the grim and grandiose debates in which he had been engaged, this simple experience was a matter of strange joy. Unconsciously he found himself aping their smirks and bows and fluttering gestures. The clown noticed him and, a few moments later, began to mime a new story. He summoned the other players and their attendant children and conveyed to them in dumb show that a new, strange creature was in their midst. Was it a dog? No. A rabbit? No. A tiger, an elephant, a pig? No. Then they must inspect it—but very, very cautiously. Finger to lips, walking on tiptoe, he led them, single file, to examine this extraordinary animal. . . .

The audience chuckled when they saw that the butt of the joke was a middle-aged fellow running to fat. Mendelius, after a moment of uncertainty, decided to join the comedy. As the actors and the children circled him he played back to them as he had once played charades with his own children. Finally, he revealed himself as a big stork standing on one leg and looking down his long beak. The audience applauded. The children laughed excitedly at their triumph. The clown and his troupe mimed their thanks. A tiny girl caught at his hand and told him:

"I knew before anybody. I really knew you were a stork!"

"I'm sure you did, liebchen."

And as he bent to talk to the little mite, Mendelius had a sudden sickening thought of what she would look like after the first blast of radiation, or a lethal infection of anthrax.

That evening at supper Katrin and Johann dominated the talk, reading an unexpected lesson to their parents. Katrin's argument was very simple.

". . . Mother has said it. If I'm old enough to go off with a man, I'm old enough to manage my own affairs. . . . Franz and I have to improve our relationship before we can think of getting married. In spite of his success with the gallery he's still very uncertain of himself . . . and I have to find a few pieces of me, too. I'm lucky. Thanks to Papa I've got financial security. . . . But for the rest I always do better if there's no one holding my hand. . . ."

"But Franz wants to marry you," Lotte objected. "He told me he's asked you several times."

"I know he does; but he wants a *Hausfrau,* someone to make him feel safe and well nourished—and reassure him that he's a genius. I don't want that role—and I don't want him to get stuck in his dependence either. He has to learn that we're partners as well as lovers."

"And what will happen," asked Johann with a grin, "if he doesn't learn as fast as you'd like, little sister?"

"Then, big brother, I find someone else!"

Lotte and Mendelius exchanged the rueful looks of parents who find themselves left far behind in argument. Mendelius asked:

"And you, Johann? Have you given any thought to my proposal?"

"A lot of thought, Father—and I'm afraid the idea doesn't work for me."

"For any special reason?"

"One and one only. You're offering to buy me out of a situation I have to handle for myself. I hate the idea of war. I see it as a vast, horrible futility. I don't want to be conscripted for gun-fodder—but I've never felt special enough to . . . well, to be exempted from the destiny of my own peer group. I've got to stay with it, at least long enough to decide whether I belong there or in opposition. . . . I'm not explaining this very well. I appreciate your care for me; but in this case, it goes further than I want or need."

"I'm glad you can be honest with us, son." Mendelius was hard put to conceal his emotion. "We don't want to run your life. The best gift we can give you is liberty and the conscience to use it. . . . So let me ask all my family a question. Does anybody object if I buy the valley?"

"What would you use it for?" Johann stared at him in surprise.

"Your father has a dream of his own." Lotte reached out to touch Mendelius' hand. "When he retires he'd like to found an academy for postgraduate studies—a place where senior scholars can meet and share the learning of a lifetime. If he wants to try it—then I support him."

"I think it's a wonderful idea." Katrin was full of enthusiasm. "I keep saying to Franz that everybody has to keep reaching out all the time. If you get too secure you go stale and fusty."

"You've got my vote, Father." Johann looked at Mendelius with a new respect. "If I can help to get the place started, count on me. . . . And if things get too rough at the University, you can always opt for early retirement."

"I'll call the lawyers first thing in the morning. They should start negotiating with the Gräfin. Next week I'll go down and look at the property. I'd like you to come with me, Johann."

"Of course."

"What about you, Lotte? Would you like to come?"

"Later, Carl. This time you and Johann should go together. Katrin and I have our own things to do."

"I'm really excited." Mendelius expounded his plan. "I'd like to talk to a good architect—a special kind of man with an interest in the ambience of living. . . ."

"We're all being very calm and logical," said Lotte abruptly. "But I've got the terrible feeling life won't turn out quite the way you expect."

"Probably it won't, liebchen; but we have to hope and act as if it will. In spite of Jean Marie's prophecies I still believe we can influence the course of human events."

"Enough and in time to prevent a war?"

There was a hint of hidden desperation in Lotte's question. It was almost as if she expected her children to be snatched suddenly from the dinner table. Mendelius gave her a swift worried look and said, with more confidence than he felt:

"Enough and in time, yes. I'm even hopeful that the publication of our piece on Sunday will focus world attention on the urgency of new initiatives for peace."

"But," Johann objected, "half the world will never see what you've written, Father."

"All the leaders will," Mendelius persisted, if only to shake Lotte out of her black mood. "All the intelligence services will read and evaluate the material. . . Never underrate the diffusion of even the simplest news item. . . . Now, why don't we clear the table and get the wash-up done. They're doing *The Magic Flute* on television. Your mother and I would like to watch it. . . ."

Halfway through the performance the telephone rang. Georg Rainer was on the line from Berlin.

". . . Carl? I think I've made sense of our amateur spies. It's clear now that Monsignor Logue passed the word that I would be working on this story. I think the surveillance was organized just to establish that fact. Now the Vatican has decided to issue its own account of the abdication. There will be a formal statement running to about three thousand words in next Tuesday's edition of *Osservatore Romano*. That means we'll be out first, and there'll be some red faces over the mistake in timing! . . . I understand the text of the Vatican release will be made available in the secular press on Monday afternoon. I'll call you if there's anything in it that affects our position. . . ."

"How do your editors feel about our piece, Georg?"

"Everyone's excited about it. Interesting though, there's a lively betting market on the kind of reaction we'll get from the public."

"How are they phrasing the bet?"

"Who will come out best in the popularity stakes—the Vatican or the onetime Pope? Listening to the office talk, I'm not sure anymore. . . . I'll be back in Rome on Monday morning. I'll call you from there. Love to Lotte."

"And to Pia."

"Oh, I almost forgot. We've decided to become engaged. Or at least Pia did and I gave my reluctant consent."

"Congratulations!"

"I'd rather be poor and free!"

"The hell you would! Thanks for calling, Georg."

"Do you want me to place a bet for you in the papal sweepstake?"

"Ten marks on Gregory the Seventeenth. We have to support our own candidate!"

A week later the verdict was in. The Rainer/Mendelius account of the abdication was received with lively interest by the public, and by the pundits with qualified respect. There was a reluctant agreement that it "clarified many issues left diplomatically vague in the Vatican account." There was question whether the authors "may not have inflated a crisis in the religious bureaucracy to the dimension of a global tragedy."

The London *Times* provided the most judicious summing-up in a leader written by its Roman Catholic editor.

. . . The authors, each within his own competence, have written an honest brief. Their history is carefully documented; their speculations are based on sound logic. They have illuminated some of the dark byways of Vatican politics. If they have tended to exaggerate the importance of a papal abdication in twentieth-century history, it must be said in their defence that the ruined majesty of Rome can play tricks with the soberest imagination.

What they do not exaggerate, however, is the perennial power of a religious idea to rouse men's passions and incite them to the most revolutionary action. It says much for the collective wisdom of the hinge-men of the Roman Catholic Church that they were prepared to act promptly and in unity against what they saw as a revival of the ancient Gnostic heresy. It says even more for the deep spirituality of Pope Gregory XVII that he chose to retire from office rather than divide the assembly of believers.

Professor Carl Mendelius is a sober scholar of world repute. His tribute to his patron and longtime friend reveals him as an ardent and loyal man with more than a touch of the poet. He is wise enough to admit that human polity cannot be directed by the visions of the mystics. He is humble enough to know that the visions may contain truths which we ignore at our peril.

It was the misfortune of Gregory XVII that he seemed to be writing prematurely the epitaph of mankind. It is his fortune that the memorial of his reign has been written with eloquence and with love. . . .

Mendelius was too intelligent a man not to see the irony of the situation. With Georg Rainer's help he had raised a monument to an old friend; but the monument was a gravestone, beneath which lay buried forever the last vestiges of influence and power which Jean Marie might have exercised. No man could have served the new Pontiff and his policies better than Carl Mendelius. It was fitting that his labours should have made him a millionaire and given him a reputation far beyond the merits of his scholarship. But the most bitter irony of all was a note of thanks from Jean Marie in Monte Cassino.

. . . I thank you both from the bottom of my heart for what you tried to do. No man could have had better advocates or more gallant friends. The truth has been told with understanding and compassion. Now the chapter can be closed and the work of the Church can proceed.

So, you must not talk as though all is lost. The yeast is working in the dough; the seed, scattered on the wind, will germinate in its own time. . . . As for the money, I grudge you not a centime of it. I trust you will spend some of it happily on Lotte and the children.

Be calm, dear friend, and wait for the words and the sign.

Yours always in Christ Jesus,
Jean Marie

Lotte, reading the letter over his shoulder, rumpled his hair and said quietly, "Leave it now, my love! You did your best and Jean knows it. The people in this house need you, too."

"I need you also, liebchen." He took her hands and drew her round to face him. "I've meddled long enough in the big world. I'm a scholar, not a gadfly journalist. . . . I'm glad we start lectures again tomorrow."

"Have you got all your stuff together?"

"Most of it." He held up a wad of typescript and laughed. "That's the first subject for this term. Look at the title: 'The Nature of Prophecy'!"

"Talking of prophecy," said Lotte. "I'll give you one. We're going to have a great season of gossip in town when Katrin goes off to Paris with her Franz. How are we going to deal with it?"

"Tell the old girls to jump in the Neckar!" said Mendelius with a grin. "Most of them gave up their own virginity in a punt under the willows!"

Every day during term time Carl Mendelius left his house at eight-thirty in the morning, walked down the Kirchgasse to the market, where he bought himself a boutonniere from the oldest character in the square: a raw-tongued grandmother from Bebenhausen. From there it was a short two blocks to the Illustrious College, which he entered always by the southeast gate under the arms of Duke Christoph and his motto: NACH GOTTES WILLEN—According to God's Will. Once inside he went straight to his study and spent half-an-hour checking over his notes, and the daily stack of memoranda from the administration office of the University. At nine-thirty precisely he was on the rostrum in the aula with his notes stacked neatly on the lectern.

Before he left the house on this first Monday of term, Lotte reminded him of the police warning to vary his route and his procedures. Mendelius shrugged impatiently. He had three streets to choose from; and lectures always began at nine-thirty. There weren't too many permutations to be made. Anyway, at least on his first morning, he wanted to sport a flower in his buttonhole. Lotte kissed him and showed him out of the house.

The ritual of arrivals was accomplished without incident. He spent ten minutes chatting in the quadrangle with the Rector of the College, then went up to his study, which, thanks to the ministrations of the housekeeper, was immaculately tidy and smelled of beeswax and furniture polish. His gown hung behind the door. His mail was stacked on the desk. The term schedules were penned on his message rack. He felt a sudden sense of relief, almost of liberation. This was home country. He could walk it blindfold.

He unpacked his briefcase, checked the texts of his day's lectures, then addressed himself to the mail. Most of it was routine material; but there was one rather bulky envelope with the President's seal on it. The superscription was faintly ominous: "Private and Confidential—Urgent—Deliver by Messenger."

Since the faculty meeting the President had been studiously silent on all matters of contention, and it was not at all impossible that he wanted to stage a set-piece battle with every order in writing. Mendelius hesitated to open the missive. The last thing he wanted was to be distracted before the first lecture of term. Finally, ashamed of his timidity, he slipped a paper knife under the flap of the envelope.

When his students came running after the explosion, they found him lying on the floor with his hand blown off and his face a bloody mess.

BOOK TWO

The voice of one crying in the wilderness:
Prepare ye the way of the Lord, make straight His paths.

—Isaiah 40:3

VIII

His Holiness Pope Leo XIV settled his bulky body deeper in the chair, propped his gouty foot on the stool under his desk and surveyed his visitor like an old and ill-tempered eagle. He announced in his harsh Aemilian accent:

"Frankly, my friend, you are a great nuisance to me."

Jean Marie Barette permitted himself a wintry smile and agreed. "Unfortunately, Holiness, it is easier to be rid of redundant kings than supernumerary Popes."

"I don't like the idea of your visit to Tübingen. I like even less the idea of your cantering around the world like some fashionable Jesuit intellectual. We made a bargain over your abdication."

"Correction," said Jean Marie curtly. "There was no bargain. I signed the instrument under duress. I put myself voluntarily under obedience to Abbot Andrew—and he has told me I must in charity visit Carl Mendelius and his family. Mendelius is critically ill. He could die at any moment."

"Yes, well . . . !" His Holiness was too seasoned a bureaucrat to court a confrontation. "I will not interfere with your Abbot's decision; but I remind you that you have no canonical mission. You are expressly debarred from public preaching or teaching. Your faculties to ordain clergy are suspended—but you are not of course prohibited from the celebration of Mass or the Sacraments."

"Why are you so afraid of me, Holiness?"

"Afraid? Nonsense!"

"Then why have you never offered to restore to me the functions of my bishopric and my priesthood?"

"Because it seemed expedient for the good of the Church."

"You realize that so far as my apostolic vocation is concerned, I am reduced to impotence. I believe I have a right to know when and in what circumstances my faculties may be restored, and I may be given a canonical mission."

"I cannot tell you that. No decision has yet been made."

"What is the reason for the delay?"

"We have other concerns, more pressing."

"With great respect, Holiness, whatever your concerns, even you are not dispensed from natural justice."

"You reprove me? Here in my own house?"

"I, too, lived here once. I never felt like an owner, but rather like a tenant—which as events proved, I was."

"Let's get to the point of this visit. What do you want of me?"

"Dispensation to live in the lay state, to travel freely and exercise my priestly functions in private."

"Impossible!"

"What is the alternative, Holiness? Surely it would embarrass you more to keep me a prisoner on my own parole at Monte Cassino."

"This whole situation is a mess!" His Holiness winced as he moved his gouty foot on the stool.

"I offer you a way out of it. Look! Rainer and Mendelius published an honest account of the abdication. They thought they were defending me; but what was the real result? Business as usual in the Church; and you settled beyond attainder in the Chair of Peter! If I tried to change that situation—which, believe me, I have no desire to do—I should make a public idiot of myself. Please! Can you not see that far from being a threat or a nuisance I may even be able to help you?"

"You can't help me by propagating these lunatic ideas about the Last Days and the Second Coming!"

"Do they look so lunatic from where you sit now?"

His Holiness shifted uneasily in his chair. He cleared his throat noisily and dabbed at his cheeks with a silk handkerchief. "Well! . . . I'll admit we're approaching a highly critical situation; but I can't give myself nightmares about it. I go on doing what falls to my hand each day and . . ."

He broke off, embarrassed by the cool scrutiny of the man he had ousted. Jean Marie said nothing. Finally His Holiness found voice again.

"Now let me see, where were we? Oh, this request of yours!

. . . If your situation at Monte Cassino isn't satisfactory, if you do want to return to private life, why don't we make an interim arrangement, *in petto* as it were, without any documents or formalities. If it doesn't work out, then we both have other recourse. Does that make sense?"

"Very good sense, Holiness." Jean Marie was studiously grateful. "I shall make sure you have no cause to regret it. Presumably the arrangement begins now."

"Of course."

"Then I leave for Tübingen in the morning. I've procured myself a French passport and returned the Vatican document to the Secretariat of State."

"That wasn't necessary." His Holiness was relieved enough to be magnanimous.

"It was desirable," said Jean Marie Barette mildly. "As a man without a canonical mission I should not want to give the impression that I had one."

"What do you propose to do with yourself?"

"I'm not quite sure, Holiness." His smile was limpid as a child's. "I'll probably end up telling the good news to children at the crossroads. But, first I must visit my friend Carl."

"Do you think . . ." His Holiness seemed oddly embarrassed. "Do you think Mendelius and his family would like me to send them a papal blessing?"

"Mendelius is still critically ill; but I'm sure his wife would appreciate the gesture."

"I'll sign the scroll and have my secretary post it first thing in the morning."

"Thank you. Do I have your Holiness' leave to go?"

"You have our leave."

Unconsciously he had slipped into the antique form. Then, as if to make amends for an unnecessary formality, he struggled painfully to his feet and held out his hand. Jean Marie bent over the ring which once he had worn in his own right. For the first time Leo XIV seemed touched by a genuine regret. He said awkwardly:

"Perhaps . . . perhaps if we'd known each other better, none of this need have happened."

"If this had not happened, Holiness, if I had not reached out for support in my solitude, Carl Mendelius would now be healthy and whole in his house!"

* * *

That same evening Anton Cardinal Drexel entertained him to dinner and their talk was of a far different kind. Jean Marie explained eagerly what he had concealed so carefully in his interview with the Pontiff.

". . . When I heard what had happened to Carl, I knew beyond all shadow of doubt that this was the sign and the summons I had been waiting for. It's a terrible thought, Anton, but the sign is always of contradiction: man in agony begging to be released from it. Poor Carl! Poor Lotte! It was the son who sent me the telegram. He felt his father would wish me near him and his mother begged me to come. I was terrified that our Pontiff would refuse permission. Having gone so far in conformity I did not want a battle at this stage."

"You were lucky," said Drexel drily. "He hasn't yet seen this stuff. Georg Rainer sent it round by messenger this afternoon."

He reached behind him to the buffet and picked up a large manila envelope filled with glossy press photographs. All of them were from Tübingen. They showed a city caught in a mediaeval fervor of pageant, piety and plain riot.

In the hospital Mendelius was shown bandaged like a mummy, with only his mouth and nostrils visible, while a nurse kept vigil by the bed and armed police stood guard at the door. In the Stiftskirche and the Jakobskirche, men, women and children knelt in prayer. Students paraded on the campus carrying crude banners: NO FOREIGN KILLERS! GUEST-WORKERS, GUEST-MURDERERS! WHO SILENCED MENDELIUS? WHY ARE THE POLICE SILENT TOO?

In the industrial sectors of the suburbs, local youths battled with Turkish labourers. In the marketplace a politician addressed a lunchtime crowd. Behind him a four-colour poster screamed the slogan: IF YOU WANT SAFETY IN THE STREETS, VOTE MULLER! . . . Jean Marie Barette studied the pictures in silence.

Drexel said, "Incredible, isn't it. It's almost as if they've been waiting for a martyr! And the same demonstrations are being made in other German cities."

Jean Marie shivered as if some squamous creature had touched him.

"Carl Mendelius in the role of Horst Wessel! It's a horrible thought. I wonder what the family thinks of all this?"

"I asked Georg Rainer. He told me the wife is deeply shocked. She is rarely seen. The daughter looks after her at home. The son gave an interview in which he said that his father would be horrified if he knew what was being done. He claimed that the tragedy was being stage-managed to create a social vendetta."

"Stage-managed by whom?"

"Extremists of the left and the right."

"Not very specific, is it?"

"But these"—Drexel tapped the photographs spread on the table—"these are terribly, dangerously specific. This is the old black magic of the manipulators and the demagogues."

"It is more than that." Jean Marie Barette was suddenly somber. "It is as if the evil that lurks in man has suddenly found a focus in this little provincial town. Mendelius is a good man. Yet he, in his extremity, is made the hero of this—this witches' sabbath! That's gallows humour, Anton, and it frightens me."

Drexel gave him a shrewd, sidelong look and began replacing the photographs in the envelope. He asked, casually enough, "Now that you are free and able to be anonymous, do you have any plans at all?"

"To visit old friends, to hear what they say about our sorry world—but always to wait for the hand's touch, to listen for the voice that will tell me where I am commanded to be. I know it sounds strange to you; but to me it seems perfectly natural. I am Pascal's thinking reed, waiting for the wind to bend me in its passing."

"But in the face of this evil"—Drexel tossed the package of photographs on to the bureau—"in the face of the other evils that will follow, what will you do? You cannot bend to every wind, or leave every shout unanswered."

"If God chooses to borrow my vagrant voice, he will find the words for me to use."

"You talk like an Illuminist!" Drexel smiled to take the edge off the allusion. "I'm glad our colleagues in the Congregation can't hear you."

"You should tell our colleagues." There was a ring of steel in Jean Marie's answer. "They will soon hear the battle cry of Michael the Archangel. '*Quis sicut Deus?*' Who is like to God? For all their syllogisms I wonder how many will rise to the challenge and confront the Antichrist? Has any of the Friends of Silence denounced the excesses in Tübingen and elsewhere?"

"If they have"—Drexel shrugged—"we haven't heard of it. But then, they are prudent men. They prefer to let passions cool before they speak. . . . However, you and I are too old to mourn over the follies of our brethren—and we're too old to cure them either. Tell me something, Jean. It may sound an impertinent question; but the answer is important to me."

"Ask it then."

"You're sixty-five years old. You've risen as high as a man can go. Today you've put yourself back to zero. You have no calling, no visible future. What do you really want?"

"Enough light to see a divine sense in this mad world. Enough faith to follow the light. That's the core of it all, isn't it? Faith to move mountains, to say to the cripple: 'Arise and walk!' "

"We also need some love to make the darkness tolerable."

"Amen to that!" said Jean Marie softly. "I must go, Anton. I've kept you up late."

"Before you leave . . . how are you placed for money?"

"Well enough, thank you. I have a patrimony, administered by my brother, who is a banker in Paris."

"Where are you staying tonight?"

"There's a pilgrim hostel over by Santa Cecilia. I lodged there when I first came to Rome."

"Why not stay here? I have a spare room."

"Thank you, Anton, but no! I don't belong here anymore. I have to acclimatize myself to the world. I may want to sit late in the piazza and talk to the lonely ones." He added with an odd humorous pathos: "Perhaps, in the last cold hour before the day-spring, *He* may want to talk to me. . . . Please understand and pray for me."

"I wish I could come with you, Jean."

"You were made for better company, old friend. I was born under a falling star. Almost, it feels as if I were going home." He gestured towards the lights that marked the papal apartments. . . . "Stay close to our friend upstairs. He is named for a lion but he is really a house-trained pussycat. When the bad times come he will need a strong man at his side. . . ."

A handshake, a brief farewell, and he was gone, a lean, frail figure swallowed up in the shadows of the stairwell. Anton Cardinal Drexel poured himself the last of the wine and pondered wryly on the aphorism of another Illuminist, Louis Claude de Saint-Martin: "All mystics speak the same language because they come from the same country."

* * *

The journey to Tübingen was a lesson in his own inadequacy. For the first time in forty years he wore civilian clothes and it took him half-an-hour to adjust the cravat under his summer shirt. In the monastery he had been cushioned by a familiar routine. In the Vatican his every move had been attended. Now he was totally without privilege. He had to shout for a taxi to take him to the airport, argue with the bustling Roman who claimed to have called it first. He had no small notes for the tip and the driver dismissed him with contempt. There was no one to direct him to the counter where he must pick up his ticket for Stuttgart. The girl had no change for his large bank notes, and he had never owned a credit card in all his clerical life.

In the Vatican the bodily functions of the Pope were carried on in sacred privacy. In the airport urinal he stood in line, while the drunk next to him sprayed his shoes and his trouser leg. At the bar, he was jostled and had coffee spilled on his sleeve; and, for a final indignity, the aircraft was overbooked and he had to argue his way into a seat.

On board he was faced with a question of identity. His neighbour was an elderly woman from the Rhineland, nervous and voluble. Once betrayed into speaking German, he was drowned in the torrent of her talk. Finally, she asked him what he did for a living. It took him a good ten seconds to frame the obvious answer.

"I am retired, dear lady."

"My husband's retired. He's become quite impossible. How does your wife take to having you round the house all the time?"

"I'm a bachelor."

"Strange that a handsome man like you never married."

"I'm afraid I was married to my career."

"What were you? A doctor? A lawyer?"

"Both," Jean Marie assured her solemnly—and solaced his conscience with a casuist's logic. He had indeed been a doctor of souls; and there was law enough in the Vatican to choke Justinian.

When he arrived in Stuttgart, he was met by Johann Mendelius, eager to welcome him, but somehow dour and strained like a junior officer, come from his first battlefield. He called Jean Marie "sir," avoiding all clerical titles. He drove carefully round the hill roads, taking the longer route into Tübingen because, as he put it, there were things to be explained before they arrived.

". . . Father is still desperately ill. The explosive in the letter bomb was sandwiched between wafers of aluminum and impregnated with tiny ball-bearings. Some of these are embedded in one eye socket, very close to the brain. We know he has lost the sight of that eye and may lose the other. We haven't seen his face; but it is obviously much mutilated, and, of course, he has lost his left hand. Other operations will be necessary, but not until he is much stronger. There is still a dangerous infection in the arm and the eye socket and the range of antibiotics that he can tolerate is very limited. . . . So we wait. Mother, Katrin and I visit the hospital by turns. . . . Mother is holding up extraordinarily well. . . . She has courage for all of us; but don't be surprised if she gets very emotional when she sees you. . . . We've told no one else you are coming except Professor Meissner. She's Father's closest friend on the faculty. . . . The way things are now, everyone in Tübingen is peddling some gossip or other. As soon as Father recovers—if he does—I'm moving him far away."

The undertone of anger and bitterness was not lost on Jean Marie Barette. He said, "I heard about the demonstrations. Georg Rainer sent photographs to the Vatican. Apparently feelings are running high."

"Too high!" The rejoinder was abrupt. "My father was well known and respected, yes! But he was never a very public man. These parades and demonstrations were not spontaneous; they were subtly and carefully organized."

"In so short a time?" Jean Marie was dubious. "By whom? And for what reasons?"

"As a propaganda piece to hide the real authors of the attempt on my father's life."

"If you will kindly pull in to the next parking bay," said Jean Marie Barette firmly, "we'll talk this out before we get to Tübingen. Unlike your father I have been a very public man—and I do not want to walk into any surprises!"

Half a mile farther on they parked between a meadow and a pinewood and Johann Mendelius gave his reading of the attempted assassination.

". . . We begin in Rome. By pure accident, Father is a witness to a terrorist killing. Big headlines, big warnings: there may be attempts to silence him or exact reprisals on him and his family. All that is clear, simple and logical. . . . Father and Mother come back to Tübingen. The criminal police contact them with renewed warnings. A drawing of my father is found in the pocket of a man killed in a bar brawl. More words of caution. . . . Meantime, the President of the University tells his senior faculty to expect a military call-up, to be ready to supply scientific specialists for the armed services and to cooperate in security surveillance of the student body. My father objects very strongly to the surveillance. He threatens to resign if it is enforced. . . . On top of that he writes the account of your abdication and is suddenly known all over the world. There is a smell of politics about the question which is not lost on our German ministries. . . . My father is no longer simply an academic—he is an international figure. In a time when the men at the top are gearing up to sell a war to the unwary public, my father could be considered dangerous. . . ."

"And as he is already under threat from an underground group, there is splendid cover for an officially sanctioned assassination!"

"Exactly," said Johann Mendelius. "And when the attempt is made, the whole town is manipulated into a protest. There's a bonus, too! Demonstrations against the guest-workers hasten the day when they can be shipped home or turned to forced labour in a wartime situation!"

"You've read me the hypothesis," said Jean Marie Barette calmly. "Now show me the proof!"

"I don't have proof, only grounds for very deep suspicion."

"For instance?"

"You say you saw photographs of student demonstrations. I saw the demonstrators themselves—and I'm certain most of them never saw the inside of a lecture hall. The newspapers published a diagram of the letter bomb, supposedly supplied by the police forensic department. The real bomb was something quite different—a highly sophisticated device fabricated with laboratory precision."

"Who told you that?"

"Dieter Lorenz. He was my father's contact in the Kriminalamt. Two days after the event, he was promoted and transferred to Stuttgart—off the case!"

"Anything else?"

"Lots of small things; but they only make sense in the context of this special town of ours. I'm not the only one who thinks like this. Professor Meissner agrees with me—and she's a very bright lady. You'll meet her at our house this evening. . . ."

"One more question. Have you said anything of this to your mother?"

"No. She has enough to worry about; and the sympathy of the townspeople helps her."

"Your father, of course, knows nothing?"

"We have no idea how much he knows." The young man made a weary gesture. "He can make sounds of recognition; he squeezes our hands to acknowledge what we say; but that's all. Sometimes I think death would be a mercy for him."

"He will survive. His real work has not begun yet."

"I wish I could believe that, sir."

"Do you believe in God?"

"No."

"That does make life difficult."

"On the contrary, it simplifies it very much. However brutal the facts may be, you don't complicate them with religious fiction."

"You've just told me a story which, if it is true, is as near to pure evil as it is possible to get. Your father is mutilated, may yet die, in an assassination attempt by agents of your own country. What is your remedy against those who treat murder as a simple political expedient?"

"If you really want the answer to that, sir, I'll show it to you tomorrow. . . . May we go now?"

"Before we do, I want a favour from you, Johann."

"Ask it, please!"

"You are the son of my dear friend. Please don't call me sir. My name is Jean Marie."

For the first time the young man relaxed and his taut features twitched into a smile. He shook his head. "That won't work, I'm afraid. Mother and Father would be shocked if I used your Christian name."

"How about Uncle Jean? It will save a lot of unnecessary explanations when you introduce me to your friends."

"Uncle Jean . . ." He tested the phrase once and again, then he grinned and nodded agreement. "So, Uncle Jean, let me get you home. We are to have an early lunch because Mother wants to take you to the hospital at three this afternoon." Johann eased the car out onto the highway and slipped ahead of a big hauler with a load of pine logs. "How long will you be able to stay with us?"

"Only a day or two; but long enough, I hope, to be of some use to your father and your mother—perhaps also to make the acquaintance of the noonday devil who has come to live in your town."

"The noonday devil!" Johann Mendelius gave him a sidelong tolerant smile. "I haven't heard that since Bible class."

"But you're not afraid of him?"

"Yes, I'm afraid." His answer was swift and simple. "But not of devils and spirit adversaries. I'm frightened of us—men and women—and the terrible destructive madness that takes hold of us all. . . . If I knew for certain who did this to my father I would kill him without a second thought."

"To what end?"

"Justice—to set the balance straight again, deter the future adversary."

"It's your father who is the victim. Would he approve?"

"Wrong, Uncle Jean! Father's not the only victim. What about Mother, Katrin, me—all the folk in the town who have been infected by this single act? Nothing will ever be the same again—for any of us."

"It seems to me," said Jean Marie deliberately, "you have a very clear idea of the nature of evil—and of the evil one as adversary. . . . But what about good? How does that present itself to you?"

"Very simply!" His voice was suddenly tight and hard. "My mother is good. She's brave and she's not a woman who finds it easy to be so. She thinks of us and Father before she thinks of herself. . . . By me that's goodness. Father is good, too. You look in his face and you see a *Mensch*, and there's always enough love to get you through the bad times. . . . But you'll see what's happened to these good people! . . . And I'm glad you're coming as plain Uncle Jean; because I don't think I'd have wanted to know you as Pope. . . ."

"That's the worst piece of logic I've ever heard." Jean Marie gave a wry chuckle. "You'd have been very flattered to know me. I was a much more agreeable fellow then than I am now. When I was elected one journalist called me the most personable of modern princes! Remember, it isn't always the prince who is the evildoer. Generally he's not clever enough to be a Satan. The real adversary is the one who whispers malice in his ear and offers to do his dirty work and keep him immune from bad report. . . ."

"But whichever is the evil one, we get him because we deserve him." Johann drove with deliberate care, as if he feared the discussion might excite him to some dangerous maneuver. "We want to be always innocent and out of the reach of malice. Father took the precautions he was told to take, but no more. An excessive care was beneath his dignity. He saw it as a triumph for terror. I don't see it that way. I walk very softly. I watch, I listen —and I carry a gun that I'm not afraid to use. Does that shock you, Uncle Jean?"

"No, it doesn't. It just makes me wonder how you will feel when you kill your first human being."

"I hope I never have to do it."

"Yet you go constantly prepared for that sole act. The man who tried to kill your father did it at a distance, mechanically, like blasting rock in a quarry. But with a pistol you will kill face to face. You will hear the cry of the victim in agony. You will see death in his eyes. You will smell blood. . . . Are you ready for that?"

"As I told you," said Johann Mendelius with wintry simplicity, "I hope the moment never comes; but, yes, I am ready for it."

Jean Marie Barette said nothing. The matter was beyond argument. He hoped it was not beyond the saving power of grace. He remembered the stark empty landscape of the vision, the planet from which mankind had obliterated itself, so that there was nothing and no one left to love.

His meeting with Lotte was strange at first. There was a moment of shock, almost of disappointment, when she saw him dressed in a layman's clothes. A sudden embarrassment held her back even from a hand's touch. He had to take her arms and draw her to him. For a split second it seemed that she would reject the embrace; then her control snapped and she clung to him, sobbing quietly, while he soothed her like a child, with small and tender words.

Katrin came home at that moment. Johann presented her to Uncle Jean, and after the first flurry of embarrassed talk, they were able to be calm together. Katrin had the morning's report on her father.

". . . I saw Doctor Pelzer. He's not very happy. The fever has flared up again. Papa doesn't respond to talk as well as he did yesterday. You know how he presses your hand when he understands something? Well, this morning I could only get an occasional response. The rest of the time he seemed to be unconscious. . . . Doctor Pelzer said I could leave. If there's any sudden change, we'll be called."

Lotte nodded and turned away to busy herself with the luncheon preparations. Katrin followed her out to the kitchen.

Johann said brusquely, "This is what it's like. We're all on a seesaw: up one moment, down the next. That's why I don't want to build up false hopes for Mother or Katrin. I don't want them clutching at cobwebs."

"You're afraid I may try to give them false hope?"

"You told me Father would live."

"I'm sure he will."

"I am not sure; so I'd rather Mother and Katrin learned to live with uncertainty. There'll be grief enough whether Father lives or dies."

"I'm your guest. Of course I'll respect your wishes."

At that moment Lotte came in carrying a linen cloth and napkins. She handed them to Johann and asked him to lay the table. She took Jean Marie's arm and led him into the next room.

". . . Katrin's doing the lunch. We can be quiet for a few minutes. . . . It's funny I can't get used to seeing you like this. You always looked so grand in Rome. It's strange to hear the children calling you Uncle Jean! . . ."

"I'm afraid Johann doesn't entirely approve of me."

"He's trying so hard to be the man of the house that he gets mixed up sometimes. He can't get it out of his head that you were somehow responsible for what has happened to his father."

"He's right. I am responsible."

"On the other hand, he knows how much Carl loves you and respects you, but he can't walk on that sacred ground until you or Carl invites him in. . . . That's difficult. I understand, because it was difficult for me, too, at first. . . . Add to all that the fear of war, the resentment that he, like so many millions, will be called to fight for a cause already lost. . . . Be patient with him, Jean! Be patient with us all. Our little world is tumbling round our ears and we are groping for something solid to hold."

"Look at me, Lotte!"

"I am looking at you."

"Now close your eyes tight. Don't open them until I tell you."

He fished in his breast pocket and brought out a small jewel case in red morocco. He laid it open on the small table at Lotte's elbow. It contained three objects, wrought in gold in the style of the Florentines of the sixteenth century. There was a small round box, a tiny flagon and a cup hardly bigger than a thimble.

"Open your eyes."

"What am I supposed to see?"

He pointed to the case.

"They're beautiful, Jean. What are they?"

"One of the privileges of the Pope used to be that he could carry the Eucharist constantly on his person. That's how he did it. The box was for the consecrated host. The flask and the cup were for the wine. There's a tiny damask handkerchief folded in the lid for the cleansing of the vessels. . . . The people of my first parish gave me the set as a personal gift on the day of my election. . . . When I was leaving Rome to come here, I felt ashamed. I had nothing to bring to you who were suffering so much on my account. So I got to Fiumicino early, said a private Mass in the airport chapel, and brought the Eucharist with me for you and Carl. I'll give you both communion at the hospital today. . . ."

Lotte was deeply moved. She closed the case and handed it back to Jean Marie.

"That says it all, Jean. Thank you. I only hope Carl will be conscious enough to understand."

"Sleeping or waking, God holds him in the palm of his hand."

"Luncheon is served," said Katrin from the dining room.

As they were seating themselves Lotte explained to her children the graceful gift Jean Marie had brought. Johann said with apparent surprise:

"I thought Father had been given the last rites."

"Of course," said Lotte, "but the Eucharist is a daily thing—a sharing of food; a sharing of life. That's right, isn't it, Jean?"

"That's right," said Jean Marie. "A sharing of life with the source of life."

"Thank you." Johann acknowledged the information without comment and asked with studied politeness, "Would you like to say a blessing for us, Uncle Jean?"

* * *

At the hospital, Lotte introduced him to Dr. Pelzer. She begged the good doctor to explain the medical situation to this old friend of the family. So it came to pass that Jean Marie Barette saw Carl Mendelius first in a series of X-ray photographs. The head which had once held the history of twenty centuries was reduced to a skull-case with broken jaws, a smashed septum and a scatter of opaque pellets embedded in the bony structure and in the surrounding film of flesh and mucous tissue. Dr. Pelzer, a tall, powerful fellow with iron-grey hair and a wary diagnostic eye, gave a commentary:

"A mess, as you see! But we can't go probing for all those foreign bodies until we have the poor devil stabilized. There's more of that rubbish in the rib cage and the upper abdomen. . . . So a prayer or two would help—and don't let the family expect too much, eh? Even if we save him, he'll need a lot of supportive therapy. . . ."

His next view was of the living man, hooked up to the drip bottles, the oxygen tap and the cardio-monitor. The head was swathed in bandages. The damaged eyes were mercifully hidden. The nasal and oral cavities were open and motionless. The stump of the severed hand lay like a large cloth club on the counterpane. The good hand twitched weakly at the folds of the sheets.

Lotte lifted it and kissed it. "Carl, my dearest, this is Lotte."

The hand closed over hers. A gurgling murmur issued from the mask of bandages.

"Jean Marie is here with me. He'll talk to you while I go and give a little thank-you gift to the ward sister. I'll be back shortly."

She tiptoed from the room, closing the door behind her. Jean Marie took Mendelius' hand. It was soft as satin and so weak it seemed that if one pressed too hard, the bones might crack.

"Carl, this is Jean. Can you hear me?"

There was an answering pressure against his palm and more helpless gurgling as Mendelius tried in vain to articulate.

"Please, don't try to talk. We don't need words, you and I. Just lie quiet and hold my hand. . . . I will pray for both of us."

He said no words. He made no ritual gestures. He simply sat by the bed, clasping Mendelius' hand between his own, so that it was as if they were one organism: the whole and the maimed, the blind and the seeing man. He closed his eyes, and opened his mind, a vessel ready for the inpouring of the spirit, a channel by which it might infuse itself into the conjoined consciousness of Carl Mendelius.

It was the only way he knew, now, to express the relationship between creature and Creator. He could not make petitions. They were all summed up in the original fiat: let your will be done. He could not bargain—life for life, service for service—because there was no vestige of self left to which he attached any importance. The important thing was the body and the agonized spirit of Carl Mendelius for whom he was now the lifeline. . . .

When at last the inpouring came, it was simple and extraordinarily sweet, like a waft of perfume in a summer garden. There was light and a strange awareness of harmony as though the music were not played but written into the texture of the brain. There was a calm so powerful that he could feel the fevered pulse of the sick man subside like seawaves after a storm. When he opened his eyes, Lotte was in the room again, staring at him in fear and wonderment. She said awkwardly:

"I didn't mean to interrupt, but it's nearly five o'clock."

"So late? Would you like to receive communion now?"

"Please, yes; but I don't think Carl can swallow the wafer."

"I know; but he can take a sip from the chalice. Are you ready, Carl?"

A pressure on his palm told him that Mendelius had heard and understood. While Lotte sat by the bedside, Jean Marie laid out the small golden vessels and put a stole around his neck. After a brief prayer he handed the consecrated wafer to Lotte and then held the tiny chalice to Mendelius' mouth. As he pronounced the ritual words "*Corpus domini*," Lotte said "Amen" and Mendelius raised his hand in a feeble salute.

Jean Marie Barette cleansed the pyx and the chalice with the damask handkerchief, folded his stole, put the case and the stole in his pocket and tiptoed out of the room.

As he stepped past the armed guards in the corridor he was accosted by a squat, ugly woman of indeterminate age, who introduced herself abruptly as Professor Meissner.

". . . We're dining together tonight at the Mendelius house; but I told Lotte I needed an hour alone with you. Will you come to my place for a drink?"

"I'd be delighted."

"Good! There's a lot to talk about."

She took his arm, bustled him into the elevator, rode the three floors down in silence, then hurried him out into the late sunshine. It was not until they were outside the confines of the clinic that she slackened her pace and began a leisurely stroll down the hill towards the old town. She was more relaxed now; but her talk was still forthright and rasping.

"You know that Carl called me in for clinical advice on your letter and your encyclical?"

"He didn't put it that way; but, yes, I knew you were involved."

"And you read my quotes in his article?"

"Yes."

"There was one they didn't use. I'm going to give it to you now. I think you're a very dangerous man. Trouble will follow you wherever you go. . . . And I understand why your colleagues in the Church had to get rid of you."

The raw brutality of the attack left him speechless for a moment. When he found voice, all he could say was, "Well . . . what do I answer to that?"

"You could tell me I'm a bitch—and I am! But it wouldn't budge me from the proposition. You are a very dangerous man!"

"I've heard the charge before," said Jean Marie quietly. "My brothers in the Vatican called me a walking time-bomb. But I'd like to know how you see the danger which I represent."

"I've thought about it a long time." Anneliese Meissner was more gracious now. "I've done a lot of reading. I've listened to a lot of tapes from colleagues who have clinical experience of religious manias and cultist influences. At the end of it all, I am forced to conclude that you are a man with a special perception of what Jung calls the collective unconscious. Therefore, you have a magical effect on people. It is as if you are privy to their most intimate thoughts, desires, fears—as indeed you are on this question of the Last Things. This subject is rooted in the deepest subsoil of the race memory. So, when you talk or write about it, people feel you inside themselves, almost as a function of their own egos. . . . As a result, everything you do or say has profound and sometimes terrible consequences. You are the giant dreaming under the volcano. When you turn in your sleep, the earth shakes."

"And what do you think I should do about this dangerous potency?"

"You can do nothing," said Anneliese Meissner baldly. "That's where your Cardinals made the mistake. Had they left you in power, the very weight of the office and its traditional methods would have damped down the magical manifestations. You would have been held at a safe distance from common folk. Now there is no damping effect at all. There is no distance. Your impact is instant—and it may become catastrophic."

"And you see no good in the power or in me?"

"Good? Oh, yes! But it's the good that comes out of disaster, like battlefield heroism, or the dedication of nurses in a pesthouse."

"You call it magic. Have you no other name for it?"

"Use any name you like," said Anneliese Meissner. "Whatever you call yourself, priest, shaman, juju man, whomever you claim to serve—the spirit of the grove, the God-man or the Eternal Oneness—you'll always be at the epicenter of an earthquake. . . . Here's where I live."

They were nearly at the top of the Burgsteige, outside an old sixteenth-century house, built of oak beams and handmade bricks. Anneliese Meissner unlocked the door and led him up two flights of stairs to her apartment, whose narrow windows looked out on the turrets of Hohentübingen and the marching pines of the Swabian uplands. She swept a pile of books off an armchair and gestured to Jean Marie to sit down.

"What will you drink? Wine, schnapps or Scotch?"

"Wine, please."

As he watched her polishing a pair of dusty glasses, uncorking a bottle of Moselle and opening a jar of nuts, he was touched by the pathos of so much intelligence, so much hidden tenderness, locked in so ugly a body. She handed him the wine and made a toast:

"To Carl's recovery."

"*Prosit.*"

She tossed off half the wine at a gulp and set down the glass. Then she made a bald and seemingly irrelevant announcement. "At the clinic we have central monitoring of all intensive-care patients."

"Indeed?" Jean Marie was politely interested.

"Yes. All vital signs are transmitted constantly to the monitor room, where a senior nurse is on duty all the time. . . . While you were with Carl, I was in the monitor room with Doctor Pelzer."

Jean Marie Barette waited. He could not be sure whether she was embarrassed or reluctant to continue. Finally he had to prompt her.

"Please! You were in the monitor room. So . . . ?"

"When you arrived Carl had a temperature of a hundred and three degrees; a pulse rate of one twenty and a pronounced cardiac arrhythmia. You were with him nearly two hours. During all that time, except for a few opening sentences, you did not utter a single word until Lotte came back into the room. By then, Carl's temperature had dropped, the pulse rate was nearly normal and the rhythm of the heartbeat was restored. What did you do?"

"I prayed, in a fashion."

"What fashion?"

"I suppose you could call it meditation. . . . But if you are trying to attribute some kind of miracle . . . please, no!"

"I don't believe in miracles. I am, however, curious about phenomena that go beyond the norms. Besides . . ." She gave him an odd sidelong glance as if she were suddenly afraid to commit herself; then she plunged ahead. "You might as well know it; everything that touches Carl, touches me. I've been in love with him for ten years. He doesn't know it and he never will. But right now, I've got to cry on someone's shoulder—and you're elected, because you're the one who got him into this mess! . . . Carl always said you had the grace of understanding. Then, maybe, you'll understand that for me, the fairy tale was reversed. It wasn't the beautiful princess and the frog-prince. It was the girl-frog waiting for the prince to kiss her and make her beautiful. I know it's hopeless and I've learned not to care too much. I'm no threat to anyone, certainly not to Lotte. But when I see poor Carl hooked up to those life-support systems, when I know how much stuff they're pumping into him, just to keep him sedated and his body functioning, then I wish I believed in miracles."

"I believe in them," said Jean Marie gently. "And they all begin in an act of love."

"But love is terrible—the same way you're terrible. If you bottle it up too long, it can blow the top of your head off. . . . Hell! I didn't bring you here to bitch you or tell you about my love life." She poured more wine and then told him, "Johann Mendelius is in big trouble."

"What sort of trouble?"

"He's putting together an underground group of students to resist military call-up, obstruct security surveillance and provide escape routes for deserters from the armed forces."

"How do you know this?"

"He told me. His father had mentioned that I would be prepared to support an underground organization among the faculty. . . . But these kids are so naïve! They don't realize how closely they're watched, how easy it is to penetrate their ranks with spies and provocateurs. They're buying and storing arms, which is a criminal offense. . . . It's only a matter of time before the police get wind of what's going on. They may know already and be waiting until all the fuss over Carl dies down."

"Johann promised he would show me what form his protest was taking. Perhaps he's thought of taking me to a meeting of this group."

"Possibly. It's because you're a Frenchman that they've named the group the Jacquerie, to recall the French peasants' revolt during the Hundred Years' War. . . . But if you take my advice, you'll stay well away."

"I'd like to keep an open mind on that. I may be able to talk some sense into Johann and his friends."

"Don't forget what I told you at the beginning. You are a very special man. Without knowing how or why, you make a potent magic; and youth is most susceptible to the witchcraft. . . . Now I want you to listen to a tape."

"What's on it?"

"Part of a clinical interview with one of my patients. I am communicating it to you under professional secrecy as Carl communicated your material to me. Agreed?"

"Agreed."

"The woman is twenty-eight, a childless divorcee, the eldest daughter of a well-known local family. The marriage lasted three years. She has been divorced for one year. She shows acute depressive symptoms, and there have been some hallucinatory episodes which are probably the sequelae of some experiments with L.S.D. in which she admits to have taken part during her marriage. . . . This tape was made yesterday. It is part of a session that lasted an hour and twenty minutes."

"And what will it tell me?"

"That's what I want to find out. It tells me one thing. It may tell you quite another."

"My dear Professor." He gave a chuckle of genuine good humour. "If you really want a profile of my character, why not start with something simple, like a Rorschach blot?"

"Because I have your profile already." The response was curt and irritable. "I've had you in my casebook for weeks now. You're a frightening phenomenon: a resolutely simple man. You say what you believe. You believe what you say. You live in a universe permeated by an immanent God with whom you have a direct and personal relationship. I don't live in such a universe, but we are both here in this room, with this tape. I want to know your reaction to it. You'll indulge me, please?"

"At your service."

"The location is my consulting room. The time: four in the afternoon. This passage occurs after forty minutes of discursive and defensive talk by the patient. . . ."

She switched on the machine. A woman's voice, low-timbred, and with a pronounced Swabian accent, picked up what was obviously a new theme in the narration:

". . . I met him one morning in the Marktplatz. I was buying grapes. He picked one from the stall and popped it in my mouth. Even though I knew how awful he could be, it made me laugh. He asked me would I like a cup of tea. I said yes I would and he took me down to that tea shop near the Nuns-House . . . you know! . . . the place you can buy teas from all over the world, even maté from Argentina. . . . He was very pleasant. I didn't feel threatened at all. The people in the shop were in and out the whole time. I agreed to try something I'd never had before: a special infusion from Ceylon. . . . I thought it was pleasant, but nothing to rave about. We talked of this and that: his work, my parents, how he was off women for a while. . . . I wondered if he'd caught anything from the last one, who was a cheap little tart from Frankfurt. I didn't say a word, but I knew he'd read my thoughts. . . . He threw the cup of tea in my face. It splashed down my blouse. He tore the blouse off, while the people in the tea shop stood by, laughing. The next thing we all joined hands and danced round the shop singing 'Boom—boom—boom,' while the big tin tea-caddies began exploding all over the place. But it wasn't tea; it was fireworks, blue and green and lots of red! . . . Then we were out in the street. I was naked and he was dragging me behind him and telling all the people . . . 'Look what the Turks did to my wife! Monsters! Bloody rapists . . . !' But when we got to the hospital there were police at the door and they wouldn't let me in because they said I had clap and the secret service never employs people with social diseases. They said he could kill me, too, if he wanted; but he said I wasn't important enough and I started to cry. . . .

"After that he took me to my house and told me to clean myself up. I had a long hot bath, then I powdered myself and put on perfume and lay on the bed, naked, to wait for him. Only it wasn't my bed. It was a beautiful circular one, soft and comfortable and smelling of lavender. After a while he came in. He went into the bathroom and when he came out he was naked and clean like me. He kissed my breasts and excited me with his hands and then he came inside me and we had a big climax which was like the tin caddies exploding in the tea shop. . . . I always close my eyes when I have a climax. This time when I opened them he was lying beside me, all bloody. His hand was on my breast, but it was just a hand with no arm or body. I tried to scream but I couldn't. Then I saw his face, it was just empty like a big red saucer. Then the bed wasn't a bed anymore, but a big black box with both of us inside it. . . ."

Anneliese Meissner switched off the machine and said, "Well, that's it!"

Jean Marie Barette was silent for a long moment, then he asked, "Who is the man in the dream?"

"Her ex-husband. He still lives in the town."

"And you know him?"

"Not very well; but, yes, I know him."

Jean Marie said nothing. He held up his glass. She refilled it for him. Then she asked tentatively:

"Any comment on what you've just heard?"

"I'm not an expert on the decipherment of dreams; but the tape did tell me something. The woman is haunted by guilt. She has knowledge which she is afraid to share with anyone else. So she dreams it, or constructs a dream about it and tells it to you. Whatever she knows is connected in some way with the Mendelius affair. . . . How am I doing so far, Frau Professor?"

"Very well. Please go on!"

"I think," said Jean Marie deliberately, "I think that you have the same problem as your patient. You know something which you're unwilling or unable to disclose."

"I'm unwilling because I'm not sure of my conclusions. I'm unable because it involves my professional integrity. You'd have the same problem with a confessional secret."

"They're both good reasons for reticence," said Jean Marie drily.

"There are others." Now she was irritable and combative.

"Please! A moment!" Jean Marie held up a warning hand. "Let's not get heated. You invited me here. I have given you my guarantee of secrecy. If you want to tell me what's bothering you, I'll listen. If not, then let's enjoy the wine!"

"I'm sorry!" It was hard for her to express any sort of penitence. "I'm so used to playing God in the consulting room that I forget my everyday manners. . . . You're right. I'm desperately worried. I don't see what I can do about it, without opening a whole new nest of vipers. Anyway, here's item one. The woman on that tape is both vulnerable and acquisitive. A young divorcee in a university town, she's had more affairs than she knows how to cope with. One of her more serious romances was with Johann Mendelius. It was finished only this summer before he left on vacation. Fortunately, neither Carl nor Lotte got wind of it. But I knew because she was my patient and I had to listen to the whole big drama. Item two is where I stumble. Her ex-husband is a man—how shall I explain it?—a man so improbable that he has to be authentic. I have a whole series of tapes on their relationship. He's the one who's selling guns to Johann and his group; and if that tape means what I think it does, he's the one who sent the letter bomb to Carl. . . . I know it sounds absurd but . . ."

"Evil is the ultimate absurdity," said Jean Marie Barette. "It is the last sad buffoonery: man sitting in the ruins of his world, daubing himself with his own excrement. . . ."

It was nearly six-thirty when he left Anneliese's apartment. As he closed the front door behind him, his attention was caught by a plaque on the building opposite, a sturdy hostelry built in the first half of the sixteenth century where the burghers of Tübingen still came to eat and drink. The plaque announced in Gothic script: "The Old Schloss Keller. Here lived Professor Michael Maestlin of Goppingen, teacher of the astronomer Johannes Kepler."

The inscription pleased him, since it celebrated the lesser-known master before the effulgent pupil. It reminded him, too, of the fear that had haunted his predecessor: that Tübingen might become the center of a second anti-Roman revolt. He himself had never had such fears. It had always seemed as fruitless an exercise to impeach a scholar for heresy as to hang out the bloody sheets after a bridal night. It further occurred to him that he ought to provide the wine for the evening meal. So he pushed open the heavy nail-studded door and went inside.

Half the booths were full of student drinkers, and a dozen burly countrymen propped up the bar. Jean Marie Barette made himself perfectly understood in *Hochdeutsch* but was totally confused by the names of unfamiliar vintages which the barman reeled off in dialect. Finally he settled on a pleasantly dry white from the Ammertal, bought two bottles and made for the exit. A call from a corner booth stopped him in his tracks.

"Uncle Jean! Over here! Come and join us!" Johann took the bottles and pushed his companions along the bench to make room for Jean Marie. He made the introductions briskly: "Franz, Alexis, Norbert, Alvin Dolman. This is my uncle Jean. Franz is my sister's boyfriend. Alvin's an American and a very good friend of Father's."

"I'm happy to meet you gentlemen." Jean Marie was cordiality itself. "May I buy you a drink?"

He signalled the waitress and ordered a round for the company and a glass of mineral water for himself.

Johann asked, "What are you doing up this end of town, Uncle Jean?"

"Visiting Professor Meissner. We met at the hospital. I walked home with her."

"How was Father this afternoon?"

"The doctor says he's improved. His temperature is down, his pulse steadier."

"That's great news; great!" Alvin Dolman seemed a little gone in his cups. "Let me know when I can see him, Johann. I've found something he'll like. It's a carving of Saint Christopher, Early Gothic. This he gets for free, as soon as he's sitting up and taking nourishment."

Jean Marie was instantly intrigued. "You are a collector then, Mr. Dolman?"

"No, sir, a dealer! But I've got the eye for the game. You've got to have the eye."

"Indeed, yes. You live here?"

"I live here, work here. Once I was married here—son-in-law to the Bürgermeister yet! But that didn't last. Old dogfaces like me shouldn't marry. We're reject china, you might say. . . . Matter of fact, your Professor Meissner was a great friend of my wife. Helped her to straighten out after the divorce."

"I'm glad to hear it," said Jean Marie. "And what kind of work do you do, Mr. Dolman?"

"I'm an artist—a technical illustrator, if you must spell it out. I work for educational publishers up and down the Rhine. On the side I deal in antique art . . . in a small way, of course. I don't have money for the big stuff."

"I thought the *company* supplied the funds." Jean Marie leaned ever so lightly on the word.

"Please?"

It was the minutest reaction—hardly the flicker of an eyelid; but Jean Marie had dealt with too many clerics and too many other subtle fellows to miss it. Alvin Dolman smiled and shook his head.

"The company? I'm afraid you've misunderstood me. I'm strictly free-lance. I accept commissions just like a portrait painter. No, sir! The only company I've ever worked for is good old Uncle Sam."

"Forgive me." Jean Marie smiled an apology. "One speaks a foreign language, but always one makes mistakes in the simplest things. . . . Johann, what time do we sit down for your mother's dinner?"

"No later than eight. Let's finish our drinks and I'll walk back with you. We're only five minutes away."

"I should be moving, too," said Alvin Dolman. "I've got a date in Stuttgart. While I'm there I'll see what I can do for you guys. But remember, it has to be cash on the line! *Wiedersehen* all!"

He climbed awkwardly to his feet and Jean Marie had to rise to let him out of the booth. As he moved to the door Jean Marie followed him. When they came out into the nearly deserted street he said in English:

"A word with you, Mr. Dolman."

Dolman swung round to face him. His smile was gone now. His eyes were hostile.

"Yes?"

"I know you," said Jean Marie Barette. "I know who you are, and what company employs you, and whose is the evil spirit that inhabits you. If I tell them inside, they will kill you with the same guns you have sold to them. So, keep your life and go from this place. Go now!"

Dolman stared at him for a moment and then laughed.

"Who do you think you are—God Almighty?"

"You know who I am, Alvin Dolman. You know everything that has been said and written about me. . . . And you know it is true. Now, in the name of God, go!"

Dolman spat in his face, then he turned on his heel and went limping hurriedly down the cobbled slope. Jean Marie wiped the spittle from his cheeks and went back into the Schloss Keller.

". . . Get rid of the guns! Every one of them is marked to convict you. Disband the Jacquerie. You are blown anyway. Dolman made you the victims of the classic intelligence plot: concentrate all the dissidents in one group, then knock them off at leisure. Meantime he was using you to cover up his own tracks as an assassin. . . ."

It was one in the morning and they were alone in Mendelius' study under the rooftops. Outside, the first chill wind of early autumn keened around the belfry of the Stiftskirche. On the floor below, Lotte and Katrin slept peacefully, unaware of the mystery play which had been enacted around them. Johann, for all his shame and weariness, could still not abandon the debate.

". . . But it doesn't make sense. Dolman's a huckster who'll trade you anything. He's a clown who laughs when an old lady falls from a bus and shows her drawers. But an assassin—no!"

"Dolman is the perfect agent-in-place." Jean Marie admonished him patiently. "As Professor Meissner says, he's so improbable he has to be authentic. . . . More! As an agent of a friendly power, concerned with Germany as its eastern frontier, he's the perfect instrument for dirty jobs like the bomb strike on your father. . . . But that's not all! I have known men highly practiced in violence who are not half as evil as their deeds. They are conditioned, bent like twigs beyond straightening. In some, a key component has been lost, so that they can never be otherwise than what they are. But Dolman is different. Dolman knows who he is and what he is and he wants to be just that. He is, truly, in the old phrase, a habitation of evil."

"How can you know that? You met him only once. I can understand Professor Meissner having an opinion about him, because she's heard all the stories from his wife. I heard them, too, many a time, in her bed; but I didn't believe them, because Dolman knew I was having her, and he encouraged me to enjoy it—and prepared me to get out when the fun was over. . . . But you? One meeting? I'm sorry, Uncle Jean. It doesn't make sense unless you know something more than you're telling me."

"I know less than you about Alvin Dolman—but much, much more about the noonday devil." He clasped his hands behind his head and leaned far back in Mendelius' armchair. "In the high places where I used to live he was a very frequent visitor—and most beguiling company!"

"That's too easy, Uncle Jean. I don't accept it."

"Very well. Let me put it another way. While you were playing love games with Dolman's wife, would you have invited a child to witness them?"

"Of course not."

"Why not?"

"Well, because . . ."

"Because you recognize innocence, even if you can't define it. You recognize evil, too; but you close your eyes to it. Why?"

"I . . . I suppose because I don't want to recognize the evil in myself either."

"At last we come to it. Now will you take some advice from your uncle Jean?"

"I'll try."

"As soon as your father can travel, move away from here. If you can complete the purchase of the Alpine property and make it fit for habitation, go there. Try to keep the family together: your mother and father, Katrin, her man, too, if he will go with you. . . . Dolman is gone. He will not come back; his company will not use him again in this region; but the company is still in business—and always in partnership with the noonday devil!"

"And where will you go, Uncle Jean?"

"Tomorrow to Paris to see my family and arrange my financial affairs. After that . . . who knows? I wait on the call!"

Johann was still uneasy and irritable. He objected, "So we're back to private revelation and prophecy and all that?"

"Well?"

"I don't believe in it. That's all!"

"But you believed in a man who tried to kill your father. You didn't believe the truths his wife told you in bed. You don't know how to smell evil from good. Does that tell you nothing about yourself, Johann?"

"You really strike for the throat, don't you?"

"Grow up, boy!" Jean Marie Barette was implacable. "We're talking about life, death and the hereafter. No one gets an absolution from reality!"

That night Jean Marie Barette had a dream. He was walking in the Marktplatz of Tübingen. He paused by a fruit stall selling beautiful black grapes. He tasted one; it was sweet and satisfying. He asked the stall holder to weigh him out a kilo. She gaped at him, horror-struck, raised her hands in front of her face and backed away. All the people in the marketplace did the same until he stood isolated in a circle of hostile humans, holding a bunch of grapes in his hand. He spoke peaceably, asking what was the matter. No one answered. He took a few steps towards the nearest person. His way was barred by a big fellow with a butcher's knife. He stopped in his tracks and cried out:

"What's the matter? Why are you afraid of me?"

The big fellow answered, "Because you're a *Pestträger*—a plague-carrier! Get out before we kill you!"

Then the crowd began to close in, forcing him inexorably towards the mouth of the alley down which, he knew, he must turn and run for his life. . . .

In the morning, red-eyed and unrested, he had an early breakfast with Lotte and then went with her to the hospital to say his farewells to Carl Mendelius. There, in a final quiet moment, he told them both:

". . . We will meet again. I'm sure of it; but where and how, God knows! Lotte, my dear, don't cling to anything here. When Carl is ready, just pack and go! Promise me!"

"I promise, Jean! It won't be hard to leave."

"Good! When the call comes, Carl, you will be ready for it. For the present, resign yourself to a long convalescence. Help Lotte to help you. Tell her you'll do that."

Carl Mendelius raised his good hand and stroked her cheek.

She drew the hand to her lips and kissed the palm. Jean Marie stood up. He traced the sign of the cross with his thumb on Mendelius' forehead and then on Lotte's. His voice was unsteady.

"I hate farewells. I love you both. Pray for me."

Mendelius clutched at his wrist to stay him. He struggled to speak. This time, painfully but clearly, he managed to articulate the words:

"The fig tree, Jean. I know now. The fig tree!"

Lotte pleaded with him. "Please, dearest, don't try to talk."

Jean Marie said soothingly, "Dear Carl, remember what we agreed! No words, no arguments. Let God make the trees grow in his own good time."

Mendelius relaxed slowly. Lotte held his hand. Jean Marie kissed her and, without another word, walked out of the room.

He was halfway to Paris, flying blind through storm clouds, when Mendelius' words made sense to him. They were an echo of the text from the Gospel of Matthew that had fallen open in his hands on the day of the vision: ". . . And from the fig tree learn a parable. When the branch is tender and the leaves come forth you know that summer is near. So, when you see all these happenings you will know that the end things are very near, yes, even at the gates!"

He felt a strange surge of relief, almost of elation. If Carl Mendelius believed at last in the vision, then Jean Marie Barette was not left utterly alone.

IX

In Paris the dream of the plague-carrier came true. His brother, Alain Hubert Barette, silver of hair, silver of tongue, a pillar of the banking establishment on the Boulevard Haussmann, was shocked to the soles of his handmade shoes. He cherished Jean Marie. He would somehow make adequate financial provisions; but to open up a forty-year-old trust, and dismantle the most complicated international arrangements—*pas possible!* Jean had come at a most inconvenient time. It would be most difficult to lodge him with the family. They had the decorators in. Odette was in a constant state of near hysteria. And the servants—my God! However, the bank would be most happy to let him use its suite at the Lancaster until he was able to make other arrangements.

How was Odette—apart from the hysteria? Well enough, but shocked—devastated indeed—by the abdication! And, of course, when Cardinal Sancerre, Archbishop of Paris, came back from the consistory and began spreading all those odd stories—that was truly an intimate distress for the whole family.

Political contacts? Diplomatic encounters? Normally Alain Hubert Barette would have been happy to act as host to such meetings; but in this precise moment—eh!—one counselled a great discretion. One did not want to risk a snub, by too direct an approach to the President or even to the high gentlemen at the Quai d'Orsay. Why not come tomorrow night for dinner with Odette and the girls and then discuss the whole question?

Meantime, the money problem . . . The bank would grant Jean Marie a substantial credit line, guaranteed by the trust, until such time as it was possible to reconstitute the arrangements.

". . . Now, let's get some documents signed so that you can

have funds immediately. I suggest—strictly between loving brothers!—that a good tailor is a first requisite and a decent shirtmaker. After all, you are still a Monseigneur and even the garments of a layman should indicate the hidden dignity."

It was one idiocy too many. It put Jean Marie in a cold, Gallic rage.

"Alain, you are a fool! You are also a snob and a tasteless, greedy little money-changer! I will not come to your house. I do not wish to have the apartment at the Lancaster. You will provide me immediately with the money I need. You will call a meeting of the trustees for ten in the morning and we will discuss in detail their past administration and their future activities. I have little time and much travel to do. I will not be inhibited by the bureaucratic nonsense of your bank. Do I make myself clear?"

"Jean, you misunderstand me. I did not intend to . . ."

"Be quiet, Alain! The less said the better. What documents do I have to sign for the immediate funds I need?"

Fifteen minutes later it was done. A very subdued Alain made the last call to summon the last trustee to the next morning's meeting. He mopped his hands with a silk handkerchief and delivered himself of a carefully modified apology.

"Please! We are brothers. We should not quarrel. You have to understand: we are all under a strain now. The money markets are going mad. We have to defend ourselves as if it were against bandits. We know there will be a war. So how do we protect the banks' assets and our own? How do we arrange our personal lives? You have been away so long, protected so long . . ."

In spite of his anger Jean Marie laughed—a gusty chuckle of genuine amusement.

"Eh-eh-eh, little brother! I bleed for you! For my part, I should not know what to do with all those trunks and strong rooms full of paper and coinage and bullion. . . . But you're right. It's too late in the day to quarrel—and it's also too late for all that silly snobbery! Why don't you see if you can get Vauvenargues on the phone for me . . ."

"Vauvenargues? The Foreign Minister?"

"The same."

"As you wish." Alain shrugged resignedly and consulted his leather-bound desk directory. He switched to a private line and tapped out a number. Jean Marie listened with cool amusement to the one-sided dialogue.

"Hullo! This is Alain Hubert Barette, Director of Halévy Frères et Barette, Banquiers. Please connect me with the Minister. . . . Apropos of the fact that an old friend of his has arrived in Paris and would like to speak with him. . . . The friend is Monseigneur Jean Marie Barette, formerly his Holiness Pope Gregory the Seventeenth. . . . Oh, I see! Then perhaps you will be kind enough to pass the message and have the Minister call back to this number. . . . Thank you."

He put down the receiver and made a grimace of distaste.

"The Minister is in conference. The message will be passed. . . . You've been there, Jean! You know the routines. Once you have to explain yourself and your current identity, you're diplomatically dead. Oh, I'm sure the Minister will return the call; but what do you want with a limp handshake and some words about the weather?"

"I'll make the next call myself." Jean Marie consulted his pocketbook and spelled out the private number of the most senior presidential counsellor, a man with whom, during his pontificate, he had maintained a constant and friendly relationship. The response came immediately:

"This is Duhamel."

"Pierre, this is Jean Marie Barette. I am in Paris for a few days on private business. I'd like to see you—and your master!"

"And I you. But it has to be in private. As to the master—my regrets, but no! The official word is out. You are untouchable."

"Where does the word come from?"

"From your principal to our principal. And the Friends of Silence have been busy at all the lower levels. Where are you staying?"

"I haven't decided yet."

"Outside the city is better. Take a taxi and drive out to L'Hostellerie des Chevaliers. It's about three kilometers this side of Versailles. I'll telephone ahead and book the accommodation for you. . . . Sign yourself as Monsieur Grégoire. They won't ask for documents. I'll call there on my way home—about eight. I must go now. *A bientôt.*"

Jean Marie put down the receiver. It was his turn to apologize.

"You're right, little brother. Diplomatically I am dead and buried. Well, I should be going. Give my love to Odette and the girls. We'll try to arrange a meal together before I leave."

"You don't want to change your mind about the Lancaster?"

"Thank you, no. If I'm a plague-carrier I'd rather not spread the infection to my family. Tomorrow at ten, eh? . . ."

The Hostellerie des Chevaliers was a pleasant surprise, a cluster of ancient farm buildings converted into an agreeable and discreet hotel. There were manicured lawns and quiet rose arbours, and a millstream that meandered under a drapery of willows.

The *patronne* was a handsome woman in her mid-fifties who waived all the formalities of registration and led him immediately to a pleasant suite with a view onto a private enclave with its own greensward and a lily pond. She pointed out that he might make his telephone calls with full security, that the refrigerator was stocked with liquor and that, as a friend of M. Duhamel, he had only to raise a finger to command the total service of the Hostellerie.

As he unpacked his one suitcase he was amused and a whit surprised to see how lightly he was travelling: one suit, a raincoat, a sports jacket and trousers, a pullover, two pairs of pajamas and half a dozen changes of shirts, underwear and socks constituted his whole wardrobe. His toiletries, his mass kit, a breviary, a missal and a pocketbook made up the rest of his impedimenta. For sustenance he had a day's supply of cash, a folder of travellers' checks and a circular letter of credit from Halévy Frères et Barette. For these he was a debtor to the bank until the trustees released some of the funds from his patrimony. At least he was free to move quickly once the call came, as it had come centuries before to John, the son of Zachary, in the desert.

What troubled him now was a growing sense of isolation and of his precarious dependence on the goodwill of friends. No matter that at the center of himself was a great pool of calm, a place, an estate, where all opposites were reconciled; he was still a man, subject to all the chemistries of the flesh, all the unstable physics of the mind.

The weapon of estrangement had been used against him in the dark and bitter days before his abdication. Now it was being used again, to render him impotent in the political arena. Pierre Duhamel, longtime counsellor to the President of the Republic, was not prone to exaggeration. If he said you were dying, it was indeed time to call the priest; if he said you were dead, the stonemasons were already carving your epitaph.

That Pierre Duhamel had been so prompt to suggest a rendezvous was itself an indication of crisis. In all the years of their acquaintance, Duhamel had observed a singular and spartan code: "I have one wife: the woman I married. I have one mistress: the Republic. Never tell me anything you do not want reported. Never try to frighten me. Never offer me a bribe. I give patronage to none and my advice only to those whom I am paid to counsel. I respect all faiths. I demand to be private about my own. If you trust me I shall never lie to you. If you lie to me, I shall understand, but never trust you again."

In the days of his pontificate, Jean Marie Barette had had many exchanges with this strangely attractive man, who looked like a prize fighter, reasoned as eloquently as Montaigne and went home to cherish a wife who had once been the toast of Paris and was now a ravaged victim of multiple sclerosis.

They had a son at Saint Cyr and a daughter somewhat older, who had earned a good reputation as a producer of programs for television. For the rest, Jean Marie made no enquiry. Pierre Duhamel was what his President claimed him to be—a good man for the long road.

Jean Marie picked up his breviary and stepped out into the garden to read the vespers of the day. It was a habit he cherished: the prayer of a man walking, at day's end, hand in hand with God in a garden. The day's psalmody began with the canticle he had always loved: *Quam dilecta.* "How lovely are thy tabernacles, O Lord of Hosts. My soul longeth and fainteth for the courts of the Lord. My heart and my flesh have rejoiced in the living God. For the sparrow hath found herself a house and the dove a nest for herself where she may lay her young ones. . . ."

It was the perfect prayer for a late-summer evening, with the shadows long, the air still and languorous with the perfume of roses. As he turned down a gravelled pathway towards another stretch of lawn, he heard children's voices, and a moment later saw a group of little girls, all dressed alike in gingham dresses and pinafores, playing a simple catching game with a pair of young teachers. On a bench nearby an older woman divided her attention between the group and a piece of embroidery.

As Jean Marie passed along the gravelled walk, one of the children broke away from the group and ran towards him. She slipped on the verge and fell almost at his feet. She burst into tears. He picked her up and carried her to the woman on the bench, who dabbed at her grazed knee and offered her a lollipop to soothe her. It was only then that Jean Marie noticed that the child was a mongol—as indeed were all the others in the group. As if sensing his shock, the woman held the child towards him and said with a smile:

"We are all from the Institute across the road. . . . This one has just come to us. She's homesick; so she thinks every man is her papa."

"And where is Papa?" There was a touch of censure in the question.

The woman shook her head. "Oh, no, it isn't what you think. He's been recently widowed. He feels, quite rightly, that she is safer here with us. . . . We have about a hundred children in the Institute. The *patronne* lets us bring the little ones here to play. Her only child was mongoloid but it died early."

Jean Marie held out his arms. The child came to him willingly and kissed him, then sat in his lap and began playing happily with the buttons of his shirt.

He said, "She's very affectionate."

"Most are," the woman told him. "People who are able to keep them in the family group find that it is like having a new baby in the house all the time. . . . But, of course, it is when the parents age and the child comes to adolescence and maturity that the tragedies begin. The boys may become very rough and violent. The girls are easy victims to sexual invasion. The future is dark for both parents and children. . . . It's sad. I am so very fond of them."

"How do you maintain the Institute?"

"We have a grant from the government. We ask fees from parents who can pay. We solicit private charity. Fortunately we have some wealthy sponsors like Monsieur Duhamel, who lives close by. He calls the children *les petites bouffonnes du bon Dieu* . . . 'God's little clowns. . . .'"

"It's a gentle thought."

"You know Monsieur Duhamel perhaps? He's a very important man, the President's right hand, they say."

"By repute," said Jean Marie carefully.

The child slipped from his knee and began tugging his hand to make him walk with her. He asked, "May I take her down to the pond to see the fish?"

"Of course. I'll come with you."

As he moved away his breviary fell from his pocket onto the

bench. The woman picked it up, glanced at the title page, then laid aside her embroidery and followed him, book in hand.

"You left your breviary, Father."

"Oh! Thank you."

He shoved it back in his pocket. The woman took the child's other hand and fell into step with Jean Marie. She said, "I have the strange feeling I've seen you somewhere before."

"I'm sure we haven't met. I've been away from France a long time."

"A missionary perhaps?"

"In a way, yes."

"Where did you serve?"

"Oh, several countries, but mostly in Rome. I'm retired now. I came home for a vacation."

"I thought priests never retired."

"Let's say I'm on retreat for a while. . . . Come on, little one! Let's go see the goldfish."

He swung the child up on his shoulder and began singing a song from his own childhood as he marched her down to the pond. The woman dropped back and stood watching them from a distance. He seemed a most pleasant man, obviously a lover of children—but when a priest, still vigorous, was retired so early, there had to be a reason. . . .

Punctually at eight, Pierre Duhamel was knocking on the door of the suite. He must be gone by eight forty-five, since he never failed to have dinner at home with his wife. Meantime he would drink a Campari and soda with Jean Marie, whom he seemed to regard with bleak amusement as a highly memorable survivor, rather like the hairy mammoth.

". . . My God! They really pegged you out and ran the steam-roller over you! Frankly, I'm astonished to see you looking so healthy. . . . What have you done now that makes them lean so hard on you? Of course, that big splash in the press didn't make you any more popular with the French hierarchy. The Friends of Silence are very strong here. . . . Then I heard that your friend Mendelius had been the victim of a terrorist bomb attack. . . ."

"A bomb attack, yes. A terrorist action, no. The thing was planned and executed by an agent of the C.I.A., Alvin Dolman."

"Why the C.I.A.?"

"Why not? Dolman was their agent-in-place. I think it was a

neat piece of work by the Americans for the Bundesrepublik. It was designed to rid them of an influential academic who was bound to cause trouble once the call-up for military service was implemented."

"Any proof?"

"Enough for me. Not enough to raise a public outcry."

"Very soon"—Pierre Duhamel stirred the liquor with his finger —"very soon you'll be able to boil your mother in oil on the Pont Royal—and nobody will blink an eye. What is being done to you is only a pale shadow of what is being planned for the repression of persons and the suppression of debate. The new propaganda chiefs will make Goebbels look like a schoolboy amateur. . . . You haven't been back in the world long enough to feel the impact of their methods—but my God, they're effective."

"Which means you agree with them?"

"Sad to say, I do. You see, my friend, on the premise that an atomic war is inevitable—and that's our military projection and your own prophecy, remember!—the only way we can control and offer any sort of protection to large masses of people is by an intense conditioning program. There's no way we can protect the people of Paris from blast and radiation or nerve gas or a lethal virus. If we announce that nasty fact, *tout court*, we'll have instant panic. So we have to keep the cities working as long as we can at all costs. If that means sweeping the streets with tanks twice a day we'll do it. If it means pre-dawn raids on dissidents or too vocal idealists we'll have them out in their nightshirts and shoot a few to admonish the rest. Then if we need some diversions—bread and circuses and orgies on the steps of the Sacré Coeur—we'll turn those on, too! . . . And there'll be no debate about any of it! We'll all be Friends of Silence then; and God help anyone who opens his mouth at the wrong moment. . . . That's the scenario, my friend. I don't like it any more than you do; but I recommended it to my President just the same."

"Then for pity's sake," Jean Marie pleaded with him, "don't you think you should look at the scenario I suggested? Surely anything would be better than the primitive brutality and bacchanalia you're prepared to offer."

"We've done our homework," Pierre Duhamel told him with wintry humour. "We're assured on the best psychiatric authority that the oscillation of tactics between violence and bacchic indulgence will have the effect of keeping the public both puzzled and amenable to authority—especially as the facts can only be evidenced by hearsay and not by reliable report in the press or on television. . . ."

"That's monstrous." Jean Marie Barette was furious.

"Of course it's monstrous." Pierre Duhamel gave an expressive shrug. "But consider your alternative. I have it with me."

He took out his wallet, extracted a carefully folded square of newspaper and smoothed it open. He went on, "This is you, as Gregory the Seventeenth, quoted in the Mendelius article. I have to presume the quote is authentic. This is what it says:

". . . It is clear that in the days of universal calamity the traditional structures of society will not survive. There will be a ferocious struggle for the simplest needs of life—food, water, fuel and shelter. Authority will be usurped by the strong and the cruel. Large urban societies will fragment themselves into tribal groups, each hostile to the other. Rural areas will be subject to pillage. The human person will be as much a prey as the beasts whom we now slaughter for food. Reason will be so clouded that man will resort for solace to the crudest and most violent forms of magic. It will be hard, even for those founded most strongly in the Promise of the Lord, to sustain their faith and continue to give witness, as they must do, even to the end. . . . How then must Christians comport themselves in these days of trial and terror?

". . . Since they will no longer be able to maintain themselves as large groups, they must divide themselves into small communities, each capable of sustaining itself by the exercise of a common faith and a true mutual charity. . . .

"Now, let's see what we have in that prescription. Large-scale disorder and chaos in social relations, to be balanced by what? Small communities of the elect, making seminal experiments in the exercise of charity and the other Christian virtues. Is that a fair summary?"

"As far as it goes, yes."

"But whatever government or leadership still exists at that time will have to take account of the barbarians first. How is it going to do that, except by the violent measures we envisage? After all, your elect—not to mention the elect of all other cults!—

will take care of themselves; or the Almighty will! . . . Let's face it, my friend, that's why your own people cast you out. They couldn't argue with the principle. It's a beautiful thought: God's people planting their garden of graces, as the monks and nuns of old did in the Dark Ages of Europe. But, at bottom, your bishops are cold pragmatists. They know that if you want law and order, you must demonstrate how bad chaos can be. If you want morality back again, you have to have Satan in the streets, large as life, so you can shout him down in full view of the terrified populace. . . . In every country in the world it's the same story; because no country can prosecute a war without a willing and conforming public. Your own Church has adopted the siege mentality: no debate, back to the simple kitchen moralities, and let's have everyone at Mass on Sunday so that we give public witness against the ungodly! . . . The last thing they want is some wayward prophet howling doom among the gravestones!"

"Even though they know the doom is coming?"

"*Because* they know it. Precisely because they know it! They cannot, any more than we, cope with the unbearable before it happens. That's the whole reason for the Friends of Silence and their counterparts in secular government!" Suddenly he was laughing. "My friend, don't look so shocked! What did you expect from Pierre Duhamel—a tranquillizer and a spoonful of soothing syrup? The Roman Catholics aren't the only ones who are opting for conformity. All the other big cults which have membership and property in the Republic have assured the government of their loyalty in the event of national emergency. . . . The reason they're all holding to the old models of experience and culture is because they have no time now to test new ones, or accustom their people to live with them."

Jean Marie was silent for a long moment. Finally he said quietly:

"I accept what you tell me, Pierre. Now answer me one question. What preparations have you, personally, made for the day when the first missiles are launched?"

Duhamel was not smiling now. He took time to frame his answer.

"This is a day in our scenario called R Day—*R* for Rubicon. If any one of half a dozen actions is taken by any major powers, then the chemistry of conflict will become irreversible. War will be declared. A global conflict will follow. On R Day I shall go home. I shall bathe my wife. I shall cook her favourite meal, open the best wine in my cellar and take a long time to drink it. Then I shall carry my wife to bed, lie down beside her and administer a poison pill to us both. . . . We're agreed. Our children know. They don't like the idea. They have other plans and other reasons; but they respect our decision. . . . My wife has suffered enough. I would not want her to endure the horrors of the aftermath—and to face them without her would be, for me, a pointless masochism."

He was being challenged and he knew it. It was the same challenge Carl Mendelius had made to him in the garden at Monte Cassino: "I have met good people who would prefer eternal blackness to the vision of Siva the Destroyer." Pierre Duhamel was an even more formidable inquisitor, because he had none of Mendelius' inhibitions. He was still waiting for his answer.

Jean Marie Barette said calmly, "I believe in free will, Pierre. I believe a man is judged by the light which has been given him. If you choose a stoic end to an intolerable situation, I may condemn the act; but upon the actor I can pass no verdict at all. I would rather trust you, as I trust myself, to the mercy of God. . . . However, I have one question."

"Ask it," said Pierre Duhamel.

"For you and for your wife, everything ends on Rubicon Day. But what about the helpless ones—your little clowns of God, for example? Oh, yes, I saw them in the garden this afternoon! I talked with their *gouvernante*, who told me you were one of their most important sponsors. So, in the bad times, what will you do? Leave them to die like chickens in a barn fire, or toss them out as playthings for the barbarians?"

Pierre Duhamel finished his drink and set down the glass. He fished out a handkerchief and dabbed at his lips. He said, with rueful formality:

"You are a very intelligent man, Monseigneur; but even you do not see the whole future. My little clowns are already provided for. Under a series of most secret political directives, persons who, by reason of insanity, incurable infirmity or other gross disability, will be a burden on the wartime state will, immediately on the outbreak of hostilities, be discreetly eliminated! Hitler gave us the blueprints for that one. We have updated them to include a compassionate rather than a brutal disposal. . . . I shock you, of course?"

"What shocks me is that you can continue to live with this secret."

"What do I do? If I try to publicize it, I am branded a madman —like you with your vision of Armageddon and the Second Coming. You see, we are both in the same sad galley."

"Then let us see how we get out of it, my friend."

"First," said Duhamel, "let's look at your problem. You are, as I said, officially untouchable. You will find it increasingly difficult to circulate. Certain countries will hesitate to give you a visa. You will be harassed at every point. Your bags will be rifled. You will have lengthy sessions with frontier officials. . . . You will be surprised at how uncomfortable life can be. So, all in all, I think we have to get you a new passport in a new name."

"Can you do that?"

"I do it all the time for people on special assignment. You are not on assignment but you are most certainly a special case. Do you have any recent photographs of yourself?"

"I have a dozen copies of the one in my present passport. I was told some countries require them for visa applications."

"Give me three of them. I'll have your passport delivered here tomorrow."

"You're a good friend, Pierre. Thank you."

"Please!" Pierre Duhamel gave him a sudden boyish grin. "My master, the President, wants you out of the country. I am instructed to do everything possible to set you on your way."

"Why should he care so much?"

"He understands theatre," said Pierre Duhamel drily. "One man walking on the water is a miracle. Two is quite ridiculous."

The image amused them both. They laughed and the tension was broken. Pierre Duhamel dropped his pose of defensive irony and began to talk more freely.

". . . When you see the battle plans laid out, it is like a vision of the inferno. No horror is absent. There are neutron bombs, poison gas, spray-borne deadly diseases. In theory of course it is all based on limited action; so that the greatest horrors are held as deterrents in reserve. But, in fact, once the first shots are fired, there will be no limit to the escalation. . . . Once you've done one murder, the rest are easy, because you have only one life in jeopardy to the hangman."

"Enough!" Jean Marie Barette stopped the conversation abruptly. "You have talked yourself and your wife into a suicide pact with a surfeit of horrors! I refuse to surrender this whole planet to evil. If we can hold one corner of it for hoping and loving then we'll do it. . . . Pierre, you hate what is being plotted. You hate your impotence in the face of the vast unreason. . . . Why not make one last act of faith and step up to the firing line with me?"

"To do what?" asked Pierre Duhamel.

"Let's shock the world into listening to us. Let's tell them first about God's little clowns and what will happen to them on Rubicon Day. You get hold of the document. I'll get Georg Rainer to arrange the press conference—and we'll face it together."

"And then?"

"Dear God! We'll rouse the conscience of the world! People always rise up against the evil done to children."

"Do they? We're nearly at the end of the century and there's still child labour in Europe, not to mention the rest of the world. There's still no effective legislation against child abuse; and women are still fighting each other and their legislators over the killing of the near-term fetus. . . . No, my dear Jean! Trust in God if you must, but never, never in man. If I did what you suggest, the press would black us out and the police would have us in the deepest *cachot* in the country inside half-an-hour. . . . I'm sorry. I am a servant of what is. When what is becomes unbearable, I make my exit. *La comédie est finie.* Give me those photographs. You'll have a new passport and a new identity tomorrow."

Jean Marie took the photographs out of his wallet and handed them over. As he did so he grasped Duhamel's hand and held it firmly.

"I won't let you go like this! You're doing a terrible thing. You're closing your ears and your heart to a clear call. It may be the last one you get."

Duhamel disengaged himself from the grip.

"You have it wrong, Monseigneur." There was a remote wraith-like sadness in his voice. "I answered my call a long time ago. When my wife fell ill and the doctor gave me the prognosis, I walked to Notre Dame and sat all alone in front of the sanctuary. I didn't pray. I gave the Almighty an ultimatum. I said: '*Eh bien*! Because she's got to wear it, I'll wear it, too. I'll make her as happy as I can for as long as she's alive. But understand, enough is enough! If you push us anymore, I'll hand back the keys to the house of life and we'll both walk out . . .' Well, He's done it, hasn't He? Even to you He didn't say, 'Tell them to reform the world or else!' You got the same message as I get every day in the presidential dispatches. Judgment Day is round the corner. There's no hope! There's no way out! So, for me, all bets are off. I'm sorry for my little clowns; but I didn't beget them and I wasn't around on creation day. I didn't mix the whole bloody explosive mess of the universe. . . . Do you understand, Monseigneur?"

"Everything," said Jean Marie Barette, "except one item. Why are you taking all this trouble over me?"

"God knows! Probably because I admire the courage of a man who can take life and all the filth of it without any conditions at all. My little clowns are like that; but only because they haven't the brains to know better. At least they'll die happy." He scribbled a number on the pad beside the phone. "That's my home telephone. If you need me, call. If I'm not available ask for Charlot. He's my majordomo and very good at improvising tactical operations. However, you should be safe here for a day or two. After that, please be very careful. People don't see them; but the dagger-men are already in the streets!"

When Duhamel had gone he fell prey to a winter fear: the prickling dread of the lone traveller who hears the wolf howls from the timberline. He could not bear the solitude of his room; so he went down to the restaurant, where the *patronne* found him a table in a quiet angle, from which he could survey the rest of the company. He ordered a piece of melon, a small entrecote, a half-bottle of the house wine, then settled down to enjoy the meal.

At least there was no menace here. The lighting was restful; there were fresh flowers on every table. The napery was spotless, the service discreet. The clients, at first glance, were affluent businessmen and bureaucrats with their assorted womenfolk. Even as he made the judgment, he caught sight of himself in a wall mirror, and realized that he, who had once worn the red of a Cardinal and the white of a Pope, was now just one more grey-haired fellow in the uniform of the bourgeoisie.

The very ordinariness of his own image reminded him of one of Carl Mendelius' earliest lectures at the Gregorian. He was explaining the nature of the Gospel parables. Many of them, he said, were records of Jesus' table talk. Their metaphors of masters and servants and meals were prompted by immediate and commonplace surroundings. Then he added a rider to the proposition: ". . . However, the familiar stories are like a minefield, full of traps and trip wires. They all contain contradictions, alienating elements, which bring the listener up short and make him see a new potential, for good or evil, in the most banal event."

In his own encounter with Pierre Duhamel, he had been quite unprepared for the finality of the man's despair. It was the more terrible because it was quite passionless. It could compass, without a tremor, the most monstrous perversities; but it would not find room for the smallest hope or the simplest joy. It was so rational a madness that one could neither cure it nor argue against it. And yet, and yet . . . there was more than one trip wire in the minefield! Pierre Duhamel might despair of himself; but Jean Marie Barette must never despair of him. He must still believe that so long as life lasted, Pierre Duhamel was still within the reach of Everlasting Mercy. Jean Marie must still make prayer for his soul, must still reach out warm hands to unfreeze his stubborn heart.

The steak was tender and the wine was smooth; but even as he savoured them, Jean Marie was preoccupied by the challenge that now presented itself. His credibility was at stake—not as a visionary, but as a simple bearer of God's good news to man. He had accused Duhamel of rejecting the good news; but was it not rather Jean Marie Barette—once a Pope and servant of the servants of God—who had failed to present it with faith and love enough? Once again, he was urged imperatively to open himself to a new inpouring of strength and authority. His reverie was interrupted by the *patronne*, who paused at his table to ask how he was enjoying the food. He complimented her with a smile.

"I've been fed like a king, madame."

"In Gascony we would say 'fed like the Pope's mule.' "

There was a gleam of mischief in her eyes, but Jean Marie was in no mood to embroider the joke. He asked, "Can you tell me, is it far from here to Monsieur Duhamel's house?"

"About ten minutes by car. If you want to go there in the morning I can have one of the staff drive you. But you should telephone first. The place is guarded like a fortress by security men and dogs."

"I am sure Monsieur Duhamel will receive me. I should like to go there immediately after dinner."

"In that case, let me call a taxi. The driver can wait and bring you back."

"Thank you, madame."

"Please! It is my pleasure." She made a show of brushing a few crumbs from the cloth and said softly, "Of course, I would much rather be feeding the Pope than his mule."

"I'm sure he'll be happy to visit you, madame—once I can assure him of your absolute discretion."

"As to that," said Madame sweetly, "all our clients trust us. We learned very quickly from Monsieur Duhamel that silence is golden! . . . For dessert may I recommend the raspberries. They come from our own garden. . . ."

He finished the meal without haste. It was almost as if he were an athlete, running with a pace-maker who would, at a given moment, hand the race over to him. His conscious attention began to shift from Duhamel to his invalid wife. It was as if she were stretching out her hand to reach him. He finished his coffee, walked to the booth and telephoned Duhamel's private number. A male voice answered.

"Who is speaking, please?"

"This is Monsieur Grégoire. I should like to speak to Monsieur Duhamel."

"I'm afraid that is not possible."

"Then will you please tell him I shall be at his house in fifteen minutes."

"That will not be convenient. Madame is very ill. The doctor is with her now; and Monsieur Duhamel is in conference with an overseas visitor."

"What is your name, please?"

"Charlot."

"Charlot, two hours ago Monsieur Duhamel named you to me as a man of confidence to whom I should turn in an emergency. This is an emergency, so will you please do exactly as I ask and let Monsieur Duhamel decide whether my visit is opportune or not? I shall be with you in fifteen minutes."

The taxi arrived in the middle of a thunderstorm. The driver was a laconic fellow who announced his contract terms for this sort of job, and once they were accepted, lapsed into silence. Jean Marie Barette closed his eyes and disposed himself to what would be demanded of him in the coming encounters.

The house of Pierre Duhamel was a large country mansion in the style of the Second Empire, set in a small park, behind a tall fence of iron spikes. The front gate was closed and a police car with two men in it was parked outside. Immediate dilemma! On the telephone he had identified himself as Monsieur Grégoire. If the police demanded his papers he would be revealed as Jean Marie Barette, a most compromising visitor. He decided to bluff it out. He rolled down the window and spoke to the nearer police officer.

"I am Monsieur Grégoire. I have an appointment with Monsieur Duhamel."

"Wait a moment!" The policeman picked up a pocket radio and called the house. "A certain Grégoire. He says he has an appointment."

Jean Marie could not make out the answer but apparently it satisfied the policeman, who nodded and said:

"You're expected. Identification, please!"

"I was instructed not to carry it on this occasion. You may check that with Monsieur Duhamel."

The policeman called again. This time there was a longish interval before clearance was given. Then, the gates opened electrically, the policeman waved him through and the gates closed again. The taxi had hardly reached the portal when the front door was opened by Pierre Duhamel himself. He was shaking with anger.

"For God's sake, man! What is this? Paulette has collapsed. There's a man from Moscow in my drawing room. What the hell do you want?"

"Where is your wife?"

"Upstairs. The doctor's with her."

"Take me to her!"

Pierre Duhamel stared at him as if he were a stranger, then he made a small shrugging gesture of surrender. "Very well! Follow me, please."

He led the way upstairs and pushed open the door of the bedroom. Paulette Duhamel, a pale, shrunken figure, was lying propped about with pillows in the big four-poster bed. The doctor stood holding her limp wrist in his hand counting the pulse-beats.

Duhamel asked, "Any change?"

The doctor shook his head. "The paraplegia has extended itself. The reflexes are weaker. There is fluid in both lungs, because the muscles of the respiratory system are beginning to fail. We may do a little for her in hospital but not much. . . . Who is this gentleman?"

"An old friend. A priest."

"Ah!" The doctor was obviously surprised but tactful. "Then I shall leave you with her for a while. She drifts in and out of consciousness. If there is any marked change, please call me instantly. I shall be just outside."

He went out.

Pierre Duhamel said with cold anger, "I want no rites, no mumbo jumbo. If she could speak she would refuse them, too."

"There will be no rites," said Jean Marie Barette gently. "I will sit and hold her hand. You can wait if you wish—unless your visitor is impatient."

"He'll be patient," said Pierre Duhamel harshly. "He needs me. He's got famine on his hands this winter."

Jean Marie said nothing. He drew a chair to the bedside, sat down, picked up the woman's slack wasted hand and held it between his own. Pierre Duhamel, standing at the foot of the bed, saw a curious transformation. Jean Marie's body became quite rigid; the muscles of his face tightened, so that, in the half-light of the sickroom, his features looked as though they had been carved from wood. Something else was happening, too, which he could not put into words. It was as if all the life inside the man were draining away from the peripheries of his body into some secret well at the center of himself. All the while Paulette lay there, a sad, shrunken wax doll, her eyes closed, her breathing shallow and full of rales, so that Duhamel wished with all his heart it would stop and she—that special and essential she whom he had loved for a lifetime—might be released like a songbird from its cage.

The wish was so poignant it seemed to put a stop on time. Whether he stood for seconds or minutes or hours Duhamel did not know. He looked again at Barette. He was changing again—the muscles softening, the taut features relaxing into a momentary smile. Then he opened his eyes and turned to the woman on the bed. He said quite casually:

"You can open your eyes now, madame."

Paulette Duhamel opened her eyes and instantly focused them on her husband at the foot of the bed. She spoke plainly, in a weak but unwavering voice.

"Hullo, *chéri.* I seem to have been foolish again."

She raised her arms to embrace him and the first thing Duhamel noticed was that the constant tremors which characterized the late stage of the disease had ceased. He bent to kiss her. When he disengaged himself, Jean Marie Barette was standing at the open door, chatting quietly with the doctor. The doctor moved to the bed, took Paulette's pulse count and auscultated her chest once more. When he straightened up, he was smiling uncertainly.

"Well, well! I think we may all relax a little, especially you, madame. This nastiness seems to be over for the moment. However, you must stay very quiet. In the morning we can think about clearing up that respiratory problem. But for now—*grâce à Dieu!*—we are out of crisis." As he walked down the hall with Pierre Duhamel and Jean Marie he became more expansive and voluble. "With this disease one never knows. Sudden collapses are not too common, but they can happen, as you saw tonight. Then, with equal suddenness, there is remission. The patient returns to a euphoric state and the degeneration slows down. . . . I have noticed often that a religious intervention, like yours tonight, Father, or the administration of the last rites, may produce in the patient a great calm, which is in itself a therapy. . . . You will remember that on the ancient island of Cos . . ."

Duhamel steered him diplomatically to the exit and then came back to Jean Marie. He was like a sleepwalker waking in a strange countryside. He was also most oddly humble.

"I don't know what you did or how you did it, but I think I owe you a life."

"You owe nothing to me." Jean Marie spoke with a spartan authority. "You are in debt to God; but since you are in contest with him, why not make the payment to your little clowns?"

"What made you come tonight?"

"Sometimes, like all the mad, I hear voices."

"Don't mock me, Monseigneur! I'm tired; and my night isn't half over."

"I'll be going now."

"Wait! I'd like you to meet my visitor."

"Are you sure he wants to meet me?"

"Let's ask him," said Pierre Duhamel—and walked him into the library to meet Sergei Andrevich Petrov, Minister for Agricultural Production in the U.S.S.R.

He was a short man, bulky as a barrel, part Georgian, part Circassian, who was born into the subsistence economy of the Caucasus, yet understood as if by animal instinct the problem of feeding a continent that stretched from Europe to China. He greeted Jean Marie with a bone-crushing handshake and a rough joke.

"So your Holiness is out of a job. What are you doing now? Playing grey eminence to our friend Duhamel?"

His smile took the sting out of the remark but Duhamel rounded on him sharply.

"You're out of order, Sergei."

"A bad joke! I'm sorry. But I have to have answers for Moscow. Do we eat this winter, or are we on short rations? Our discussion was interrupted; so I am sharp-tempered."

"It's my fault," said Jean Marie. "I came uninvited."

"And made me a private miracle," said Pierre Duhamel. "My wife is past the crisis."

"Perhaps he will make one for me. God knows I need it." Petrov swung round to face Jean Marie Barette. "For Russia, two bad seasons make a catastrophe. When there's no feed grain we have to slaughter the livestock. With no reserves of bread grains we have to ration civilians to feed the armed forces. Now the Americans and Canadians are cutting off supplies. Grain is classified as war material. The Australians are selling all their surplus to China. So, I'm running round the world offering gold bullion for wheat. . . . And, would you believe it, I can hardly find a bushel?"

"And if we sell it to him," Duhamel added the sour afterthought, "we are perfidious France breaching the solidarity of Western Europe, and exposing ourselves to economic sanction by the Americans."

"If I don't get it somewhere, the Army has the final excuse it needs to precipitate a war." He gave a humourless chuckle and flung out his hands in a gesture of despair. "So, there's a challenge to a miracle worker!"

"There was a time," said Jean Marie, "when my good offices might have meant something among the nations. Not anymore.

If I attempted now to intervene in affairs of state, I should be written off as a crank."

"I'm not so sure," said Sergei Petrov. "The whole world's a madhouse these days. You're original enough to provide some diversion. . . . Why don't you call me tomorrow at the embassy? I'd like to talk with you before I go back to Moscow."

"Better still," said Pierre Duhamel, "why don't you call him at the Hostellerie des Chevaliers? I wouldn't trust a laundry list to your embassy switchboard—and I'm trying to protect our friend as far as I can. . . . Now, if you'll excuse us, Jean. We've got a long night ahead."

He pulled the bell rope by the fireplace and an instant later Charlot was at the door, ready to conduct the guest to his taxi. Jean Marie shook hands with the two men.

Petrov said with a grin, "If you can multiply loaves I'll give you my job tomorrow!"

"My dear Comrade Petrov," said Jean Marie Barette. "You can hardly write God out of the Communist manifesto and then expect him to show up every harvest time!"

"You asked for that, Sergei!' Pierre Duhamel laughed and said to Jean Marie, "I'll pass by tomorrow with the documents. . . . Perhaps by then I'll have found words to thank you."

"I have a meeting at my brother's bank in the morning. I expect to be back by early evening. Good night, gentlemen."

The impassive Charlot conducted him to the door. The taxi driver was drowsing in his cab. The police car was still parked at the gate. Far away in the garden he heard the baying of hounds, as the security men checking the perimeter flushed a fox out of the shrubbery.

By the time he had finished his prayers and his preparations for bed it was one in the morning. He was desperately tired; but he lay a long time, wakeful, trying to understand the strange otherworldly logic of the evening's events. Twice now—once with Carl Mendelius and again with Paulette Duhamel—he had experienced the inpouring, the offering of himself as a conduit, through which a gift of comfort was made available to others.

It was a sensation quite different from that associated with the rapture and the disclosures of the vision. Then he had been literally snatched out of himself, subjected to an illumination, endowed with a knowledge which he had in nowise solicited or desired. The effect was instant and permanent. He was marked and burdened by it forever.

The inpouring was a transient phenomenon. It began with an impulse of pity or love, or a simple understanding of another's profound need. There was an empathy—more, a mode of identity—between himself and the needy. It was himself who urged mercy upon the Unseen Father, through the merit of the incarnate Son, and he offered the same self as the vessel through which the gifts of the Spirit might be passed. There was no sense of miracle, of magic or thaumaturgy. It was an act of love, instinctive and unreasoned, through which a gift was passed or renewed.

But though the act was a free dedication of himself, the impulse that prompted it came from elsewhere. He could not say why he had offered himself as a mediator for Paulette Duhamel and not for Sergei Petrov, upon whom depended matters of vast consequence: famine and the pestilence of war. Petrov made jokes about miracles—but he wanted one desperately. Offer him half a loaf on the winter ration and he would happily sing the doxology with the Patriarch in Moscow.

So why the difference? Why the prompting towards the frail one, the facile refusal of the other? It was not an act of judgment, it was an unreasoned response—the reed bowing to the wind, the migrant goose responding to the strange primal prompting that bade him begone before the winter.

Once, a long time ago, while he was still a junior in the Sacred College, he had strolled with Carl Mendelius in a villa garden overlooking Lake Nemi. It was one of those magical days, the air vibrant with the hum of cicadas, the grapes full on the vine, the sky washed clean of clouds, the pines marching like pikemen across the ridges. Mendelius had startled him with a strange proposition:

". . . All idolatry springs from a desire for order. We want to be neat, like the animals. We mark out our territories with musk and feces. We make hierarchies like the bees and ethics like the ants. And we choose gods to set the stamp of approval on our creations. . . . What we cannot cope with is the untidiness of the universe, the lunatic aspect of a cosmos with no known beginning, no visible end and no apparent meaning to all its bustling dynamics. . . . We cannot tolerate its monstrous indifference in the face of all our fears and agonies. . . . The prophets offer us hope; but only the man-god can make the paradox tolerable. This is why the coming of Jesus is a healing and a saving event. He is not what we should have created for ourselves. He is truly the sign of peace because He is the sign of contradiction. His career is a brief tragic failure. He dies in dishonour; but then most strangely, He lives. He is not only yesterday. He is today and tomorrow. He is as available to the humblest as to the highest. . . .

"But look what we humans have done with Him. We have bloated His simple talk into a babble of philosophies. We have inflated the family of His believers into an imperial bureaucracy, justified only because it exists and cannot be dismantled without a cataclysm. The man who claims to be the custodian of His truth lives in a vast palace, surrounded by celibate males—like you and me, Jean!—who have never earned a crust by the labour of their hands, never dried a woman's tears or sat with a sick child until sunrise. . . .

"If ever they make you Pope, Jean, keep one small part of yourself for a private loving. If you don't, they'll turn you into a Pharaoh, mummified and embalmed before you're dead. . . ."

The summer landscape of the Alban hills merged into the contours of the dream country. The sound of Mendelius' voice faded behind the piping of the nightingales in the garden of the Hostellerie. Jean Marie Barette, dispenser of mysteries beyond his own frail grasp, lapsed into sleep.

X

He woke refreshed and immediately regretted his involvement with the moneymen. He reached for the telephone to call Alain at the bank and cancel the meeting of trustees; then he thought better of it. New in the world, already in quarantine as a plague-carrier, he could not afford to lose any line of communication.

In this last decade of the century, bankers were better equipped than any other group to chart the progress of mankind's mortal disease. At every day's end their computers told the story and no amount of rhetoric could change the grim passionless text: gold up, the dollar down, rare metals booming, futures in oil and grain and soybeans climbing through the roof, equities on the seesaw, confidence eroding every week towards the panic point.

Jean Marie Barette remembered his long sessions with the financiers of the Vatican, and how bleak a picture emerged from all their cabalistic calculations. They bought gold, but sold mining shares, because, they said, that was market advice. The real story was that the black guerrillas in South Africa were strong, well trained and well armed. If they could blow up an oil refinery they could certainly explode the deep tunnels of the mines. So you bought the metal and got rid of the threatened asset. One of the most potent arguments against the publication of his encyclical had been that it would put the markets of the world in a panic and expose the Vatican itself to enormous financial loss.

Jean Marie had come out of every meeting wrestling with his conscience, because his clerical experts, like all others of their ilk, were forced to speculate, without distinction, upon the moralities and immoralities of mankind. It was one domain of the Church's life where he approved of secrecy—if only because there was no way he could justify or even explain the faint bloodstains on every balance sheet, whether they came from exploited labour, a rough bargain in the market, or a reformed villain buying a first-class ride to heaven.

The trust which his father had set up to preserve the fortune he had accumulated for his family was a substantial one. Jean Marie's share of the funds was administered in a special fashion. The capital remained untouched, the increment was at his disposal. As a parish priest and later as a bishop he had dedicated it to works connected with the welfare of his flock. As Pope he had used it for charities and gifts to people in personal crisis. He still believed that while social reform could only be accomplished by effective organizations soundly financed, there was still no substitute for the act of compassion, the secret affirmation of brotherhood in affliction. Now, he himself had to make claim for sustenance. He was sixty-five years old, statistically unemployed —and in need of a minimal liberty to spread the word that had been given to him.

There were four trustees, with whom he must deal. Each was a senior official of a major bank. Alain introduced them with appropriate ceremony; Sansom from Barclays, Winter from the Chase, Lambert from the Crédit Lyonnais, Mme. Saracini from the Banco Ambrogiano all' Estero.

They were all respectful, all a trifle wary. Money lived in strange houses; power was controlled by unlikely hands. Besides, they were being called to account for their stewardship—and they wondered how well this onetime Pope could read a balance sheet and a profit-and-loss account.

Mme. Saracini was their spokesman: a tall, olive-skinned woman in her late thirties, dressed in a suit of blue linen, with lace at her throat and wrists. Her only jewellery was a wedding band, and a gold jabot brooch set with aquamarine. She spoke French with a faintly Italianate lilt. She also had a sense of humour and was obviously prepared to exercise it. She asked innocently:

"Forgive me, but how do you like to be addressed? It can't be Holiness. Should it be Eminence or Monseigneur? It cannot possibly be Père Jean."

Jean Marie laughed. "I doubt there's any protocol. Celestine the Fifth was forced to abdicate and after his death they canonized him. I'm not dead yet so that doesn't apply. I'm certainly less than an Eminence. I've always thought Monseigneur was an unnecessary relic of monarchy. So, since I'm living as a private person, without a canonical mission, why not just Monsieur?"

"I don't agree, Jean." Alain was upset by the suggestion. "After all . . ."

"After all, dear brother, I have to live in my skin and I do like to feel comfortable. . . . Now, madame, you were going to explain the mysteries of money."

"I'm sure," said Mme. Saracini with a smile, "you understand there are no mysteries at all—only the problems of maintaining a firm capital base and an income that keeps ahead of inflation. . . . This means that there is need of an active and vigilant administration. Fortunately you have had that, since your brother is a very good banker. . . . The capital, valued at the end of the last financial year, is some eight million Swiss francs. This capital, as you will see, is divided in a fairly stable ratio: thirty percent real estate, both urban and rural, twenty percent equities, twenty percent prime bonds, ten percent in art works and antiques and the remaining twenty percent liquid in gold and short-term money. . . . It's a reasonable spread. It can be varied at fairly short notice. If you have any comments, of course . . ."

"I have a question," said Jean Marie mildly. "We are threatened with war. How do we protect our possessions?"

"So far as commercial paper is concerned," said the man from the Chase, "we all have the most modern storage and retrieval systems, triplicated and sometimes quadruplicated in strategically protected areas. We've hammered out a common code of interbank practice that enables us to protect our clients against document loss. Gold, of course, is a strong-room operation. Rural land is perennial. Urban developments will be reduced to rubble, but, again, war-risk insurance favours the big operators. Art works and antiques, like gold, are a storage job. It might interest you to know that for years now we've been buying up disused mine workings and converting them for safe deposits. . . ."

"I am comforted," said Jean Marie Barette with dry irony. "I wonder why it has not been possible to invest similar money and similar ingenuity for the protection of citizens against fallout and poison gas. I wonder why we are so much concerned with the retrieval of commercial paper and so little with the proposed mass murder of the infirm and the incompetent."

There was a moment's stunned silence and then, with cold anger, Alain Hubert answered his brother.

"I will tell you why, brother Jean! It is because we, unlike many others, keep the bargain we have made with our clients—of whom you are one. Others may do ill—monstrously ill!—but you cannot blame us because we do well! I think you owe me and my colleagues an apology!"

"You're right, Alain." Jean Marie responded gravely to the reproof. "I beg your pardon—yours, too, madame, gentlemen! . . . But I hope you will permit me to make an explanation. I was shocked yesterday, shocked to the marrow!, to learn that, in this my homeland, there are plans for the elimination of the handicapped, immediately war breaks out. . . . Do any of you know of this matter?"

The man from the Crédit Lyonnais pursed his lips as though someone had put alum on his tongue.

"One hears all sorts of rumours. Some of them are based on fact; but the facts are not fully understood. If you calculate to kill a million people with a single atomic blast, and contaminate a huge peripheral area, then you have to count on some form of mercy killing for survivors beyond hope. . . . In the general chaos, who's going to draw the lines? You have to leave it to the officer in charge of the area, whoever he turns out to be."

The man from Barclays was a mite more subtle and urbane.

"Surely, my dear sir, the scenario for chaos which you set down in your own writings is almost the same as that prepared by our secular governments. The difference is that they are called upon to provide practical remedies and they do not have the luxury of moralizing about them. Even you cannot moralize about triage in a front-line hospital. The surgeon, walking down the line of wounded, is the sole arbiter of life and death. 'Operate on this one, he will survive! This one is second on the list, he may survive. Give that one a cigarette and a shot of morphine, he will die!' . . . Now, unless you are under the enormous stress of that adjudication, I submit, sir, that you have no standing in the immediate case. . . ."

Before Jean Marie had time to rebut the argument, Mme. Saracini came to his rescue. She said with bland humour:

"You see, my dear Monsieur Barette, you have, until this moment, lived a very sheltered life. You must understand that God gave up making land millions of years ago. So, if you've got a piece of real estate you hang on to it. The oil's running out with the rest of the fossil fuels. So, you have to fight to get your share. Rembrandt's dead and so is Gauguin. So, there aren't any more of their pictures. But human beings—pouf! There are too many of us already. We're due for a little genocide; and if the overkill is exaggerated then we can soon start breeding again—with some help from the sperm banks, which are housed in our vaults."

She made such a black comedy of it that they had to laugh; then, when the tension had relaxed, she pushed straight ahead into the trustees' report, which showed that Jean Marie Barette could live like a prince on his income. He thanked them for the courtesy, apologized for his lapse of manners and told them that he would draw on them only for his personal needs and let the trust pile up until Judgment Day.

The men of Barclays and the Crédit Lyonnais and the Chase took their leave. Mme. Saracini stayed behind. Alain had invited her to make a foursome at lunch with Odette, Jean Marie and himself. While they were waiting for Odette, Alain served sherry and then left them, while he took a telephone call from London. Mme. Saracini raised her glass in a silent toast and then delivered a cool reproof.

"You really were quite unpleasant to us. Why?"

"I don't know. Suddenly I was seeing two images on a split screen: all those whirring computers in their underground caverns—and, above, the bodies of children burned in front of an ice-cream parlour."

"My colleagues won't forgive you. You have made them feel guilty."

"Will you?"

"I happen to agree with you," said Mme. Saracini, "but I can't make frontal attacks. I'm the girl who makes them laugh first and see sense afterwards—when their manhood isn't threatened."

"Is my information right or wrong?"

"About euthanasia for the incompetents? It's right, of course; but you'll never prove it; because, in a strange subconscious fashion, all Europe is consenting to the conspiracy. We want an exit for ourselves and our loved ones when things get too horrible to bear."

"Do you have any children, madame?"

"No."

"And your husband?"

"He died a year after our marriage."

"Forgive me! I didn't mean to pry."

"Don't distress yourself. I'm glad you were interested enough to ask. As a matter of fact, I believe you know my father."

"Do I?"

"He is called Vittorio Malavolti. He's serving twenty years in prison for bank fraud. As I remember, he handled a great many transactions for the Vatican—cost you a lot of money, too! . . ."

"I remember. I hope you have been able to forget."

"Please! Don't be facile with me! I don't want to forget. I love my father. He is a financial genius, and he was manipulated by a lot of men whom he still protects. I worked with him. He taught me all I know about banking. He set me up clean with clean money. I bought the Banco Ambrogiano all' Estero when it was a hole-in-the-wall in Chiasso. I cleaned it up and built it up and made some strong alliances and every year I pay five percent of my father's personal debts, so that when he comes out—if he comes out!—he'll be able to walk down the street like a man. . . . And that reminds me. Don't you dare patronize your brother! He helped me get started. He pushed me into situations like this trusteeship. If he sometimes looks like a fool, it's because he married the wrong woman. But Pope or no Pope, he put you down this morning when you deserved it! That makes for respect!"

He was startled by her vehemence. Her hand was unsteady and a little runnel of liquor slopped over the side of her glass. He gave her the handkerchief from his top pocket to mop it up. He asked mildly, "Why are you so angry with me?"

"Because you don't know how important you are—especially now that you're out of office. Those articles in the newspapers made people love you. Even those who didn't agree respected you and paid attention. Sansom, the Barclays man, quoted your writings back at you this morning—and, believe me, he hardly reads anything but the financial pages! . . . So, when you do something unpleasant, you disappoint a lot of people."

"I'll try to remember it," said Jean Marie, and added with a grin, "It's a long time since I've had my knuckles rapped."

She blushed like a schoolgirl and made an awkward apology. "I've got a sharp tongue, too—and a sort of proprietory interest."

"Have you indeed?"

"Way back in the fourteenth century both my husband's family and mine were friends and correspondents of the Benincasa and of Saint Catherine herself. They supported her in her efforts to get your namesake Gregory the Eleventh back from Avignon. . . . It's a long time ago, but we Sienese are jealous of our history—and sometimes a little mystical about it." She put down the glass, fished in her handbag and brought out a notebook. "Give me your address and telephone number. I want to talk to you again."

"About anything in particular?"

"Would my immortal soul be important enough?"

"Most certainly." He acknowledged defeat with a smile and gave her the information.

And that, for the moment, was the end of their talk. Alain came in with Odette, elegant, expensive, dropping names like summer raindrops. Alain gave Jean Marie a conspiratorial wink and then left him to carry the burden of Odette's monologue until they arrived at the restaurant. Luncheon was an uneasy meal. Odette dominated the talk, while Alain remonstrated feebly against her more obvious snobberies. Mme. Saracini left before the coffee. Odette sniffed and pronounced a disdainful valediction:

"Extraordinary woman! Quite attractive—in an Italian sort of way. One wonders what domestic arrangements she's made since her husband died."

"It's none of your business," said Alain. "Let's be family for a while. What are your plans from this point, Jean? If you propose to stay in France you'll need some kind of permanent establishment: an apartment, a housekeeper . . ."

"It's too early for that. I'm still too public a figure—and obviously embarrassing to old friends. It's best I keep moving for a while."

"You should also keep silent for a while," said Alain moodily. "You are used to making big pronouncements from the top of the ladder; but, you can't do that anymore. What you said at our meeting will be all over town by evening. That's why I attacked you. I can't afford to be associated with subversive talk. . . . It's much more dangerous than you realize."

Odette chimed in, positive and omniscient as always.

"Alain's right! I was talking to the Defense Minister the other night. He's a very attractive man; though his wife is quite impossible. He said that what we needed now was not controversy but sound, businesslike diplomacy and quiet negotiation while the armed forces prepare themselves."

"Let's all understand something," said Jean Marie Barette

firmly. "I became a priest to preach the word, to tell the good news of salvation. That's not something I can be prudent about, or safe, or even kind! And I have to give you the same message as I preach to the rest of the world. The battle between good and evil is already joined; but the good man looks like a fool, while evil wears a wise man's face and justifies murder by impeccable statistics!"

"Our Cardinal doesn't say that." Odette was ready, as always, for an argument. "Last Sunday he gave the television sermon on the coin of the tribute. He said it's a matter of priorities. We obey the law as a means of serving God—and even if we make mistakes in good faith, God understands."

"I'm sure he does, my dear," said Jean Marie. "And I'm sure the Cardinal has his own reasons for being so bland—but it isn't enough! It isn't half enough!"

"We should go," said Alain diplomatically. "I have a two-thirty appointment with the Finance Minister. He's seeking our advice on the best way of launching a defense bond issue!"

He had promised himself an afternoon of simple and private pleasures—an hour of book hunting along the quais, a stroll among the artists in the Place du Tertre. He had been away so long, and this was home. Even if the family were difficult he should be able to take his ease in his own natal place.

The book hunt was rewarding. He found a first edition of Verlaine's *Fêtes galantes* with an autographed quatrain pasted inside the cover. Verlaine had always haunted him: the sad, lost drunk who wrote angel songs and lived in hell with Rimbaud, and who, if there were any justice in the universe, must be singing canticles of joy at the footstool of the Almighty.

The Place du Tertre was at first a disappointment. The painters had to eat and the tourists had to take home a piece of Paris and the canvases were cynically vulgar. But, in the least-favoured corner of the Place, he came upon a curiosity: a twisted, dwarfish girl, hardly more than twenty, dressed in a sweatshirt and jeans, etching on a glass plate with a diamond point. On the table beside her were specimens of her work: a goblet, a mirror, a punch bowl. Jean Marie picked up the goblet to examine it. The girl cautioned him roughly:

"If you drop it you pay for it!"

"I'll be very careful. It's beautiful. What does the design represent?"

She hesitated for a moment, as if afraid of mockery, then explained, "I call it a cosmos cup. The goblet's a circle, the sign of perfection. The lower part is the sea, waves and fishes. The upper is the land, wheat and vines. It's a representation of the cosmos. . . ."

"And where are the humans in the cosmos?"

"They drink from the cup."

The conceit pleased him. He wondered how far she would embellish it. He asked again, "Does God figure in the design?"

She gave him a swift, suspicious look. "Is it important?"

"It's interesting, at least."

"Are you a Christian?"

Jean Marie chuckled. "I am, even if I don't look like one."

"Then you'll know that the fish and the vine and the wheat are symbols of Christ and the Eucharist."

"How much is the piece?"

"Six hundred francs." Then she added defensively, "There's a lot of work in it."

"I can see that. I'll take it. Can you pack it safely for me?"

"Yes. It won't be elegant, but it will be safe."

She set down the work she was doing and began packing the goblet in a stained cardboard box filled with plastic pellets. Watching her, Jean Marie noticed how thin she was, and how, with the small effort, the sweat broke out on her forehead, and her hands fumbled unsteadily with the fragile piece. As he counted out the money he said:

"I'm a sentimental collector. I always like to celebrate with the artist. Will you join me for a drink and a sandwich?"

Again she gave him that wary sidelong look and said curtly, "Thanks, but you paid a good price. You don't have to do me favours."

"I was asking you to do me one," said Jean Marie Barette. "I've had a rough morning and a nervous lunch. I'd be glad of someone to talk to. Besides, it's only three steps from here to the café."

"Oh, very well."

She shoved the parcel into his hands, called to a nearby painter to watch her table, then walked with Jean Marie to the café at the corner of the Place. She had a curious, hoppity gait which slewed her almost in a half-circle with every pace. The spinal curvature was grossly pronounced, and her head, elfishly beautiful, was comically mismatched, as if set askew by a drunken sculptor.

She ordered coffee and a Cognac and a ham roll and a hard-boiled egg. She ate ravenously, while Jean Marie toyed with a glass of Vichy water and tried to keep the conversation alive.

"I had another piece of luck this afternoon: a first edition of Verlaine's *Fêtes galantes.*"

"You collect books, too?"

"I love beautiful things; but these are gifts for other people. Your goblet will go to a lady near Versailles who has multiple sclerosis. I'll write and explain the symbolism to her. . . ."

"I can save you the trouble. I typed up a little piece about it. I'll give it to you before you go. . . . Strange you should ask me where God came in."

"Why strange?"

"Most people find the subject embarrassing."

"And you?"

"I gave up being embarrassed a long time ago. I accept that I'm a freak. It's easier for me, it's easier for people if I take my oddity for granted. Sometimes it's hard though. Up here on the Place you get all types. There are some weird ones who want to sleep with crippled women. That's why I was a bit sharp with you. Some of the weird ones are even older than you."

Jean Marie threw back his head and laughed till the tears ran down his face. Finally he managed to splutter, "Dear God! And to think I had to come back to France to hear it!"

"Please! Don't make fun of me! Things can get very rough up here, believe me!"

"I do believe you." Jean Marie recovered himself slowly. "Now, would you mind telling me your name?"

"It's signed on the piece—Judith."

"Judith what?"

"Just that. In the community we use only first names."

"The Community? You mean you're a nun?"

"Not exactly. There are about a dozen of us women who live together. We're all handicapped in one way or another—not all physically! We share what we earn. We look after each other. We're also a kind of refuge for young girls of the quarter who get into bother. It sounds primitive, and it is; but it's very satisfying and we feel it puts us close to the early Christian idea. After what you paid for the cosmos cup, you deserve to be remembered tonight at the meal prayer! What's your name? I like to keep a list of people who've bought my work."

"Jean Marie Barette."

"Are you anybody important?"

"Just remember me in the meal prayer," said Jean Marie. "But tell me one thing. How did this—this community of yours start?"

"That was strange. You remember some months ago the Pope abdicated and a new one was elected. Normally it wouldn't have meant very much. I've never met anyone higher than a parish priest. But that was a bad time for me. Nothing seemed to be going right. There seemed to be a connection between that event and my life. You know what I mean?"

"I know very well," said Jean Marie with feeling.

"A little while afterwards I was working in my studio. I had a little mansard apartment down the road from here. A girl I know, a model who works for some of the painters, staggered in. She was drunk and she'd been raped and punched about and her concierge had thrown her out. I sobered her up and took her to the clinic to be patched up, then I brought her back to my place. That night she turned very strange—remote and hostile and—how do I say it?—disconnected. I was frightened to be near her and yet I didn't dare to leave her. So, just to get her interested in something, I started carving a little doll out of a clothes peg. I made three altogether; then we sat down and made dresses for them, as though I were the mother and she the child. . . . That night she slept quietly in my bed, holding my hand. Next day I got two friends to share the day with her; and so it went on until she came back to normal. By then we had a little group and it seemed a pity to break it up. We worked out that we could save money and live more comfortably if we lodged as a family. . . . The religious part? Well, that seemed to come in quite naturally. One girl had been in India and had learned meditation techniques. I'd been brought up in a convent and I rather liked the idea of meeting for family prayer. Then one of the girls brought home a worker priest she'd met in a brasserie. He talked to us, lent us books. Also, if we were bothered at night we'd telephone him and he'd arrive with a couple of his friends from the factory.

That was a help, I promise you! Well, after a while, we managed to work out a pattern of living that suited us. Few of us were virgins. None of us is sure whether we're ready for a long-term relationship with a man. Some of us may get married. But we're all believers and we work at trying to live by the Book. . . . So there we are! I'm sure it doesn't mean too much to you, but for us, it's a peace-giving thing. . . ."

"I'm very glad to have met you," said Jean Marie Barette. "And very proud to have your cosmos cup. Would you accept a gift from me?"

"What sort of gift?" The old wary look was back.

He hastened to dispel her fears. "The Verlaine I found today. There is a line in it that might have been written about you. It's in the poet's own handwriting." He took the small volume from his pocket and read her the quatrain pasted inside the jacket . . . " '*Votre âme est un paysage choisi. . . .*' " He asked very humbly, "Will you accept it please?"

"If you'll dedicate it for me."

"What sort of dedication?"

"Oh, the usual. Just a little word and your autograph."

He thought about it for a moment and then wrote:

FOR JUDITH, WHO SHOWED ME THE UNIVERSE IN A WINE CUP.
Jean Marie Barette,
lately Pope Gregory XVII

The girl stared, unbelieving, at the classic script. She looked up, searching for mockery in his smiling face. She said tremulously:

"I don't understand—I . . ."

"I don't understand either," said Jean Marie Barette. "But I think you have just given me a lesson in faith."

"I don't know what you mean," said the small, twisted girl.

"It means that what I was trying to tell the world from Vatican Hill, you have accomplished from a mansard in Paris. Let me try to explain. . . ."

. . . And when he had finished telling her the whole long story, she stretched out an emaciated hand, rough from the etcher's tools, and laid it over his. She said with an urchin grin:

"I hope I can tell it to the girls the way you've explained it to me. It would help if I could. Every so often they get fed up, because our little family seems so pointless and disorganized. I keep saying that there's one good thing about hitting rock bottom. The only place to go is up!" Her smile faded and she added gravely, "You're down there now; so you know. Would you like to come home to dinner?"

"Thank you; but no!" He was careful not to disappoint. "You see, Judith my love, you don't need me. Your own hearts have taught you better than I ever could. Already you have Christ in the midst of you."

The evening traffic was murderous; but he rode back to the Hostellerie on a white cloud of serenity. Today, if ever in his life, he had seen how the Spirit pre-empted all the plans of high men. This tiny group of women, maimed and threatened, had made themselves a family. They had asked no patent, no rescript. They had love to share and they shared it. They needed to think; they thought. They found an impulse to pray; they prayed. They found themselves a teacher in a workers' bar; and girls in trouble came to them, because they felt the warmth of the hearth fire.

The group might not be stable. It had no guarantees of continuity. There was no constitution, no sanction to give it legal identity. But what matter? It was like the campfire in the desert, lit at nightfall, quenched at dawn; but while it lasted it was a testimony to human sojourn to the God who visited man in his dreams. Once again the voice of Carl Mendelius wove itself into his reverie:

". . . The Kingdom of God is a dwelling place for men. What else can it signify but a condition in which human existence is not only tolerable but joyful—because it is open to infinity. . . ."

How better could one express the phenomenon of a small, twisted girl who engraved the cosmos on a wine glass and made a family for hurt women under the rooftops of Paris?

When he arrived at the Hostellerie his first act was to telephone Tübingen. Lotte was at the hospital but Johann was at home. He had good news.

"Father's condition is stable. The infection is under control. . . . We're still not sure about his sight; but at least we know he'll survive. Oh, another piece of news! The valley's ours. The contracts were signed today. I'm going down next week to talk to surveyors and architects and engineers. And I've been deferred from military service on compassionate grounds! How are things with you, Uncle Jean?"

"Good, very good! Will you give a message to your father? Write it down like a good fellow."

"Go ahead."

"Tell him from me: 'Today I was again given a sign. It came from a woman who showed me the cosmos in a wine glass.' Repeat that please."

"Today you were again given a sign. It came from a woman who showed you the cosmos in a wine glass."

"If ever you get a message that purports to come from me, it must carry that identification."

"Understood! What are your movements, Uncle Jean?"

"I don't know—but they may be hurried. Remember what I told you. Get your family out of Tübingen as soon as you can. My love to you all!"

"And ours to you. What's the weather like in Paris?"

"Threatening."

"Same here. We disbanded our club as you suggested."

"And got rid of the equipment?"

"Yes."

"Good! I'll be in touch whenever I can. Remember me kindly to Professor Meissner. *Auf wiedersehen.*"

He had hardly set down the receiver when Pierre Duhamel came to deliver his new passport, and a new identity card, inscribed to J. M. Grégoire, *pasteur en retraite.* He described to Jean Marie their uses and limitations.

". . . Everything is authentic, since you once bore the name Gregory. You are a minister of religion. You are pensioned off. The numbers on the documents belong to a series used for special categories of government agents—so no French immigration officer will want to ask questions. Foreign consulates will not raise too many problems about granting a visa to a retired clergyman travelling for his health. . . . However, try not to lose the documents, try not to get into trouble and have them impounded. That could be embarrassing to me. . . . Apropos of which, my dear Monseigneur, you opened your mouth very wide with the bankers this morning. The lines were buzzing as soon as they got back to their offices. . . . Once again you are named as a dangerous gadfly."

"And you, my dear Pierre, are you of the same mind about me?"

Duhamel ignored the question. He said simply:

"My wife sends you her thanks. She is in remission again and more comfortable than she has been for a long time. The curious thing is that even though she appeared to be unconscious, she remembers your visit and describes what you did, most vividly, as a 'caress of life.' Under other circumstances I could be very jealous of you."

Jean Marie ignored the tiny barb. "I bought a small gift for you both."

"There was no need." Duhamel was touched. "We are already in your debt."

Jean Marie handed him the cardboard box and made a smiling apology. "I wasn't able to have it gift-wrapped. You can open it if you want."

Duhamel snapped the string, opened the box and took out the goblet. He examined it with the care of a connoisseur.

"This is lovely. Where did you find it?"

Jean Marie recounted his meeting with Judith, the maimed one, in the Place du Tertre. He gave him the paper which explained the symbolism of the design, and told of the curious little community of women.

Pierre Duhamel listened in silence and made only a single terse comment: "You're working very hard to convert me."

"On the contrary," said Jean Marie firmly. "I'm called to give witness, to offer the gifts of faith and hope and loving. What you do with them is your most private affair. . . ." His tone changed to one of pleading and desperate persuasion. "Pierre, my friend, you've helped me. I want to help you. What your wife called the caress of life is something very real. I felt it today when this girl, who looks like a caricature of womanhood, laid her hand on mine and invited me into her special world. . . . This great stoic courage of yours is so—so barren, so desperately sad!"

"I'm in a sad business," said Pierre Duhamel with arctic humour. "I'm a funeral director, preparing the obsequies of civilization. That demands a certain grand style. . . . Which reminds me. . . . Tomorrow I shall be asked to sign a document requiring Grade A surveillance of a certain Jean Marie Barette."

"Classified as what?"

"Anti-government agitator."

"And you will sign it?"

"Of course. But I'll hold it up for a few hours so that you can make suitable arrangements."

"I'll leave here tomorrow morning."

"Before you go"—Duhamel handed him a slip of paper—"call this number. Petrov wants to talk to you."

"About what?"

"Bread, politics—and a few fantasies of his own."

"When we met in Rome I liked him. Can I still trust him?"

"Not as far as you can trust me. But you'll find him much more agreeable. . . ." For the first time he relaxed. He held the cosmos cup in his hands and turned it round and round, studying all the details of the etching. Finally he said, "We will drink from it, Paulette and I. We'll think of you and the little *bossue* on the Place du Tertre. . . . Who knows? It's good enough theatre to suspend our disbelief. . . . But, you understand, this is the bad time—the day of the black battalions. If you fall into their hands, I can't help you at all."

"What does your President think of all this?"

"Our President? For God's sake! He's the same as every other president, prime minister, party leader, duce or caudillo. He's got the flag tattooed on his back and the party manifesto on his chest. If you ask him why we have to go to war, he'll tell you that war is a cyclic phenomenon, or you can't make an omelette without breaking eggs or—God rot him in hell—war is the archetypal orgasm: agony, ecstasy, and the long, long quiet afterwards. I've often wondered why I shouldn't kill him before I kill myself. . . ."

"Why do you stay then?"

"Because if I weren't there, who else would get you your passport—and who else would tell what goes on in the madhouse? I must go now! Make sure you've gone too, before midday tomorrow!"

Jean Marie Barette reached out and clamped firm hands on Duhamel's broad shoulders. "At least, my friend, give me time to thank you."

"Don't thank me," said Pierre Duhamel. "Just pray for me. I'm not sure how much more I can take!"

When he had gone, Jean Marie dialled the number for Sergei

Petrov. A woman's voice answered, in French. A moment later Petrov was on the line.

"Who is this?"

"Duhamel gave me a message to call you."

"Oh, yes! Thank you for being so prompt. We should meet and talk. We have interests in common."

"I believe we may have. Where do you suggest we meet? I may be under surveillance. Does that bother you?"

"Not greatly." The news did not seem to surprise him too much. "So, let me think! Tomorrow at eleven, does that suit you?"

"Yes."

"Then let's meet at the Hotel Meurice, Room five eighty. Come straight up. I'll be waiting for you."

"I have all that. Until tomorrow then."

But over the rest of tomorrow and all the days afterward there was still a very large question mark. Before the surveillance began, he had to find himself a bolt-hole, a place where he could sleep secure, from which he could communicate and travel quickly. Alain could help; but that relationship was already uneasy, and Odette was no model of discretion. He was still ruminating over the problem when the telephone rang. Mme. Saracini was on the line. She was cheerful and abrupt.

"I told you I wanted to talk to you again. When and where can we meet?"

Jean Marie hesitated for a moment and then told her, "I've been informed by a reliable source that as of tomorrow I shall be under Grade A surveillance as an anti-government agitator."

"That's madness!"

"It is, however, a fact. So I need a secure place to stay for a while. Can you help me?"

The answer came back without a second's hesitation. "Of course! How soon could you be ready to move?"

"In ten minutes."

"It will take me forty-five minutes to get to you. Pack your bag. Pay the bill. Be waiting at the front entrance."

Before he had time to thank her, she had rung off. He packed his few belongings, explained to the *patronne* that a sudden change in his personal situation dictated his brusque departure, paid his account, then sat down to read his breviary until Mme. Saracini arrived. He felt very calm, very trustful. Step by step he was being led to the proving ground. By a curious trick of association

—Saracini, Malavolti, Benincasa, we Sienese—he was reminded of the words which the twenty-five-year-old Catherine had written to Gregory XI at Avignon: "It is no longer time to sleep, because Time never sleeps, but passes like the wind. . . . In order to reconstruct the whole, it is necessary to destroy the old, right down to the foundations. . . ."

The woman who picked him up at the entrance to the Hostellerie looked ten years younger than Mme. Saracini, president of the Banco Ambrogiano all' Estero. She wore slacks and a silk blouse and a head scarf, and drove a convertible, custom-built by the most famous Italian designer. She locked his suitcase into the trunk and whisked him away with a scream of tires, before any curious guest had time to notice the car or its owner. Once on the road, however, she drove with studious care and a sharp eye for police traps, while she instructed him briskly in her plans.

". . . The safest place in Paris for you is my house—precisely because it is a house. There are no other tenants, no concierge and I can guarantee the loyalty of my domestic staff. I entertain a lot; so there's a constant coming and going of people. Any visitors you have will pass unnoticed. You will have your own apartment—a bedroom, a study and a bathroom. It has a direct telephone line and its own private stairway to the garden. My staff are underemployed; so they can easily look after your needs."

"This is most generous of you, madame; but . . ."

"There are no buts. If the arrangement doesn't work, you leave. Simple! And would you please call me by my given name, Roberta!"

Jean Marie smiled to himself in the darkness and said, "Then, Roberta, will you let me point out that there are certain risks in harbouring me."

"I'm happy to accept them. You see, I know you have a work to do. I want to be part of it. I can help more than you realize at this moment."

"Why do you want to help?"

"That's one question I'm not prepared to answer while I'm driving; but I will answer it, when I get you home."

"Try this one then. Do you think it's good for your reputation to have a man in residence?"

"I've had others, far more scandalous," she told him bluntly. "It's twenty years since my husband died. I didn't live like a nun all that time. . . . But, things happened to make me change. My father went to prison. I went through a very bad patch with someone I loved very much and who one night went crazy in my arms and nearly killed me. Then there was you. When you were Pope, I felt the same way about you as my father used to feel about the good Pope John. You had style. You had compassion. You didn't go round shouting discipline or damnation. Even when I was living pretty wildly I always felt there was a way back, as there was with my father when I'd been a naughty girl. Then, when you abdicated and I heard some of the inside story from your brother, Alain, I was furious. I thought they'd broken you; until your friend—what's his name?—wrote that wonderful piece about you."

"Mendelius?"

"That's it! . . . And then somebody passed him a letter bomb! It was then that I began to see how things fitted together. I started to go to church again, read the Bible, pick up friends that I'd dropped in the wild days, because they seemed too earnest or stuffy. . . . But we're off the track. First we install you in your apartment; then we feed you. Afterwards we talk about the future and what you need to do."

He was tempted to chide her, tell her that, while he needed help, he was not prepared to be managed. He thought better of it. He changed the subject.

"I've been provided a second passport and an identity card in the name of Jean Marie Grégoire. It's probably best if we use that name with your staff."

"I agree. There are three altogether: a man and wife and a daily maid. They've all been with me a long time. . . . We're nearly home now. My place is just off the Quai d'Orsay."

Three minutes later she stopped in front of a porte-cochère closed by a steel gate, which opened to a radio signal. The garage was on the left of the entrance and an interior stairway led to the floors above. His suite was a pair of rooms, the one a large studio lined with books, the other a bed-sitting room with a bathroom between. Outside was a balcony from which he could look down on the central atrium, which had been converted into a rock garden with a fountain in the center.

"It's not quite the Vatican," said Roberta Saracini. "But I hope you'll be comfortable. Dinner in thirty minutes. I'll send someone to fetch you."

She came in person, dressed in a house gown of some rich brocaded material, stiff as a benediction cope. She led him into the dining room, a small but beautifully proportioned room, with a coffered ceiling and refectory furniture of Spanish mahogany. The meal was simple but exquisitely cooked, a country pâté, a filet of sole, a mousse of blueberries. The wine, he told her, was much too good to waste on M. Grégoire, *pasteur en retraite*. To which she answered that the pastor was in retirement no longer and it was time to discuss what he wanted to do.

". . . I know what I must do: spread the word that the last days are upon us and that all men of goodwill must prepare for them. I know also what I must not do: make confusions or dissensions among honest believers, or undermine the principles of legitimate authority in the Christian community. . . . So, first question: how do I resolve the problem?"

"It seems to me, you've already found the solution: a new identity. After all, it's the message that's important, not the man who proclaims it."

"Not quite. How does the messenger establish his authority?"

"He shouldn't try," said Roberta Saracini. "He should put the word about, as the early Disciples did, and trust to God to make it fruitful."

There was more than piety in the way she said it. There was a total confidence, as if she had herself made proof of the proposition.

He told her, "I agree with the principle; but how do I, a man unwelcome in his own country, deprived of a canonical mission, preach the word without a breach of the obedience which I owe to the Church?"

Roberta Saracini poured coffee and handed the cup to him across the table. She offered brandy. He refused it. She explained carefully:

"I'm a banker, as you know. As a banker I have holdings in a lot of diverse enterprises: mining, fabrication, travel, advertising, entertainment, communication. So, once you are sure of what you want to say . . ."

"I have always been sure of that."

"Then we can find a hundred ways, a thousand voices, to spread the news."

"That will cost you a fortune."

"What if it does? Who's going to keep accounts after Rubicon Day?"

"How do you know about Rubicon Day?"

"I have my sources. You don't think I gamble blind in the market?"

"I suppose not."

He was still uneasy, though the explanation made sense enough. He himself would not name his sources, even to a close friend.

"There are ample funds available for whatever you want to do. I'd like to introduce you to some of my people in publishing, television and advertising. Consider them as your voices. Tell them what you want to say. You'll be surprised what ideas emerge. . . . You're looking dubious. Why? Where would the modern papacy be without television—or the American presidency for that matter? Isn't it a moral duty to use all the gifts that are placed at our disposal?"

Once again, most strongly, he was reminded of that young Sienese woman of the fourteenth century who had written to Pierre Roger de Beaufort-Turenne, Gregory XI . . . "*Siatemi uomo, virile e non timoroso* . . ." "Be a man for me, virile and not a coward!"

He was silent for a moment, considering his decision. "How soon can I meet your experts?"

"Tomorrow evening."

"And how far can I trust them?"

"The ones who sit at this table you can trust, as you trust me."

"Then, will you answer the question I asked on the way here: why do you want to help a man who is telling the end of the world?"

She did not fumble with the answer, she gave it to him, flat and unadorned.

"Because he is a man, just that! All my life I've been waiting for someone who will stride out into the storm and shout against the wind. I watched you this morning at the bank. You were so angry I thought you would burst; but you had the grace to say you were sorry for bad manners. For me that's reason enough."

"Not for me," said Jean Marie Barette. "Nobody's so strong all the time. Nobody lasts so long. The man I followed as Pope —I stood by his deathbed and watched him puking up his lifeblood and crying 'Mama, Mama, Mama!' The newspapers said he was calling on the Virgin Mary. He wasn't. He was calling for his mother in the dark. . . . Don't build on me, Roberta! Build on yourself! You're not some sad *dévote* in the middle of the menopause. I'm not some troubled priest wondering why he's wasted his whole life in celibacy."

"Tell me what you are then!" said Roberta Saracini with sudden anger. "Let's be good Jesuits and define the terms!"

"I have been given a call to proclaim the Last Things and the Coming of the Lord. I have answered the call. I seek the means to make the proclamation. You have offered me shelter and funds and experts to help me. I have accepted with gratitude; but I have nothing to give in return."

"Have I asked for anything?"

"No, but I have to warn you—and believe me it is an act of love!—you must never expect to possess any part of me—or hope to manage me in any fashion."

"For God's sake! Why do you think you have to warn me?"

"Because when we first met you talked of being mystical about your own past, about your family connection with Saint Catherine of Siena. It seemed to me a very significant prelude. You were offering me the same kind of support that she had offered Gregory the Eleventh, to bring him back from Avignon to Rome. But one can't repeat history and one can't duplicate relationships. That Gregory was a mincing man, a vacillator and a coward. I have many faults, but I am not such a man. I am called to walk a desert road. . . ." She started to protest but he stayed her with a gesture. "There is more, so please let me say it. I am not ignorant of the life and works of your little saint. I wrote my doctoral thesis on the great women mystics. I have read the *Dialogo* and the *Epistolario*. Catherine wrote much and beautifully about love, human and divine. Nevertheless, there are dark passages in her relationships that none of her biographers has wholly explained. She is too exotic for my taste; possibly because I am French and she never liked the French. But I think that once or twice she pushed the young men of her *cenacolo* too far. She was dreaming divine love when they were still struggling to make sense of the human variety—and that's when the tragedies occurred. So . . ." He smiled and shrugged. "Like good Jesuits we have defined the terms and spelled out the rules of the game. Am I forgiven?"

"Yes. But not easily." She raised her glass in a silent toast and tossed off the rest of the wine. "It's late. I have to be at work early in the morning."

"I have to go out, too. I have a meeting with the Russian Minister for Agricultural Production."

"Petrov? I've had bank dealings with him. He's tough but decent. However, he's in a desperate position. If he can't get enough grain for winter, he's a ruined man."

"And our world is one hour closer to midnight."

He rose and held back her chair. When she stood up she turned and took his hand and kissed it in the old-fashioned style.

"Good night, Monsieur Grégoire."

He accepted the gesture without comment.

"Good night, madame, and thank you for the shelter of your house!"

XI

In Room 580 of the Hotel Meurice, Jean Marie Barette, once a Pope, talked with Sergei Andrevich Petrov, Minister for Agricultural Production in the U.S.S.R. Petrov looked tired and crumpled, as if he had shed his clothes on the bedroom floor and climbed into them the next morning. His eyes were red and rheumy. His voice was hoarse and his skin exuded a smell of stale liquor. Even his sense of humour was wearing thin.

". . . You think I look a wreck? I am. Twelve, fifteen hours a day for weeks now, I'm travelling, talking, pleading, squawking for husks of grain like a starving parrot! But no one wants to sell to me. So I walk down the ladder to stage two. What do I ask for now? Intervention, mediation—what they call in the trade 'good offices.' It occurred to me you might be willing to help."

"Willing, yes," Jean Marie answered without hesitation. "How useful is another matter. In the democracies the leader of the opposition still has a strong voice and a lot of bargaining power. With me it's different. I'm just a *pasteur en retraite*. Put it another way. How would you react if I came asking favours from you in Moscow?"

"Better than you think. You have much respect everywhere. Will you try to help? The position is desperate. Famine is the horror nobody understands until it happens. Look at Africa! The warnings had been there for years, but nobody paid any heed! . . . From the Sahara to the Sachel to the Horn, suddenly thousands were dying. Now that threat hangs over us—except that for us it's dearth in winter! We'll just about get through it;

and then, as soon as the thaw comes, I promise you the rockets will be launched and our armies will move south towards the oil fields of the gulf, west through the great Hungarian plain, by sea towards India, the Philippines and Australia. It's like an axiom of mathematics. The only way to stave off disorder at home is to march against the enemy abroad. . . . The Western powers and the Chinese are playing that dangerous game the English call brinkmanship. Well, it's not a sport that you enjoy with an empty belly. So, once again, will you try to help?"

"Yes, of course I will try; but I can't work in a vacuum. I need a briefing. I need a list of trading points which your people are prepared to concede in return for urgent supplies. You, too, play the game on the edge of the precipice and you can be just as stupid as any in the West! So, I need a piece of script, however elementary, that gives me authority to act as broker in the market."

"That may be difficult."

"Without it, the rest is impossible. Come, Comrade Petrov! I can make press statements, sermons, appeals. I did it every Sunday in Saint Peter's Square! I made special diplomatic speeches on every tour. But that's the same as you making a May Day Speech on Marxist-Leninist ideology and the solidarity of the People's Soviets! It puts no meat in the stew! But with a brief in my hand, one that you can repudiate if I botch it—*Bien!* At least I will be received as an emissary with respect."

"Would you be prepared to come to Moscow?"

"Yes—provided I get a friendly invitation from the men at the top and I'm not harassed at every step by the K.G.B."

"That won't happen, I promise you."

"When would you want me there?"

"As soon as possible; but I have to stick my toe in the water just to see that there are no crabs waiting to bite it off. How can I get in touch with you?"

"Through my brother, Alain, at the bank, Halévy Frères et Barette." He scribbled the address on a desk pad and passed it to Petrov. "Alain won't know where I am; but I'll be in touch with him from time to time."

Petrov folded the paper and put it into his pocketbook. He said, "Would you join me in a drink?"

"Thank you, but it's a little early for me."

"I need one. I know I've been hitting it hard the last few

weeks; but what's a man to do at the end of another lousy day with the begging bowl? You don't get any medals for effort in this business—just fish-eyed stares and 'Tut-tut, Comrade! There must be something constructive you can do!' I know there isn't and they know there isn't; but they're safe in the Kremlin shuffling their papers while I'm wearing out shoe leather and patience."

"I thought you had some hope with Pierre Duhamel."

"So far that's all it is—hope! He's trying to work out some complicated scheme by which we purchase cargoes while they're in transit and divert them to Baltic ports. It's the size of the operation that's the problem—unless Duhamel is playing dirty. . . . What do you think of him?"

"I think he's trying to play clean in a dirty game."

"It could be. What about that drink?"

"Suggestion," said Jean Marie Barette.

"Let's hear it."

"Forget the drink. Order coffee for two. Give me your size and I'll go down and buy you a new shirt and underwear. Then you send your suit out to be pressed and take a long, hot bath while you're waiting for it."

Petrov stared at him in disbelief.

"You're telling me I'm unclean?"

"I'm telling you, dear Comrade, that if I were under the gun as you are, I'd change twice a day, never drink till after sundown—and let it be known that anyone who thinks he can do my job better is welcome to it."

"Only one problem with that prescription."

"What's that?"

"Whoever takes my job will want my head as well—and I don't want to part with it just yet. . . . But you're right about the rest of it. I'm size forty. You go buy the clothes. I'll order the coffee. It usually takes a while to get room service anyway."

"I thought you were staying at the embassy," said Jean Marie Barette.

"I am," said Sergei Petrov. "I keep this place for—private contacts."

"Are you sure they are private?"

"As sure as I can be. I know the room is not bugged. . . . On the other hand, that scares me more than anything."

"Why?"

"Because it could mean nobody really gives a damn what I do. I could be a sitting duck, just waiting for someone to knock me off. . . . Not that it would matter very much. The whole human race has a pretty limited run anyway."

"Precisely how long do you give it?"

"Let's see. We're now in September. If I can't get grain before the winter, the Army will march immediately after the spring thaw. If I get it, then there's a breathing space, but not too long, because there's still the problem of fuels and energy, and every big nation has a plan for pre-emptive strikes if the oil fields are threatened. . . . At worst we've got six, eight months—at best, eighteen. It's not a pretty thought, is it?"

"I'll go buy the clothes," said Jean Marie. "Any preference in colours?"

Sergei Andrevich Petrov burst into a bellow of laughter.

"I wish the old comrades could see me now! Ever since the revolution the Vatican has been a burr in our breeches. Now I have the Pope buying my underwear!"

"And what's odd about that?" asked Jean Marie with bland innocence. "The first one peddled fish in Israel."

As he went about the simple business of buying socks and underwear, he was struck not only by the comedy of the situation, but by the macabre recklessness of it. Born in the mid-twenties, he had been too young for military service with the French Army, and he had been forced to flee to the mountains to avoid conscription for forced labour under the Germans. He had fought with the Maquis and begun his seminary training a year after the end of hostilities. But one of his most vivid memories was the nightmare period when the Germans began to pull out and the whole edifice of occupation began to collapse. It was like a Walpurgisnacht of drunkenness, cruelty, heroism and complicated insanities.

Now he was seeing the same thing again—the operatic disorders in Tübingen, assassination by decree, Pierre Duhamel, the trusted servant of the Republic, conniving at secret horrors in the vain hope of preventing greater ones, and now Sergei Petrov, trying to break a blockade of the grain market and drowning his despair in vodka. It was the madness-in-little which was the most sinister of all. Famine in the Horn of Africa? Eh! What was it? A natural purge of surplus population from marginal land—that is, until you picked up a child with a belly like a balloon and arms like matchsticks and hardly enough heartbeat to pump air into its lungs. Then you cursed God and cursed man, his errant creature, and primed the bombs to blast the whole mess into oblivion!

Whereupon, with sublime irrelevance, he decided that brother Alain was right. He did need some new clothes. If he were shopping for Petrov he might just as well spend a little care on himself. There was no point in going badly dressed to one's own funeral.

That night, Roberta Saracini had three guests home to dinner. They came in work clothes and brought briefcases, an artist's folio and a video tape machine. They had the purposeful air of professionals who knew exactly what they were about and needed no advice from the unskilled. The oldest of the three was a big, florid-faced fellow with a broad smile and a shrewd eye. Roberta introduced him as Adrian Hennessy.

". . . No relation to the Cognac. He's American, speaks seven languages, and makes expensive sense in all of them. He arrived from New York this morning. If you and he can get along he will direct our operation."

The second guest was a mannish young woman whose features looked vaguely familiar. This one was the surprise packet.

". . . Natalie Duhamel, our expert on films and television. I believe you know her father."

"I do."

Jean Marie was nonplussed. The young woman gave him a cool smile and a well-rehearsed definition.

"My father and I have an excellent relationship. He doesn't produce my shows and I don't write his reports to the President. In matters of confidence, he doesn't ask, I don't tell—and vice versa!"

"It's a very precise arrangement," said Jean Marie Barette.

"And this"—Roberta Saracini presented her third guest, a stripling youth who might have modelled for the Delphic charioteer—"this is Florent de Basil. He designs, he paints, he makes beautiful songs."

"In short, a genius." He had the ready innocent smile of a child. He took Jean Marie's hand and kissed it. "I can't tell you how much I've wanted to meet you. I hope you'll be able to give me time to do a portrait."

"First things first, my love," said Roberta Saracini. "It's half-an-hour to dinner. Why don't we start work over cocktails?"

Adrian Hennessy opened his briefcase and brought out a tape recorder. Florent de Basil produced a sketch pad. Natalie Duhamel sat placidly watching. Hennessy took a swallow of liquor and stated categorically:

"We talk off the record first. If we don't agree the terms of reference we enjoy our dinner and call it a day. If we agree, then we start work forthwith. First item. How do we call the subject? That's you, sir. Remember, certain materials like notes and tape recorders have to be carried around, therefore, they can be lost. So, we don't want real names."

"My name is Jean Marie . . ."

"Then let's change it to American: John Doe. Next, the aim of our project. As Roberta has explained it, you have a message which you wish to deliver to the world. You are concerned, however, that you should not be seen to propagate this message as an official teacher of the Roman Catholic Church."

"That's an accurate summary. Yes."

"But it is still incomplete. It ignores the heart of the problem: that as a onetime Pope you still wear the aura of your office. There is no way you can make public declarations without coming into conflict with the present incumbent—who, by the way, is the least inspiring of orators. So the question is, how far are you prepared to risk that conflict?"

"Not by a single step," said Jean Marie Barette.

"I like a man who knows his own mind," said Hennessy with a grin. "But a message has to be delivered by someone; and that someone has to have some authority. After all, you don't read the letters of John Doe in church . . . you read Saint Paul and Saint Peter and Saint James. . . ."

"I don't agree," said Jean Marie. "I'm sorry; but I've had this argument ad nauseam. I almost ended believing it. Not now! Not ever again! Listen. . . ." Suddenly he was a man on fire. The listeners hung on his every word, and gesture. Hennessy reached forward and switched on the tape recorder. ". . . If each of us were locked in a silent room, deprived of all sensory reference, we should very soon become disoriented and, finally, insane. The person who would probably endure longest would be the one who was practiced in withdrawal, in meditation, whose life had an outside reference to God. I met several such people during my pontificate, three men and one woman who had been confined as religious agitators and tortured by sensory deprivation. . . . The fact is that we live only in communion—not only with our present but with the past and the future as well. We are haunted by a whole poetry of living, by lullabies half remembered and the sounds of train whistles in the night and the scent of lavender in a summer garden. We are haunted by grief, too, and fear, and images of childhood terror and the macabre dissolutions of age. . . . But I am sure that it is in this domain of our daily dreaming that the Holy Spirit establishes His own communion with us. This is how the gift is given, which we call grace: the sudden illumination, the sharp regret that leads to penitence or forgiveness, the opening of the heart to the risk of love. . . . Authority is irrelevant here. Authority is the one-eyed man in the kingdom of the blind! It can command us to everything except love and understanding. . . . So what am I trying to tell you?" He gave them a grin of self-deprecation. "Peter is dead and Paul is dead and James the brother of the Lord. Their dust is blown away by the winds of centuries. Were they large men, little men, fair or dark? Who knows? Who cares? The testimony of the Spirit, made through them, still endures." He quoted softly, "Though I speak with the tongues of men and of angels and have not charity, I am become like a sounding brass or a tinkling cymbal. . . ."

There was a long silence in the room. Jean Marie looked from one to the other, seeking a response. Their faces were blank, their eyes downcast. Finally it was Hennessy who spoke. He switched off the tape. He addressed himself not to Jean Marie but to his colleagues.

". . . I don't need to see the man who said that. I can read it, listen to it, and make my own image. Natalie?"

"I agree, totally. Imagine that with lights, makeup, cues—all the mechanics. He'd look like a whore playing a virgin—with all respect to you, Monseigneur! What do you think, Florent?"

The young man was curiously subdued. He said, "No images, certainly. I found myself hearing music—something very simple, like the old ballads that told about love and knightly deeds. . . . Perhaps I should modify that. The image should not be of the speaker. It could be of his audience. Can we think about it for a while?"

"I'm a banker," said Roberta Saracini. "But you gave me a thought, Adrian. You said, 'You don't read the letters of John

Doe in church.' Would you read a letter from this John Doe? Would you listen if he sent you a message on tape?"

"You're damn right I would!" He scribbled a note on his pad. Then he turned to Jean Marie and made a rueful apology. "I know this must sound very impertinent—treating you like some kind of puppet to be manipulated."

"I'm used to it," said Jean Marie equably. "Our people at the Vatican are experts in high theatre; and some of our masters of ceremonies were real tyrants. Don't worry! I'll let you know when I've had enough!"

"Letters!" said Natalie Duhamel. "They used to be a very fashionable form of literature."

"Still are," said Hennessy. "*Letters of Junius, Lettres de mon Moulin, Letters to The Times*! Trouble is to find editors with guts enough to run them in spite of present censorship. We could certainly find enough book publishers to run a series. . . . Could you write them, Monseigneur?"

"I've been writing them all my clerical life," said Jean Marie. "Pastoral letters, encyclicals, letters to clergy and conventual nuns. I'd welcome a change of style."

"You could also talk them onto tape?"

"Of course."

"I'm scared," said Natalie Duhamel. "Who's going to listen to sermons?"

"Was that a sermon?" The young man pointed dramatically at the tape.

"No, but can he sustain the style? . . . Can you, Monseigneur?"

"I'm not aware of style." Jean Marie was crisp and definite. "I have things to say, about living and dying. They have to be spoken heart to heart."

"If you write letters," said Hennessy boldly, "to whom do you address them? That's where you come back to authority. The editor asks, 'Who is this fellow?' The public asks, 'What the hell does he know?' "

"And you may not be dealing with editors at all," said Natalie Duhamel. "You may have to go back to the *samizdat* and the underground press or even to the wall posters of China! But Adrian's right. A letter begins 'Dear X. . . .' Who is X in this case?"

"If you're writing about the end of everything," said Florent de Basil, "it seems a pointless self-contradictory exercise. Who can do anything about the final event?"

"You're right," Jean Marie agreed with apparent good humour. "With whom do you correspond then—God?"

"Why not?" Jean Marie savoured the thought for a moment. "Where else do we turn at world's end? It's what a child might do: write letters to God and post them in a hollow tree. You could call them *Last Letters from a Small Planet*!"

"Stop right there!" Hennessy's command was like a whipcrack. He looked around at the small assembly. "Don't anybody say a word until I ask for it. The title is beautiful. I love it." He turned to Jean Marie and asked, "Could you write those letters?"

"Of course. It's not difficult." He made a small joke of it. "After all, I do talk to the Almighty every day. I don't have to learn a new language."

"How soon could you begin putting something on paper?"

"Tonight, tomorrow morning, whenever."

"Then please! One letter a day—a thousand to twelve hundred words—until further notice. Leave it to us to find the hollow tree—and an international distribution."

"One elementary question." It was Natalie Duhamel who asked it. "Who will be the author of these letters? What character and under what name? That's basic to our promotion."

Jean Marie offered a half-serious suggestion. "I can't be a child again; but I've often felt small. Why don't I sign myself 'Jeannot' . . . Little John?"

"It sounds a little clownish to me," said Roberta Saracini.

"Then let's go the whole way! Let's admit that there is such a thing as a divine folly. I'll sign myself 'Jeannot le Bouffon'! Johnny the Clown."

"Why demean yourself?" Roberta was still unhappy. "Why step so far out of character that no one will know who you really are?"

"Because then no one can accuse me of ambition or rebellion. . . . And, who but a child or a clown would write letters to the Almighty?"

"I agree with the man!" said Hennessy. "And if we can't make Johnny the Clown a household name around the globe, I'll blow my brains out. What do you say, Natalie?"

"I can see a way to visualize the whole thing if Florent can come up with a logo."

"A logo and the music, my love—and even a counterpoint

theme: 'Johnny the Clown is so simple. Why are the rest of us so complicated? . . .'"

"Let's not talk it into the air," said Hennessy. "And let's not distract the author! He's the inspired one. We're the technicians. . . . How long to dinner, Roberta? I'm starving!"

He could not believe it was so easy to write the letters. As Pontiff he had been forced to weigh every word, lest it deviate by a hair's breadth from the definitions of ancient councils: Chalcedon, Nicaea, Trent. He could not discredit the decretals of his predecessors, however much he disagreed with them. He must not speculate; he could only hope to illuminate the traditional formulae of faith. He was the fount of authority, the final arbiter of orthodoxy, the looser and the binder—himself more stringently bound than any, a tomb-slave to the Deposit of Faith.

Now, suddenly, he was free. He was no longer *Doctor et Magister* but Johnny the Clown, wide-eyed among the mysteries. Now he could sit and smell the flowers, watch the waterspout and, the fool of God, safe in his buffoon dress, dispute with his Maker.

Dear God,

I love this funny world; but I have just heard the news that You are going to destroy it; or, worse still, You are going to sit up in heaven and watch us destroy it, like comedians wrecking a grand piano, on which great masters have played Beethoven.

I can't argue with what You do. It's Your universe. You juggle the stars and manage to keep them all in space. But please, before the last big bang, could You explain some things to me? I know this is only one tiny planet; but it's where I live and, before I leave it, I'd like to understand it a little better. I'd like to understand You, too—as far as You'll let me—but for Johnny the Clown, You'll have to make it all very simple.

. . . I've never really got it clear in my mind where you fit in. No disrespect, truly! But You see, in the circus where I work, there's an audience and there's us, the people who do the tricks, and there are the animals, too. You can't leave them out because we depend on them and they on us.

Now, the audience is wonderful. Most times they're so happy and innocent you can feel the joy coming out from them; but sometimes you can smell the cruelty, too, as if they want the tigers to attack the tamer, or the aerialist to fall from the high trapeze. So, I can't really believe You're the audience!

Then there's us, the performers. We're a mixed bunch: clowns like me, acrobats, pretty girls on horseback, the people on the high wire, the women with the performing dogs and the elephants and the lions and—oh, all of it! We're a grotesque lot really: good-hearted, yes, but sometimes crazy enough to murder each other. I could tell You tales . . . but then You know, don't You? You know us like the potter knows the vase that he's turned on his own wheel.

Some people say You're the owner of the circus and that You set up the whole show for Your own private pleasure. I could accept that. I like being a clown. I get as much fun as I give. But I can't understand why the owner would want to cut the ropes of the big top and bury us all underneath it. A mad person might do that, a vengeful villain. I don't believe You can be mad and make a rose, or vengeful and create a dolphin. . . . So You see, there is a lot of explaining to do. . . .

The more he wrote, the more he wanted to write. It was not a literary exercise. He was not teaching anyone. He was engaged in the most primitive pastime of all, the contemplation of paradox, the reasoning of a simple man with ultimate mystery. He was expressing himself with a peasant's vocabulary, far different from that of the philosophers and the theologians. He did not have to invent new symbols or new cosmogonies like the Marcians and the Valentinians. He was a man in love with old and simple things—ripe grain rubbed in the hands, apples picked fresh from the tree, the first sweet savour of spring love. They were the more precious, because they would soon be lost in the doomsday chaos. As Pope he had written for women—mandates, prescriptions, counsels. Never before, in all his clerical career, had he written so tenderly about them.

. . . They tell me their secrets because I'm a clown with big boots and baggy pants and I'm always afraid. They're not ashamed to admit that they're afraid, too. They don't feel ridiculous either—even when they've made fools of themselves with a man. I'm much more foolish than they'll ever be, with my big mouth and my crybaby eyes. They just want to love and to be loved, and nest like the birds and make beautiful children. . . . But they hear the ghostly horsemen riding in the night—war, plague, famine—and they ask why they should breed babies to die at a dry breast or burn up in a bomb flash. They cannot walk safe in the streets; so they learn to fight like men and carry weapons against rape. They watch the men making war dances and they despise them. When the men get angry, they despise them the more; and the loving becomes sour or strange.

They want to know what's gone wrong with Your world . . . and why they don't see You sometimes on the street corner where Your Son used to be centuries ago, talking to the passersby, telling the truth in fairy tales. What can I tell them? I'm just Johnny the Clown! The best I can do is make them laugh by falling flat on my face or walking slap-bang into a custard tart! . . .

Will You think about all these things and try to give me some kind of answer? I know we've talked often. Sometimes I've understood. Sometimes I haven't. But right now I'm scared and I'm tripping over my big boots to run and hide.

This letter will be posted in the hollow oak at the bottom of the meadow—right near the place where we keep the circus horses.

I'll keep writing because I have a lot more questions to ask. These may be the last letters You'll ever get from our small planet; so, please don't shut down the world before I can make some sense of it.

Your puzzled friend,
Johnny the Clown

By evening he had written five letters, twenty pages of script in all, and it was only sheer physical fatigue that made him stop. It was still early. It would be pleasant to take a stroll along the quais. Then, with a small shiver of fear, he remembered that now he was the subject of Grade A surveillance and the trackers would be casting about to pick up his scent. He could not risk compromising Roberta Saracini by a trifling act of self-indulgence. Instead he called Adrian Hennessy.

". . . If you have time this evening, I'd like you to see what I've written."

"How much have you got?"

"Five letters. Something better than six thousand words."

"My God! You are industrious. I'll be over in twenty minutes."

"Would you do me a favour? On your way, pick up a basket of flowers for Roberta and a card to go with them. I'd do it myself, but I'm not supposed to leave the house."

"Better still: let me have them delivered direct from the florist. What do you want to say on the card?"

"Just: 'To say my thanks, Jeannot le Bouffon.'"

"Got it! I'm on my way."

In eighteen minutes he was at the door, brisk, blunt and businesslike. Before he read a line of the manuscript he laid down another set of ground rules.

'This is the big game: no compliments, no concessions. If it's good I say so. If it's bad we burn it. In between? Well, we think about it."

"Very proper," said Jean Marie placidly, "except you can't burn anything you don't own!"

Hennessy glanced quickly through the manuscript.

"Good! For a start it's legible. Why don't they teach handwriting like this anymore? I want to be alone for half-an-hour. That will give you time to read vespers in the garden. You might remember me when you come to the *Domine Exaudi.*"

"With pleasure."

He was hardly out of the door before Hennessy was deep in his reading. Jean Marie chuckled quietly to himself. He felt like a sceneshifter on a Japanese play, he was dressed in black and therefore to be ignored. He did, however, make remembrance of Adrian Hennessy at the *Domine Exaudi.* He said, "Please! Let me be able to trust him! I'm not sure in my judgments anymore."

The judgment that Hennessy passed on the manuscript was brief and final.

"That's what you promised. You moved me—and I've got boiler plate around my heart."

"So what happens now?"

"I take these, have them copied and a couple of file copies sent to you. I retain the original holographs in case we have to authenticate. Natalie and Florent read them and come up with ideas for special audio-visual treatments. Meantime, I'm looking for newspaper, magazine and book outlets—in all languages. You will continue writing—and may God guide your pen! As soon as we've got concrete situations, we'll present them to you for approval. . . .

Your flowers are ordered. Is there anything else I can do for you?"

"I'm under Grade A surveillance as a political agitator—or at least I will be as soon as my whereabouts are known. I'd like to get out and stretch my legs, eat in a restaurant; but my face is too well known. Any suggestions?"

"Easiest thing in the world." Hennessy consulted his pocket-book and then made a telephone call. "Rolf? Adrian Hennessy. I've got a job. . . . Immediate. Highest scale for payment. Let me see . . . I'll read him off to you. Age: sixty-five, grey hair reasonably abundant, fair complexion, features thin but fine-boned, eyes blue, very slim. Well, the point is he's anchored to the house and he'll soon be chewing the carpet. . . . Yes, he is well known, so it's a whole transformation scene . . . but not the Hunchback of Notre Dame, for God's sake! He still wants to eat in a public place. . . . Have you got a pencil? I'll read you the address. . . . How long will it take you to get here? . . . Fine, I'll wait. . . . That's right. He's one of mine—and very close!" He put down the receiver and turned to Jean Marie. "Rolf Levandow, Russian-Jewish, best makeup man in the world. He'll be here in half-an-hour with his box of tricks. When he's finished, your own mother wouldn't know you without a voice-print."

"You amaze me, Adrian Hennessy."

"I am what you see. I give what I'm paid for: total service! That's the chalk line. Nobody steps over it unless I ask them—even you, Jeannot le Bouffon!"

"Please!" Jean Marie held up his hands in protest. "I wasn't asking to hear your confession!"

"You've heard it, anyway." Adrian Hennessy was suddenly strange and faraway. "I know how to arrange any service you want, from a lipstick promotion to a liquidation. I walk some pretty wavy lines; but I don't cross up my clients, and nobody owns enough of me so that I can't toss the contract back on the desk and walk out. . . . But let's talk about you for a moment. A couple of months ago you were one of the high men, spiritual leader of half a billion people, absolute monarch of the smallest but most important enclave in the world. That's an enormous power base. With it, you had a whole, worldwide organization of clergy, monks, nuns and parochial laity. Yet you surrendered it all! . . . Now look at you! You can't go for a stroll except in disguise. You're the houseguest of a lady lion-hunter. You're depending on her to buy you print-space and air-time that once you could have had for free. I have to ask myself what sense this makes to you."

Jean Marie considered the question for a moment and then shook his head.

"Let's not play dialectic games, Mr. Hennessy. An eagle can talk sense with a canary but a canary with a goldfish, never! They live by diverse modes in diverse elements. I have had an experience which has changed me completely—for better or worse is not the question. It is simply that I am different."

"How? In what particulars?" Hennessy, cold-eyed, pressed the question. "I need to know the man I'm serving."

"I can tell you only by simile," said Jean Marie quietly. "Do you remember the gospel story of Jesus raising his friend Lazarus from the dead?"

"I remember it."

"Think about the details: the sisters in grief, in fear of what might be revealed when the tomb was opened. '*Iam foetet,*' they said. 'Already he stinks!' Then the tomb opened. Jesus called. Lazarus stepped out, still wrapped in the cerecloths. Have you ever thought how he must have felt, as he stood blinking in the sunlight, looking anew on a world from which he had taken his last leave? . . . After what happened to me in the garden at Monte Cassino, I was like Lazarus. Nothing could ever be the same as it was before."

"I think I understand," said Hennessy dubiously, "but even if you've changed, the world hasn't. Never forget that!"

"Why do you call Roberta Saracini a lion-hunter?"

"Because I'm trying to be polite." Hennessy was suddenly snappish. "In my country they use a dirtier word for women who chase male celebrities. Don't mistake me! She's a good client and you need her! But part of me is an old-fashioned Irishman and I hate to see a priest tied to a woman's apron strings."

"You have bad manners and a dirty mouth!" Jean Marie was angry and harsh. "I presume you said all this to Madame Saracini before you began taking her money?"

"I did." Hennessy was unmoved. "Because it's my job to point out the land mines before you both step on them. Since her father was put away, Roberta's got religion. She works at it, as she works at everything else. It helps her and I'm glad. But before that—and I know!—cocktails with Roberta meant breakfast in bed as well. . . . So you, Monseigneur, can very easily get caught in the slipstream of her past. You're under Grade A surveillance, because the government is looking for nails to put in your coffin. If you think I've got a dirty mouth, wait till you hear the government brand of pornography! . . . Simple example! You ordered flowers for Roberta. A gentleman's gesture to his hostess; no harm in it at all! But how would you feel if someone planted a gossip item: 'What high Catholic dignitary is sending flowers to what lady banker whose daddy once took the Vatican for a reputed fifteen million?' . . . That's only one of the risks."

"I am grateful for your care," said Jean Marie with mild irony. "But I suggest that there is no recourse against malice and evil report."

"Don't patronize me!" Hennessy was suddenly furious. "It happens I do care! I believe what you say! I want it heard! But I don't want my Church shamed in the city square."

"Forgive me!" Jean Marie made a rueful apology. "I warned you. I haven't changed for the better."

"At least you've got fire in your belly," said Hennessy with a sour grin. "Next time I'll choose my words more carefully."

The makeup man arrived—a big, swart, bearded fellow who looked like an Old Testament prophet and was just as eloquent and peremptory. Disguise, he explained at length, was a matter of illusion. Complicated makeup was for the stage or the screen. Very few women knew how to use cosmetics properly, even though they applied them every day. Rolf Levandow would certainly not trust an elderly gentleman of sixty-five to do a successful maquillage. . . . So, let's see! Head this way, head that! A pity to change the hair. It would be a kind of mutilation. Presumably Jean Marie was not entering himself for a concourse of elegance. On the other hand, he could not pass for a workman—not with those thin shoulders and flat belly and soft hands. Well then! A retired professor, a magazine critic, something in the arts! . . . Again the idea was to create a local identity; so that the man behind the bar and the girl at the newspaper kiosk and the waiter in the brasserie would swear that he was familiar and safe. Finally, Jean Marie found himself looking into a mirror at a slightly seedy scholar, who wore a Basque beret, gold pince-nez with a moiré ribbon and a pair of gum-pads that gave him a rabbit-faced look. As the makeup man explained, a literary magazine under the arm would help; an inexpensive cane was optional; and a certain air of parsimony was recommended, like counting out his coins from a little leather purse. Practice would suggest other embellishments. He should try to enjoy it as a game. If he wanted a change for any reason, then it could be arranged. Frequently one found the subject got bored with a single identity. He would leave his card . . .

"Break it up, Rolf!" said Hennessy. "My friend and I have lots of work to do. I'll walk you to the taxi rank."

When he came back Jean Marie was still studying himself in the mirror. Hennessy laughed.

"It works, doesn't it? I told you he was the best. And it would pay you to keep in touch with him—for more reasons than make-up."

"Oh?"

"He's an Israeli agent, a member of Shin Beth. This job is a useful cover. He travels a lot with film people and does regular work for French television. He recognized you instantly. He says the Israelis are well disposed towards you. They understand prophets in exile! Who knows, you may find him helpful. I should be on my way."

"When will I hear from you?"

"As soon as there's anything to report. You keep working on the letters."

"I will. Could I ask a small service?"

"Sure!"

"Let me walk with you as far as the quai. I have to get used to this new fellow with the pince-nez and the beret!"

It was the simplest of pleasures to stroll along the river, watch the hopeful anglers and the lovers hand in hand and the tourists in the *bateaux mouches* and the sunset splendours drenching the grey pile of Notre Dame. There was a childlike fun, too, in the disguise game. He bought, for a few francs, a battered volume of *Les Trophées* and a cane with a dog's-head handle. Thus protected, as if by a cloak of invisibility, he sauntered along, happy as any literary gentleman who, even if he were pinched by inflation, still got the best out of his autumn years.

It was an agreeable fantasy and it carried him through to the last ceremony of the afternoon, when he settled himself under the awning of a sidewalk café, ordered coffee and a sweet pastry and divided his attention between the passersby and the lapidarian verse of José Maria de Hérédia. He found that the old Parnassian had worn well and that he himself could still be moved by that last poignant moment between Anthony and Cleopatra on the eve of the battle of Actium.

Et courbé sur elle, l'ardent imperator
Voyait dans ses yeux clairs étoilés de points d'or,
Toute une mer immense où fuyaient des galères.

The grave and fateful beauty of the image matched his own mood of elegy. It seemed a blasphemy even to contemplate the ruin of Paris, this so human city, the extinction of all its serene beauties. And yet, come Rubicon Day, the sentence would be irrevocable—and any man who had lived in Rome knew how fragile was the fabric of the greatest empire and how quiet the dead were in their urns and catacombs. Then he heard the voice. It was close and to his left, a hearty American baritone expounding the art of *bouquinage*:

". . . You don't go at it as if you're turning out Grandmother's attic. You decide on one set of prints you'd really like to own. It doesn't matter if they're as rare as hens' teeth. That's just the starting point. It tells the man you're serious, that you've got money to spend and it will pay him to take time and show you what he's hiding under the counter. That's the way I worked in Germany and . . ."

As the monologue rolled on, Jean Marie fished for money in his wallet and turned his head slowly as if to signal a waiter. He remembered the dictum of Rolf Levandow. Disguise was illusion. Even if someone thought he recognized you, he was still put off by the unfamiliar features. You had to capitalize on that, stare him down, snub him if he greeted you.

Alvin Dolman was seated at the next table, deep in talk with a young woman dressed in bright summer cotton. As Jean Marie raised his hand to signal for the check, Dolman looked up. Their eyes met. Jean Marie remembered that he was wearing pince-nez and that, very probably, Dolman could not see his eyes. He turned away slowly; then, as if impatient to be gone, shoved a ten-franc note under the saucer, gathered up his book and cane and edged his way past Dolman's table towards the street. Mercifully Dolman had not paused in his monologue.

". . . Now you have to remember the kind of things that usually turn up on the bookstalls. I met a guy today—the one next to where you were standing—who specializes in ballet designs. That's not my line, but . . ."

. . . But the noonday devil was in Paris and Jean Marie Barette could make some disturbing guesses at his current employment. Ten paces away from the café he let his book fall to the pavement. As he bent to retrieve it, he looked back. Alvin Dolman was still deep in talk with the girl. He seemed to have made some progress. He was now holding her hand. Jean Marie Barette hoped she would be responsive enough to keep him interested—at least until he himself was safe in his own bolt-hole.

There was a message waiting for him. Madame would be late home. He should order whatever he wanted for dinner. He settled for coffee and a chicken sandwich, to be served in his room. Then he bathed, put on pajamas and dressing gown and began work on another letter. Now he was dealing with that most contentious of subjects: the divisions on matters of faith between men and women of goodwill.

Dear God,

If You're the beginning and the end of it all, why didn't You give us all an equal chance? In a circus, You know, our lives depend on that. If the riggers make a mistake, the trapeze artists die. If the man with the thunderflash doesn't do it right, I lose my eyes.

But, You don't seem to look at things that way. A circus travels, so we get to see how other people live—and I mean good people who love each other and love their children and really deserve a pat on the head from You.

Now, here's the thing I can't understand. You know it all. You made it all. But everyone sees You differently. You've even let Your children kill each other; just because they each have a different description of Your face at the window! . . . Why do we all use different marks to tell us we're Your children? I was sprinkled with water because my parents were Christians. Louis, the lion tamer, had a little piece cut off his penis because he's a Jew. Leila, the black girl who handles the snakes, wears an ammonite around her neck, because this is the magical snake-stone. . . . And yet, when the show is over and we all sit at the supper table, tired and hungry, do You see much difference between us? Do you care? Are you really very upset when Louis, who is getting old and scared, creeps into Leila's bed for a little comfort, and Leila, who is really quite ugly, is glad to have him?

I seem to remember that Your Son enjoyed eating and drinking and chatting with people like us. He liked children. He seemed to understand women. It's a pity nobody bothered to record very much of his talk with them—a few words with his mother, the rest was mostly with girls who were on the town, one way and another.

What I'm trying to say is that You're shutting down the world without really giving us a chance to overcome the handicaps You've given us. . . . I have to say that. I wouldn't be honest if I let the matter pass. Somewhere up near the North Pole there's an old woman sitting on an ice floe. She's not suffering. She's fading slowly away. Her family have put her there. She's content, because this is the way death has always been arranged for the old. You know she's there. I'm sure You're making it easy—more easy perhaps than for some other poor old dear in a very expensive clinic. But You've never told us very clearly which situation You prefer. I like to believe it's one with the more loving in it!

On the other hand—I have to tell You this—I sat today in a café. Next to me was a man I know to be truly inhabited by a spirit of evil. He's treacherous. He's destructive. He's a murderer. How will You judge him? How will You make the judgment known to all the rest of us? We do have a right to know. I don't have children, but if I ever had any they wouldn't be just playthings, would they? Life itself would confer rights on them—at least according to our small standards. I'd hate to believe that Yours were any lower.

So please—I know I'm pushing hard tonight, but I'm tired and I'm scared of that evil man with the happy voice and the sweet smile—please tell me how and when You're going to hear the case of Creator versus creature—or should it be the other way round? Or perhaps You could call the whole thing off and turn it into a love feast?

That's strange! I've never thought to ask before. Can You, God, change Your mind? If not, why not? And if You can, why didn't You do it before we all got into such a terrible mess? I'm sorry if I sound rude. I don't mean to be . . .

. . . Once again, without warning, he was on the high peak, among the black mountains of the dead planet. Once again he was empty, alone, prey to an unendurable sadness, a shame, as if he alone were the author of all the desolation about him. There was no respite, no appeal, no forgiveness. There would be no rapture, no fiery whirlwind, no exquisite agony of union with the Other. He himself was the dead center of a dead cosmos. He could not weep. He could not rage. He could only know that this was all there was to know: himself anchored to a barren rock in the desert of eternity.

Suddenly he felt a touch on his flesh, a tug at his dangling fingers. He looked down. It was the little girl from the Institute, the little clown of God, with her vacant, trusting smile. His heart melted to her. He snatched her up and held her close. She was his life-spark. He, her last protection against the vacancy of a cold planet.

They could not stay here on the peak. There must be caves to shelter them. He began to walk, stumbling down the dark stony slope. He felt the child's cheek against his own, her warm breath, like a tiny wind, ruffling his hair. As he walked, the well-spring of emotion began to flow again. He was aware of pity and terror and tenderness and a fierce rage against the Other who had dared to desert this tiny helpless creature in a place which was no-place.

Finally he came to the mouth of a cave, within which, most strangely, he could see a tiny light, like a star reflected in the black water of a tarn. He held the child closer and closer, as if to cover her with the armour of his own skin, and strode towards the light. It grew larger and brighter until it dazzled him and he was forced to close his eyes and stand quite still like a blind man in a new place. Then he heard the voice, strong and calm and gentle.

"Open your eyes."

He did so and saw, seated on an outcrop of rock, beside a small fire, a young man of the most extraordinary comeliness. He was naked except for a breechcloth and sandals. His hair, golden and abundant, was caught back with a linen band. Beside him on the rock was a platter of bread and a cup of water. He held out his arms and said:

"I'll take the child."

"No!" Jean Marie felt a sudden lurch of fear and stepped back against the farther wall. He eased himself down into a sitting position and cradled the child in his arms. The young man stood up and offered the bread and the cup. When Jean Marie refused he began feeding the child morsels of the loaf and tiny sips of liquid. From time to time he stroked her cheek and smoothed the hair away from her eyes. He asked again:

"Please, let me hold her. She will come to no harm."

He took the child and made a little dance with her, until she laughed and fondled his face and kissed him. Then suddenly she was not a mongol anymore, but perfect and beautiful like a princess doll.

The young man held her up to be admired. He smiled at Jean Marie and told him:

"You see! I make all things new!"

"Where are all the rest? The flowers, the animals, the people?"

"Here!"

He held the child up above his head. She stretched out her hands. The walls of the cave dissolved into a prospect of meadows and orchards and streams, silver in the sun. The young man said chidingly:

"You have to understand. The beginning and the end are one. The living and the dying are a single act because life is renewed by death."

"Then why must the dying be so terrible?"

"Man makes his own terrors, not I."

"Who are you?"

"I am who I am."

"I've never understood that."

"You should not try. Does the flower contend with the sun, or the fish with the sea? That's why you're a clown and you break things and I have to put them together again."

"I'm sorry. I know I make a mess. I'll go now."

"Don't you want to kiss your daughter?"

"Please! May I?"

. . . But when he reached out his arms to take the beautiful child, she was not there. The man and the girl and the cave and the magical meadows were all gone. He was back in his own room. Roberta Saracini was standing by the desk with a tray in her hand.

"I saw the light under your door. I thought you'd like some hot chocolate before you went to bed. When I came in you were asleep at your desk."

"I had a big day—one way and another. What time is it?"

"Just after ten."

"Thank you for the chocolate. How was your evening?"

"Most interesting! We've been invited to share in the financing of a new industrial project in Shanghai. The Chinese financial delegation entertained us at the embassy. Ours is a mixed group: British, Swiss, American and, of course, a consortium of bankers from the European Economic Community. The Chinese are very shrewd. They want as wide a spread of investment as possible. They also believe that war is inevitable and they have crash programs for enterprises that can make military materials. . . . Your name came up in the war talk."

"How?"

"Let me see if I can remember exactly. Oh, yes. . . . The Americans were talking about danger periods and trigger incidents that could set off a war—Rubicon Day in fact! They make no secret of the fact that they regard the Chinese as their natural allies. In fact, I'm sure one or two of their delegation were intelligence people. Anyway, a man named Morrow, who used to be Secretary of State but is now with Morgan Guaranty, mentioned your prophecies and the articles about your abdication. He asked the Chinese how accurate they thought you were. One of them—a director of the Bank of China—laughed and said, 'If he is a friend of the Jesuits he is very accurate indeed.' He reminded us that it was the Jesuit Matteo Ricci who first introduced into China the sundial, the astrolabe and the method of extracting square and cube roots from whole numbers and fractions. . . . He was very interested when I told him that I knew you and was, in fact, a trustee of your estate."

Jean Marie mourned silently over the indiscretion. He wanted to say something but he was tired and the milk was already spilt anyway.

Roberta Saracini went on, "Morrow said he would like to see you again. Apparently you had dealings together at the Vatican. I told him you were in touch with me from time to time and I would pass the message."

"My dear Roberta!" He had to speak now and he could not temper the words. "I'm deeply grateful for all your help; but you have just committed a monumental folly. The French want me under surveillance. This afternoon I stood within a pace of the C.I.A. man who tried to kill Mendelius. I still don't know whether he recognized me. Now you, at a diplomatic gathering, announce that you are my trustee and I am—I quote!—in touch with you from time to time. From tomorrow your phone will be tapped and your house watched. . . . I have to move! Tonight! How long will it take to get to the airport?"

"At this hour—forty minutes. But where . . . ?"

"I don't know and it's better you don't either. First thing in the morning get in touch with Hennessy and my brother, Alain. Tell them I'll make contact as soon as I can. I've got to pack."

"But the letters, the whole project . . ."

". . . Depend on me! So I need a safe place and secure communications. Will you drive me to the airport? Taxi calls can be traced."

"At least let me say I'm sorry."

She was near to tears. He took her face in his hands and kissed her lightly on the cheek.

"I know you didn't mean it. I've put you in a dangerous game and you can't be expected to know all the rules. When I'm settled we'll find a safe way to communicate. I still need your help."

"I'll get the car out. Hurry with your packing; the last planes leave at midnight."

On the face of it, a midnight flight to London was a folly of desperation, but if he could arrive without detection he could be safe while he worked on the letters and cast about among old friends for any who might believe in his mission and be prepared to cooperate in it.

He had always admired the British, though he had never wholly understood them. The subtleties of their humour often escaped him. Their snobberies always irritated him. Their dilatory habits in commerce never failed to amaze him. Yet they were tenacious of friendships and fealties. They had a sense of history and a tolerant eye for fools and eccentrics. They could be land-greedy and money-mean and capable of extraordinary social cruelties; yet they supported great charities; they were humane to fugitives; and they counted privacy a right and not a privilege. Give them a cause they understood, put liberties they valued at risk, and they would take to the streets by thousands or walk in solitary dignity to the headsman's block.

On the other hand—and he admitted it with wry humour—as Gregory XVII, he had never been a great success with the British. They had, over the centuries, developed a working relationship with the Italians, whose arts they bought, whose fashions they aped, whose talent for high rhetoric and low-keyed compromise was akin to their own. On the other hand, they looked on the French as a prickly lot, stiff-necked, uppish and politically immoral, who lived too close by for comfort, had an uncomfortable taste for grandeur and a cynical skill in pursuing it.

So, to his singular regret and occasional irritation, Jean Marie had made good friends but exercised small influence in the British Isles. In the end, he had been happy to leave the conduct of the local Church to Matthew Cardinal Hewlett, who, as one of his Curial colleagues put it, "is probably the least risky man for the job. He has zeal without fire, intelligence without talent, never makes an argument if he can avoid one, and has no redeeming vices at all." Hewlett had never joined The Friends of Silence; but at the fateful consistory he had cast his vote for abdication and justified it with a characteristic quip. "If our Pontiff is a madman we're well rid of him. If he's a saint we won't lose him. I see no problem at all. The sooner he's out, the better!"

All in all, Matthew Cardinal Hewlett was not quite the man to call at two in the morning and ask for bed and breakfast. So, with the help of a taxi driver, Jean Marie Barette found lodging in a reasonable hotel in Knightsbridge and slept dreamlessly until noon.

XII

There were peacocks on the lawn and swans on the lake and the gold of early autumn in the woodlands as Jean Marie Barette walked in the manor garden with a man in whom he had confided much during his papacy, and who now was to be his first publisher in the English language: Waldo Pearson, old-time Catholic, onetime Foreign Secretary in the Conservative Cabinet, now chairman of the Greenwood Press.

Adrian Hennessy was there as well, with his folio of illustrations, recordings of the *Letters* in French and English, and fully orchestrated tapes of the theme for Johnny the Clown, composed by Florent de Basil. He had also brought a certified document from the Banco Ambrogiano all' Estero, guaranteeing an initial half-million sterling, to be spent on the promotion and exploitation of *Last Letters from a Small Planet.* Jean Marie ventured the wry comment that perhaps the money was more eloquent than the author. Waldo Pearson uttered a frosty disclaimer:

". . . We are very close to the time when money will have no meaning anymore. In a nuclear conflict, we stand to lose two-thirds of the population of these islands. No government can come to terms with that catastrophe—no Church either, as you have found! So they choose, as a matter of policy, to ignore it. In the *Letters,* you have found a way to discuss the terror that confronts us without creating panic or contention. You will be judged as a prophet and not as a banker."

"And glad I am to hear you say it, Waldo!" Hennessy put on his most syrupy brogue. "Because it's me that represents the bankers and devil a dollar will you get until you've demonstrated the quality of your own publishing and promotion!"

"I've told you before." Pearson was determined to have all his reservations on the record. "We're confident of an exceptional distribution. The advance we're paying reflects that. The newspaper serialization will help, too—and, of course, the advertising funds you're providing. But you're still asking me to fight with one hand behind my back! No television, no press interviews, no revelation at all of the author's identity! I see no sense in that."

Before Hennessy had time to answer, Jean Marie stepped into the argument.

"Please! There are good reasons. If my identity is known, I may seem to put myself in conflict with the present Pontiff. I do not want that. More: I am writing in response to what I believe to be divine command. I have to rest on that act of faith and be content that the tree be recognized by its fruits. Finally, the only thing I can control is the integrity of the published text. I cannot put myself at the mercy of interviewers who may distort my message by false, biased or incompetent report."

"In short, Waldo"—Hennessy grinned like a happy leprechaun—"no way! No how!"

Waldo Pearson shrugged. "Well, it was worth a try! When may we expect the finished manuscript?"

"In two weeks."

"Good! Is the author satisfied with the English translations?"

"I am, yes. They are both fluent and accurate. . . . May we change the subject a moment? There is something else on which I should like your advice."

"Please!"

"There are several people in England whom I received while I was in office. Could you arrange for me to meet them again—and would you permit me to have the meetings here in your house?" Before Pearson had time to answer, he went on to explain. "I live in a modest hotel under an assumed name. I cannot invite known personages to such a place; but I still believe I can be of service in the crisis that faces us all. For example, Sergei Petrov has asked me to mediate in the matter of the grain embargo. However, I have no means of knowing whether I am acceptable to any other parties. You have held cabinet rank, Mr. Pearson; how would you react to me?"

"Difficult to say." Pearson, the politician, was a more prickly animal than Pearson the publisher. He began to reason aloud.

"Let's take it by debit and credit. You're a defeated leader, a Roman Catholic cleric, a Frenchman, a self-styled prophet—all handicaps for a political negotiator in today's market!"

Jean Marie laughed, but made no comment. Pearson went on with his accounting.

"On the credit side, what do we have? You're a practiced diplomat. You can have no personal ambitions; your good behaviour after the abdication did not pass unnoticed! You're a free agent. The memorial which Rainer and Mendelius wrote about you took some of the mist out of your mysticism." He chuckled over his own schoolboy pun. "So, let's sum it up. If I were Foreign Secretary I should most certainly receive you. If you told me the Russians had invited you to mediate a case with me, I'd be very skeptical. I'd reason like this. You are, prima facie, an honest broker. Conversely or obversely, I'd wonder whether the Russians had turned you, or why they hadn't picked someone with more muscle in the market. Then I'd argue that if they were desperate enough to use an outsider like you, we ought to be able to drive a hard bargain. So, all in all—yes! I'd receive you with interest—and bypass you as soon as possible!"

"That makes good sense," said Jean Marie. "Now back to my first question. Would you be willing to arrange a few meetings for me—here in your house?"

"Of course! You tell me whom you want and I'll invite them down. Please remember that you yourself are welcome here at any time."

"There's something else to remember." Hennessy was uneasy. "If you don't want to reveal yourself as the author of *Last Letters*, how are you going to explain your presence in the house of a prominent British publisher?"

"We explain nothing," Pearson cut in briskly. "I let drop the information that we're discussing a possible book . . . I'd certainly like to raise the question of an autobiography."

"I'm afraid," said Jean Marie. "that's a project for which I should have neither the taste nor the time."

"There are others that may interest you. I've been trying for years to find someone who can do me a clear and unrhetorical book on the nature of religious experience. We're seeing a phenomenon in England which deserves more notice than it's getting. While the traditional churches are losing clergy and congregations at an alarming rate, the cults are flourishing. . . . Let me show you something." He walked them round the corner of the house to where the woodland opened onto a vista of hill pasture, at the end of which, perched on a rounded knoll, was a large mansion in the Palladian style. Pearson's commentary was spirited but unhappy.

". . . That place for instance! It used to belong to a good friend of mine. Now, it's the headquarters of a group who call themselves the Family of the Holy Ones. They're a cult like the Moonies, the Soka Gakkai, the Hare Krishna. They proselytize actively. They have a very strong conditioning regimen, based on excessive labour and constant surveillance of the neophyte. Lots of young people are attracted to them. They're very rich. . . . Like some of the other groups they are now arming themselves, stockpiling food, medicines and weapons against Armageddon Day. If they survive, they and others like them could be the warring barons of the post-nuclear age. . . . That's what the Catholic hierarchy were afraid of when you wanted to publish your encyclical. Matt Hewlett brought back a copy from Rome. He came down especially to talk to me about it. He stood just where you're standing now and said, 'That's where Gregory the Seventeenth is going to lead us, whether he understands it or not. Cromwellian Christianity, pikes, muskets and all!' "

"And did you believe him?" asked Jean Marie quietly.

"At the time, yes."

"What has happened to change your mind?"

"Several things. Having been in politics and seen how hard it is to make democracy work, I've often been tempted towards dictatorships of one kind or another. As a publisher I've seen how people can be conditioned to habits and points of view. To my regret I've often been seduced into manipulative exercises in politics and commerce. . . . Then Hennessy brought me your first letters. There's a passage in the fourth one which I learned by heart . . . 'When a man becomes a clown he makes a free gift of himself to the audience. To endow them with the saving grace of laughter, he submits to be mocked, drenched, clouted, crossed in love. Your Son made the same submission when He was crowned as a mock king, and the troops spat wine and water in His face. . . . My hope is that when He comes again, He will still be human enough to shed a clown's gentle tears over the broken toys—that once were women and children.' "

Pearson broke off as if embarrassed and stood a long time

staring across the green folds of the land towards the Palladian mansion. Finally he admitted with odd emotion:

"I suppose you could say that was the moment of my conversion. I've always been a communicating Christian—but only because I kept my mind resolutely shut against some of the more horrifying consequences of belief: like a universe where the animals devour each other to live, and torturers are public servants, and the best offer to agonized mankind is 'Take up your cross!' . . . But somehow your words managed to release me from that credal despair and set me wondering again, looking with new eyes at an upside-down world!"

Adrian Hennessy said nothing. He reached for a handkerchief and began to polish his spectacles vigorously.

Jean Marie Barette said with grave gentleness, "I know what you feel; but it's a very fragile joy. Don't lean on it too hard; otherwise it may snap under your weight."

Pearson gave him a swift, probing look. "You surprise me! I should have thought you'd want to share the joy, however fragile."

Jean Marie held up a hand in deprecation. "Please don't misunderstand me! I am truly happy when anyone is granted the kind of insight that gives new meaning to his profession of faith. I was simply warning you, out of my own experience, that the comfort you now feel may not last. Faith is not a matter of logic; and the moment of intuition does not always repeat itself. One has to expect long periods of darkness and, often, a destructive confusion!"

Waldo Pearson was silent for a moment; then, with surprising bluntness, he said to Hennessy, "Adrian, I want to talk privately with our friend. Why don't you leave us for a while?"

"No problem!" Hennessy seemed unperturbed. "I'll take the car and drive down to the Nag's Head for a drink with the locals! Talk anything you like except contracts. That's my business!"

Waldo Pearson led Jean Marie down to the edge of the lake, where a pair of white swans floated serenely in and out of the reedbeds. He explained himself haltingly:

"We're at the beginning of—well—a fairly intimate relationship. Author and publisher can never live satisfactorily at arm's length —at least not an author like you and a publisher like me. Just now I felt—rightly or wrongly—that something important was being left unsaid between us. . . . It seemed strange that you felt the need to utter a warning about my—my spiritual health."

"I was equally concerned with my own," said Jean Marie. "It would not take much at this moment to convince me that I am suffering from a monstrous delusion."

"I find that hard to believe. You've been so adamant in your convictions. You've given up so much. You write with such deep emotion."

"Nevertheless, it is true." Jean Marie plucked a reed from the lakeside and began to shred it restlessly as he talked. "I have been in England three weeks now. I live in a comfortable hotel that looks out on an old-fashioned square, with a garden in the middle where children play and young mothers bring their babies. I work in the morning. In the afternoon, I walk. In the evening I read and pray and go to bed early. I am very free, very relaxed. I have even made friends. There is an elderly Jewish gentleman who brings his grandson to play ball in the garden. He is a fine scholar in the Rabbinical tradition. When he found that I knew Hebrew he was ready to dance with joy. Last Friday I went to a Sabbath supper in his house. Then there is the concierge, who is Italian and talkative and always ready for a little gossip. . . . So you see, my life is pleasant and I am almost converted to this extraordinary equanimity of the British . . . some of whom really do believe that God is an Englishman of impeccable taste who never lets any mess get quite out of hand. . . . But, suddenly, I have realized that this is a quite insidious temptation. I can be silenced, not by enemies, not by authority—but by my own comfortable indifference! I can believe that just because I have written a few pages which will be widely published, I have given full witness and earned the right to dream out the rest of time until Judgment Day. That's one side of the medal. The other is equally sinister, though in a different way. As I write the *Last Letters from a Small Planet*, I am expressing myself, my relationships with God and the human family. I am not teaching a body of doctrine. I am not proposing a theological argument. I am not a pastor concerned for the well-being of his flock. I am out of office, you see; I am half-laicized; I even celebrate the Eucharist for myself alone; which really makes little sense of the sacramental act. . . Now, without warning, a pit opens under my feet. Even as I wrote the lines that so moved you I was thinking: Is this true? Is that what I really believe? . . . The end of civilization I do see as possible and proximate. But the Parousia, the Second Coming, that will make all things new? I do not know how to come to terms with the concept of a God-man, risen and glorified, presiding in eternal calm over the agonizing dissolution of our earthly dwelling place. Whenever, now, I try to reason about it, I smell blood and see demon faces from the frescoes of ancient temples. I wish, sometimes, I could forget it all and talk to my old rabbi while we watch the children play. . . ."

"And yet," said Waldo Pearson quietly, "that isn't what you write. What appears on the page is the talk of a confident child with a loving father."

"So which am I?" asked Jean Marie with an odd half-humorous pathos. "The equable Englishman, doubting Thomas, the deluded prophet, or the clown who is himself a child at heart? . . . Or, perhaps, I am none of these, but something quite different."

"What, for instance?"

Jean Marie crumpled the last shreds of the reed in his fist, tossed them into the water and watched them bobbing in the wake of the regal swans. It was a long moment before he answered the question.

"I set out to make myself a thinking reed, pliant to the wind of the Spirit; but a reed is also a hollow tube through which other men may pipe a music alien to me."

Waldo Pearson took his arm and guided him away from the lake towards an old-fashioned hothouse set against the weathered brick wall of the garden.

"Our grapes are ripe. I'm very proud of them. I'd like you to try a bunch."

"Do you make your own wine?"

"No. These are table grapes." As casually as he had slid off the subject Pearson came back to it again. "It seems to me what you are trying to explain are the symptoms of an identity crisis. I understand that. I've been through it. After twelve years in the House, five of them in cabinet, I felt lost, disoriented, empty—and, I suppose, open to manipulation. It's a little frightening; but I didn't feel, as you seem to do, that it was a situation tainted with evil."

"Did I say that?" Jean Marie swung round to face him. He was puzzled and concerned. Pearson, however, did not retreat.

"Not in so many words; but you seemed to imply it. You said 'a music alien to me.'"

"You're right, I did. That's the core of the matter. All apocalyptic literature refers to false prophets deceiving the elect. Can't you feel the horror of the idea? . . . What if I were one of them?"

"I don't believe it for an instant," said Waldo Pearson firmly. "Otherwise I would not publish your book."

"I don't believe it either," said Jean Marie. "But I do feel myself to be a battleground, still in dispute. I am drawn to a safe indifference. I am tempted to lose all faith in a loving deity. I am afraid that my new and very fragile identity may suddenly explode into fragments."

"I wonder," said Waldo Pearson as he opened the glass door of the orangery. "I wonder if your so rigid obedience isn't a mistake. Contention is healthy and necessary—even in the Church—and self-imposed silence can be very demoralizing. I found that in Cabinet. You had to speak up or be killed."

"There's a difference." Jean Marie relaxed into good humour again. "You didn't have to deal with God in the Cabinet room."

"The hell we didn't!" said Waldo Pearson. "He was sitting right there in the P.M.'s chair."

They both laughed. Pearson snipped a bunch of big black grapes, divided it and offered a handful to Jean Marie, who tasted them and nodded approval.

"I've got a proposal to make to you." Pearson was adept at swift changes of subject. "You need a forum and some access to the decision-makers in this country. I need a substitute speaker for dinner at the Carlton Club. I did have the Prime Minister but he has a summit meeting in Washington. I need someone with weight and interest. It's three weeks from now. You'll probably be finished the *Letters*. It's a closed function. Everything said is off the record—and the rules have never been broken. . . . The members all belong to what you call in France *le Pouvoir*—though they're rather less drastic in its exercise. Please? You'd do me a favour; and you can certainly propagate the message."

"What should I talk about?"

"Your abdication. The reasons and the aftermath. I want to see my colleagues' faces when you tell them that God spoke to you! I'm not joking. They all invoke Him. But you're the only man I know who claims a private revelation and has put his head on the block to give witness to it. They'll be expecting some wild-eyed zealot! Tell me you'll do it!"

"Very well. If I'm to speak in English I'll need to write a text. Will you check it for me?"

"Of course! I can't tell you how happy I am. . . . And are we agreed, the reason for your presence is that we are discussing plans for a book, possibly several books?"

"Agreed."

"Splendid! Now let me tell you about these grapes. The vine was struck from cuttings taken from the Great Vine at Hampton Court. . . ."

It was all so especially British and understated that Jean Marie missed the significance of the invitation. Because he was more interested in the folklore of Waldo Pearson's estate, he forgot to tell Adrian Hennessy about the Carlton Club until they were halfway back to London. Hennessy was so startled that he almost slewed the car off the road.

"My God! The innocence of the man! Don't you understand what's happened to you?"

"I've been invited to speak at dinner in a gentlemen's club," said Jean Marie amiably. "I assure you I'll cope with the occasion. It's not nearly so formidable as a public audience in Saint Peter's or a papal visit to Washington!"

"But it can be a hell of a lot more important for you," said Hennessy irritably. "Pearson's a shrewd old fox. He invites you to the Carlton Club, the stronghold of Conservative politics. He sets you as substitute speaker for the Prime Minister at one of the three most important political dinners of the year. That's as close as you'll ever get to canonization by the English. If you make a good speech—and if you don't fall down drunk or toss chicken bones at the chairman—you're made! You can lift a telephone and talk to anyone anytime in Whitehall or Westminster—and you won't be nearly as vulnerable as you are now! The word will be around the chanceries that in Britain you're a protected species. That will have an immediate effect in France; because whatever happens in the Carlton Club is studied very carefully on the other side of the Channel. Petrov's going to hear about it, too; and the Americans. The members of the Carlton bring the guests they want to educate."

"Hennessy, my friend, if ever I am re-elected, you'll be my Cardinal Camerlengo!"

"Not unless you change the rules on celibacy! I'd have done

well in the Renaissance; but not in this day and age! . . . Which reminds me— What are you going to wear to the Carlton Club dinner?"

The question took Jean Marie by surprise.

"What am I going to wear?"

"Precisely. All the other gentlemen will wear dinner jackets and black ties. How are you going to present yourself—as a cleric or a layman? If you go as a cleric, will you wear any sign of rank? A red stock, a pectoral cross? If you go as a layman, you certainly can't go in hand-me-downs from a rental company. I see you laughing, Monseigneur; but the question's important. French protocol is clear and trenchant: tictac and you know who's who in the pecking order! But the English—God bless their cotton socks! —do it differently. You can be elegant and despised, shabby and admired, eccentric and respected. If you're a genius you can even wear last year's soup on your lapels! They'll be watching you like a hawk to see how you perform in costume drama!" He swung out to overtake a juggernaut trailer. "The fate of nations may hang on the cut of your *smoking*."

"Then let's give it the attention it deserves," said Jean Marie Barette cheerfully. "Can you find me a good Italian tailor? I need someone with a sense of theatre."

"The best," said Hennessy. "Angelo Vittucci. He can make a fat Bacchus look like Mercury in tights! I'll take you to see him tomorrow. You know, Monseigneur . . ." He pulled the car onto the motorway and pushed down hard on the accelerator. "I'm beginning to get very fond of you! For a man of God you've got a good worldly sense of humour!"

"You know what Pascal said: '*Diseur de bons mots—mauvais caractère!*' "

"Why?" asked Hennessy with enormous gravity. "Why do bad characters make good company?"

"We're the mustard on the meat!" said Jean Marie with a grin. "It would be a dull world if nothing needed mending and nobody needed saving! We'd both be out of a job!"

"If you'll pardon the expression"—Hennessy with a clear road ahead of him was prepared to enjoy himself—"you're the one who's out of a job! I'm trying to get you gainfully employed. . . . Now sit back and listen to this song again. I really believe it could be a hit!" He slipped a cassette into the tape deck and a moment later they were hearing Florent de Basil's theme song

"Johnny the Clown." The tape was designed to demonstrate several different treatments of the song. It stood up solidly under all of them. The words were simple, the rhythm catchy; but the melody had an odd plangent quality that tugged at the heartstrings.

"Big boots, floppy clothes,
Painted face, button nose,
That's Johnny the Clown.

"Johnny, Johnny, bounced and humbled,
Johnny, Johnny, trounced and tumbled,
Johnny kicked and Johnny clouted,
Johnny chased and Johnny routed,
Who says thanks for all the laughter,
Gives you hugs and kisses after?
Johnny, are you lonely too?

"Comic smile, goggle eyes,
Who knows if he laughs or cries?
Just Johnny—Johnny the Clown!"

When the song ended, Hennessy switched off the tape and asked, "Well, how does it sound this time?"

"Still charming," said Jean Marie. "Haunting, too. How do you propose to use it?"

"We're discussing a contract now with one of the biggest recording companies. They'll do a special production with one of their singing stars and launch it just before the book is published. Then, if my guess is right, the song will be picked up by other singers and should go climbing up the charts. It will provide an immediate audio link with the visual publicity on the book."

"Our young friend Florent has a very attractive talent; perhaps instead of my speaking at the Carlton Club, we should send him to sing there."

"First lesson in show business," Hennessy admonished him. "Never pass up a good booking. You may not get asked again!"

Two days later, alerted by telephone to the change in Jean Marie's circumstances, Brother Alain arrived in London. As usual he was full of irrelevant solicitudes. Was not Jean's hotel a shade too modest? Should he not entertain some of the old Catholic nobility, like the Howards of Arundel and Norfolk? If it could be arranged for the French ambassador to be invited to the Carlton Club, the climate in Paris would change immediately.

Jean Marie listened patiently and agreed to take these momentous matters under advisement. He was grieved to hear that Odette had been stricken with the grippe, delighted that one of his nieces would soon announce her engagement and that the other had taken up with a young man of excellent prospects who worked in the Ministry of Defense. It was not until they were halfway through dinner at Sophie's—a small retreat in a cul-de-sac off Sloane Street—that Alain began to talk freely about his personal concerns.

". . . I tell you, Jean, the money markets have gone mad. There is a mountain of gold in Swiss vaults and the price has gone through the roof. We are covering commodity deals all round the globe—base metals, rare metals, mineral oils, vegetable oils, beet sugar, cane sugar, timber and coking coal. . . . There aren't enough ships to carry the stuff; so we're making loans on bottoms that should have rusted through years ago and the insurance companies are charging mad money to insure the vessels and the cargoes. Even so, how do you make the payments with currencies swinging ten percent in a day? . . . God should not hear the words I say, Jean; but we need a war, just to halt the nonsense."

"Never fear, little brother!" Jean Marie was in a winter of sadness. "We're going to have one! Paris will be a priority target. Have you thought what you're going to do about Odette and the girls?"

Alain was shocked by the question. "Nothing! We conduct our normal lives."

"Bravo!" said Jean Marie. "I'm sure you'll end with pure hearts and blank minds, still believing the blast that hit you was hot air from a hair dryer. Get out of Paris, for pity's sake, even if you have to rent a hut in the Haute Savoie!"

Alain was a picture of dignity affronted. "We can't all join the panic of the Gadarene swine!"

Once again, Jean Marie had to reproach himself for the old sibling rivalry. "I know! I know! But I love you, little brother, and I'm concerned for you and your family."

"Then you must try to understand where our concerns lie.

Odette and I have had our bad years. At one stage we were seriously thinking of breaking up."

"I didn't know that."

"I took care you didn't! Somehow we both managed to hold on. We're solid now. The girls are older and they've paired off with decent fellows. That's a satisfaction, if not a triumph. So far as Odette and I are concerned, there isn't too much to interest us in a refugee life in the mountains! We'd rather enjoy what we have and take our chances with the rest of Paris."

Jean Marie shrugged agreement. "It makes sense. I should not try to prescribe anyone else's life."

"I think you ought to take an interest in Roberta's." He said it in so flat and peremptory a fashion that Jean Marie was startled.

"What sort of interest?"

"Compassion, for a start. Her father died three days ago in prison."

"I didn't know. Why didn't someone tell me?"

"I didn't know myself until a couple of hours before I left Paris. I didn't want to throw it at you the moment I arrived. The terrible part is that he was murdered, stabbed by another inmate. The general belief is that the killing was organized from outside, probably by accomplices in the bank fraud."

"Dear God! . . . How is she taking it?"

"According to her assistant, very badly. She'd built everything on the fact that she was paying off her father's debts and giving him a chance of an honourable life later. I think you should call her and, if you can, persuade her to come to London for a few days."

"I hardly think that's appropriate!"

"To hell with appropriate!" Alain was angry. "You owe it to her! She took you into her house. She's financing your project with her own money. She adores the ground you walk on! . . . If you can't pick her off the floor, dry her tears and play Dutch uncle for a few days, then frankly, brother Jean, you're a fraud! I've heard you say a hundred times, charity isn't collective. It's thou and I . . . one to one! And if you're worried about some kind of sex scandal at sixty-five, then all I can say is you're more fortunate than I am!"

Jean Marie gaped at him for a moment in utter disbelief. Then, without a word, he got up and walked across to the cashier's desk.

He laid a ten-pound note on the counter and asked if he might make an urgent call to Paris. The girl handed him the phone. He tapped out Roberta's number. A few moments later her manservant answered. He regretted most deeply that Madame was indisposed and was accepting no calls.

"Please!" Jean Marie pleaded with him. "This is Monsieur Grégoire. I am calling from London. Will you beg her to speak with me?"

There was a long, ominous silence and finally Roberta Saracini came on the line. Her greeting was pale and distant. He told her:

"Alain is with me. He has just told me the news of your father. . . . I imagine your line may be tapped. I don't care. I know how you must be feeling. I want you to come over to London. . . . Immediately! Tonight if you can make it. I'll book you a room at my hotel. . . . Yes, the same address Hennessy gave you. . . . No, I do not agree! This is no time to be alone; and with me at least you don't have to spell the words. . . . Good! I'll wait up for you! . . . *A tout à l'heure*!"

He put down the phone, then called his own hotel to reserve a room. The cashier gave him his change. He walked back to the table and answered Alain's unspoken question.

"She's coming over tonight. I've booked her into my hotel."

"Good!" said Alain brusquely. "And don't waste too much time over the obsequies! Show her the town. She loves pictures. There seems to be some good theatre. . . ."

"Why not let me plan my own tour, little brother?"

Alain Barette seemed suddenly to have turned into a wit. He raised his glass in an ironic salute. "Well, you're not really used to going about unchaperoned, are you?"

Jean Marie burst out laughing. "You and I have a lot to learn about each other!"

"And not much time to do it." Alain was moody again. "There's something else. Petrov came to see me. He wants a talk with you. I told him you were out of the country and any meeting would have to be outside the frontiers. I offered to carry a message. This is what he told me. The project for your visit to Moscow is under consideration at the highest level. So far, reactions are favourable. Once a decision is made he will contact me and I will pass the message to you."

"How does he look?"

"Ragged! He's under enormous strain."

"I wonder how long he can hold up," said Jean Marie thoughtfully. "When you get back, arrange another face-to-face meeting with him. Tell him of my engagement to speak at the Carlton Club. Explain that it may give me an opportunity to explore the situation on the grain embargo with people in positions of influence. At least they will tell me whether it is possible to reopen a dialogue. . . . How much success has Petrov had with Duhamel?"

"He thinks it may be possible for Duhamel to divert a Canadian shipment of about a quarter of a million bushels of hard wheat, originally intended for France That's a drop in the bucket and the ship is still in mid-Atlantic. So, who knows if it's just a delaying tactic. Duhamel is a champion at that game."

"Have you spoken with Duhamel?"

"Briefly, to let him know I was coming to visit you. He sent round a note which he asked me to put into your hands."

He handed an envelope across the table. Jean Marie opened it. The message was written in Duhamel's impatient script.

My friend,

Each day we come closer to the Rubicon. Our plans for the day of the crossing are unchanged, even though Paulette's remission continues and we are able to enjoy more together. We are grateful beyond words for this privilege. We cannot, however, accept it as a bribe for an act of submission which we are not yet prepared to make.

You are still listed for Grade A surveillance in France. The Americans have also become interested in you. Our people have had requests for information from a C.I.A. operator named Alvin Dolman. He left last week for the United Kingdom. His cover is that of personal assistant to former Secretary of State Morrow, who now works for Morgan Guaranty.

I asked a friend of mine in British intelligence to run a check on Dolman, as I thought he might be a double. We know he isn't; but it helps to muddy the waters.

Paulette sends her love. Take care,

Pierre

Jean Marie folded the note and shoved it in his breast pocket. Alain watched him with somber, brooding eyes.

"Bad news?"

"I'm afraid so. The man who tried to kill Mendelius is in London. He's a C.I.A. man called Dolman. They have planted him with Morrow of Morgan Guaranty."

"I shall call Morgan Guaranty and tell them about it." He announced it so pompously that it sounded like a line of bad comedy. Jean Marie noted, with some surprise, that brother Alain was getting drunk. He said with a laugh, "Truly, little brother, I don't recommend it."

Alain's sensibilities were wounded. "I don't want to find myself sitting next to a killer at a bankers' conference."

"I wonder how often you've done it, unaware."

"*Touché*." Alain acknowledged the point with a salute and then signalled the waiter for more wine. He asked, "And what are you going to do about the Dolman fellow, Jean?"

"Tell Hennessy and Waldo Pearson—then forget it."

"Hoping that one or the other will provide you with some protection—or remove Dolman from the scene."

"In some fashion, yes."

"So, when he is found dead in his apartment or run down by an automobile, how much guilt will you carry? Or will you turn away like Pilate and wash your hands?"

"You're playing rough games tonight."

"I'm trying to see what you're made of—after all, we haven't spent much time together these last thirty years." Again there was a surprise for Jean Marie. Brother Alain could be morose and maudlin in his cups. "You've always been the high one—parish priest, bishop, Cardinal, Pope! Even now, people defer to you because of what you used to be. I see it all the time in my business. Prince Cul de Lapin, who's never done a day's work in his life, gets better treatment than a successful tradesman with half a million francs in his account." He was having a little difficulty now, getting the words out. "What I mean is, it's like ancestor worship! Great-grandpa is the wise one, he's dead! You're not dead; but—God!—you do pronounce on a lot of things you don't really understand."

"I'm going to pronounce on you, brother mine! *T'es soûl comme une grive!* You're drunk as a thrush. I'm taking you back to the hotel."

Alain was near toppling as Jean Marie paid the check and hurried him outside. They walked two blocks before Alain was able at last to get his feet in rhythm. Back at the hotel, Jean Marie helped him to his room, undressed him down to his underthings, rolled him onto the bed and covered him with the counterpane. Alain submitted to the whole performance without a word; but, as Jean Marie was about to let himself out, he opened his eyes and announced, apropos of nothing at all:

"I am drunk; therefore I am. The only time I can prove it is when I'm away from Odette. Don't you find that curious, Jean?"

"Much too curious to debate at midnight. Go to sleep. We'll talk in the morning."

"Just one thing . . ."

"What?"

"You've got to understand Roberta's problem."

"I do."

"You don't. She had to believe her father was some kind of saint, doing penance for other people's sins. Fact is, he was a real bastard. He never had a thought for anybody but himself. He ruined a lot of people, Jean. Don't let him ruin her from the other side of the grave."

"I won't. Good night, little brother. You're going to have a beautiful hangover in the morning."

He tiptoed out and went downstairs to wait for Roberta Saracini.

Her appearance shocked him. Her skin was dry and opaque. Her eyes were red, her features pinched tight over the bone structure. Her movements were jerky, her speech hurried and voluble as if silence were a trap to be avoided at all costs.

He had reserved a small suite for her on the same floor as his own. He ordered coffee for two and waited in the salon while she freshened herself after the journey. She came back on a new floodtide of talk.

". . . You were right, of course. It's crazy to stay shut up in that big house! It's amazing the number of people who take those late-night flights. Where's Alain? How long is he staying? He's worried as we all are about the fluctuation in the currency market. I suppose he's told you that. . . ."

"He told me," said Jean Marie gravely, "that you were in deep distress. I see that you are. I want to help. Will you let me, please?"

"My father's dead—murdered! You can't change that. Nobody

can. I have to get used to the idea, that's all!"

She said it defiantly, as if daring him to pity her. She was tight as a fiddle string, ready to snap under the first touch of the bow. Jean Marie poured coffee and passed her a cup. He talked on, gentling her down from the high pitch of near-hysteria.

"I was so grateful when you agreed to come. It told me you were prepared to trust me. It gave me the opportunity to say my thanks for what you are doing, also to share with you some exciting things: the last stages of the *Letters,* the speech I'm to make at the Carlton Club, and new friends I've made in London. . . . I want to go to the Tate and the Royal Academy and the Tower of London, and Cardinal Wolsey's palace at Hampton Court and oh, so many other places. We'll do it together. . . ."

She gave him an odd, wary look.

"You talk as if I were a little girl. I'm not. I'm a grown woman, whose father was stabbed in a jail corridor. That makes me bad company for man or beast."

"You're hurt and lonely," said Jean Marie firmly. "I have no practice with women; so I'm probably going about this all the wrong way. I'm not trying to pat you on the head like a bishop or give you a papal blessing—which I'm not entitled to do anyway. I'm offering you an arm to hold when you cross the street and a shoulder to cry on when you feel like it."

"I haven't shed a tear since I heard the news," said Roberta Saracini. "Does that make me an unnatural daughter?"

"No, it does not."

"But I'm glad he's dead! I hope he's burning in hell!"

"Because you've already judged him," said Jean Marie with crisp authority. "And you have no right to do that! As for burning in hell, that's always bothered me, like a pebble in my shoe. Sometimes in the press I'd read about parents maltreating little children, breaking their bones, burning them on hot stoves, for some naughtiness, real or imagined. I've never been able to imagine God our Father, or His so-human Son, damning his children to burn in eternal fire. If your father were here now for judgment, and his fate were in your hands, what would you decide for him, forever and a day?"

Roberta Saracini said nothing. She sat, tight-lipped, eyes downcast, clasping her hands together to stop their trembling. Jean Marie pressed her.

"Think of the worst crimes that have ever been committed —the massacres of the Holocaust, the genocide in Kampuchea and Brazil. . . . Can they ever be expiated, even by an infinity of similar terrors? They cannot. The prisons of this world and the next could not accommodate the malefactors. I believe—and I have been shown only the faintest glimmer of what is to be—that the final Coming and the final Judgment itself must be acts of love. If they are not, then we inhabit a chaos created by a mad spirit, and the sooner we are released from it into nothingness, the better."

Still she did not answer. He went and sat beside her on the floor. He took her hand and held it firmly in his palm and said, "You haven't been sleeping very well, have you?"

"No, I haven't."

"You should go to bed now. We'll meet at breakfast and start our holiday immediately after."

"I'm not sure I want to stay."

"Will you say a small prayer with me?"

"I'll try." The answer was low and tremulous.

Jean Marie gathered himself for a moment and then, still holding her hand, intoned the prayer for the departed.

"God, our Father,
We believe that your Son died and rose to life.
We pray for our brother Vittorio Malavolti,
Who has died in Christ.
Raise him at the last
To share the glory of the Risen Christ.
Eternal rest give to him, O Lord,
And let perpetual light shine upon him."

"Amen," said Roberta Saracini, and began to weep, quiet healing tears.

For the next five days they played tourists, gorging themselves on the simpler pleasures of London. They strolled by the Serpentine, watched the changing of the guard at Buckingham Palace, spent a morning at the Tate, an afternoon at the British Museum, an evening at a Beethoven concert in the Albert Hall. They took a river excursion to Greenwich and another to Hampton Court.

They went window-shopping in Bond Street, spent a morning with Angelo Vittucci, who promised to design Jean Marie a suit "so discreet that a cherub could not be scandalized, yet so beautifully fitted you will think you have grown a new skin!"

Roberta Saracini was, at first, desperately moody—happy as a child one moment, the next, buried in a deep pit of depression. He learned quickly that logical talk made no impression on her: that gentleness, distraction and an occasional curt chiding were the best remedies. He made discoveries about himself, too: how far he had travelled from Vatican Hill, how many small joys had passed him by when he was the puzzled shepherd of a faceless flock. The *Letters*, on which he worked late at night, became more poignant, as each Arcadian day made time and tenderness and the tears of things more precious.

Roberta had decided that she would stay out the week, leaving London late on Sunday evening so that she could be back at work on Monday morning. The forecast promised fine weather —a brief extension of the Indian summer before the first frosts came in. Roberta suggested a picnic. She would hire a car, pack her luggage in the trunk. They could spend the whole day in the country. Jean Marie could drop her off at the airport on the way back to London. So, it was agreed.

Early on Sunday morning, Jean Marie said Mass at a side chapel in the Oratory Church, where the sacristan had come to know him simply as Père Grégoire, an elderly French priest who wore a beret and looked rather like a benevolent rabbit. Then, with Roberta at the wheel and a picnic basket made up by the hotel, they drove out to Oxford, Woodstock and the Cotswold country beyond.

It was still early and the Sunday traffic had not yet begun to build up; so they were able to turn off the highway and meander through small villages still rubbing the sleep out of their eyes, and rolling farmland brown with the last stubble or dark after the first plowing. Their pleasure was in the small wonders: the ribbon of mist that lay along a hillside, the grey tower of a Norman church, climbing out of the huddle of a tiny hamlet, an apple tree by the roadside laden with red-ripe fruit, free to the passerby, a child perched on an ancient milestone, nursing a doll.

Somehow, it was easier to talk while they were driving. They did not have to look at each other. There was always a new distraction to bridge the betraying silence.

Roberta Saracini touched his arm and said, "I feel so much better than when I arrived. Things make more sense. I can cope better. I have you to thank for that."

"You've been good for me, too."

"I don't know how; but I'm glad anyway."

"How do you feel about your father now?"

"I'm not sure. It's all a sad kind of mess; but I know I don't hate him."

"What holds you back?" He prompted her firmly. "You love him; no matter what he was or what he did, he paid his own price—and he gave you enough to get started, too. Say it! Say you love him!"

"I love him." She resigned herself to the proposition with a smile and a sigh which might have been relief or regret. Then she added the postscript. "I love you, too, Monsieur Grégoire."

"And I love you," said Jean Marie gently. "That's good. That's what it's all about. 'My little children, love one another.'"

"I hope," said Roberta Saracini, "you didn't have to be commanded to it."

"On the contrary," said Jean Marie—and left the rest of it unsaid.

"How do you feel about women—not necessarily me, in particular? I mean, you've been a celibate all these years and . . ."

"I've had a lot of practice at it." Jean Marie was douce but very firm. "And part of the practice is that you don't flirt and you don't play dangerous games and, most important of all, you never tell lies to yourself. I feel about you as any man feels about an attractive woman. I've been happy in your company and flattered to have you on my arm. There could be more; but precisely because I love you, there won't be. We were set to walk on separate paths. We've met most pleasantly at the crossroads. We'll part, each a little richer."

"That's quite a sermon, Monseigneur," said Roberta Saracini. "I wish I could believe half of it."

He glanced across at her. She was driving steadily, eyes fixed on the road, but there were tears on her cheeks. She turned to him and asked bluntly:

"What made you become a priest in the beginning?"

"That's a long story."

"We've got all day."

"Well! . . ." Immediately he was closed-in and reluctant. "The only person to whom I've ever told that was my confessor. It's still a painful subject."

"It was tactless of me to ask. I'm sorry."

They drove the next half-mile in silence; then, without further prompting, Jean Marie began to talk, slowly, musingly, as if he were putting together in his mind the pieces of a puzzle.

". . . When I first joined the Maquis I was very young—just arrived at military age. I wasn't religious. I was baptized, communicated and confirmed in the Church; but there it stopped. There was a war; life was catch-me-if-you-can. With the Maquis I was a man overnight. I carried a rifle, a pistol and a killing knife. Unlike the older ones who could sometimes slip into town, I was forced to stay out in the hills and the countryside; because if I got picked up in a city raid I'd be shipped out to forced labour in Germany. I did courier duty at night, of course; because I was young and could move fast and outrun the curfew patrols. . . . Before, I had had girl friends and some experience of sex—just enough to make me want more. Now I was without a woman and my companions mocked me, as older men do, calling me the little virgin and the choirboy. . . . Old, bawdy stuff, harmless enough, but very difficult for a youth who knew he might never live to enjoy a manhood. . . .

"Well, one of my regular courier routes took me to a farmhouse near a main road. All troop movements in the area had to pass the place; so the farmer's wife kept a list, which we collected every three days, and passed on to Allied intelligence. I never went to the house. There was a shepherd's hut and a sheep pen about half a mile away, on the brow of a hill. I'd lie up there and tie a rag to a sapling for a signal. After dark, the woman would come up with the messages and food for me and for the boys in the hills. Her name was Adèle, she was somewhere in her thirties, childless; and her husband was missing since the first days of the *Blitzkrieg*. . . . She ran the farm with two old men and a couple of sturdy girls from nearby families. . . .

"On this particular day I arrived late. I was scared and shaken. There were lots of German patrols out and twice I was nearly picked up. To make matters worse, I'd gashed my leg on some barbed wire, and I was scared of tetanus. An hour after sunset Adèle came. I was never so glad to see anyone in my life. She, too, had had a bad day, no less than three raids with troops stamping in and turning over the place. She washed my leg with wine, and bandaged it with strips from her petticoat. Then we drank the rest of the wine and ate supper together and afterwards made love on the straw mattress. . . .

"That I remember as the most wonderful experience of my life—a mature passionate woman and a frightened youth, in a single ecstatic hour, in a world full of monsters. Whenever afterwards I have talked about charity, the love of God for man and man for God and woman for man, I have done it in the light of that single hour. From curate to Pope I have remembered Adèle every morning in my Mass. Whenever I have sat in the confessional box and heard sad people tell the sins of their love lives, I have remembered her and tried to offer my penitents the gift of knowing that she gave to me."

He fell silent. Roberta Saracini swung the car into a lay-by, from which the land dropped away into a vista of farmland, and scattered coverts and walls of weathered ashlar. She wound down the window and stared out on the tranquil scene. Not daring to look at Jean Marie, she asked with singular humility, "Do you want to tell me the rest of it? Where is Adèle now?"

"Dead. She left me before midnight. When she got home there were Germans in the house again. They were drunk on her wine. They raped her and nailed her to the table with a kitchen knife. . . . That was how I found her when, eager to renew the night's loving, I broke all the rules and crept down the hill to see her at six in the morning!

"That was the day I decided I had a debt to pay. Later, much later, I decided that the exercise of the whole office of the priesthood was the best way to do it. The passion of Christ became very real to me as a drama of brutality, love, death and living again. I have never regretted the choice; nor, in spite of the horror that followed, have I been able to regret the wonder that Adèle and I shared. My confessor, who was a wise and gentle man, helped me to that. He said, 'The real sin is to be niggardly in love. To give too much is a fault, easily forgiven. What you knew, your Adèle knew, too—that you had shared a moment of strange grace. I am sure she remembered it at the end.' . . . Look at me, Roberta!"

She shook her head. She was sitting, chin on hand, eyes averted, staring out at the sun-dappled countryside. He reached out and turned her tearstained face towards him. His eyes were tender, his voice full of compassion. He admonished her gently.

"I'm old enough to be your father—so you can adopt me as a Dutch uncle if you like! For the rest, remember what I told you at the beginning. *On ne badine pas avec l'amour.* One doesn't trifle with love. It's too wonderful and too terrible! . . ."

He handed her his pocket handkerchief to dry her eyes. She accepted it, but faced him with a last blunt question.

"After all that, how is it possible that your best friend, Carl Mendelius, is a German?"

"How is it possible," asked Jean Marie, "that you and I are sitting here, because your father cheated the Vatican out of millions and was killed in a prison corridor? . . . The biggest mistake we've all made through the ages is to try to explain the ways of God to men. We shouldn't do that. We should just announce Him. He explains Himself very well!"

The day before the function at the Carlton Club he went with Adrian Hennessy to deliver the manuscript of *Last Letters from a Small Planet.* He laid it on Waldo Pearson's desk and said, "There you are. It's done. Good or bad, it's a heart-cry. I hope someone hears it."

Waldo Pearson weighed the package in his hands and said that he was sure, yes, very sure, that someone would hear the heart-cry. Then he handed Jean Marie the typescript of the English version of his speech for the Carlton Club.

Jean Marie asked him, "What do you think of it? Does it make sense?"

"It makes frightening sense. It makes wonderful sense. I cannot say how the audience will take it."

"I've read it," said Adrian Hennessy. "I love it. I'm also scared. There's still time to make changes if you will consent to them."

He glanced at Jean Marie, who nodded agreement. "I know I am talking to new people in a new idiom. Be honest with me! I am your guest at your club. If I am overstepping the proprieties of the occasion, I must know."

"There is no breach of the peace or the decencies," said Waldo Pearson. "Hold to the text!"

"Will there be questions afterward?"

"There may be. We generally allow them."

"Will you please make sure I understand them before I answer? I am fluent in English but sometimes, in moments of stress, I think in French or Italian."

"I'll see you through it. There's a lot of interest."

"Do you have a guest list?" Hennessy asked the question.

"Afraid not. When there's a big attendance, as there will be this time, the members have to ballot for guest places. I have, however, invited the Soviet ambassador—and Sergei Petrov, if he should happen to be in London. If he appears it will be a sign that he is still viable politically. I have also invited Morrow, because I knew him when he was my opposite number in Washington. I suggested he might like to bring a colleague—which leaves it open for him to present Dolman if he chooses. For the rest, it's an impressive list: members of Cabinet, diplomats, heads of industry, press barons. So you'll have a wide sampling of religions, nationalities—and moralities as well."

Hennessy added an ironic footnote. "Maybe the Holy Ghost will give you the gift of tongues."

"I used to talk about that with Mendelius." Jean Marie picked up the joke and embellished it. "He used to say that it was probably the least useful of all the gifts of the Spirit. If a man was a fool in one language, you'd never make him wise in twenty!"

They all got a laugh out of that. Waldo Pearson produced champagne. They drank a toast to *Last Letters from a Small Planet* and to a quondam Pope who was about to be tossed to the lions in the Carlton Club.

Jean Marie Barette gripped the edges of the table lectern and surveyed his audience, packed into the principal dining room at the Carlton Club. He had met only a few of them—a privileged group entertained by Waldo Pearson to sherry in the committee room. Waldo, he found, ruled the Conservative stronghold with an iron fist. He would not have his most exotic guest mauled and put upon in the vacuous preambles of cocktail time. He had professed himself delighted with Jean Marie's choice of dress—a black jacket buttoned to the neck, with a minimal display of Roman collar and a simple silver pectoral cross. The dress expressed the import of his opening words.

". . . I stand before you a private man. I am a cleric ordained to the ministry of the Word in the Roman Catholic Church. I have, however, no canonical mission; so that what I say to you in this assembly is my private opinion and must not be construed as either the official teaching of the Church or as a statement of Vatican policy."

He gave them a grin and a Gallic gesture to take the weight off the words.

"I am sure you will need no elaboration of this point. You are all political men, and—how do you say it in English?—a wink tells as much as a nod to a blind mule."

They gave him a small chuckle to warm him—and to tempt him, too. If he were fool enough to trust this audience, he would not be worth anyone's attention in the morning. His next words jolted them out of their complacency.

"Because I am a man, I have experience of fear, love and death. Because I have been, like you, a political man, I understand the usages of power and its limitations, too! Because I am a minister of the Word, I know that I am peddling a folly in the marketplace and that I risk to be stoned for it. . . . You, too, my friends, are peddling follies—monstrous insanities!—and all of us risk to perish by them!"

There was a deadly quiet in the room. For this single moment he held them hypnotized. They understood the arts of the forum. They knew that this man was a master; but if his thought proved unworthy of his orator's talent, they would shout him down as a mountebank. Jean Marie thrust forward with his argument.

"Your folly is to promise a possible perfection in the affairs of men—an equitable distribution of resources, an equal access to seaways, airways and strategic land routes, a world, in short, where every problem can be solved by an honest broker, an inspired leader, a party apparat. You make the promise as a necessary step to power. You choose to ignore that you are playing with dynamite.

"You raise illusory hopes. You excite expectations you cannot fulfil. Then, when you see that the deluded people are turning against you—presto!—there is a new solution: a cleansing war! Now, suddenly, you are not givers of gifts. You are janissaries imposing the edicts of the sultan. If the people will not obey the dictate, then you will make them do it! You will lop them, limb by limb, like Procrustes, until they fit the bed on which they writhe tormented. But they will never fit it. The golden age you have promised will never come. . . .

"You know it! In a most terrible act of despair you are resigned to it! Already you have counted the cost: so many millions in New York, in Moscow, in Tokyo, in China, in Europe. The aftermath, the desert which will be called peace, you have elected to ignore, because who will be left to care? Let the bandits subdue the populace. Let the casualties die. There will be a new dark age—a new Black Death. In some far-distant future there will, perhaps, be a renaissance; but who cares, because we shall never see the wonder of it.

"Do you think I exaggerate? You know I do not. If the embargo on grain is not lifted, the Soviet Union will come near to starvation this winter—and her armies will march at the first thaw. Even if they do not, a movement by any power towards the oil fields in the Middle East or the Far East will precipitate a global conflict. I do not know the battle order, as some of you do; but you will recognize that I touch close to the core of the matter. . . . I make no plea to you. If your own good sense, the promptings of your own heart when you look at your children and your grandchildren, do not move you to action to avert the holocaust, then—amen! So be it! *Ruat coelum*—let the heavens fall!

"I have sought only to define your folly; which is to believe that man can construct for himself a perfect habitat, and that every time he fails, he can destroy what he has done like a sand castle and begin again. . . . In the end the constructive impulse is overmastered by the destructive one. And all the time the tide creeps in relentlessly, to obliterate the small beach-head on which we play! . . ."

He could not tell whether they approved or disapproved. All he knew was that the silence held and their ears, if not their hearts, were still open to him. He went on, more quietly and persuasively.

"Now let me tell you of my folly, which is the reverse of yours, but which served only to compound it. When I was elected Pope, I was both humbled and elated. I believed that power had been placed in my hands, the power to change the lives of the faithful, to reform the Church, to mediate perhaps in the quarrels of nations and help to maintain the precarious peace we enjoy. All of you know the feeling. You experienced it when you were first elected to office, given your first embassy, your first cabinet post, or when you bought your first newspaper or television station. A heady moment, is it not? And the headaches are all in the future!"

There was a small chuckle of assent. They were glad of the

relief. The man was more than a rhetorician. He had a saving grace of humour.

"There is a catch of course—a trap into which we all step. What we have is not power but authority—which is a horse of a different colour! Power implies that we can accomplish what we plan. Authority signifies only that we may order it to be accomplished. We pronounce—*Fiat*! Let it be done! But by the time the ordinance filters down to the peasant in the rice paddy, the miner at the coal face, the slum priest in the *favela*, it has lost most of its force and meaning. The definitions in which we enshrine our dogmas and our moralities are touchstones of orthodoxy. Whether we be Popes, ayatollahs or party preceptors, we dare not abrogate them; but their relevance to man in his extremity is minimal. What theology can I teach to a girl who is dying with a septic abortion? All I can give her is pity, comfort and absolution. What do I say to the boy revolutionary in Salvador whose family has been shot by the soldiers in the village square? I can offer nothing but love, compassion and an unprovable proposition that there is a Creator who will turn all this madness into sanity, all this sorrow into eternal joy. . . . So you see, my folly was to believe that somehow I could exercise at once the authority which I had accepted, and the beneficence to which my heart prompted me. It was an impossibility, of course—just as it is impossible for a foreign minister to denounce the obscenities of a dictator who supplies his essential raw materials.

"It is in this context that I want to explain my abdication, which, painful as it was at the time, I now neither mourn nor protest. In an experience which came unbidden and unexpected, I was given a revelation of the Last Things. I was given a command to announce them as imminent. I myself was and am absolutely convinced of the authenticity of this experience; but I neither had nor have any means of proving it. So, my brother bishops decided that I could not legitimately hold the office of Pontiff and, at the same time, assume the role of a prophet and proclaim an unauthenticated private revelation. I say nothing of the means they took to procure my abdication. These are at most a footnote to a history that may never be written.

"I do, however, say this. I am glad, now, to have no authority; I am glad to be no longer obliged to defend the formulae of definition; because the authority is too limited, the formulae too narrow to encompass the agony of mankind in the last days and the magnitude of the Parousia—the promised Coming.

"It may be that there are those among you who, like me, have become conscious of the limitations of power and the folly of mass murder. It is to these that I m—"

Suddenly he was aware that the words he was saying were not words at all, but a single childish sound, repeated over and over: "ma . . . ma . . . ma . . . ma." He felt something tugging at his trouser leg. He looked down and saw his left hand flapping helplessly against his thigh. His vision was blurred. He could not see the audience. Then the room canted and he lurched forward across the table. After a certain confusion of motion and time he heard two voices very close to him. One of them was Waldo Pearson's.

"That was quite eerie. It sounded like glossolalia. Only yesterday we'd been talking about the gift of tongues."

"It's a typical symptom of C.V.A."

"What's C.V.A.?"

"Cerebro-vascular accident. The poor devil's had a stroke! . . . That ambulance is taking a hell of a time!"

"Midday traffic," said Waldo Pearson. "What are his chances?"

"Ask me in three days."

The words reminded Jean Marie of resurrection. Instead he lapsed into darkness.

BOOK THREE

Believe not in every spirit, but test the
spirits to know if they be of God; for
many false prophets are about in the world.
—First Epistle of St. John 4:1

XIII

Now he was another man in a strange country. The country was very small. It had four white walls, two doors and a window. There was a bed, on which he lay, a small table beside it, a chair, a chest of drawers with a mirror above it in which the man in the bed was reflected. He had a curiously lopsided look, like a before-and-after advertisement for liver salts. One side of his face was mobile and upturned, the other dragged slightly downward into an expression of dolour or distaste. One hand lay motionless on the white counterpane. The other roved restlessly, exploring contours and textures and distances.

There was at least one other inhabitant of this new country: a rather plain young woman in a nurse's uniform who appeared often to take his pulse and his blood pressure and listen to his chest. She asked him always the same simple questions: "How do you feel? What is your name? Would you like a drink?" The strange thing was that while he understood her perfectly, she did not seem to comprehend a word he said—although she did give him a drink, holding him up so that he could suck the liquid through a plastic straw. And she held a bottle to his penis so that he could make water. When he did so, she smiled and said, "Good, very good," as if he were a baby learning the act of peeing. She always used the same exit line: "Doctor will be back to see you soon." He tried to remember who the doctor was and what he looked like; but the effort was too great, so he closed his eyes and tried to rest.

He was too disturbed to sleep; not disturbed about anything in particular, but anxious, as though he had lost something precious and were groping for it in a fog. Every so often he would feel that he was close to it and close to knowing what it was; but the moment of discovery never came. Then he would feel like a man in a cellar with the trapdoor locked above his head. Finally, the doctor arrived, a lean grey-haired fellow who displayed a kind of offhand concern.

"My name is Doctor Raven. Can you repeat it for me? Raven."

Jean Marie tried several times but succeeded only in saying, "Ra . . . Ra . . . Ra . . ."

The doctor said, "Never mind. You will do better soon. Just nod if you understand me. I am speaking English. Do you know what I am saying?"

Jean Marie nodded.

"Can you see me?"

A nod.

"Smile at me. Let me see you smile."

Jean Marie tried. He was glad he could not see the result. The doctor looked into his eyes with an ophthalmoscope, tested his reflexes with a little rubber mallet, checked his blood pressure and auscultated his chest. Then he sat on the edge of the bed and delivered himself of a small lecture. Jean Marie was reminded of the discourse with which the rector of his seminary used to greet each batch of newcomers.

". . . You are a lucky man. You are alive. You are rational and you have some of your faculties intact. It is too early to know what damage has been done inside your skull. We have to wait two or three days before we know whether this is one episode or whether others may follow. You have to trust us and try to accept that for a little while you are helpless. This is the Charing Cross Hospital. Your friends and relatives know where you are. But they know you must have no visitors and no disturbance at all until we get you stabilized. Have you understood that?"

"Ma . . . ma . . . ma . . . most," said Jean Marie, and was absurdly pleased with himself.

The doctor, too, gave him a smile and a pat of approbation. "Good! That's promising. I'll be back to see you in the morning. Tonight they'll give you something to help you sleep."

Jean Marie tried to say thank you. He found he had forgotten the words in English. In French he could only get as far as "*Mer . . .*" He struggled with it until he wept in frustration and the nurse came in to pump an opiate into his arm.

* * *

After four days it seemed he had made enough progress for them to initiate him into the games of the new country. But first they had to find him a French-speaking assistant to teach him the rules. He was having enough trouble with phonic jumbles and word blocks, without launching him into a mania of mixed tongues.

The assistant was a handsome fellow in his early thirties, trim as an athlete, with the olive skin of a Mediterranean man, and an incongruous head of golden hair that looked as though it had been inherited from some long-dead Nordic crusader. He came from what he vaguely described as the Middle East. He confessed to being fluent in English, French, Arabic, Hebrew and Greek. He had built himself a modest career in medical circles in London by acting as interpreter, male nurse and physiotherapist to the polyglot groups who inhabited the metropolis. The neurologist introduced him as Mr. Atha. Together they began a series of games, all designed to map the damage to the sensorium, the part of his brain which perceived sensations. For a man who had once been, by dogmatic definition, the infallible interpreter of God's message to men, it was shocking to find how fallible he was, and in how many simple matters.

Asked to close his eyes and raise both arms horizontally in front of him, he was amazed that only one arm obeyed him fully while the other stayed, like the hand of a stopped clock, at twenty-five minutes to the hour.

Asked to tell where he was pricked with both points of a pair of dividers, he found some of his identifications were wildly astray. Worse, he could not even find the tip of his nose with his left hand.

However, there were some hopeful signs. When his feet were tickled his toes turned in. This, Mr. Atha explained, showed that his Babinski reflex was functioning. When the inside of his thigh was tickled, his scrotal sac contracted. This, he was told, was also good because his cremaster reflex was in working order.

Then came a most unhappy moment. Mr. Atha asked him to repeat for the neurologist the words of the old song:

"Sur le pont, sur le pont,
Sur le pont d'Avignon."

He found, to his horror, that his mouth was full of treacle, and what came out was a burble of phonic nonsense.

Once again he began to cry. The neurologist admonished him firmly. He was lucky to be alive. He was twice lucky to have suffered so little impairment. The prognosis was hopeful, provided he was prepared to be patient, cooperative and courageous —virtues quite beyond his capacity at that moment.

Mr. Atha translated it all into more soothing French and volunteered to stay with him until he was calm again. The neurologist nodded approval of the idea, patted Jean Marie's good hand and went about his other business; which, as Mr. Atha explained, included many patients far worse off than Jean Marie.

". . . I work with them, too; so I know what I am talking about. You can swallow. You have no double vision. You have control of your bowels and your urine. . . . Eh! Think how much that means! Your speech will improve; because you and I are going to practice together. You see, with the doctor, you are trying to show that you are not damaged. You are determined to prove it by a sudden burst of oratory. When it doesn't happen, you despair. We're going to start from the fact that you are damaged. We are going to repair the trauma together. . . ."

He was not only persuasive; he had an enormous quality of repose. Jean Marie felt the weight lifting off the top of his head, the fog dissipating from inside his skull case. Mr. Atha talked on quietly.

". . . You used to be Pope, they tell me. So you must remember the Scripture: 'Unless you become as little children, you shall not enter the kingdom of heaven.' Well, you're like a child now. You have to learn simple things from the beginning. You have to admit that you can't cope with complicated ones for a long while yet. But in the end you will grow up again, just as a child does. You're in kindergarten now. As the weeks go on, you'll climb through the grades. You'll learn to dress yourself, get your bad arm and leg moving again—and above all, you'll talk. You can talk now, if you take it slowly. Let's pick something very simple: 'My name is Jean Marie.' Now, one word at a time. . . ."

Somewhere in the long night hours, when the only sounds were the footfalls of the night nurse and the only light was the beam of her torch focused on his face, he learned another lesson. If he tried to remember things, they always eluded him. If, however, he lay quietly, making no effort at all, they crept up on him, and sat about him like woodland animals in a child's picture book.

They were not always in the right order. Drexel was next to the little mongol child. Mendelius was mixed up in some bishops' conference in Mexico, Roberta Saracini was drinking out of the cosmos cup; and the little twisted girl was selling prints to Alvin Dolman. But at least they were all there. He had not lost them like an amnesiac. They were pieces of a pattern in a kaleidoscope. One day they would shake themselves into a familiar order.

There was something else, too. As with the vision in the monastery garden, he was aware of it in a fashion that escaped verbal definition. Somewhere at the deep core of himself—that sorry fortress so beset and bombarded and ruined—there was a place of light where the Other dwelt, and where, when he could withdraw to it, there was communion of love, blissful but all too brief. It was like—what was it like?—deaf Beethoven with his head full of glories, Einstein bereft of mathematics to express the mysteries he understood at the end. There was another wonder, too. He could not command his limp hand or his numb leg, and only sometimes his halting tongue; but, in this small place of light and peace, he could command himself, dispose freely of himself, as a lover to the beloved. It was here that the pact was made. "Whatever you have laid on me I accept. No questions, no conditions! But please, come Rubicon Day, give light and a taste of joy to my friend Duhamel, and his wife. He is a good one. He has been niggardly only to himself!"

The first danger point was past, the neurologist told him. Fingers-crossed-and-pray-a-little, this was a one-off episode and he should make a good recovery. There would be sequelae, of course, handicaps and inhibitions of one kind and another; but, in general, there were good hopes that he could return to a normal life. But not yet! Not nearly yet! He must be trained, harder than any athlete. Mr. Atha would not only explain, but would drive him through the exercises, hour after hour, day after day. Visitors? Well, wouldn't it be better to wait awhile, until he could display to them a certain competence? Sometimes visitors got more distressed than the patients.

". . . Besides," Mr. Atha added his own good reasons, "you're an important man. I'd like to feel proud of you the first day you go on display. I want you dressed right, talking right, moving right . . . with panache, yes?"

"Panache!" said Jean Marie, and the word came out clear as a bell note.

"Bravo!" said Mr. Atha. "Now let's get the nurse in. The first thing we have to do is teach you to sit on the edge of the bed and then stand by yourself."

It sounded so simple that he could not believe the effort and the humiliation of it. Time after time, he crumpled like a rag doll into the arms of Mr. Atha and the nurse. Time after time, they stood him up and gradually withdrew their support until he was able to remain erect for a few moments. When he was weary they sat him back on the bed and showed him how to roll himself into a recumbent position and ease himself off the pressure points where bedsores might begin.

When he had mastered the overture, they began to teach him the opera: how to walk with tiny shuffling steps, how to exercise his left hand with a rubber ball, a whole series of operations with mechanical equipment in a large gymnasium. It was here that he understood, as Mr. Atha had told him, just how fortunate he was. He noted something else, too: the boundless patience which Atha dispensed to his motley group, and how quickly they reacted to his smile and his word of encouragement.

Atha made him participate in the small, disjointed community life of the gymnasium—by tossing a ball to one, making halting conversation with another, demonstrating to a third a movement which he himself had mastered. Brief as they were, these social interludes left him exhausted; but Atha was adamant.

". . . You will renew your own resources only by sharing them. You cannot expect to spend all this time of healing in a hermetic world and then emerge a social animal. If you get tired of talking, touch people, smile, share your awareness of things—like that pair of pigeons cooing on the window ledge. It may not worry you; but half the people here are terrified that they will no longer be attractive to those who love them, that they will be sexually impotent or even, in the end, a hateful burden to their families. . . ."

"I am sorry." Jean Marie managed to get the words out. "I will try to do better."

"Good!" said Mr. Atha with a smile. "You can relax now. It's massage time!"

There was one set of games which gave him real pleasure. The neurologist called them gnostic sensibility tests. In fact, they meant the recognition, by touch alone, of textures and weights, shapes flat and solid. The pleasure in this game was that the sensibilities did become perceptibly sharper and his guesses came closer to the objects that produced the sensation.

His attention span became longer, too, and he was able to enjoy the mass of letters and cards which had piled up, unread, in the top drawer of his bureau. When his concentration lapsed, Mr. Atha would read them to him and help him to frame a simple reply. He would not write it, however. Jean Marie must do that himself. Mr. Atha would supply the words and phrases that lost themselves momentarily from his vocabulary or jumbled themselves with others in some synaptic short circuit.

Now he had newspapers delivered—English and French—and enjoyed scanning them, though he retained lamentably little of what he read. Mr. Atha consoled him in his calm fashion.

". . . What do you want to retain? The bad news that tells you man is dismantling civilization brick by brick? The good news is here, right under your nose! The blind see. The lame walk. Sometimes even the dead are jolted back to life . . . and if you listen hard enough, you'll hear echoes of the good news."

"You . . . you are a . . . different man!" said Jean Marie in his halting fashion.

"You meant to say 'strange.'"

"So I did."

"Then say it now."

"Strange," said Jean Marie carefully. "You are a very strange man."

"I also bring good news," said Mr. Atha. "Next week you may begin having visitors. If you tell me whom you want to see I'll make a list and get in touch with them for you."

Brother Alain was invited first, because Jean Marie felt that the family tie should be respected and now there was no reason left for sibling jealousy. They embraced awkwardly, because of Jean Marie's useless arm. After the first verbal exchanges, Jean Marie made it plain that he would rather listen than talk; so

Alain hurried through the family news until he came to where his own heart was anchored: the Bourse, with all its transactions and its rumours.

". . . Now we are in the big-scale barter business. Oil for grain, soybeans for coal, tanks for iron ingots, meat for yellow powder uranium, gold for everything! If you've got commodities we can find a buyer for them. . . . But why am I running on like this? How long do you expect to be in this place?"

"They do not say." Jean Marie had found by now that he did better with simple announcements, fabricated in advance. "I don't ask. I wait."

"When you do get out, you're welcome to come to us."

"Thank you, Alain. No! There are places for . . . for . . ." He groped for the word and almost grasped it. "Rehab . . . rehab . . ."

"Rehabilitation?"

"Right. Mr. Atha will find me one."

"Who is Mr. Atha?"

"He works here with stroke victims."

"Oh!" He was not callous or indifferent. He was simply a stranger in a strange country. "Roberta sends her love. She'll be over in a few days."

"Good. Glad to see her."

It was the most he could manage. Alain, too, was glad to be dispensed. After a few more exchanges and some long silences they embraced again and parted, each wondering why he had so little to say to the other.

The next day Waldo Pearson came. He was attended by a manservant, laden with unexpected treasures: six author's copies of *Last Letters from a Small Planet*, one leather-bound volume for the author himself, a tape recorder and two best-selling versions of "Johnny the Clown," one by a male vocalist, the other by a well-known female singer with full chorus. He also brought a bottle of Veuve Clicquot, a bucket of ice, a set of champagne glasses, a jar of fresh caviar, toast, butter and the full text of Jean Marie's speech at the Carlton Club, also bound in leather. Waldo was in his best "come-and-he-cometh-go-and-he-goeth" mood.

"My father had two strokes—they didn't call them cerebrovascular accidents in his day!—so I know the form. Chat when you want. Be silent when you feel like it. Do you like the book? . . . Handsome, isn't it. The subscriptions are rolling in. It's the biggest thing we've had in twenty years. We're assured of rave reviews and big ones, too! I'm only sorry we can't have you at our launching party. Hennessy called. He tells me the reaction in the Americas and on the Continent is the same. He says he'll see you on his way back from New York. You've really touched a nerve. . . . And everyone's whistling the song. I even sing it in my bath. . . . Champagne? Can you manage the caviar, too? . . . That's very good! You really do cope. I was determined you'd have champagne and caviar if I had to feed it to you with an eyedropper. . . ."

"I'm very touched. Thank you." Jean Marie was surprised at his own fluency. "I'm sorry I made such a scene at the club."

"That was most curious." Pearson was instantly grave. "Some of the audience were hostile. Many were deeply moved. None was able to be neutral. I sent copies of the full text of your address to all members and to their guests. The replies, pro and con, were illuminating. Some expressed fear; others spoke of a religious impact; yet others spoke of the contrast between the power of your message and the modesty of your personal demeanor. By the way, did you hear from Matt Hewlett? He said he was going to write. He thought you might be embarrassed if he came to see you."

"He wrote. He told me he had offered nine days of masses for me. The Pontiff cabled and some members of the Curia. Drexel wrote a long . . . long . . . long . . . Forgive me. The simplest words fail me sometimes."

"Relax!" said Waldo Pearson. "I'm going to play you the song. I prefer the woman's version. See what you think."

"Can you get me a copy for Mr. Atha?"

"Of course; but who is he?"

"He's a ther . . . therapist. I can't tell you what he does for all of us. He's a god . . . godsent man! I must autograph a book for him. Does it matter now if I'm known as the author?"

"I don't believe it matters a damn anymore," said Waldo Pearson. "The charitable will find God in the book. The bigots will be sure you're stricken for your sins. So everyone will be happy."

"Did . . . did Petrov get his grain?"

"Some, but not enough."

"I've lost count of time. I can't remember events . . ."

"Be glad! The times are out of joint. Events outrun our control."

Jean Marie reached out to grasp his hand. He needed the reassurance of human contact. The thought he had been trying to grasp for weeks was finally clear to him. He pieced it out with desperate care.

"He showed me the Last Things. He told me to announce the Parousia. I gave up everything to do it. I tried. I truly tried. Before I could get the words out, He struck me dumb! . . . I don't know what He wants now. I am so confused."

Waldo Pearson held the frail hand between his palms. He said gently:

"I was confused, too. I was angry. I found myself shaking a fist in His face and demanding to know, why? Why? Then I read *Last Letters from a Small Planet* and I realized that was your testimony. It was all there in black and white. Whatever you said or failed to say at the Carlton Club was postscript and dispensable. . . . I remembered something else, too. The first precursor, John, called the Baptizer, came to a strange end. While the Messiah, whom he had announced, was still walking free in Judea, he was murdered in Herod's dungeon and his head presented on a dish to a belly dancer. All he had from his Messiah was a praise that became an epitaph. 'Among men that are born of women there is none greater than John the Baptizer. . . .'"

"I'd forgotten that," said Jean Marie Barette. "But then I forget so many things."

"Have some more champagne," said Waldo Pearson, "and let's listen to the music."

The next day, new plagues afflicted him. He was sitting in his wheelchair, scanning the headlines in the morning paper, when Mr. Atha came in to say that he would be absent for a while. He had to go abroad to deal with some of his father's affairs. Jean Marie's therapy session would be conducted by a woman assistant.

". . . And when I come back," said Mr. Atha, "I want to see a vigorous, vocal man."

Jean Marie was a prey to sudden panic. "Where . . . where are you going?"

"Oh, a number of capitals. My father's interests are extensive. . . . I'm taking your book to read on the aircraft. Come now! Don't look so glum!"

"I'm afraid!"

He blurted out the word before it eluded him. Mr. Atha would not bend to the appeal.

"Then you must confront the fear! All the work we have done together is to one end: to make you walk, talk, think and work for yourself. Courage now!"

But, the moment Mr. Atha walked out the door, his courage deserted him. Depression, black as midnight, settled over him. Even the place of light was blotted out. He could not find his way back to it. As the day went on, he found himself sinking deeper and deeper into a condition of despair. He would never get well. He would never leave the hospital. Even if he did, where would he go? What would he do? What was the point of all these efforts, if they produced nothing but the ability to put on a jacket, talk elementary inanities, shuffle along a straight line on a concrete pavement?

For the first time he began to contemplate death, not merely as a release from misery, but as a personal act of termination to an intolerable situation. The contemplation produced an extraordinary calm and a mind clear as the long, cold light of the northern latitudes. It was simple logic to proceed from the contemplation of the act to a speculation on the means by which it might be accomplished. Only when the nurse came in did he realize, with a shock of guilt, how far his morbid reverie had taken him.

He was sufficiently scared by the experience to mention it to the doctor when he looked in on his evening round. The doctor perched himself on the edge of the bed and talked round the subject.

". . . I was beginning to think you'd been lucky and sidestepped this particular crisis. It was clear to all of us that your religious background had given you resources which most people don't possess. . . . But there's no telling how, or when, a depressive illness is going to strike."

"You mean I have another sickness?"

"I mean," the neurologist explained patiently, "you have just described the classic symptoms of acute depression. If these symptoms are allowed to pass untreated, the depression will develop into a chronic condition, constantly aggravated by your present handicaps. The departure of Mr. Atha was simply a trigger incident. . . . So we're going to intervene before things go too far. We'll try you with moderate doses of a euphoric drug. If it works—fine! If not, there are other prescriptions. However, if you can beat the black devils without too much psychotropic intervention, so much the better; but don't try to be brave or bold. If you feel fearful, unable to cope, tell the nurse, tell me, immediately. Promise me!"

"I promise." Jean Marie said it firmly and clearly. "But it is hard for me to feel so dependent."

"That's also my biggest problem as a doctor. The patient is at odds with himself. . . ." He hesitated and then offered a curious question. "Do you believe man has a body and a soul, which get separated at the moment of death?"

Jean Marie pondered the question for a moment, fearful that a new fog-swirl might obscure the answer for which he was reaching; but—God be thanked!—the light held. He said with surprising fluency:

"That's the way the Greeks expressed man: spirit and matter, dual and divisible. As a module it served very well for a very long time. But, after this experience, I don't know . . . I'm not aware of myself as two elements: a musician playing a piano with notes missing, or, conversely, a Stradivarius violin played badly by a schoolboy. I'm me—one and undivided! Part of me is half-dead; part of me is totally dead and will never work again. I'm . . . de . . . de . . ."

"Defective," said the neurologist.

"Yes," said Jean Marie. "Defective."

The doctor reached for the chart clipped to the end of the bed and scribbled a prescription for remedy against the black devils.

In a rare flash of his old humour, Jean Marie said, "Don't you offer an incantation to go with the medicine?"

Against what happened to him next, no medicine and no incantation availed. Two days after Mr. Atha's departure, an hour before noon, Waldo Pearson and Adrian Hennessy came to see him. Their enquiries about his progress were solicitous but brief. Waldo Pearson offered an apology.

"I'd hoped to spare you this; but it was impossible. We have to seek injunctions in Great Britain, on the Continent, in the

United States—wherever else we can get them. We need your signature on the bills of complaint."

Jean Marie looked from one to the other in puzzlement. He asked, "What am I complaining about?"

Adrian Hennessy unlocked his briefcase. "Brace yourself for a shock, Monseigneur!"

He laid on the bed a large scrapbook and a paperbound volume. The title was *The Fraud.* The author was one Luigi Marco. The jacket was stamped "Uncorrected Proof Copy." The publisher was Veritas S.p.a., Panama. Hennessy held up the book.

"This little confection has been circulated to all international press agencies. It is due to be published worldwide, in twenty languages, on the day that we publish *Last Letters* in each country. We want to get injunctions to stop publication. However—and this is the nasty one!—some of the gutter press have already picked up the serial rights and are running the juicier sections of the story. The serious newspapers and the television networks can't ignore the fact of publication. They stand on their right to comment on the material. We have to file libel suits to prevent a further spread of the scandal."

"But what is the scandal?"

Waldo Pearson took up the burden of explanation. "The book, appropriately titled *The Fraud*, purports to be the true story of your career, from your earliest youth until now. It is a careful and very skilful blend of fact, fiction and scurrilous innuendo. The author's name is, of course, a pseudonym. The whole thing is a highly professional smear job, like those so-called documentaries about spies and defectors or political scandals which rival propaganda services turn out to discredit each other. The publisher is a hollow corporation registered in Panama. The printing was done in Taiwan by one of the houses that produce such things on contract. Bound copies of the book were then airfreighted to major countries. . . . Someone has laid out a mint of money on research, writing, translation and manufacture. . . . Some of the photographs were taken with a telescopic lens, which indicates that you were under professional surveillance for a long time."

"What sort of photographs?" Again Jean Marie had to explode past the phonic block.

"Show him!" said Waldo Pearson.

Hennessy, with obvious reluctance, flipped through the press cuttings in the scrapbook. There was a shot of Jean Marie with the twisted girl in the Place du Tertre. The angle was such that his face was close to hers and it was easy to assume that they were lovers *tête-à-tête.* There were several shots of Roberta Saracini and himself arm in arm, in Hyde Park, on the riverboat, and strolling in the gardens at Hampton Court. There was one shot of himself and Alain emerging from Sophie's restaurant, looking like a pair of elderly drunks. A black fury took possession of him and he almost choked on the question.

"What . . . what about the text?"

Waldo Pearson shrugged helplessly. "What you might expect. They've done a very thorough job of research and a very clever job of muckraking, so that you show up as a thoroughly bad type who is also a little crazy. . . . On that point they've managed to get hold of two reports from doctors who examined you before your abdication. There are also various other exotic details."

"For instance." Hennessy leafed through the volume. "They found someone who served with you in the Maquis. There was some story about you and a farmer's wife who was later found raped and murdered. Of course, the locals blamed it on the Germans; but . . . They're very good with the buts. Your best friend is Carl Mendelius of Tübingen but the suggestion is that you helped to procure his release from the priesthood because of a homosexual association. The fact that you defended him against charges of heresy and officiated at his wedding only reinforces the innuendo. . . . That's the horrible thing about this kind of job. The scandalmonger doesn't have to prove anything. He just plants the dirty idea. If you kiss your mother at a railway station it has to be incest."

"What do they say about Roberta?"

Hennessy frowned with distaste. "Her father swindled the Vatican Bank out of millions. The funds were never traced. You are known to have a substantial patrimony, of which Roberta Saracini is the trustee. Trusteeships in France are a matter of public record. When you went to Paris you lodged in her house. After that you're photographed in England holding hands with her in the park—and you're living here under an assumed name. . . . Do you want any more?"

"No. Who did all this? Whose idea was it? How did they get all this information? Why?"

"Let's reason through it." Waldo Pearson tried to calm him. "Adrian and I have talked to a lot of well-informed people and we believe we've come up with an explanation that fits all the available evidence. . . . Are you sure you're up to this?"

"Yes!" Jean Marie was clearly under strain but he forced the words out. "Take no notice of me! Just talk!"

Waldo Pearson talked on in the monotone of a man who brings bad news.

"From the moment you claimed a private revelation of the Last Things and made moves to publish it in a letter to the faithful, you were a dangerous man. You know what happened in the Church, and how bitter the Friends of Silence became. But outside, where the nations were actively preparing for a nuclear war, it was much worse. You, with your visions of horror and of judgment, became an instant threat to the myth-makers.

"They were preparing the public to participate in a competition of nuclear destruction, a game, a diabolical game, in which each side commits the same butchery for the same non-reason!

"Your vision, which made you seem a madman, was, in fact, the only available sanity. You saw the horror. You told it! Before the public grasped the thought, you had to be silenced.

"But that was not so easy. You were an active contentious man. In Germany, you blew the cover of a C.I.A. operative, an important agent-in-place. In France, your own country, you were instantly in the black book, under Grade A surveillance. You were watched in England, too; but I was a fairly respectable patron; and I stood surety for you with our government.

"All the time, however, you were a burr in the breeches of the mighty; because just when the war drums were booming, you might shout out that the king had no clothes—and after the first big bang, he might not have any subjects either.

"There was a question, as both Adrian and I discovered from different sources, of having you liquidated. It was a fairly unanimous recommendation. When it was known that your book was in preparation, the decision to liquidate you was rescinded. Another plan was made: to discredit you utterly. . . . You have seen how it was done."

"How did they manage to get all this material so quickly?"

"Money!" said Adrian Hennessy brusquely. "Put enough operatives in the field at once, hand out enough spending money, and you can have anyone's secret life in a month. Given a hostile situation in the Church, given top-level cooperation from governments, the job is as easy as boiling an egg."

"But who organized it?"

"Dolman was the boy who put it together and he had a special reason for making it work. You knew he had tried to kill Carl Mendelius."

"It makes sense, all of it."

"It also raises a problem."

"Please!" said Jean Marie with absolute clarity. "Please do not hold anything back."

"Even if we get restraining injunctions," said Adrian Hennessy, "we'll have only temporary relief. We'll have to fight a series of court cases in the major countries. That will cost a lot of money. You'll have to pay most of it out of your own resources. . . . And, since we're now in the dark ages and will soon be living under emergency regulations, there's no guarantee, even in England, that you'll get a fair trial from either the jury or the judiciary!"

Jean Marie thought for a moment and then said slowly:

"I have the funds. If it takes my last sou, we must fight this obscenity on any battleground we can find! I am not so naïve as to believe we can win; but we have to be seen to fight—and with my money and no one else's. Waldo, I only hope this will not damage your publication of *Last Letters*."

"No!" said Waldo Pearson. "If anything we'll get more press space, more lively debate. In the end it will come down to a private judgment in each reader's mind: could the author of the *Letters* possibly be the same rascal who is portrayed in this piece of garbage?"

"Meantime, we should get the documents signed." Hennessy was fishing them out of his briefcase. "Unless you want to read through a mountain of legalese, you'll have to take our word that the papers are well drawn by the best legal talent in England, France and the United States."

"I take your word." Jean Marie was already signing the first pages. "But look! To provide all the background for this libel, many people who knew me well must have supplied information."

"Obviously!" said Waldo Pearson. "But the mere fact that they gave information to an interviewer doesn't make them your enemies. You don't know what fiction was employed to make them talk. They may have thought they were doing you a favour. They could have been simple gossips. The Vatican is full of those! Hennessy and I are your allies; but we talk about you! I'm sure we've dropped phrases and opinions that found their way into this false indictment! . . . I'm afraid you just have to accept what's happened, make the best fight you can and then tell the bastards to go to hell. You can't afford to become paranoid."

"I am defective," said Jean Marie. "I am not paranoid. On the scale of the last catastrophe I am a minimal quantity. What happens to me is a non-event. I am troubled for people like Roberta, who will suffer hurt because their names are linked with mine in this libel. When I was Pope, every one I touched felt blessed. Now, I am truly a plague-carrier infecting even my closest friends. . . ."

That night, for the first time, he asked for a drug to make him sleep. In the morning he woke later than usual, but refreshed and clearheaded. At the therapy session he found that he was walking more confidently, that his damaged arm was responding quite well to messages from the motor centers. His speech pattern was consistently clear and he had rarely to grope for a word. The therapist encouraged him.

". . . . This is the way it happens in cases with a good prognosis. They improve rapidly; they seem to drag for a long while; then there is another major improvement which generally continues along a regular upgrade. I'll report to your doctor. He'll probably order a series of new tests. Then . . . well, let's not rush things! The trick, now, is to enjoy the improvement, but not push yourself too hard. You're still not ready to play football; but—come to think of it!—we could start you swimming!"

Jean Marie walked back, unaided, to his room. When he got there he was tired but triumphant. Whatever terrors he had to face now, at least he could confront them on his own two feet. He wished Mr. Atha were there to share this first, real victory. He lay on his bed and made a series of telephone calls to tell the good news. He drew a blank on every one. Carl Mendelius' phone was disconnected; Roberta Saracini was in Milan; Hennessy was back in New York; Waldo Pearson was in the country for a few days. Brother Alain was available, but preoccupied. He was happy to hear of Jean Marie's progress. The family would be happy, too. Please, please, keep in touch! . . .

Which brought Jean Marie, by a round turn, face to face with the problem of his own future. However much he was improved, however small his residual disabilities, he was still a man of sixty-five, rising sixty-six, victim of a cerebral episode, liable to another at any time.

Whatever the outcome of the court cases, he would emerge discredited—more so than if he were guilty of all the misdemeanors and misfeasances attributed to him. The world was fond of rascals; it had no patience with incompetents. On the face of it, therefore, Jean Marie Barette would be exactly what his passport called him: *pasteur en retraite*, a retired priest, whose best expectation would be a chaplaincy in a hospital or a cottage in the country, where he could amuse himself with his books and his garden. By evening the black devils were at him again and the doctor had to read him a lecture on manic-depressive swings and how to handle them. The lecture ended with a surprise.

". . . I've ordered an encephalogram for the day after tomorrow. If that reads the way I hope it will, we could think about discharging you within a few days. There's not too much more we can do for you. You'll need quarterly checkups, regular exercise and, for the beginning at least, some reasonable support in your domestic situation. You might care to think about that. We'll chat again tomorrow, eh?"

When the doctor had gone, he checked the calendar in his notebook. It was the fifteenth of December. In ten days it would be Christmas. He wondered where he would spend it, and how many more Nativity Days the world might see, because Petrov had not had his grain and the Soviet armies would move at the first thaw.

He chided himself. Not five minutes ago the doctor had told him he must not sit brooding. It was nearly visiting time. He tidied himself with great care, changed into fresh pajamas—just to prove that his new skills were not an illusion—put on a dressing gown and slippers, picked up his stick and began a careful but ostentatious promenade down the corridor, waving greetings at his companions from the therapy sessions.

What was it Mr. Atha had said? We must have panache! The English always translated it as style, but it had much more flourish than mere style. Flourish! That was good! Now he was coordinating two languages. He should try to get a little practice in German, too, before he met again with Carl Mendelius. Lotte's last letter—when was it dated? What had she said about their plans and movements? He retraced his steps along the corridor, acknowledging the compliment of the night nurse: "Well! Aren't you the clever one!" and the salute from the Jamaican orderly: a hop, a step, a shuffle and the invitation "Come dancin', man!"

He rummaged in the drawer of the bureau, found Lotte's letter—a whole sequence of small movements executed without trouble!—then sat down in his wheelchair to read it. The date was December 1.

. . . Our dear Carl gets stronger every day. He has become very skilful with the prosthetic device which replaces his left hand and there is very little he cannot do for himself. Unfortunately he has lost the sight of one eye and he now wears a black patch. This, with the other damage to that side of his face, gives him the look of a very sinister pirate. We have a family joke. When we need money, we can put Papa in a television serial like "Treasure Island" or "The Spanish Main"!

Johann and Katrin and a small party of their friends have been down in the valley for a month now. They are trying to make the main buildings habitable and stock up with essential supplies before winter closes in. Carl and I will go down next week to join them. We have sold our house here, fully furnished; so all we shall have to take with us are Carl's books and the few personal things that still mean something in our lives. I thought it would be a wrench to leave Tübingen after all these years; but it isn't. Wherever we go now—Bavaria or the South Seas—it doesn't matter too much.

And how are you, dear friend? We have all your cards. We trace your progress by the handwriting—and, of course, we have the messages from your kind friend in England, Waldo Pearson. We can't wait to get a copy of your book. Carl is dying to talk to you about it but we understand why you are timid about using the telephone. I am always so, especially when foreigners are on the line. I stammer and stutter and shout for Carl.

When will they let you out of hospital? Carl insists, and so do I, that you come straight to us in Bavaria. We are your family—and Anneliese Meissner says it is most important that you move directly from hospital into a secure environment.

She, too, may spend some of the winter vacation with us in Bavaria. She is very attached to Carl. They are good for each other and I have learned not to be jealous of her, as I learned not to be jealous of you. As soon as you know when you are to be discharged, send a telegram to the Bavarian address we gave you. Fly straight to Munich and we shall pick you up at the airport and bring you to the valley.

Carl gets anxious sometimes. He is afraid the frontiers may be closed before you are ready to come to us. There is great tension everywhere. More and more British and American troops are being moved into the Rhineland. One sees many military convoys. The tone of the press is frankly chauvinist and the atmosphere at the University is very strange. There is a constant recruitment of specialists and, of course, all the security surveillance which Carl and Anneliese so feared. The extraordinary thing is that so few students object. They, too, are affected by the war fever, in a way one would never have expected. It is a shock to hear all the old clichés and slogans! I thank God every day Johann and Katrin are out and away. . . . The madness infects us all. Even Carl and I find ourselves using phrases we have heard on radio or television. It is as if all the old dark Teuton deities were being called up from their caverns; but then I suppose every nation has its underground galleries of war gods. . . .

A raw, transatlantic voice interrupted his reading.

"Good evening, your Holiness!"

He looked up to see Alvin Dolman, leaning against the doorjamb and grinning down at him. Dolman, too, was dressed in pajamas and dressing gown, and he carried a package wrapped in brown paper.

For a moment Jean Marie was stunned by the sardonic insolence of the man. Then he felt a wild rage boiling up inside him. He fought it down with a brief, desperate prayer that his tongue would not fail him and leave him shamed before the enemy. Dolman moved into the room and perched himself jauntily on the edge of the bed. Jean Marie said nothing. He was in command now. He would wait for Dolman to declare himself.

"You look well," said Dolman amiably. "The ward nurse tells me you'll be discharged very soon."

Jean Marie was still silent.

"I came to bring you a bound copy of *The Fraud*," said Dolman. "Inside it you'll find a list of the people who were really happy to sell you out. I thought you might get a kick out of that. It won't help you in court; but then nothing helps in a case like this. Whatever verdicts you get, the mud will stick." He laid the package on the bedside table; then, he picked it up again and partially unwrapped it. "Just to prove it isn't booby-trapped, like the one I sent to Mendelius. There's no need for that in your case, is there? You're out of the game for good."

"Why have you come?" Jean Marie's voice was cold as hoarfrost.

"To share a joke with you," said Alvin Dolman. "I thought you'd appreciate it. The fact is, I go into surgery tomorrow morning. This was the only hospital in London that could take me in a hurry. I've got a cancer on the large bowel; so, they're going to cut out a part of my gut and give me a little bag to carry around for the rest of my life. I'm just tossing up whether it's really worth the sweat. I've got all the tools for a quick, painless exit. Don't you think it's funny?"

"I ask myself why you hesitate," said Jean Marie. "What is there in your life or in yourself that you find so valuable?"

"Not too much," said Dolman with a grin. "But we're building up to one hell of a drama—the big bang that wipes out all our past and maybe the future, too! It might be worth waiting for a grandstand seat. I can still opt out afterwards. You're the man who prophesied it. What do you think?"

"For the little my opinion is worth," said Jean Marie, "this is what I think. You are scared—so scared that you need to play this silly game of mockery! You want me to be afraid with you —of you! I am not! . . . Rather I am sad; because I know how you are feeling, how pointless everything looks—how useless a man can seem to himself! This is only the second time we have met. I know nothing about the rest of your life or what you have done to other people. But how do you feel about what you did to Mendelius and to me?"

"Indifferent!" The answer was prompt and definite. "That's line-of-duty stuff! It's what I'm trained for; it's what I do. I don't question the orders I get. I make no judgments about them—good or bad, sane or insane. If I did, I'd be in the booby hatch! Mankind is a mad tribe! There's no hope for it. I found a profession in which I could profit from the madness. I work for what is, with what is. I deliver on every contract. The only things I don't deal in are love and resurrection! But in the end, I'm at least as well off as you are. You've been peddling salvation through the Lord Jesus for two thousand years—and look at where it's got you!"

"You are here, too," said Jean Marie mildly. "And you came by your own choice. That argues more than indifference."

"Curiosity," said Alvin Dolman. "I wanted to see how you were looking. I must say you've worn pretty well!"

"Still not enough!"

"O.K. Here it is!" Dolman cocked his head to one side like a predatory bird surveying its victim. "When all this started, I was the one who recommended killing you. I put up a dozen simple plans. Everybody shied away, except the French. They've always believed in quick, painless solutions. However, Duhamel intervened. He gave you a special passport and put the word about that he'd chop anyone who tried to chop you. Once you were in England liquidation seemed a less profitable solution. When you had your stroke it was clearly unnecessary. . . . The argument was that it would be better to discredit you than to make you a martyr.

"I never thought so. When I got the news yesterday that I'd have to have surgery and that I'd be carrying around my own excrement for the rest of my life, I thought, why not kill two birds with the one stone—you first, me afterwards?

"I remembered that evening in Tübingen when you said you knew me and the spirit that dwelt in me. I don't think I've ever hated anyone so much as I hated you at that moment." He fished in the pocket of his dressing gown and brought out a gold pen. He displayed it to Jean Marie. "This is Death in one of his more elegant dresses—a capsule of lethal gas sufficient to carry us both off—unless I cover my nose like this while I blow the stuff at you."

He covered his nose and mouth with a handkerchief and extended the pen, point forward, towards Jean Marie's face.

Jean Marie sat very still, watching him. He said quietly, "I came to terms with death a long time ago. You are doing me a kindness, Alvin Dolman."

"I know." Dolman stuffed the handkerchief and the pen back in his pocket and made a comic gesture of resignation. "I guess I just needed to prove it to myself!" He reached out and picked up the half-opened packet from the table. He said with a shrug, "It was a bad joke anyway. I'll be getting back to my room."

"Wait!" Jean Marie heaved himself slowly out of his chair and stood up. "I'll walk to the elevator with you."

"Don't bother! I can find my own way."

"You lost your way a long time ago." Jean Marie's tone was somber. "You will never find it by yourself."

Dolman's face was suddenly transformed into a pale mask of rage. "I said I'd find my own way back!"

"Why are you so angry over a courtesy?"

"You should know that!" Dolman was grinning now, a rictus of silent glee that was more terrible than the laughter. "You told me in Tübingen you knew the name of the spirit that dwelt in me!"

"I do know it." Jean Marie spoke with calm authority and an odd quirky humour. "His name is Legion. But let's not overplay the drama, Mr. Dolman. You are not possessed by devils. You are a habitat of evils—too many evils for one aging man to carry inside himself!"

The taut grinning mask crumpled into a tired, middle-aged face—the face of an aging *clochard* who had used up all his chances and now had no place to go.

"Sit down, Mr. Dolman," said Jean Marie gently. "Let's treat with each other like simple human beings."

"You miss the point," said Alvin Dolman wearily. "We call up our own devils because we can't live with ourselves."

"You're still alive. You are still open to change and to God's mercy."

"You're not hearing me!" The tight, twisted grin was back again. "I may look like everyone else; but I'm not. I'm of a different breed. . . . We're killer dogs. Try to change us, try to domesticate us, we go mad and tear you to pieces. You're lucky I didn't kill you tonight."

He walked out without a word. Jean Marie went to the door and watched him limping down the long corridor with the brown-paper parcel under his arm. He was reminded of the old tale of the lame devil who roamed the city at night, lifting the roofs off houses, to display the evil that dwelt there. So far as he could remember, the lame devil never found any good anywhere. Jean Marie wondered sadly whether the lame devil was purblind or just too clear-sighted to be happy. Unless one believed in a beneficent Creator and some kind of saving grace, the world was a good place to be out of—especially if you were a middle-aged killer with a cancer in the gut.

That night he offered his Compline prayer for Alvin Dolman. Next midday he telephoned Dolman's ward nurse, only to be told that Mr. Dolman had died during the night of an unexplained cardiac arrest and that an autopsy was being arranged to establish the cause of death. His papers and his personal effects had already been retrieved by an official from the United States Embassy.

Jean Marie could not deal so curtly with a man who, however evil, was an element in the divine economy. Lives had been terminated, lives damaged, lives perhaps enriched, however momentarily, by Dolman's presence on the planet. It was not enough to pass the loveless judgment of the Puritans: "Pardon was offered; pardon was rejected; he took the inevitable walk to the Judas tree."

Jean Marie Barette—once a Pope—had too much experience of paradox to believe that the Almighty dispensed frontier justice. Whatever the Scriptures said, it was not possible to divide the world into white hats and black hats. He himself had been granted a revelation—and been reduced to a cold-eyed contemplation of suicide. He had been given a mission to proclaim the Last Things and, at the moment of announcement, had been struck dumb. So, perhaps it was not too strange to see in Dolman's suicide an act of repentance, and in his visit, a victory over the killer who lived in his skin. Were there not the tales old Grandfather Barette used to tell, of men bitten by mad dogs? They knew that death was inevitable; so, rather than infect their families, they blew their brains out with a hunting gun or locked themselves in a mountain cabin and howled themselves to death.

Once again Jean Marie was back to the dark, terrifying mystery of pain and evil and who was saved and who was not and who was ultimately responsible for the whole bloody mess. Who spawned the man who trained the killer dog? And what cosmic emperor looked down, in everlasting indifference, on the baby-child which the dog tore to pieces? . . .

It was still only noonday; but the midnight blackness enveloped him again. He wished Mr. Atha were there to walk him to the gymnasium and talk him out of the darkness towards the center of light.

XIV

Mr. Atha stepped back into his life as casually as he had stepped out of it. That evening, while Jean Marie was eating supper, he walked in, looked Jean Marie up and down like an exhibit at a flower show and smiled his approval.

"I see you've made splendid progress." He laid a small package on the tray. "That's your reward."

"I missed you." Jean Marie held out both hands to greet him. "Look! Both working! Did you have a successful trip?"

"It was—busy." Mr. Atha was as evasive as ever about himself. "Travel is very difficult now. There are delays at every airport and much intervention by the police and the military. People are mistrustful and afraid. . . . Look at your present."

Jean Marie unwrapped the package and found a pouch of soft leather, inside which was a small silver box, intricately engraved.

Mr. Atha explained, "The design is made up of the invocations to Allah. There is an old man in Aleppo who used to make them. Now he is blind. His son engraved this one. Open it."

Jean Marie opened the box. Inside, nestling in a bed of white silk, was an ancient ring. The setting was gold, the stone a pale emerald with the head of a man carved on it, cameo-fashion. The stone was worn and scratched like a pebble abraded by the sea. Mr. Atha told him the story.

"This was given to me by a friend in Istanbul. He says it is certainly of the early first century and it probably comes from Macedonia. There is a half-effaced inscription in Greek on the back of the stone. You need young eyes or a magnifying glass to make it out; but it says, 'Timothy to Sylvanus. Peace!' My friend thought it might have some connection with the Apostle Paul and his two companions Sylvanus and Timothy. . . . Who knows? I had the whimsical idea that since you gave up the Fisherman's ring, you might like to have this one instead."

Jean Marie was deeply moved. Behind Mr. Atha's "whimsical idea" there was so much and so gentle a care. Jean Marie slipped the ring onto his finger. It fitted comfortably. He took it off and laid it in the silver box. He said:

"Thank you, my friend. If my blessings count for anything, you have them all." He gave a small, unsteady laugh. "I suppose one does need a certain amount of faith; but wouldn't it be wonderful if it really were a gift from Timothy to Sylvanus? They were in Macedonia together. It's clear from Paul's letter to the Thessalonians. Let me see if I can remember it. . . . 'Paul and Sylvanus and Timothy to the Church of the Thessalonians: in God the Father and the Lord Jesus Christ.'" He frowned, fumbling for the next words. . . . "Sorry, I'm blocked on the rest of it."

"'. . . Grace to you and peace!'" Mr. Atha completed the quotation. "'We give thanks to God always for you all.'"

Jean Marie stared at him in surprise. He said, "I knew you were a believer. You had to be."

He used the French word *croyant*. Mr. Atha shook his head.

"No, I am not a believer. It happens that I was brought up in the Jewish tradition; but the act of faith is not one I personally can make. As for the passage in Thessalonians, I looked it up when my friend told me the provenance of the ring. It seemed so very appropriate: 'Grace to you and peace!' . . . Now, let us talk about you. You've had all your tests and the results are good."

"Yes, thank God! The doctors say they could discharge me immediately. However, they'd prefer I stay here for three or four more days. I can go out in the daytime and return in the evening. That way they can monitor my first reactions to physical and psychic stress."

"And you'll be surprised how much of both you'll get," said Mr. Atha.

"Will you stay with me? Take me about in London—perhaps fly with me to Munich and hand me over to my friends? I want to be with them for Christmas. I'm sure they'd be glad to have you, too. I don't want to take you away from other people who need you; but I'm out of practice in the simplest things."

"Enough!" said Mr. Atha. "You have me! I'd always intended to stay with you until you were properly recovered. You're a rather special client—in spite of your bad reputation!"

"That has to mean . . ."

"Yes, I've read the other book, too," said Mr. Atha. "It has, I understand, been suppressed by injunction in some countries; but where I've been it was freely available—and selling well! The thing is a disreputable caricature."

"Even so, it will harm a lot of people," said Jean Marie moodily. "Especially Roberta."

"Not too much," said Mr. Atha. "It will be forgotten before the year is out."

"I wish I felt so confident."

"It is not a matter of confidence, but of simple fact. Before New Year's Day we shall be at war."

Jean Marie gaped at him in total amazement. "How can you say that? Every estimate I ever heard gave us at least until spring, possibly well into the summer."

"Because," Mr. Atha explained patiently, "all the estimates were based on textbook evaluations—a conventional war by land, sea and air, escalating to a limited use of tactical nuclear weapons—with the big ones held in reserve for bargaining. The logic of history says you don't start that kind of war in the winter—certainly not between Russia and Europe or Russia and China! But I'm afraid, my friend, that the logic of history is already out the window. This time they will start with the big firecrackers, on the premise that whoever hits first wins and that the outcome will be decided in a week. . . . How little they know!"

"How much do you know?" Jean Marie was wary now. There was a sharp edge to his question. "What proof can you offer?"

"None," said Mr. Atha calmly. "But then, what proof could you offer for your vision—or even for what you wrote in *Last Letters from a Small Planet*? Believe what I tell you! It will happen—and there will be no warning. What we are seeing now—troop movements, civil defense exercises, meetings of ministers—is all grand opera. It's tradition; people expect it; so their governments are giving it to them. The reality is much different: men in concrete caverns, far below the earth, men in capsules far above it, waiting on the last fatal command. . . . Did you hear the evening news?"

"No, I missed it."

"The French President arrives here tomorrow, for emergency talks at Downing Street. Your friend Duhamel will be with him."

Jean Marie set down his fork with a clatter. "How do you know Duhamel is a friend of mine?"

"He is mentioned in *The Fraud.*"

"Oh!" Jean Marie was embarrassed. "I've never read the book. . . . I wonder if Duhamel would agree with your interpretation of global events."

"I hardly think it matters."

"It matters to me," said Jean Marie testily. Then instantly he apologized. "I'm sorry; that was rude. There's a long story between Duhamel and myself. I don't want to bore you with it."

"I am never bored," said Mr. Atha. "I am too much in love with this small world. Tell me about Duhamel."

It took a long time in the telling, from the moment of his first call from brother Alain's office, to Duhamel's resolve to end it all on Rubicon Day and the cosmos cup that was the symbol of the bond between them.

When the story was ended, Mr. Atha added his own footnote. ". . . So now you'd like it all tidy and tied with a pink ribbon: Duhamel and his wife safe in the arms of Everlasting Mercy. Yes?"

"Yes!" said Jean Marie flatly. "It would be good to know something was tidy in the economy of salvation."

"I'm afraid it never is," said Mr. Atha. "The mathematics are too complicated for human calculation. . . . I must leave you now. I'll pick you up here at ten-thirty in the morning, clothed and in your right mind!"

It was extraordinary how, in the shadow of Mr. Atha's prediction, the simplest pleasures became exquisitely precious: the sight of children playing in the park, the faces of women window-shopping, the tinsel and the glitter of Christmas decorations, even the grey drizzle that drove them to seek shelter in the snuggery of an English pub.

With Mr. Atha he felt the same kind of companionable ease that he had enjoyed in the early years of his friendship with Carl Mendelius. Yet there was a difference. With Mendelius there were always the explosive moments—of anger at an injustice, of excitement at some newly grasped idea, of emotion at a glimpse of hidden beauty. Mr. Atha, on the contrary, was inexorably calm, like a great rock in a turbulent sea. He did not communicate emotion. He understood it. He absorbed it. What he gave back was an almost physical sensation of peace and repose.

If Jean Marie were surprised, Atha would somehow enlarge the surprise to wonder, the wonder to a serene illumination. If Jean Marie were saddened—as he was by moments—at the sight of a derelict sleeping rough in an alley, a youth soliciting on a street corner, a child with the marks of cruelty or neglect, Mr. Atha would transmute the sadness into a hope which, even under the threat of Armageddon, seemed not incongruous.

". . . In poorer and simpler countries we respect beggars and honour madmen. The beggars remind us of our own good fortune and the madmen are blessed by God with visions denied to others. We experience cataclysms but see them in terms of continuity rather than of termination. . . . The strange thing is that men who have unlocked the secrets of the atom and of the spiral helix will now use those secrets to destroy themselves. . . ."

"What is in us that brings us inevitably to the precipice?"

"You were taught it from a child. Man is made in God's image. . . . That means he is a creature of almost unbelievable resources, of frightening potential."

"Which he always misuses."

"Because he will not come to terms with his mortality. Always he believes he can cheat the hangman."

"I thought you told me you were not a believer."

"Nor am I," said Mr. Atha. "Belief is impossible to me."

"Relatively or absolutely?" Jean Marie teased him with a theologian's question.

"Absolutely," said Mr. Atha. "Now, let's take a taxi. Waldo Pearson wants you at the Carlton Club at twelve forty-five precisely."

"You were invited, too."

"I know. I'm duly flattered; but I'm sure Pearson and Duhamel would like to have you to themselves."

"Duhamel? I didn't know he was going to be there."

"I suggested it," said Mr. Atha amiably. "After all, it is a farewell meal. . . . I'll pick you up at two-thirty."

It was strange to be back in the room where he had been

stricken, a little embarrassing to exchange nods or greetings with the men who had witnessed his collapse. This luncheon was another moment of testimony, given in the understated English fashion, but trumpet-clear to everyone familiar with the rituals of the realm. Waldo Pearson was saying, "This man is still my friend; the things you have read about him are lies; if any of you thinks otherwise let him raise his voice and tell me so!"

The presence of Pierre Duhamel was also a potent witness to his good character. The President of the Republic was lunching at Downing Street. His most trusted counsellor was very visible at the Carlton Club, giving the lie to a libel about Jean Marie Barette. But Duhamel dismissed the issue over the soup.

". . . Pouf! A nothing! A graffito on the ruins, with no one left to read it! Don't you agree, Waldo?"

"Regrettably I do," said Waldo Pearson. "We're facing a grim Christmas and a very dubious New Year. You could be as villainous as the Borgias now, Jean, and no one would give a damn."

"I am told," said Jean Marie carefully, "that we may not see a New Year."

Pearson and Duhamel exchanged anxious glances. Duhamel asked with dry irony, "Another vision?"

"No," said Jean Marie with a shrug of deprecation. "This time it was Mr. Atha, my therapist."

"In that case," said Waldo Pearson with obvious relief, "we can enjoy lunch. I recommend the rack of lamb and a bottle of the club's Burgundy. I chose it myself and you won't get better at the President's table."

Jean Marie was not to be put off so blandly, even by Waldo Pearson. He turned to Pierre Duhamel and put the barbed question, "How far are we from Rubicon Day?"

"Not very far." Duhamel answered without hesitation. "Troops of the Warsaw Pact are already mobilized in Europe. Soviet troops are also deployed in depth along the frontiers with China, Iran, Iraq and Turkey. The dispositions and strengths correspond with their known battle order and stage two of combat readiness."

"And what is stage two?" asked Jean Marie.

"Basically it means they're ready to meet any attack during winter and can be quickly reinforced for an offensive in early spring. Which is what we all expect."

"They're following the textbook," said Waldo Pearson. "Right down to the small print."

"But just suppose there's a different textbook," said Jean Marie quietly. "The order of battle is reversed and the big bang comes first."

"The way the Russians are disposed indicates they won't do that." Waldo Pearson spoke with solid John Bull conviction.

"What if we are the ones with the different textbook?"

"No comment," said Pierre Duhamel.

The waiter presented the wine, Waldo Pearson sniffed it, tasted it, announced that he was still proud of it and ordered it to be poured. He raised his glass to toast Jean Marie.

"To your continued good health and the continued success of the book."

"Thank you."

"I read it." Pierre Duhamel was eager in his praise. "Paulette, too! She laughed and wept over your little clown. Me? I began by admiring the cunning of your invention and the elegance of your style. Then I found myself arguing with your Jeannot—sometimes for him, sometimes against. In the end—well, how does one say it?—the book didn't solve the problems of this lousy twentieth century, but it did leave a good taste in my mouth. . . . Like your wine, Waldo!"

"My thanks to you both." Jean Marie raised his own glass. "I am blessed in my friends."

"The lamb!" said Waldo Pearson. "We get the first cut! That's why I like to be here right on time."

Jean Marie was bemused. Pearson's insistence on the trivia of the meal table seemed odd and out of character for a man so forceful and intelligent. But when Pearson left the table to take a telephone call, Duhamel explained it with a very Parisian aside.

"So British! He knows this is good-bye. He doesn't know how to say it. So he talks about the rack of lamb! Dear loving God! What a race!"

"I'm an idiot," said Jean Marie; and to cover his embarrassment he asked hastily, "What do you hear of Roberta?"

"Nothing. She is always away."

"If you see her, give her my love."

"I will."

"And to Paulette, too."

"Jean, my friend, let me give you one last piece of advice."

"Go ahead!"

"Think of yourself! Don't worry about me, Roberta, Paulette, anyone else! We all have a telephone line to our private God—whoever He may be! If He's there, He'll talk to us. If not, the whole game's a *blague*. Here! Have some more wine! . . ."

". . . Was it a good lunch?" asked Mr. Atha.

"It was good-bye," said Jean Marie Barette. "We walked out. We shook hands. I said, 'Thank you for a pleasant meal.' Waldo said, 'Delighted to have you, my dear chap.' Duhamel said, 'What horrible exit lines!' We laughed and went our separate ways."

"It sounds appropriate," said Mr. Atha. "I've picked up our plane tickets and booked a car to take us to the airport. The flight leaves at eleven. Allowing for the normal hour's delay, we should be in Munich by two in the afternoon. When we get back this evening I'll get you to sign checks for the medical bills and for staff gratuities. That way you won't be fussed in the morning."

"And then it finishes! Another chapter of my life closed—just like that!"

Mr. Atha shrugged. "Going away is dying a little and dying is very simple. There is a saying among the desert people: 'Never wave good-bye to the caravan. You will follow it soon.' . . . Now, we have to buy you some warm clothes; otherwise you'll freeze in that Alpine valley."

It was snowing hard when they landed in Munich, the last plane in before the airport closed. There was a long queue at passport control. The frontier police were checking meticulously on all foreigners. Jean Marie wondered whether his name was listed in the black book of undesirables; but finally he was waved through the barrier into the customs hall, where there was another pile-up of harassed travellers. Mr. Atha steered him to the exit and then went back to wait for the baggage. A moment later Jean Marie was caught in a bear-hug embrace by Johann Mendelius.

"Uncle Jean! You made it! You look wonderful! Mother and Father wanted to come in but the roads are bad; so I had to bring the jeep and use chains to get through the pass."

Jean Marie held him at arm's length and looked at him. There was no boy left in him now. He was a man, all muscle and sinew. His face was weather-beaten, his hands hard and calloused. Jean Marie nodded his satisfaction.

"Yes, you'll do! You look like a real countryman!"

"Oh, I am! Peasant to the boot soles! We've had a big scramble to make the place habitable for the winter; but we did it! Don't expect anything too grand though. All we guarantee is country cooking and warm shelter."

"You'll find me easy to please," said Jean Marie.

"All your people arrived safely."

"My people?"

"You know; the ones you sent with your password: 'the cosmos in a wine glass.' There were three groups, nine people in all. They've settled in very well."

Some elemental instinct warned Jean Marie not to make a discussion about it. The mystery would explain itself as soon as he arrived in the valley. He simply nodded and said, "I'm glad they caused no trouble."

"On the contrary."

"How are your mother and father and Katrin?"

"Oh, they're fine. Mother's gone rather grey; but it suits her. Father tramps around like a captain on the quarterdeck, inspecting everything with his one good eye, and learning to hold tools with that mechanical grip of his. Katrin's two months pregnant. She and Franz decided to wait and ask you to marry them."

Mr. Atha pushed through the crowd with a trolley of baggage. Johann stared at him gape-mouthed, and then burst into laughter.

"I know you! You're the one who . . . Uncle Jean, this is quite extraordinary. This man . . ."

"Don't tell him now!" said Mr. Atha. "Save it awhile. Surprises are good for him."

"I agree!" Johann laughed again and took Jean Marie's arm. "It really is worth waiting for."

Together they shepherded Jean Marie through the crowd and out to the pickup zone. When Johann hurried off to bring the jeep from the parking area, Jean Marie faced Mr. Atha with a veiled reproof.

"I think, my friend, there are lots of things about you that need explaining."

"I know," said Mr. Atha in his easy fashion. "But I'm sure we'll find a better time and place to do it. . . . That's a fine young man!"

"Johann? Yes. He's matured so much since I last saw him." A sudden thought struck him. He groaned aloud. "It's Christmas Eve! I've been so preoccupied with myself I forgot to buy any presents for the family—or for you. I feel very bad about that."

"I don't need presents and you pay me to remember! I bought some things before we left. They're wrapped. All you have to do is write on the cards." He smiled and added, "I hope I chose the right things."

"I'm sure you did; but this time I'd rather not have any surprises. What did you buy?"

"For Frau Mendelius, head scarves and lace handkerchiefs; for the young man, a ski sweater; for the girl, perfume; for the professor, a prismatic magnifier for easy reading. Did I do right?"

"Magnificently. You have my eternal gratitude. But you are still not dispensed from explanations."

"I promise you will get them. I hope you will understand," said Mr. Atha. "Here's Johann."

They helped Jean Marie into the Jeep, bundled him up in a blanket and a sheepskin pelisse and set off along the autobahn to Garmisch.

Johann talked eagerly about the small community in the valley. ". . . Our intentions were vague. Papa had this idea of founding a postgraduate academy. I thought of it as a place where my friends and I could hide out, if we got into trouble with the authorities. You'll remember that was in the days when we were buying arms from Dolman and setting up an underground at the University. . . . Then, of course, everything changed. We had to help Papa rebuild his life and this seemed a good place to do it.

"Eight of us came down to start making the buildings habitable. We camped in the lodge and worked from sunup to sunset. The place is far off the trunk routes as you will see. So we didn't expect many visitors. But they started dribbling through—young people mostly, but some older ones. We put it down to the fact that Bavaria is full of tourists in the fall. There's the Bierfest and the opera and all the fashion shows. So we got all sorts of callers: Italians, Greeks, Yugoslavs, Vietnamese, Poles, Americans, Japanese. They said they'd like to stay and help. That was great. We were terribly short of labour. We made a simple rule: work and share. It's amazing! So far we've held together and we're quite a mixed community, as you'll see!"

"Did people offer any special reason for joining you?" asked Jean Marie.

"We don't enquire," said Johann. "If they want to talk. we

listen. I suppose it would be true to say that most of them have some hidden scars."

"And they'd like to be born again without them," said Mr. Atha.

"Yes, you might put it like that," said Johann thoughtfully.

When they reached the first Alpine foothills, Johann turned south and began a long, winding ascent along a country road already deep in snow. Just before the road ran out and became a rutted timber-track through the pinewoods, there was a small wayside shrine, the usual carved wooden crucifix with a gabled canopy above it. Johann slowed the car.

"That's where we first met Mr. Atha, when we were hiking through here on our way to Austria. We asked him if he knew a good camping spot. He pointed us up the track we're taking now. . . . Hang on, Uncle Jean! It gets rough from now on!"

It was, in fact, fifteen minutes of jolting and jerking that threatened to shake the teeth loose from their heads; but when they broke out of the timber, they saw a high black wall of rock, with snow piled white in the crevices, and through it a defile, cut clean as if with a giant axe. The defile was perhaps a hundred meters long. The far end was closed with a palisade of split logs hung on huge hinges of hand-forged iron. Johann got out of the jeep, swung the palisade open and drove through it into a large saucer-shaped depression fringed with black crags that gave place, tier by tier, to pinewoods and the wilder growth of the lowlands round the lake. Johann stopped the jeep. Mr. Atha got out to close the barrier. Johann pointed down through the snow swirls.

"You can't see much in this murk. The lake is bigger than it looks from up here. The lights you can see through the trees come from the main lodge and the cabins which are strung out on either side of it. The waterfall is on the far side and the old mine entrance about fifty yards to the left. . . . There's such a lot to show you But let's get you home. Father and Mother will be biting their fingernails! . . ."

Mr. Atha climbed into the jeep and they jolted down a deer track towards the sparse yellow lights.

"We have you to ourselves until dinnertime," Lotte told him happily. "Carl laid it down like the laws of the Medes and Persians! No reception committee! No visitors! No interruptions until we had had our own time with our own Jean Marie! Johann promised to entertain your Mr. Atha. The others are busy decorating the Christmas tree, cooking for the dinner tonight. . . . We've all had to get used to less house-room and less privacy; but, at Christmas, it's rather pleasant and tribal."

They were sitting round an old porcelain stove in what had once been the servants' sitting room in the lodge. The furniture consisted of a small pine table, piled high with books, a wooden stool and three battered armchairs. They were drinking coffee laced with brandy and nibbling on cupcakes, hot from the oven.

Lotte had aged rapidly in a few short months. The last traces of youth were gone and she was now a silver-haired matron with soft, motherly features and the ready smile of a woman at peace with herself and her world. Mendelius had slimmed down; but he was still a solid, vigorous man. One side of his face was ravaged—scarred and stained by tiny fragments which had ruptured the vesicles; but his black eye-patch gave him a raffish air and there was humour still in his lopsided smile. He professed himself not unhappy with Jean Marie Barette.

". . . The limp is a nothing! It's just enough to make you look like a distinguished war veteran! The face? Well, I wouldn't know you'd had a stroke. Would you, Lotte? Anyway, beside me, you look like Donatello's *David*! . . . Still, there's a lot of life left in us both, old friend! What do you think of this place? Of course, you can't see a thing with the snowstorm; but it's all very exciting. We've got forty people here now, including four children. You'll meet them before dinner. And it will be a good dinner, I promise you! Johann and his boys hauled in nearly fifty tons of supplies last month. The woods are full of deer. We've got four milch cows in the barn. You'll smell them tonight, because your room is right over the byres. . . . You'll say midnight Mass for us, of course. Not everybody's Christian. We get over that by what we call 'a communion of friends' at the evening meal. Anybody who feels uneasy can avoid it by coming late. The rest of us sit together and hold hands in silence. If anyone feels like saying a public prayer, he or she says it. If someone wants to make a testimony or ask for an accounting of our common day, this is the time to do it. We end with the recitation of the 'Our Father.' Most people join in. Then we dine. . . . It seems to work. There's something else you should know." Mendelius straightened up in his chair. His tone was a shade more formal. "The deeds of the valley are in my name and Lotte's, with reversion to the children. However, we felt that since most of our people are young, I was no longer appropriate as a leader; so, by common consent, Johann is the head of the community."

"It works very well," said Lotte eagerly. "There is no longer a rivalry between Carl and Johann. They respect each other. Johann constantly seeks advice from Carl and me. He listens carefully—but in the end he makes the decisions. However, we'd all like you to take the place of honour, sit at the head of the table, that sort of thing!"

"No, my dear Lotte!" Jean Marie reached out to touch her cheek. "You have it wrong. I am the servant of the servants of God. I'll sit with you and Carl—old friends, wise enough to let the young cut their teeth on the barbed wire!"

Suddenly, as if a fuse had blown, the affectionate talk was over. Mendelius reached out his good hand and gripped Jean Marie's wrist. He said grimly:

"This is all too bland, Jean! We both know it. I hear the same kind of chat every day among our people here. Everything's sweetness and light. God help us! You'd think we were young lovers building our dream houses!"

"Carl, that's not fair!" Lotte was indignant. "We talk simple things to take our minds off the terrible ones we can't control. And why shouldn't we enjoy what we're doing here? There's a lot of sweat going into this place—and a lot of love, too. Only sometimes you're too crotchety to see it!"

"I'm sorry, liebchen. I don't mean to be bad-tempered. But Jean understands what I'm trying to say."

"I understand you both," said Jean Marie. "The short answer is that all the news is bad. The best hope is that hostilities will not begin until spring. The worst prediction, made by my friend Mr. Atha, and half-confirmed by a 'No comment' from Pierre Duhamel, is that the Americans might attempt a pre-emptive strike with the big missiles, even before the New Year."

There was a long moment of silence. Lotte stretched out her hand to touch her husband.

Carl Mendelius said, "If that happens, Jean, then everything will be tossed into the witches' cauldron: nerve gas, germs, lasers, every weird horror in the arsenals of the world."

"True," said Jean Marie. "Even so, you could be safe here for a very long time."

"But that's not the point, is it, Jean? That's not where all this began—as a plan for mere survival. If it were, I don't think Lotte and I would have taken the trouble. I don't think you would either. We've both become familiar with Brother Death; and he's not half the terrifying fellow he's made out to be. All this began with your vision and the message they wouldn't let you proclaim: centers of hope, centers of charity for the aftermath. Well, now that you're here, what do we do?"

"Carl, he's only just arrived!" Clearly Carl Mendelius' frustrations were no new thing to Lotte. "But we can tell him what we've been doing. You said it yourself: you can't give water from an empty bucket. So we're all preparing ourselves for the services we can best offer—in no matter how small a way. Anneliese Meissner is training some of the young men and the girls in practical medicine—even in homeopathic remedies which are available from local plants. She has them fired with enthusiasm by the example of the barefoot doctors in Chinese rural areas. One of the people Johann brought in is a young engineer who is working on a scheme to use the waterfall for generating power. . . . I've started classes for the children, and Carl is working on an idea for preserving a record of what we do here and the problems we encounter. . . . I know it's all small and elementary but it's . . . it's shareable! Even if the world does fall apart, sooner or later we'll have to try to make contact with the remnants near us. When we do, we must have something to offer; otherwise hope's dead and charity's empty!"

It was the longest speech Jean Marie had ever heard her make, and the finest affirmation of all she had learned as a woman.

"Bravo, Lotte! You should be proud of this girl, Carl!"

"I am." Carl Mendelius was good-humoured again. "I just get jealous because she's so much more useful than I am. I mean it! I'm a very learned fellow. But what's it worth beside a woman who can make medicine from herbs or a man who can make electricity from a waterfall?"

"Oh, I'm sure there's some use we can make of you." Lotte stood up and kissed Mendelius on the forehead. "I'm going to see what progress they're making in the kitchen."

When she had left, Jean Marie asked him a question.

"Where would you say the name Atha comes from?"

"Atha?" Mendelius repeated the word a few times and then

shook his head. "Truly, I've no idea. This is the friend who came with you?"

"Yes. He's very vague about himself—and a lot of other things as well. He says he comes from the Middle East. He was brought up in the Jewish tradition and he's a nonbeliever. . . . But, Carl, he's a unique man. He's young, as you see. He can't be older than the mid-thirties. Yet he has so much maturity, so much inner endurance. When I was at my lowest, I clung to him like a drowning man. I felt he was carrying me to safety on his back. It was very strange. He slipped so easily into my life that it was as if I had known him forever. One gets the impression of immense knowledge and most varied experience. Yet he never exposes any of it. I'll be very interested to see how you react to him."

"Atha . . . Atha . . ." Carl Mendelius was still toying with the name. "It certainly isn't Hebrew. But it does ring a faint bell somewhere. . . . I don't know why; but ever since I've been in hospital, my memory isn't nearly as good as it used to be."

"Mine isn't either," said Jean Marie. "The only consolation is that there are lots of things we need to forget!"

Mendelius pushed himself out of his chair and held out a hand to pull Jean Marie to his feet.

"Let's take a stroll and see who's around. Then you won't have to face a long line of new faces at dinnertime."

In what had once been the dining room of the lodge, a big log fire was blazing and Advent candles in their sprays of greenery were set at the windows. In one corner there was the traditional Nativity tableau: wooden figures of the Virgin, Joseph and the Christ Child with the shepherds and the animals watching about the manger. Opposite was a large Christmas tree dressed with tinsel and baubles. The rest of the room was taken up by benches and trestle tables where bustling young men and women were setting places for dinner. Mendelius, fumbling for names, settled for an offhand introduction:

"Friends, this is Father Jean Marie Barette. . . . He'll be available later for confessions, counsel—or just agreeable company! You'll have plenty of time to get to know him. . . ." In an aside to Jean he added, "I know it's a comedown; but we're too small to afford a Pope or even a bishop! And we don't want to frighten off the customers!"

Jean Marie finished the old, clerical joke for him: "Not before we collect the Christmas offerings!"

The kitchen boasted a large, ancient wood oven and a half-dozen eager cooks preparing poultry, vegetables and sweetmeats. One of them was Katrin, covered in flour to her elbows. She held up her face to be kissed and made a joke of her condition.

"Would you believe it! Me of all people! At first I was panic-stricken but now I'm really happy. So is Franz. You'll see him later. He's sawing logs in the barn. You will marry us, Uncle Jean?"

"Who else is there?"

"Well, if you hadn't come, we were going to have a kind of public binding."

"It's the same thing," said Jean Marie, "except mine comes with benefit of clergy."

In the far corner, Anneliese Meissner was mixing a concoction in a large copper pot. Jean Marie said his greetings and then stuck his fingers in the pot.

"Punch!" she told him. "My own recipe. Not to be served to anyone under eighteen or persons not covered by life insurance." She held the ladle up for him to taste. "Well? What do you think?"

"Lethal!" said Jean Marie.

"You get one small glass, no more. I hope you're doing all the things you were told." She fixed him with a shrewd professional eye. "You look pretty good. . . . Only the tiniest touch of facial paresis. Give me your left hand. Grip hard! . . . You'll do. I'll check you over tomorrow, when I've recovered from the hangover I shall undoubtedly have. It's good to see you!"

It was still snowing but Carl Mendelius was eager to keep moving. He handed Jean Marie a sheepskin coat and a pair of snow boots, then took him out to give him a quick look at the contours of the tiny settlement: the lake frozen and snow-covered, with an upturned boat on the strand, the waterfall still flowing but festooned with icicles, the mouth of the ancient mine tunnel.

"It goes in a long way," Mendelius explained. "There are still some large outcrops of bloodstone. We've got all our stores in there: canned foods, seed stocks, tools. It's the best possible protection against blast or direct radiation. . . . The fall-out, of course, depends on the winds. I would guess Munich must be the nearest big target. . . . Would you like to meet the children? They're in this cabin. Some of the women are looking after them.

We don't want to spoil the surprise of the Christmas tree."

But when Mendelius pushed open the door and stood aside to let him enter the cabin, Jean Marie had his own big surprise. Mr. Atha was seated in a chair with his back to the door. He had a small child on his lap. Three others were seated on the floor in front of them and behind the children were four women, all absorbed in the story. One of them made a hushing signal with her hand. Mendelius and Jean Marie crept in on tiptoe and closed the door silently. Mr. Atha went on with his story.

". . . You haven't been there; but I have. This place where the shepherds were watching their sheep is a hillside, very bare and cold. It didn't have trees like you have here, just stones and coarse grass, hardly enough to feed the sheep. The shepherds were lonely. I've spent a lot of time in the desert and I can tell you it is very frightening at night. So, one shepherd sang a little, and the one farther away picked up the song, and then another one, until they were all singing together like angel voices. Then they saw the star. It was big—big as a melon!—and it hung so low that they could almost reach up and pick it out of the sky. It was bright too; but soft-bright, so that it didn't hurt their eyes. And it hung right over the cave where the baby had just been born. So the shepherds walked towards the star, still singing, and they were the first visitors that little family of Jesus, Mary and Joseph ever had in Bethlehem of Judah. . . ."

There was a momentary hush and a big "Ah! . . ." from the children as the story ended. Then Mr. Atha stood up and turned to greet the newcomers. The child in his arms was the little mongol from the Institute at Versailles. One of the women was the *patronne* of the Hostellerie des Chevaliers; another was Judith, the little twisted one who made the cosmos cup.

Jean Marie was struck dumb with shock. He stammered and stuttered, as he had after the palsy.

"How . . . How did you get here?"

"You sent for us," said Judith. "Mr. Atha brought the message."

Jean Marie turned to Mr. Atha. "How did you know the password? I told it to no one except Johann."

"Take the child," said Mr. Atha. "She wants you."

He handed the little girl to Jean Marie and immediately she began fondling him, gurgling with pleasure. He found voice again as he crooned to her. "Eh, my little clown!"

It was only then that he was able to greet the others, and he embraced them like a father parted too long from his family. To the *patronne* he said, "Now, madame, you really have the silly mule and not the Pope!"

Mr. Atha's voice steadied him against the rush of emotion.

"These folk are my Christmas gifts to you. I invited others, too, in the same way. You'll meet them later, but you won't know them. They were clients of mine who needed special help. I hope you don't mind my small stratagem, Professor Mendelius."

"It's Christmas." Mendelius was laughing at Jean Marie's happy discomfiture. "It's always been open house at our place!"

"Thank you, Professor."

"Your name interests me, Mr. Atha. It's not Hebrew. What is its origin?"

"Syriac," said Mr. Atha.

"Oh," said Carl Mendelius, and was too polite to ask any more questions of so laconic a guest.

Dinner began with a ceremony of children. Jean Marie carried the little clown girl in his arms to show her the Christmas tree and the Nativity stable and the sparks dancing from the big pine logs. She would not leave him; so, before the meal could begin, her high chair had to be placed next to him.

Johann stood at the head of the table with his mother on his right and Anneliese Meissner on his left. Carl Mendelius was next to Lotte; Jean Marie sat next to Anneliese with the child beside him. Opposite him on the other side of the table was Mr. Atha, with Judith on one side and Katrin Mendelius on the other. Johann opened the proceedings with a formal request.

"Will you give us a blessing, please, Uncle Jean."

Jean Marie crossed himself and recited the grace, noting as he did so that Mr. Atha did not make the sign of the cross, as some did; though he did chime in with the "Amen" at the end of the prayer.

Then the feast began, ample, cheerful and noisy, with everyone primed on Anneliese's punch and fuelled with Rhine wine. It was arranged, Johann had told Jean Marie, to come to the coffee by ten-thirty, so that the children could be got to bed and the adults have a chance to sober themselves before the Christmas Mass at midnight. By ten the assembly had settled into a sentimental mood. Johann Mendelius stood up and rapped on his glass for attention. Even in the afterglow of the wine he had an air of confidence and authority. He said:

"My friends, my family. This won't be a long speech. I want first to wish you all the best of good things for Christmas and our life afterwards in this valley. I thank you all for the hard work you did to get us ready for winter. Next, I want to welcome Uncle Jean and tell him how glad we are to have him. When I saw him last, months ago, I had reservations about all the things he stood for. Now, I'd like him to know I have fewer reservations and a lot more convictions about what makes a good man. Finally, I'd like to say thank you to Mr. Atha, who first pointed me up the track to this place and now has brought us not only our most distinguished but also our most beloved citizen." He gestured towards Jean Marie and the child in the high chair beside him. There was a small burst of applause. He went on, "From a chance remark which he made while we were chatting this afternoon, I gather that Mr. Atha is one of those unfortunate people whose birthday falls on Christmas Day. Normally he gets only one present instead of two. Well, this time, we'll make sure he gets two presents!" He held up a bottle of red wine and a bottle of white and passed them down the table with a greeting. "Happy birthday, Mr. Atha!"

There was cheering and clapping and calls for a speech. Mr. Atha stood up. In the glow of the candles and the firelight he looked like a figure from some ancient mosaic, revealed in a sudden splendour of bronze and gold. Abruptly there was silence. He spoke not at all loudly; but his voice filled the room. Even the little buffoon child was still, as if she understood every word.

"First I have thanks to give. Tomorrow is indeed my birthday and I am happy to celebrate it here with you tonight. I have promised explanations to my friend Jean Marie, and it is proper that you should hear them, too, because you are sharers in the same mystery. . . . First, you should know that you are not here by your own design. You were led here, step by step, on different roads, through many apparent accidents; but, always, it was the finger of God that beckoned you.

"You are not the only community thus brought together. There are many others, all over the world: in the forests of Russia, in the jungles of Brazil, in places you would never dream. They are all different; because men's needs and habits are different. Yet they are all the same; because they have followed the same beckoning finger, and bonded themselves by the same love. They did not do this of themselves. They could not, just as you could not, without a special prompting of grace.

"You were prompted for a reason. Even as I speak, the adversary begins to stalk the earth, roaring destruction! So, in the evil times which are now upon us, you are chosen to keep the small flame of love alight, to nurture the seeds of goodness in this small place, until the day when the Spirit sends you out to light other candles in a dark land and plant new seeds in a blackened earth.

"I am with you now; but tomorrow I shall be gone. You will be alone and afraid. But I leave my peace with you and my love. And you will love one another as I have loved you.

"Please!" He urged them to cheerfulness. "You must not be sad! The gift of the Holy Spirit is gladness of heart." He smiled and the room seemed to light up. He joked with them. "Professor Mendelius and my friend Jean Marie are puzzled about my name. So much for scholarship, my dear Professor! And how quickly even Popes forget their Scripture! You were looking for one word. There are two. You will know them when I remind you. *Maran Atha. . . .* The Lord comes!"

Jean Marie was instantly on his feet. His voice was a high challenge.

"You lied to me! You said you were a nonbeliever!"

"I did not lie. You have forgotten. You asked was I a believer. I answered that I was not. I said at another time that the act of faith was impossible for me. True?"

"True."

"And still you do not understand?"

"No."

"Enough!" Carl Mendelius spoke out, angrily in defense of Jean Marie. "The man is tired. He has been ill. He is not ready for riddles!" He turned to Jean Marie. "What he is saying, Jean, is that he cannot believe because he knows. They taught you that in first-year theology. God cannot believe in Himself. He knows Himself as he knows all the work of His hands."

"Thank you, Professor," said Mr. Atha.

Jean Marie stood silent, as the full meaning of the words

dawned upon him. Once again he challenged the man across the table.

"You have called yourself Mr. Atha. What is your true name?"

"You have to tell me!"

There was, again, the odd, abrupt silence. Out of it Jean Marie spoke.

"Are you the promised one?"

"Yes, I am."

"How do we know?"

"Sit down, please!"

Mr. Atha sat down first. Without a word he drew a trencher of bread towards him and poured wine into a cup. He broke a piece off the bread and held it in his hands over the cup. He said, "Father, bless this bread, fruit of Your earth, the food by which we live." He paused and then began again. "This is my body. . . ."

Jean Marie stood up. He was calm now and respectful, but still undaunted.

"Sir, you know that these are very familiar words, most sacred to us all. You know enough of our Scriptures to remember that the early disciples recognized Jesus in the breaking of bread. You could be using that knowledge to deceive us."

"Why should I do that? Why are you so mistrustful?"

"Because our Lord Jesus himself warned us: 'There will arise false Christs and false prophets who will show great signs, so as to deceive even the chosen. . . .' I am a priest. The people ask me to show them Jesus Christ. If you are He, you must give me what you gave your first disciples, a legitimizing sign!"

"Isn't all this enough?" The gesture embraced the whole room and the valley. "Doesn't this legitimize me?"

"No!"

"Why not?"

"Because there are communities which call themselves godly, but which exploit people and twist them into hate. We are not tested yet. We do not know if the gift is true or treacherous."

There was a long silence; then the man who called himself Jesus held out his hands.

"Give me the child!"

"No!" Even as he recoiled in fear, Jean Marie knew it was all presaged in the dream.

"Please let me hold her. She will come to no harm."

Jean Marie looked around the assembly. Their faces told him nothing. He lifted the child out of the high chair and passed her across the table. Mr. Atha kissed her and sat her on his knee. He dipped a crust of bread in the wine and fed it to her, morsel by morsel. As he did so, he talked, quietly and persuasively.

"I know what you are thinking. You need a sign. What better one could I give than to make this little one whole and new? I could do it; but I will not. I am the Lord and not a conjuror. I gave this mite a gift I denied to all of you—eternal innocence. To you she looks imperfect—but to me she is flawless, like the bud that dies unopened or the fledgling that falls from the nest to be devoured by the ants. She will never offend me, as all of you have done. She will never pervert or destroy the work of my Father's hands. She is necessary to you. She will evoke the kindness that will keep you human. Her infirmity will prompt you to gratitude for your own good fortune. . . . More! She will remind you every day that I am who I am, that my ways are not yours, and that the smallest dust mote whirled in darkest space does not fall out of my hand. . . . I have chosen you. You have not chosen me. This little one is my sign to you. Treasure her!"

He lifted the child from his lap, and passed her back across the table to Jean Marie. He said gently:

"It is time to give witness, my friend. Tell me! Who am I?"

"I am not sure yet."

"Why not?"

"I am a fool," said Jean Marie Barette. "I am a clown touched in the head. . . . Truly!" He looked around at the little company. He tapped his skull. "A little part of me up there doesn't function anymore. I limp, like Jacob after his wrestle with the angel. I drop things. Sometimes I open my mouth and nothing comes out. I chase the words as a child chases bu . . . bu . . ." At the last moment he seized on the word. "Butterflies! So you must be simple with me. Tell me: can you really change your mind?"

"Why do you ask?"

"Abraham bargained with God for Sodom and Gomorrah. He said, 'If there be a hundred or twenty or ten just men in the cities, will you spare them?' And God, so the Scripture said, was very reasonable about the whole affair. Our Jesus who was of the seed of Abraham said that whatever we ask will be given us. We should knock at the door and clamour to be heard. But there's no point in that if there's no one inside—or if the one inside is a mad spirit whirling heedless with the galaxies!"

"Ask then!" said Mr. Atha. "What do you want?"

"Time." Jean Marie Barette held the child close to him and pleaded as he had never pleaded in his life before. "Enough to hope, work, pray, reason a little longer together. Please! If you are the Lord, do you want to march into your world like the old barbarians on a carpet of dead bodies? That would be surely an unworthy triumph. . . . This child is a great gift; but we need all the children and time enough to deserve them. Please!"

"And what can you offer me in return?"

"Very little," said Jean Marie with bleak simplicity. "I am diminished now. I have to think in small ways; but, such as I am, you can have me!"

"I accept," said Mr. Atha.

"How much time will you give us?"

"Not too much—but enough!"

"Thank you. Thank you from us all."

"Now are you ready to testify?"

"Yes, I'm ready."

"Wait!" It was Carl Mendelius who uttered the final challenge. For all his ravages and his wounds he was still the doughty old skeptic of Rome and Tübingen. "He has promised nothing, Jean. He has uttered only words familiar to us for centuries. I can list their sources for you, every one! He talks as though time is in his gift. You abdicated because you had no patent of authority for your prophecy. Why do you accept less from this man?"

There was a murmur of approval from the small assembly. They looked first at Mr. Atha sitting calm and composed in his place, then at Jean Marie, clasping the child close to him and rocking back and forth in his chair. Lotte Mendelius got up from her place to take the child from him. She said, so softly that only he could hear:

"Whatever you decide, we love you."

Jean Marie patted her hand and surrendered the little girl. He gave Carl Mendelius the old sidelong grin which acknowledged all the things they had shared in the bad times in Rome. He said, "Carl, old friend, there's never enough evidence. You know that. You've been digging for it all your life. We make do with what we have. From this man I have had nothing but good. What more can I ask?"

"The answer, please." Mr. Atha prompted him firmly. "Who am I?"

"I believe," said Jean Marie Barette, and prayed for a steady tongue. "I believe you are the Anointed One, the Son of the Living God! . . . B-but . . ." He stumbled and recovered himself slowly. "I have no mission, I have no authority. I cannot speak for my friends. You will have to teach them, as you have taught me."

"No!" said Mr. Atha. "Tomorrow I shall be gone about my Father's other business. You must teach them, Jean!"

"How . . . how can I with this halter on my tongue?"

"You are a rock of a man!" said Mr. Atha. "On you I can build a small standing place for my people!"

EPILOGUE

Pierre Duhamel stood at the window of the President's chamber and watched the snow falling over Paris. He fumbled in the pocket of his jacket and his fingers closed round the tiny enamelled comfit box, which held the two gelatin capsules: the passport to oblivion for Paulette and himself. The sensation gave him a weary kind of comfort. At least Paulette would not need to suffer anymore and he himself would be spared the sight of Paris in the aftermath. He wanted to be quit of this long, despairing deathwatch and go home to bed.

The man he had served for twenty years sat behind him at the great desk, chin propped in his hands, staring sightlessly at the documents in front of him. He asked, "What time have you got?"

"Five minutes to midnight," said Pierre Duhamel. "It's a hell of a way to spend Christmas Eve."

"The President promised to call me from the White House the moment he'd reached a decision."

"I think he's reached it already," said Pierre Duhamel. "He'll tell us just as they're pushing the last button."

"Nothing we can do about that."

"Nothing," said Pierre Duhamel.

Out of the silence that followed, the telephone shrilled. The man at the desk snatched it up. Duhamel turned back to the window. He did not want to hear the death sentence read. He heard the phone replaced and then the long exhalation of relief from his master.

"They've called it off! They think they see a breakthrough with Moscow."

"What's the next deadline?"

"They haven't set it yet."

"Thank Christ!" said Pierre Duhamel. "Thank Christ!"

Somehow it sounded like a prayer.